Cate Green grew up in Buckinghamshire and lived in Manchester and London before moving to France over twenty years ago. She now lives and writes just outside Lyon, France's second city and gastronomic capital.

Her debut novel *The Curious Kidnapping of Nora W* was inspired by her late mother-in-law, a resilient and feisty Holocaust survivor who lived almost as long as Nora herself. It won the 2019 Exeter Novel Prize.

Cate is a broadcast and print journalist and copywriter with over twenty years' experience in international radio, television and corporate communications. When not writing or running around after her three daughters, she is often sampling local food and wine, swimming lengths to make up for it, or getting lost in Venice.

 twitter.com/saracategreen
 instagram.com/categreenwrites
 facebook.com/Cate%20Green

THE CURIOUS KIDNAPPING OF NORA W

CATE GREEN

One More Chapter
a division of HarperCollins*Publishers*
1 London Bridge Street
London SE1 9GF
www.harpercollins.co.uk
HarperCollins*Publishers*
Macken House, 39/40 Mayor Street Upper,
Dublin 1, D01 C9W8, Ireland

This paperback edition 2023
First published in Great Britain in ebook format
by HarperCollins*Publishers* 2023
1

A catalogue record of this book is available from the British Library

ISBN: 978-0-00-856252-6

Printed and bound in the UK using 100% Renewable Electricity
by CPI Group (UK) Ltd

For Rose, Claire, Ruby and Maya, the next generation, with love.

Author's Note

The initial inspiration for *The Curious Kidnapping of Nora W* was my late mother-in-law, Norma Celemenski née Kryger. Norma was born in 1925 in Lodz. She was still living in the city at the time of the Nazi invasion of Poland and was walled up inside the ghetto there along with her family and tens of thousands of other Polish Jews. Her father died there of starvation in 1943. Just over a year later, she and her mother were deported to Auschwitz. Her mother was shot and killed on the platform as she got off the train. Norma became a slave worker because she was deemed to have the young eyes and hands necessary for making precision bombs. One of her brothers was also murdered in the Holocaust. Another brother and her sister survived.

After the war, Norma became a refugee and later a nurse in Sweden. She eventually left to find her sister in France and then sailed with her husband, Heinryk, and their two young children to Montreal, where they ran a shop very much like the one in this novel, open 7 days a week (except for the Jewish New Year and Yom Kippur) and also called Henry's Fruit.

Like Nora in the novel, Norma was resilient, determined - and stubborn. She lived well into her nineties and, towards the end of her life, some began to wonder if she might not actually be indestructible. It was her resilience and spirit that gave me the idea of writing about a survivor, a woman who might take a personal revenge against the perpetrators of the Holocaust by becoming the oldest person in the history of the world.

Two other women are also part of the inspiration for the book: Mahbubeh and Imane, both refugees from Iran and Syria respectively, who shared my family's home for a few months when they arrived in France and who have become dear friends. Like Norma, they are paragons of resilience. Because of war and religious intolerance, they have been forced to leave their home, their country, most of their family and their friends. Yet rarely have I ever seen them with anything other than a smile on their lips.

The Curious Kidnapping of Nora W is not a historical novel. It is not a novel about the victims of war and injustice. It is a novel about survivors of war and injustice and their lives as ordinary people with an extraordinary past. The friendship between Nora and Arifa is a small tribute to the three women who inspired it.

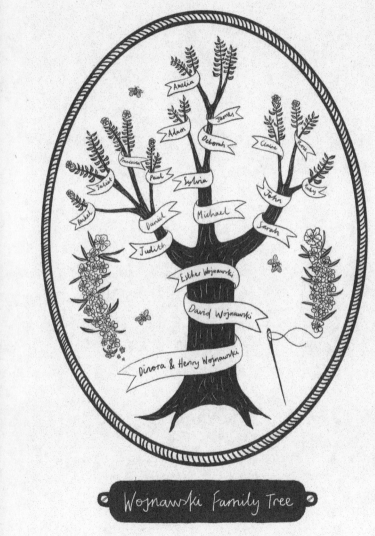

Amelia
James
Adam
Deborah
Claire
Rose
Francesca
Paul
Sylvia
Ruby
Juliet
John
Rachel
Daniel
Michael
Sarah
Judith
Esther Wojnawski
David Wojnawski
Dinora & Henry Wojnawski

Wojnawski Family Tree

ONE

Eighteen days and counting

Morning

My great-grandmother has only eighteen days to go. There's no need for alarm though. The doctors have not predicted her precise date of death, nor has she threatened hyper-geriatric suicide on that specific date. No, in eighteen days' time she will become the world's oldest person. Ever.

Dinora Wojnawski was born on 10th November 1896 and if she makes it to 24th April 2018 (and her doctors are confident) she will be 122 years and 165 days old. Thus demolishing the record set by Jeanne Calment, who was born in Arles in romantic Provençal France and died there too, in August 1997. The records state that in 1888, Mademoiselle Calment was the last living person to have knowingly met Vincent van Gogh. The story goes that he came to her father's shop a hundred years before to buy canvas for his paintings and that our thirteen-year-old Jeanne found him particularly ugly. At the time, nobody thought to ask the hideous painter customer to pay for his supplies in artworks, but since Mademoiselle married into money, she had little, if any, regrets on that score. These are just a few facts that differentiate Jeanne Calment, currently the oldest person the world has ever seen, from my great-grandmother.

Dinora (known to her intimates as Nora and to all her grand, great-grand and great-great-grandchildren as our traditional yiddisher Bubby) was born in Lodz, Poland in the relatively carefree days before the two world wars. Less romantic than Provence, you will agree. It seems certain that she will die in Pinner, Middlesex, since that is where she now resides, in the Cedars Care Home, conveniently located on the Metropolitan Line with fast trains into central London and not a majestic conifer in sight. As far as we know, she has never met any world-famous painters, living or dead, although Elton John did come to the Cedars for her 120th birthday celebrations (Wikipedia notes that Elton, aka Reginald Kenneth Dwight, was born and raised in Pinner). He sang the rather inappropriate 'Candle in the Wind'. I suppose he was thinking of all the ones on the cake.

A little less than a hundred years and a thousand miles separate Nora from Lodz today and her life has been at least as full as Jeanne Calment's, if rather less sheltered. Although much of that is another story entirely.

A further important difference between these two supremely senior citizens is that my great-grandmother did not marry well. By that I do not mean, as her remaining family apparently believed, that my great-grandfather was a good-for-nothing. Rather that he had little or no pockets, let alone any *zlotys*, left when he arrived in Britain fresh from the war (note the ironic use of the word fresh) and failed to earn much more than a pittance in the grocery that he and his wife ran just off Brick Lane, until retiring to the flat above the shop.

(Henry's Fruit, as it was called, is now a trendy street art café, rumoured by some to belong to Banksy.) Money was certainly scarce back then, but these days there is uncertainty, not to say speculation, among her grand, great-grand and even great-great-grandchildren about just how much we all stand to inherit, if and when mortality finally catches up with the apparently indestructible Nora. An old miser is how my mother has been known to describe her, but then she's always claimed the Wojnawski side of the family welcomed her with less than open arms. Careful, Bubby would say. Careful enough for the happy couple to put their hard-earned savings to one side to buy a rental flat here, a rental flat there, so she must have cashed in big time thanks to the East End of London's soaring property prices when, several years after Henry's death, the family gently suggested she sell up and move to the Cedars. And that makes the guess-how-many-zeroes game even more of a puzzle. I'm not going to lie, the pound signs have occasionally been known to flash across my mind, but Bubby is Bubby and I love her from the top of her bald head to her tired old toes. I for one would be happy for her to keep us all guessing until her great-greats have produced their own heirs to any possible fortune. Which is one of the reasons that I was the natural choice as the family's Guinness-Book-of-Records-party-organiser-in-chief.

Yes, it is I, Debs Levene, née Wojnawski, and the family's go-to party organiser/peace negotiator who hath been tasked with project managing, nay choreographing, the celebrations to mark this miracle of miracles:

- *Set the date – piece of cake [check]*
- *Book the rabbi (no service planned, but of course – as my mother is at pains to remind me – no self-respecting North*

3

London Jewish World Record party would be complete
without a rabbi) – [check]
- *Choose and book the venue (another piece of cake since the*
  Cedars only has one function room) – [check]
- *Liaise with the UK and worldwide keepers of the records*
  of records at guinnessworldrecords.com – [check]
- *Book the caterer without causing a fatal family feud –*
  (just about) [check]
- *Select and send the invitations – (and I stand by my*
  choice of design, tasteful yet Jewish) [check]
- *Contact Elton John's manager re reprise (but with*
  different song) – but Elton unavailable [check]
- *Direct rehearsals of choral performance by great-great-*
  grandchildren to replace Elton [ongoing]

You get the picture. There will be the twenty-one direct descendants. These include Grandpa David wheeled down from his studio on the fifth floor of the Cedars (Bubby is on the third floor, closer to the medical facilities) and a big contingency from Canada, my aunts Judith and Sarah having headed to the far north with their families, leaving pretty much all elderly relative considerations to Daddy, me and (if there are martyrdom points to be scored) Mummy. Likewise, my brother Adam, who, as befits a good Jewish son, will be bidding a brief farewell to his New York law firm for the occasion. Then there will be at least a *minyan* from each of Bubby's synagogues in East London and Middlesex, none of her own friends (all dead) and instead, apparently, the family of her favourite carer, Arifa. Arifa, like most of the other care professionals at the Cedars, recently arrived in Britain from somewhere in the south where Judaism is definitely not the official religion. Unlike some of my immediate family members

(OK, Mummy and Adam) I do try to keep the centuries-old animosity between our peoples out of the equation, but I did almost say when hell freezes over to that one. I mean, Arifa may be Bubby's latest hero, but she's paid to have gentle hands and be patient, isn't she? *She* doesn't spend hours shopping around to bring her her favourite herring and gladioli, listening to her ramble on about the old days in the East End or complaining that her son never comes to visit. *I* do. And I do it out of love and family loyalty and, with the relatives on the other side of the Atlantic and my parents mostly at loggerheads (if and when they communicate at all), I seem to have become the family glue. But then you can't refuse the not-quite-deathbed wishes of your own great-grandmother, can you?

Anyway, today is my turn (again) to visit Her Royal Bubbyness. And to administer the weekly pop-in on Grandpa David too. A quick round of pleasantries with the usual suspects in the lift and the doors open at floor three. Dinora Wojnawski lives in studio 318. An auspicious address under any circumstances (eighteen is a lucky number in the Jewish tradition, for those of you who are not of the faith) and especially today, with eighteen days to go before we raise our glasses of Guinness. (Champagne too expensive. No, just kidding!) The residents' names are neatly written on pieces of card that are slotted into little holders next to their door. Handier to remove and change than engraved brass plaques, though, given the price of a month at this place, the real thing would have been more elegant. They are also allowed to hang something personal on their door, other than a *mezuzah*, obviously, and Bubby has pained James, my husband, by refusing to replace her chosen decoration with an exquisite wax crayon rendering of the Cedars' grounds by our daughter,

Amelia, aged five. She has clung on to a cheap, wood-mounted, pastel-coloured photograph of a square in lovely Lodz.

I knock, just hard enough for Lodz to wobble precariously, and go in without waiting, because the little light above her door that saves visitors from personal hygiene moments is green. And there she is. And it gets me every time. This tiny figure, swallowed up by the sheets and protective pillows of her medical bed. Tiny, but with steel in the bones that carried her first from Lodz to unthinkable places and then to London. And after that, when the doctors said she was far too old and infirm for home care (not to mention the cantankerous behaviour that made it impossible to find home *carers*), here to this bed that she says she hates but where we have said she must stay because we love her. *I* love her. I press my hand to my mouth to keep my voice steady and then, 'Hello, Bubby,' I call.

'Who is it?' she says, turning her head towards me.

I don't know if Arifa is on duty today, but whoever it is has remembered to put her wig on, and despite her hollow cheeks and almost lightless eyes, there is our Bubby. The matriarch who has made it to the age of 122 years and 147 days. Who has driven us all mad, told us our chopped liver needs salt, taught every single one of us over the age of fourteen to play poker and who will probably outlive us all. I reach for the tissues in my bag.

'It's me,' I say and hope her old ears don't pick up on the lump in my throat, 'Deborah. I've brought you flowers.'

'Who?'

'Deborah, little Michael's daughter. You know, your favourite foolish girl.'

6

'Oh, that one. And why have you brought me flowers? Haven't you got any vodka in your bag?'

'Bubby! You know you're not allowed to drink anymore. I can get you a cup of tea, if you like.'

'Ho!' Her laugh is thin and shaky and catches in her chest. 'I know I'm not allowed vodka before sundown, you foolish girl. I'm not senile. Thank goodness one of us has a sense of humour.'

I laugh too. I run some water, put the gladioli in her washbasin and then sit on the chair next to her bed. I kiss her cheek. Warm, crumpled paper. Paper, scissors, stone. Paper beats stone and Bubby has a wig to hide the various victories of scissors, fear and very old age.

'So does my favourite horrible old lady want a cup of tea?'

'No tea. I don't want to be calling for a bedpan while you're here, do I? Just a chat with you will be lovely. How are your little ones?'

I'm pretty sure Bubby remembers which of her eight great-grandchildren I am when she tries, but she makes no pretence of knowing how many great-greats she has, who they belong to and what they are called. And frankly, why would she?

'You mean Amelia, Bubby. She's fine. She made you another drawing, can you see? It's her cat, Domino.' (I will put the masterpiece in the recycling on the way out.) 'Those are its ears and there's its tail and I think those black blobs are its paws.'

'I hope she's better at maths than drawing.'

Bubby is not known to mince her words. Even where five-year-old family artists are concerned. It's one of the long list of faults my mother (her granddaughter-in-law) finds in her and one of the many things that I hug her for on the rare occasions she lets me.

'Oh, you horrible old lady,' I laugh. 'I know you can hardly see what I'm showing you. And in case you've forgotten, Amelia is still only five years old.'

'Five is plenty old enough to know how to draw, you foolish girl. Your father was painting family portraits in oils at that age.'

'You mean Grandpa David, Bubby. I remember you telling me that story when I was five or six and you caught me trying to paint the kitchen wall in your flat above the shop,' I say. (And that was just the first time I remember you telling me about your only son's many talents, I don't say.) 'You tried to be angry with me, but I could tell from the look in your eyes that you didn't mean it. And you made me honey cake.' I squeeze the bones where her fingers used to be. I used to love the Sunday stories and the honey cake. And I still love that look in her old, almost blind eyes.

'It was a good shop.'

'Yes, it was, Bubby.'

'And you remember how you used to help your *Zeyde* with the weighing and the measuring? Ho! He used to scold you if you measured out too many herrings.'

She closes her eyes and claps her hands. I clap too, but I don't remember. It wasn't me. *Zeyde* was pushing ninety by the time I came along, so this must have been Aunt Judy. Or Sarah.

'Does she like herring?'

'Who? Me?'

'No, you foolish girl. Your little one. The painter.'

'I don't know. I don't think she's ever tried them.'

'Never tried herring? And she's three already?'

I try to keep my nod serious. Herring is sacred. And as my mother has always told me, age is just a number.

'So why the wait? You want her to grow up with a good brain? Learn to paint even?'

There goes that look in her eyes again.

'You're right, Bubby, I'll pick up some herring on the way home. But don't worry, Amelia's father and I are already sure that she is destined to follow in his footsteps and become a doctor. Or a lawyer.'

'That's a blessing.'

'Yes, it is, isn't it? No pressure or anything, Bubby.'

'What's that you say?'

'I said lovely weather we're having. Spring. Which reminds me, your Guinness Book of Records party should be on a lovely spring day. It's in eighteen days' time, did you remember?'

'Of course I remember. I'm not senile.'

'I know, Bubby. And what are you looking forward to most? The cake?'

'No.'

'The rabbi then?'

'Don't be ridiculous.'

'The family.'

'Oy, the family. Everyone together? Recipe for disaster.'

Senile? Bubby? She's more lucid than the lot of us.

'What then? You must be looking forward to something.'

'I must, must I?'

'Well, I hope so. We're all doing our best to make it a happy day for you.'

Now what's she up to? I mean we truly do want it to be a happy day for her – plus there's the ridiculous amounts of time I'm spending running around checking things off lists, negotiating peace over menu choices and phoning rabbis.

'Well, I'm not looking forward. Not at all.'

9

'Oh. Oh dear, Bubby. Is there something special you want?'

Something special? I'll give her something special, between the bloody choir and the bill from the kosher bloody caterer.

'Yes, there is.'

'Go on.'

'I want it cancelled.'

I laugh. She has such an impish sense of humour!

She sighs. 'It is not a laughing matter.'

It isn't? Eighteen days to go. Fifty per cent cancellation fees kick in at thirty days.

'But, Bubby!'

Full fee penalty at fifteen days. Caterers threatening sanctions over food waste. The entire family (well, mostly Mummy) telling me I've crashed and burned.

'I'm not having it. I'm not having complete strangers walking into this residential care home for the dying and pinning a ribbon on me!'

'There won't be a ribbon, I promise.'

'Are you a complete idiot, Esther?' (That's my grandmother, her late daughter-in-law and another of the women that is rumoured to have said my mother wasn't good enough for her son.)

'I'm Deborah, Bubby.'

'That's what I said. Well, are you?'

'I suppose I must be.'

'Yes, I suppose you must. Now listen very carefully, young lady. There will be no Gilbert and Sullivan party for Dinora Wojnawski at the Cedars on the 24th of April two thousand and eighteen. *Host tu farshteyt?*'

I don't think I do understand.

'No rabbi, no cake, no future doctors. *Bupkis! Farshteyt?*'

'Nothing. Yes, I got it.' It's true, I am beginning to get it now and there's a lump in my throat to prove it. All those hours on emails and phone calls. All those weeks imagining the future smile on Bubby's face. 'But Bubby…'

'Who's doing the catering? Who's organising this whole *meshuggeh* idea?'

'I am.' And for a moment I'm glad her tired old eyes can't see that the lump has spilled over onto my cheeks.

'Good. Because you're going to have to bloody well find a way of unorganising it, aren't you?'

TWO

Eighteen days more

Morning

I worry when I see Mrs Wojnawski agitated like this. I know that she does not like to eat so early. Eleven thirty is time for a snack to keep me going when the shop is busy, she will always tell me, even though I know the shop is closed now for many years. Maybe a little herring and vodka on a Sabbath Saturday, she says. Well, today is Sunday and I don't think it is her lunch that has made her pull off her wig and snap at me to give her peace when I knocked at her door. On Sundays there is always someone from her family to come and visit, mostly the great-granddaughter who likes to show me that she knows best what is good for Mrs Wojnawski. Sometimes it goes well and sometimes not.

I try again.

'I would be happy if you would eat a little. You know that on a Sunday we always have a roast for you. Some meat and roast potatoes and a good sauce.'

I have never seen a Sunday roast since I came to England, except here at the Cedars, and if this grey meat and wet cabbage is what they are famous for then I hope nobody will offer me one for lunch. A foolish thought, I hear my mother tell me in my head. She is right – who would invite me to their home here in London?

'It is still hot,' I tell her, only a small lie. 'You should eat it while it's hot.'

'I need a headscarf,' she says. 'You don't see that my head is cold?'

'I will find you one, of course,' I say. I want to soothe her agitation, but I know that if I ask her what is troubling her it will only make even more trouble. They gave me some papers to read and train me when they gave me the job here. How to help the old people feel relaxed and not so lonely, the papers said, but also always stay polite and respectful. I did read them, of course, but mostly I thought how could the others who work here not know already about keeping respect for the elders? And I thought about how it was with my own people at home, staying in their own place and sharing it with their family or following their children if they found a job and went away to live in the city.

'This is a beautiful one,' I say. 'The one that is the colour of sand with the blue and purple flowers. I think you told me it was a gift from your son.'

'My Dovid is a good boy. Always good to his mother.'

'Of course he is. We are both lucky women to have fine sons. And this is a fine scarf. It is made of silk. It will keep your head warm.'

She reaches out for it and when she holds it to her cheek, the soft folds show the wrinkles in her skin even deeper.

'You know my Dovid? Have you met him? Where? He is a good boy, but he doesn't come to see me here.' She takes the scarf in both of her hands and pulls at it between her fingers. 'They've shut me up in here and he won't come to see me. My own son and he doesn't see how much it hurts my heart to stay here. This place with the doctors and the smells of bad food, when I should be back in the old neighbourhood, in the shop with Dovid and Henry.'

For a woman so old, Mrs Wojnawski's mind is sharp like my sewing needles, but I know that she can mix things up, forget the order of things sometimes when she is agitated, when she thinks about her son David – or Dovid the way she calls him – or the home she had with her family. She has told me they lived right over their shop then, and many times she has said she wishes to go back there, to the east of London, near the part where now I have my flat, with my son. But I know that in this country it is not so easy for the old people to stay with their family. And she is more than 122 years now; of course she is too old and weak to go back.

'I know why he doesn't come,' she says. 'They won't let him; they don't want me to see him. They say it will trouble me, but they are the ones with the trouble. And now they want to make me wear ribbons and dance and eat cake with the rabbi. Ach! You think I want to dance? You think I like ribbons? I am telling them they should forget it. I am the one to decide if I want to eat cake and when I see my boy.'

Her fingers are pulling faster and I try to put my hand over hers, but she pushes it away. Every time I am with her, the strength in her bones is a new surprise. So is the way she always likes to keep her fingernails nice. Neat, with pink polish.

'Which one are you and why have you come into my room? You want me playing records and having parties too?'

'I'm Arifa,' I say. 'I'm your carer, here at the Cedars. And I don't want you to do anything you don't want to do.'

'Arifa.'

'Yes, that's right. Arifa. You asked me to put your headscarf on for you.'

She puts a hand to her head and then strokes the scarf again.

'My head is cold.'

Now she lets me put my hand on hers and I keep my voice the way I hear my mother's voice inside my head. 'Of course. Here is your scarf. Let me make your head warm for you.' I fold the scarf into a triangle and knot it behind her neck, the way she likes it. I leave my hand against the silk for a moment and she covers it with hers. I know that the papers they gave me would say that now I should ask her to eat her lunch. I want her to eat. I know she must. She needs to keep up her strength, the way they say, but I think she wants a little quiet after the agitation from her son and whoever came from her family this morning. Then she will eat some of the grey roast dinner.

'Would you like to listen to some music?' I ask her.

She smooths the scarf close around her head and checks the knot that I tied at the back.

'Thank you, Arifa. I would like that,' she says. 'I think you know the one I like to listen to.'

Yes, I know it. I know that I only need to press play on the remote control and it will start up again. And I know what she told me. That this was the music that she used to dance to with her husband and their friends so many years ago, before she came to England and before she went to the places that she has never told me about. I have seen the blue numbers on her arm and I will listen if she wants to talk about them, but I will never ask her. I respect her, even more than the way it says in my training.

'Is that loud enough for you?'

She nods and holds her hand out. I pass her the remote control and she waves it a few times to the beat of the music. Dance music that has violins instead of our *ouds*, and clarinets that she tells me can laugh or cry. She stops counting the beats and shuts her eyes. I leave her lunch where she can reach it and turn for the door.

'Arifa?'

'Yes, Mrs Wojnawski?'

'Will you pass me my photo of Henry and me?'

It is a beautiful photo in black and white, in a frame with swirls that make me think of the patterns in a mosque. It is Mrs Wojnawski's wedding day and she has thick black hair covered with flowers.

'Thank you,' she says, but she doesn't open her eyes. I think the music must help her to see herself and her proud, happy husband.

My bones and skin were so tired that they pulled me down into the wood and bits of straw padding like I was a huge stone dropped into a river. But the rush of the water in my ears was not enough to stop the sound of the other women crying, praying, sometimes even laughing when they found they could share a memory with somebody. The only way to stop it was to shut my eyes and listen in my head to the music that they played when Heinryk stood before me, because now I was his own wife and we were in the centre of the dance in the celebrations.

I had only one moment to look into his eyes and see the shine there and feel the safety of the circle we made together because – hey! – the music began. The violins and clarinets, the clapping and the singing, and round we went, circled by the crowd that had come to cheer for our marriage and forget for the evening whatever it was they needed to forget. And even though I knew it was coming, that moment of whirling among them was a rush of laughter but also some fear. I looked around for my mother and father to see if they could catch me if I fell, but my eyes found Heinryk again, whirling with me and reaching for the white handkerchief in my hand. Heinryk's fingers hooked into mine even though we both knew how the rabbis taught that until we were alone, later tonight, we must only touch the handkerchief. His smile and his fingers making a lock that couldn't be broken even though the music and the clapping grew faster as the dance turned, and the singers shouted that we must all rejoice and be happy and sing. My hair flew into my eyes, thick and black, the hair that Heinryk said was like a precious cloth to make a cloak out of. That he told me he would wrap around his wrists, his neck, his own shoulders, once we were married. And that meant now, so I didn't need to look around for my parents to help me or to scold me, because here was my bright future dancing with me, full of clapping and song.

'Dinora, stop, you are singing too loud.'

The hand on my arm was not Heinryk's. This one was thin, with no strength, but all I wanted to feel were Heinryk's fingers, with the handkerchief wrapped between us. All I wanted to hear was the freylekh, our wedding song. I pushed the bony hand away, but it came back, like a bird's claw tight on a branch. I couldn't see who this was, but when I went to lift my hair out of my eyes, all I felt was my bare forehead. My bare forehead and my bare head, just with a few patches of rough stubble where Heinryk had seen black silk, fit for a cloak.

17

I only heard that I had started to wail when the bird's claw clamped over my mouth.

'Dinora,' it said, 'you have to be quiet now.'

I opened my eyes and saw someone I recognised but I didn't know. What was she doing at my wedding?

'I was dancing with my husband and there was music,' I told her. I think it was a woman, even though she had no hair.

I reached out to touch her head, but then pulled my hand away. She caught it and put it to her head. This time I felt the wail well up from inside me, swelling like it was trying to burst my lungs, but I pressed my lips together and the other ghost woman nodded at me. I turned and slid my bones and skin off the wooden rack and stood to face her, both of us in the rough uniforms that they told us to wear when they took our clothes. On one side, our hands slid together, on the other, mine took her shoulder, hers held my waist. Now I knew her. This was Luba, from Kutno, not so far from Lodz although I never saw her there. She came to this place before me, she knew all of the rules and all the punishments. They said she had cried for four of her own children, but that she was still living because of the kernel of hope inside her that maybe they were not all lost. To the rest of us, Luba was our kernel of hope that maybe there was some kind of a future after these huts with their wooden racks for beds, their filth and their hunger. After the fear and the stink of the smoke and the prayers that please, God, please, let our children not be in it. She nodded at me again. We both heard the ghost violins as they began and then the clarinets joined them. They were not laughing in a freylekh at a wedding, this music had tears in it, but Luba and I turned together in a circle, our eyes closed so that we could feel our hair lifting in the dirty air of the hut as we danced.

When I go back to see if Mrs Wojnawski has been able to eat her lunch, the music is still playing, and I wonder how she can sleep with such dancing sounds in her ears. But the older folk have their own ways and, although I am sure it isn't true, some of her family and some of the others who work here say she is not just confused, but deaf too.

The tray is still on the table with wheels that I pushed close to her bed. It is all still there, the traditional roast beef, minced into small pieces and the matching grey roast potato mush. It must be completely cold now, but I want to try again to ask her to eat some. Maybe she is not sleeping. I go a little closer. Her breathing is steady. She has one hand resting at the bottom of her neck. The other is on the frame that holds her wedding photo. And I see that she has been crying. I catch my own breath because I know that this proud woman will not want the shame of somebody who works here knowing her sadness. I leave the tray and turn for the door. I will tell them on the next shift to be careful, that Mrs Wojnawski has not eaten her lunch.

'Arifa.'

'Mrs Wojnawski? I thought you were sleeping.' I turn back.

'I never sleep. I'm too old.'

'Ah, I see. You haven't eaten your lunch,' I tell her.

'Oy! I don't need any lunch either,' she says and lifts the frame to show me. 'Did you see my photograph?'

'I certainly did,' I answer. 'You made a beautiful couple.'

'*This* was a party. This was a celebration!' She pulls the scarf from her head and waves it in the air. 'We had dancing. Henry and I tricked everybody, holding hands under the handkerchief. And now that I am old, they want me to have more celebrations, but I've told them that I won't have it. I will leave and go back to my flat if they try to make me.'

She takes the photograph and holds it like a mirror.

'How can it be good to celebrate being so old? How can

19

there be a party without Henry? He loved my hair so much. He wanted to make it into a cloak.' Now she is whispering, but when she looks at me her voice is stronger. 'Arifa, I asked you to find me a headscarf. And please look for my coat. I want to go out.'

THREE

Eighteen days and counting

Afternoon

I hear the doorbell ring and the front door open and close and I can just make out James murmuring something along the lines of 'not too sure it's a good time'. Then the click of heels hurrying down the hallway. The living room curtains are drawn and the lights are out, but Sylvia Wojnawski doesn't do concerned taps at closed doors.

'Deborah, darling, whatever are you doing in the dark?'

Switching on the lights is one way of trying to get an answer.

'Hello, Mummy.' I shuffle up into a semi-prone position on the sofa and reluctantly remove my eye mask.

'Just look at your eyes!'

They are red. And my mother can't see it, but my throat is raw and I've been through a family box of tissues over the thought that Bubby doesn't want her celebration. The one I've been racing around party-planning and perfecting for the last God knows how long. It isn't the fifteen minutes of Guinness

World Record fame and it isn't the grateful smiles and thank yous – well not that much. This was my own small bit of Wojnawski family lore and big bit of love for Bubby, and even James couldn't stop the tears, when all that usually takes is me being folded into his Dior-scented chest.

'I know,' I say, because I also know family lore won't work on Mummy, especially where Bubby's concerned.

'But why didn't you call me? If it wasn't for James, I would already have been on my way into the West End.' A pause. 'Matinée tickets for *The Tina Turner Musical* with Carol, but no matter, darling.'

Mental note to James: never call my mother outside of scheduled times, you know that for God's sake. Just never. He's sat through enough of my rants about Adam and favourites, and the fact that nothing I do has ever been good enough, to know better.

'But it does matter, Mummy. There was no need for you to miss the show.' James also knows that Mummy is the last person I would have called if I hadn't switched my phone off before retiring to the safety of drawn curtains and sofa, but I aim for a placatory smile. 'I don't remember you being a fan of Tina Turner.'

She isn't, but you can bet she will be from this day forward, at every possible opportunity for airing family grievances with Carol, or Zita, or anybody else who appears to be willing to commiserate over the ineptitude of her ever-bungling daughter.

'Always open to new ideas. So important to learn and change, darling.'

My mother has given up Sunday matinée tickets and is now sitting on my coffee table next to my sofa. Unheard of.

'Now then, what have you gone and done to Bubby?'

Eye mask. Strangulation. Mother. Possible?

'What have *I* gone and done to Bubby?'

'Yes, that is what I said.' Sharp intake of breath. Her, not me. My rolling-of-eyes-at-my-mother days are over. 'James said that the party was off, and we all know how much she was looking forward to it. You're the *maître d'* and today was your turn to visit. Ergo.'

James. James! Stick to the bloody script!

'That's not exactly how it went.' Play for time, Debs. 'Look, I don't suppose you'd like a cup of tea now you're here, would you, Mummy? A cappuccino? Oh, Meelie and I made some lovely cupcakes together this morning.'

'Don't you try fobbing me off with Amelia.' She actually tutted, but it was worth a try. 'My grandmother-in-law is about to turn 128 or some other scientifically-implausible age and knock some Frenchwoman off her *record mondial* and now – and goodness knows how you've managed it – the celebrations have been cancelled?' She clutches her trademark real-if-not-heirloom pearls for emphasis. '*Ce n'est pas possible*, Deborah.'

'I know.' What I don't know is why I put up with my mother and her certainty that it must always be my fault. Psychoanalysis has never appealed, but Daddy's anything for a quiet life approach sometimes has its limits.

'So what are you doing about it?'

I hold up my eye mask and point to the bottle of Pinot Grigio on the coffee table that I hoped would take the edge off Bubby's bolt from the blue, if not off a rescue visit from Mummy. I brace myself for the next salvo, but she reaches over and squeezes my hand. I squeeze my eyes shut and shake my head, but I know she can see the tears. And now my mother is sitting next to me on the sofa and pulling me into an actual hug against her Sunday matinée faux-Chanel jacket. It's almost as if some part of her, somewhere, does think family lore is worth crying over. Unheard of.

We are on the way back to the Cedars. James is driving and my mother is riding shotgun. I am safe (ish) in the back seat, next to a large bag containing a tin of homemade cupcakes, a bottle of vodka and one of tonic (deadline too tight for fresh herrings) and the framed photograph of all the great-greats taken at my cousin Juliet from Canada's wedding last summer. Amelia, adorable in a spangled Boden dress in the photo, has been left behind to play with the other Amelia next door.

I am rather glad to be out of earshot of most of my mother's narrative on the streets of northwest Greater London and their inhabitants (of course that's what she's talking about) and James seems to be redeeming himself with many a nod and the occasional appropriate comment. *Well, I never! Who'd have thought it? Of course, Sylvia, of course.* Or similar. I was given just enough time to freshen up and reapply my make-up before leaving, so now I am playing guess-the-price whenever we pass an estate agent's board in an effort to ensure that my smoky eye effect does not slide into panda.

'Deborah?'

I drag my thoughts away from an estimation of a not very desirable '30s semi conversion with paved off-street parking (formerly front garden). Can't be more than £350,000 for a first floor flat on the A404, surely.

'Sorry, Mum?'

'I was asking whether you had investigated alternative venues.'

Oh, run out of local gossip then.

'Well, no, we all agreed on the Cedars' function room. Reasonable and convenient. Direct wheelchair access by lift. I had no idea that the resident super-centenarian was about to stage a rebellion.'

'Very droll, darling. Glad to see you've cheered up.'

She looked it. Not.

'So no contingency plans at all then?'

'Not really.'

'Typical.'

Thanks.

'Although, I must say the old crone really has gone and landed us up to the neck in the proverbial creek this time, hasn't she?'

'Mummy!' I burst out laughing and James' shoulders shake as he grips the wheel.

'It's no joke! Your father was suggesting we send an invitation to the Mayor of London the other night. That got me thinking Downing Street or even Buckingham Palace. After all your great-grandmother is an international phenomenon. I was just worrying about the security, and now look.'

'It might have been a little late for those invitations in any case.'

'I hardly think you of all people are in a position to give me lessons in logic just now, Deborah.'

This time I would have rolled my eyes but there is a vanity mirror in her sun visor and she is looking in it at my reflection.

'No, we need to stick together. We are family and our family has always stuck together.'

Yes, I suppose when we are up to our neck in the proverbial creek, we always have.

'We need a proper plan.' She looks at my reflection even

harder. 'Especially since no contingency plan for the bookings has been made.'

Ah. The Wojnawski glue is rather less adhesive when it comes to everyday opportunities for point scoring.

'I have such a plan,' she continues.

Being the driver, James' sun visor is of no use, but our eyes meet in the rear-view mirror. They are wide.

'Yes, Mummy?'

'I will talk her out of it.' A pause for dramatic effect and then, 'James!'

This, as my husband slams on the brakes to avoid hurtling into the car in front: it had slowed to accommodate the real-time traffic conditions, whereas his eyes had been unable to tear themselves away from the rear-view mirror at the announcement of my mother's proper plan.

'Sorry, Sylvia. You were saying.'

'Would you please keep your eyes on the road!'

'Yes, of course. Sorry about that.'

'As I was saying. My plan.' A small cough. 'You two can accompany me up to the third floor, but I will speak to Bubby alone.'

Perhaps James and I should wait in the ecumenical prayer room on the ground floor in that case.

'I will take her the vodka and begin with a little chat about my weekend, just the way I would on a normal visit.'

My mother's normal visits to Bubby happen about once every other leap year, but I say nothing.

'That way I can ease the subject of the Guinness party into the conversation and tell her how much we are all looking forward to celebrating her life, remembering Henry and hearing anecdotes about the shop and the people of the East End of London.'

Henry is of course my great-grandfather, born Heinryck, and the East End is about as exotic to my mother as Lodz.

'I am famed as a dinner party hostess adept at making people feel they are the centre of attention and I am sure that what works with guests from many different walks of life in a dining room in Harrow-on-the-Hill will work with an elderly lady who, let's face it, has not always had an easy life, has not always had the chance to shine.'

I am trying hard not to catch James' eye again in the rearview mirror as my mother turns in her seat to look at me. I think she may be expecting applause.

'Oh. Yes. Yes, that sounds like an excellent approach. Empathetic.'

'I beg your pardon?'

'*Em*pathetic, Mummy. You're always looking at things from the other person's point of view.'

Thou shalt not bear false witness. Thou shalt honour thy father and thy mother. The Ten Commandments can sometimes be confusing.

'Yes, so important, Deborah. One of the most important things that I have tried to impart to you and your brother. So glad you see that now.'

Despite the distractions of the 'proper plan', James has by now managed to back the Audi into a space in the Cedars' car park. I wish that, like my brother Adam, I was an ocean away in my Brooklyn apartment. But I am not. We are here and my mother's ingenious strategy is about to spring into action. I reach for James' hand because James is a doctor with excellent bedside manners and he works wonders when it comes to instilling feelings of confidence. We look into each other's eyes *sans* rear-view mirror. Mutual support will have to do then.

A few steps ahead of us and, as yet unencumbered by the

bottle of alcohol that is to seal the deal, Mummy whisks through the automatic entrance doors and strides over to the lift. She is determined, but does not confuse haste with speed or considerations of good manners and waits for James to press the up button. The doors open and eject a gaggle of other Sunday visitors, none of whom seem in the least affected by concerns over having an extremely stubborn and unempathetic elderly relative. Nods and smiles of varying degrees of sincerity are exchanged and then it is our turn. Another button for James to push. The doors close. Three floors can sometimes feel forever, can't they, and I avoid catching anyone's eyes in the lift mirror by holding James' hand and thinking back to that badly located flat I was trying to price on the horribly noisy A404.

Ping. Studio 318. Photo of Lodz. The red light is on, but Mummy grabs the vodka, touches the *mezuzah* and kisses her fingers. I look at James. Surely she won't – there could be a bedpan in there. But she does. Of course she does. She is Sylvia Wojnawski and no matter, darling!

'Bubby, my dear, how are you today?'

She shuts the door behind her, presumably hoping to secure the exclusive rights to the tales of her proper and successful plan, but then there is a shout. A very loud one.

'Deborah! James! God help us!'

James shoves himself through the door and I scurry in behind him. My mother is sitting on the floor by Bubby's bed and the vodka bottle is spinning wildly beside her. My great-grandmother is not in the bed and Mummy's face is an entirely uncharacteristic picture of panic.

She looks up and waves a sheet of A4 paper at us.

'Deborah. James. Do something, will you? That bloody old crone has gone and done a runner!'

FOUR

Eighteen days and counting

Evening

The A4 was the discharge form now sitting on the scratchy blue blanket that covers my grandfather's malfunctioning and probably horribly scrawny legs. A few paragraphs above the signatures that were shown to us with not a little ceremony by the Cedars Sunday duty manager, a Mr Darren Simpkins, is a statement that is about as accurate as the Book of Genesis. 'Next of kin: Mr David Jakob Wojnawski, born 26th March 1927 and sound of mind', it says. I've checked the date and, yes, the form was signed today, so God alone knows how much money Dr Pamela Chalmers M.D. (also on duty on this momentous Sunday) must have handed over for the right to use those two magic initials. Because Grandpa David's mind is about as sound as a three-legged racehorse and I can prove it.

'Grandpa?' I say and pick up the limp bag of fingers splayed on the bedcover. Not a flicker. 'Grandpa?' This time I take a deep breath and force myself to keep my eyes open as I bring my face in line with his. Grandpa was not the most handsome of men, even in his prime, a sad fact that family tradition puts down to the permanent scowl etched onto his face by the generally appalling temper induced by his marriage to my late grandmother, Esther. The same tradition that prefers to hush up the inevitable psychological damage that has been passed down through the war-torn generations and wreaked havoc on pretty much all of us, on all sides of the family, as far as I can see. So for Grandpa David, the difficult Wojnawski disposition is blamed on Grandma Esther. Grandma and the fact that, in his youth, he was declared to be some kind of mathematical genius destined for Oxbridge and Nobel prizes, but ended up wasting his talents on a life behind the counter in a Jewish grocery in the East End. Whatever the emotional duress inflicted by history and family, close-up, aged ninety-or-so, my grandfather is not the prettiest of sights.

'Grandpa?'

'Who's there?' The words are barely audible and are accompanied by shuddering lips and flecks of spittle. I do not flinch.

'It's me. Deborah. You remember "Oom-pah-pah" don't you? You know, from that film, *Oliver!* We used to love to sing that one!'

'Oliver. Oliver?'

I'm not sure, but I do think *Oliver!* has got something working behind his wrinkled forehead.

'Oom-pah-pah, oom-pah-pah, that's how it goes…'

'That's it, Grandpa David, well done! They all suppose what they want to suppose, when they hear oom-pah-pah!'

Mercifully, his surprisingly ear-splitting singing voice has trailed off under mine. So yes, OK, there is some glimmer of memory in there. But sound of mind? Dr. Chalmers will know exactly what she can do with her phoney medical qualifications when I've finished with her!

'We did love that one, didn't we, Grandpa? But never in front of Bubby, isn't that right?'

'What's that? Rubbish?'

'Bubby, Grandpa. Bubby.'

His ancient mouth twists back into that familiar scowl and I pull my head away.

'Really, Deborah, must you be so thoughtless?'

I had almost forgotten that Mummy and James had taken the trip up to the fifth floor with me. And now Mummy has pulled Grandpa's wheelchair over to his bed and is sitting in it. Her sense of drama must have won out over her rules on decorum and dignity.

'David, dear? David, this is Sylvia.'

A hint of a pause to see if he remembers her? None.

'David, you really must see that it was a terrible mistake to sign this form. A terrible mistake.'

She picks up the form and waves it at him.

'Because Bubby's gone now. She's disappeared. We don't know where your mother is, David.'

Well, we know where my mother is and her attempts to spell things out for my grandfather don't seem to be working. The flicker has gone and he is still scowling into space.

'David, honestly!' She springs out of the wheelchair and grabs at his arm. 'You know, we do need you to sign another form...'

'Sylvia, just a minute. I think it's time for Grandpa David's nap.'

I don't know if James saw me clap my hand over my mouth, but he has gently put an arm round Mummy's shoulders and is turning her away from the bed. Her face is a vivid shade of London bus, but for once she is following doctor's orders.

'Oh, you bloody Wojnawskis,' she mutters. 'Vindictive and bloody-minded, the lot of you.'

'Mummy, I don't think Grandpa David could hear you,' I say.

'Of course he could hear me. Vindictive, I'm telling you. If there's a grudge to be borne, you Wojnawskis will bear it and don't think I don't know that, Deborah.'

Daddy's don't-mention-the-war claim about Mummy's let's say 'brittle' manners is that it is in large part down to her relationship (or lack thereof) with her late mother-in-law (not to mention her still living grandmother-in-law), her own mother having died not long after their wedding. But even so!

'He's always felt hard done by. Always sure he would never live up to Bubby's expectations.'

But that's par for the course for anyone with a Jewish mother, isn't it? It is for me in any case.

'Always played the martyr.'

Ok, now I know we're in Jewish mother territory. Especially mine.

'James, we really must find a way of having a new form signed.'

———

We didn't and now the photocopy of the discharge form is gracing our kitchen table, weighed down by three definitely half-empty glasses of vodka and no tonic. The black scrawl of Grandpa David's signature sits alongside Bubby's at the end of the page, just above the more legible penmanship of that bloody fucking Darren Simpkins. (Yes, vodka and my mother's certainty that the failure of her plan is my fault, combined with the disappearance of a closely related soon-to-be world record holder, are all things that make me swear.)

James has his Mac out on the table. D. Simpkins Esq agreed to inform us (so very good of him) that Mrs Wojnawski left the Cedars in the excellent care of her exceptional carer, Ms Arifa Hashmi, but did not agree to divulge (the idiot) this eminent person's address or phone number. Confidential information under the Data fucking Protection Act of nineteen fucking ninety-eight. Well, Saint Arifa is going to need protection – I knew there was more to her game than soft hands and fucking bedpans! And little does Darren know that my brother and three of my cousins are lawyers and will soon be tearing up every last punctuation mark of that bloody discharge form and his fat fucking arse along with it. But I digress. James has his Mac out on the table.

'Arifa with an "a", is that right?'

'Yes, darling, an "a" at the beginning and an "a" at the end. Like Amelia in fact. And Hashmi is h-a-s-h-m-i.'

'Nothing for Arifa Hashmi London on Google.'

Nightmare.

'I'll have a look at Facebook.'

Nothing. I mean there are Arifa Hashmis out there, but none of them are ours. Unless they are commuting to Pinner from Northampton, Michigan or Islamabad. Ditto Twitter and Instagram. Nightmare, nightmare, nightmare.

'Isn't there a phonebook dot com?' I say.

'You think so? Nobody's listed in phone books anymore,' he answers.

'Worth a try though, isn't it?' Come on, James!

Bingo! There's an A. Hashmi in Camden. Potentially a tad

expensive for a carer at the Cedars, and yes, I'm right. The A is for Ahmed.

'I'll call him though,' says James. 'No law against having a wife with the same initial.'

He does.

'Hello, Mr Hashmi?'

Mummy suddenly clutches my hand. One surprise after another today and I almost miss the end of the call.

'Yes, I see. Sorry to have bothered you.'

I leave my hand in Mummy's. James takes the other one. Mine, not Mummy's.

'I'm sorry, darling, I don't know what to suggest next,' he says. 'I don't suppose any of the family know much about this Arifa, let alone where she lives, but we could text them.'

'Call the police, that's what we should do. This is bodysnatching of the very worst kind!'

'I think you mean kidnapping, Mummy. Bodysnatchers tend to rob graves and the whole point of Bubby is that she's still alive.' I tap Grandpa David's signature on that bloody photocopy. 'And I'm not sure the police are going to be interested once they take a look at this little gem.'

A phone bursts into life and we all jump. Vivaldi's *The Four Seasons, Spring*. Mummy enjoys seasonal ringtones. She grabs it.

'Hello? Michael?'

'Put it on speakerphone!' I hiss.

Mummy makes batting movements at me and listens, her mouth open. Which would have been comical for its sheer impossibility under other circumstances.

'No! Stepney? But that's ridiculous!'

It is rather a long way from Pinner, I grant you, but I have heard people live there.

'Right. Right. We'll meet you there. Just the tiniest minute. Pen!' she hisses back at me.

I scrabble around in my bag and James beats me to it, sliding the discharge form across the table at her in lieu of notepad.

'Cornwood Drive. Got it. Yes, number seventy-one. I think whoever gets there first had better wait outside. See you there then, bye.'

Amelia L. is a little clingy when I explain that she is having a sleepover at Amelia B.'s next door, but a promise of a first-day-of-the-holidays-trip-to-Pizza-Express tomorrow does the trick. That and Mummy (hers, not mine) tucking her up with Froodle, her faded and just the right kind of stinky cuddly frog, in bunk beds with Amelia B. 'Two Amelias, one up, one down, Mummy!' There's a catch in my throat as I reach in for another kiss. James and I really will have to do something about her being so clingy.

In the back of a (vodka-induced) black cab, there is no escape from Mummy's running commentary, this time along the lines of 'how could she do this to me?' but I am between her and James and married couples snuggle up in times of need, don't they, so his warmth and informed medical opinion on the sheer physical robustness of the old bird help drown her out.

I realise with something of a mental jolt that I haven't been back to the East End for over twenty years. Sunday visits switched to the Cedars when Bubby left the flat above the grocery, and the newfound hip-and-happeningness of Brick Lane has never quite appealed enough to tempt me away from my preferred shopping venues: Hampstead and the Shepherd's Bush Westfield. I try to see if there's anything I recognise by peeking round James' chest, but it's getting dark. The cabby's sat nav says 'four minutes to go' and 'Commercial Road'. Mostly two or three storey brick buildings with shop fronts that have those loud signs across the top and are usually late night mini-marts or bargains galore or takeaways. Quite a lot of the ones around here are clearly proud to be halal. A couple of turns and here we are on Cornwood Drive. We all peer out of the windows. Looks as though number seventy-one is somewhere in the middle of the long row of squat purpose-built flats that have nothing appealing about them (whatsoever) in the last grey light of day.

James pays and we are greeted by what even I recognise is not a pedigree dog peeing against a bollard put up to stop people blocking the entrance to the flats with their cars. A horn honks and there is Daddy.

'Daddy, what are we going to do? What are we going to do?'

He wraps me in a hug that is almost as comfortable as James's.

'Why didn't you call us sooner if you had Arifa's address?'

'I'm so sorry, darling, I know you were all on pins, but I didn't switch my phone on until I was back in the car. The trout scarper at the slightest noise. Anyway, we're here now.'

'Yes, we are.' Sunday fishing at the reservoir is Daddy's idea of heaven. Peace and quiet and a good excuse to turn his phone off. Nightmare.

He and James shake hands and there's an air-kiss on the cheek for Mummy.

'So how do we do this?' he says.

I can feel my mother gathering her thoughts, and probably

36

her pearls, and this really is no time for another one of her proper plans.

'You go first, Daddy,' I say. 'After all you're the only next of next of kin this side of Canada.'

Arifa's living room is tiny, especially when reorganised around an ancient lady in an electric wheelchair. Mummy and Daddy have been offered the sofa, I am perched on one arm and James is on the other. Arifa has brought in a stool from the kitchen. There is untouched tea and biscuits on a small table to one side.

'I said be quiet.' Bubby cuts short Mummy's ongoing plan to honour Zeyde Henry's memory. 'I will be the one holding the record.'

Is it me, or is her Polish Jewish accent stronger now that she's back on home turf?

'I will be the oldest of the world. That the world has ever known. Not you, not you and not even Rivkah Mendel.' She lives in studio 303 at The Cedars, if I remember rightly, and is eons younger than Bubby. 'That gives me my right and my say in how we will do this thing, wouldn't you agree?'

Three heads nod along the sofa. Mummy goes to speak, but Daddy presses his hand on hers.

'I am not deaf yet, but I do not hear you,' says Bubby.

'Yes, Bubby, of course that gives you the right to have your say,' says my father, 'but what about your health? We're simply worried about you and your wellbeing, you know. What about the risks of being away from the care of the Cedars?'

'I have the care of the Cedars, right here, right here in this room.'

We all turn and stare at Arifa, who seems to be wishing she and her stool were back in the kitchen.

'Arifa is a wonder, a *feyne meydel*. Such a good, kind girl, I cannot say it enough. All of you, yes, you come and see me, tell me, Bubby, *you* are a wonder. Once a month, once a fortnight. Maybe once a week if I am fortunate. But Arifa, she is with me almost always.'

It's called a job, Bubby.

'Yes, she is paid to do it.'

What? I didn't say that bit about the job out loud, did I?

'But not so very much. Her hands are gentle; her voice is soft; she is not in a hurry. She likes to listen when I talk to her about the old ways, and she will try to beat me at a game of cards. She laughs when I tell her her people are bad people.'

Now we are staring at Bubby.

'Because she knows I am making a joke. She knows that I have lived, ach, so many years. Too many years, too long to see bad people anymore. I do not see so much now, but I see people, that is all. Arifa is a *feyne meydel* and she will care for me here. In the old neighbourhood so that I can be with my David, my Dovid, again after all these years. Arifa, where is the boy?'

FIVE

Seventeen days more

Morning

It is ten o'clock and Mrs Wojnawski is sleeping. Here, in my bed, in this flat in Cornwood Drive. Nora. She is so old that I feel it would be best to call her Mrs Wojnawski, but I am happy that she has told me no, here I must say Nora. Her name is so difficult with all those Ws and Js. How tired she must be after all these years and this morning after such an adventure. It has made me tired too. Why is it that my heart is shaking me even though I know I am doing nothing wrong? Nora's mind can be confused, but it can also be clear and her body is thin like a thread, but one that is made of steel. A true wonder. I do believe she has the right to live her last times in the way she wants, but my heart was feeling too strong for my own body when she signed the paper and Mr Simpkins was shaking her hand and saying goodbye. I was calmer when it was time to wheel her out of the taxi and into the flat. These are familiar, daily tasks: residents must be transported or transferred from chair to bed or their shower stool. This needs no thinking and it soothes me.

There is a loud knock at the door as I am folding the sheets from the sofa.

'Nasir,' I call, 'go and see who it is.'

I guess who it is before I hear the voice and I go into the hallway.

'Open the door, Nasir. Let Mrs Levene come in.'

She has her little daughter with her – of course, it is half term. Amelia, I think. She is four or five and very pretty with her curls and her fluffy purple jacket. But she is shy, holding on to her mother's leg. Of course she is.

'Good morning, Mrs Levene,' I say.

'Hello, Arifa,' she says. She looks tired too and still not happy, but this is not a surprise. And it is not a surprise to see her here this morning.

'I'm sorry, I wasn't expecting you, but please come in. This is Amelia, is that right?'

'Yes. Say hello, Amelia.'

The little one tries to hide behind her mother's leg.

'It doesn't matter. I'm happy to see you, Amelia.' I smile, but my visitors do not. 'Please, come through.'

I show them into the kitchen. It is small, but I am not ready to bring this woman to the living room and let her see that I have been sleeping on the sofa. Amelia says no to some juice and no to water, but her mother says she will have a cup of tea. I have made baklava to welcome Nora yesterday and am glad to be able to present this hospitality. I believe I have a good idea of what Mrs Levene thinks of me and my home.

'Meelie, darling, I need to have a little chat with Arifa,' she says. 'Why don't we see if there's somewhere you can do some colouring?'

The child is sitting on her mother's knee. She shakes her head and tries to hide again.

'Perhaps she would like to play with my son. Nasir,' I call, 'come and show Amelia my phone.'

'Ah. Amelia isn't actually allowed to play with phones. We feel she's a bit young for that.'

'I see. I'm sorry.'

Nasir has come into the kitchen and now Amelia looks round her mother's arm.

'I could have a quick go, couldn't I?' she says, very quiet.

'As you wish,' I say.

'Amelia…'

'Please, Mummy?' This time louder.

'Amelia, you know our rules about phones.'

No, her mother is not happy to be here and not happy that I should try to have her change her rules. Amelia knows that too. And at her age, she knows what loud noise can do to mothers.

'Oh for goodness sake. Just this once then. But it's a treat, Amelia, just today. And only until I've had my chat with Arifa.'

The child jumps down so fast I almost laugh, but I know her mother has serious things to say. She is looking hard at me across the table. So hard I reach up and touch my hair. How is it this woman can make me wish I was wearing my hijab when that is one of the only things I am happy to have left behind?

'Would you like milk and sugar?'

'Milk please, no sugar.'

I have a small jug and I know that in England polite people use ones like this for milk with their tea. I put it on the table and pour the tea, but she doesn't let me finish.

'Arifa, you just can't do this to us,' she says.

'I think you mean the situation with Mrs Wojnawski?' I say it slowly to try and say that difficult name right and because I am not used to this quick anger that her family uses. With my own family, yes, I am used to some anger, but not with people that I only know a little.

'Yes, of course I mean the situation with my great-grandmother. Why else would I be here?'

'I understand. It is her wish, Mrs Levene,' I say. 'I tried to argue. I asked her to think of her family, but this is her wish. It is hard to reason with her.'

I think she knows this.

'Well, you should have tried harder!'

And I think she knows this would not work.

'It's simply irresponsible. What about her health, have you thought of that? I hardly need remind you that she is a very old lady. Very, very old, Arifa. The family all agree. She needs swift access to proper medical care in the event of any kind of health issue, however minor.'

I would like to answer, but she is too quick.

'And that is what she has at the Cedars. Your home is clean and comfortable. Quite adequate for you and your son, of course. But surely you can see the risks for Mrs Wojnawski.'

She is right, it is enough for us now. We are grateful to be here.

'I understand you, Mrs Levene. These are things that I said to her. She would not listen.'

'You know that my husband is a doctor, don't you? All it would take is a medical examination and his signature and back she will go. You could get into quite a lot of trouble.'

Again, she is right, I think. Tarek would not have liked me to do this, but he is gone and that has made me understand more about the things that make a good life.

'But Mrs Wojnawski is not willing to return to the Cedars, Mrs Levene. There is an excellent English hospital close by here, if we have a problem, but I think she will not need to go there.' Nora's body is strong like steel. It is her heart that needs to rest. 'I will take care of her, this I can promise you. She has told me she would like to visit some of the old places again. She would like to show them to my son. We have talked about my son many times and she was asking to meet him.'

'Your son? How very lovely that she wanted to meet your son, Arifa. I'm sure he is very excited to visit my great-grandmother's old haunts.' Her laugh is like a snort. 'And what about my daughter? What about me, my brother, my father? My father is Mrs Wojnawski's grandson, you know.' She makes a pause and stirs her tea. 'She is our family history. We love her.'

Now her voice is quieter and I see that what she says is true. This family has its own history of war and they sometimes use it like a weapon, sometimes like a shield. I think they mostly want to protect themselves from the scars that this history made on Nora's body and in the hearts of her children and her children's children. And I can see behind her armour that Mrs Levene wants to keep her great-grandmother safe too. I think I can tell her that Nora knows she loves her, but her daughter runs back into the kitchen.

'Mummy! Nasir showed me how to make a picture on his phone. And he printed it out for me. See? It's for Arifa. It's a drawing of Nasir playing with Domino. Look, she likes him.'

'That's lovely, darling, but if it's for Arifa you should give it to her, don't you think?'

The child looks at her mother to be sure. She nods and smiles. What else can she do?

'See, Arifa?' Amelia comes and stands beside me. 'This is

Domino and this is Nasir. He knows cats like playing with wool so I put lots of wool all over the page. That's the red and yellow.'

'I see that. Thank you so much, Amelia. Can I keep it?'

'Yes, it's for you, like I said.'

'Thank you. I will put it on the fridge. Can you find a magnet?'

She does. It has a bright photo of the Citadel taken for tourists before the war.

'This one's pretty, Mummy.'

'Yes, darling, it is. It looks very old, doesn't it?'

'Where is it?'

'I think it must be in Arifa's country. Is that right, Arifa?'

'Yes.' What must I tell this woman about my country?

'Very nice.'

'It is a very old castle in Syria.' Amelia is just a child; I should say something. 'In my city, Aleppo. It is an important Syrian city.'

'Yes, I've heard of Aleppo,' Mrs Levene says. 'It's been on the news. And that's why you and Nasir – isn't that your son's name? – have come here, to Britain, is it?'

'Yes,' I say.

'I see.'

So. I am happy that she does not want to talk about this either.

'Can I do another drawing on the phone, Mummy? One for you?'

And she is happy that her daughter did not ask to make a drawing for Nasir.

'Alright, darling. But it's the last one. We're going soon. I just need to have one more chat with Arifa, OK?'

She nods and runs back out of the kitchen.

'Will you have some more tea, Mrs Levene? Some baklava?' I say.

'No, Arifa. I don't want tea. I'm sure your baklava is delicious, but what I want is to see my great-grandmother. Have you thought about her dietary needs? About whether she can digest baklava and all that chilli and those spices you cook with?'

She reaches into her bag.

'Here. There's some chicken soup and some herring. The kind of food she's has been eating for well over a hundred years, that's part of *her* culture, Arifa. The kind that she loves and that has kept her healthy.'

I think this package is a test, a fight to see who can take the best care, but then I see that her hand pushing it across my kitchen table is shaking a little. When I look into her eyes there is a cloud in them. I see that she was once a young girl who ate the chicken soup around the table listening to stories from her great-grandmother. But then she looks up at me again and the cloud turns back into ice.

'Don't misunderstand me, Arifa,' she says and there is no more shake anywhere, in her hand or her voice. 'This is purely an emergency supply to make sure my great-grandmother eats some healthy food this morning.'

I keep my mouth shut. How can I battle with this woman? Did her family teach her not to trust other people while they were teaching her to make chicken soup? I will not tell her how my own family also learned to cook together, from my own great-grandmother down to me, how my fridge is already full of the food Nora has asked for or how she told me she is the only one with the right recipe for her soup.

'As I said, I want to see my grandmother. Immediately. I

came here this morning to bring her back to the Cedars, and the sooner the better.'

The anger is back, but I have made my promise to Nora.

'Mrs Wojnawski is sleeping.'

'So let's wake her up then.'

'She is old. She has a routine. I cannot change it.'

'Her routine didn't worry you yesterday.'

'You are angry. I understand and I am sorry. But you are wrong. I worried about her, but she is stubborn. I think that is the word you say. First, I try to change her mind, but then I try to respect her. She is an older person and this I respect. But you are right that yesterday she has no routine. Your great-grandmother is tired from that, from the moving around and all the feelings. So much feeling for her, for you and your family. This morning she is tired. I cannot wake her.'

I touch the pendant that Tarek gave me when our son was born and make myself keep looking at Mrs Levene.

'Considerate of you to think of our feelings,' she says. 'You didn't think you should show a little respect for our wishes? Ask for our permission?'

'Mrs Wojnawski has asked to leave of her own wish. Mr David Wojnawski has agreed. He is her son.'

'Mrs Wojnawski's wish. Mr Wojnawski agreed. I see. Mr David Wojnawski is almost ninety, Arifa, and often can't remember where he is, let alone where his mother should be living. I suppose you respected him because he was an older person too.'

I know I must listen. She is the one with the right to be angry. To use her anger as a shield for her fear.

'Well, in my family we respect our elders too, in case you were wondering, but we also respect the people who love them and have been caring for them for many years. I have been caring for my great-grandmother for many years, Arifa. Didn't you think it was necessary to contact another family member, perhaps one who is still able to look after themselves?'

'Mr Simpkins phoned your father,' I say. 'I think three times and there was no answer. Then he tried your telephone also, but again no answer. Mrs Wojnawski was upset. She was wanting to leave quickly. Mr Simpkins had the paper. So we went.'

What else can I tell her? I have made my promise.

'And who will look after her when you are on duty at the Cedars, have you thought of that?'

'I will not go to the Cedars. I will stay here with Mrs Wojnawski.'

'I see. Out of the goodness of your respectful heart.'

'I will be paid.'

So, now she knows this.

'And who is paying you?'

'I cannot say.'

'For God's sake, Arifa, this is my great-grandmother we're talking about!'

'I am sorry. I have a contract. I have been told this is private.'

I have been told also how this family talks about money, but this is private too.

'Well, I think I will have a talk to Mrs Wojnawski about her private arrangements. Right now.'

She stands up and the tea with milk that she did not drink splashes onto my table.

'She is asleep, Mrs Levene. This is my home.' I stand also. 'I ask you to respect and not to go where you are not invited.'

I look at her, right into her eyes. We can both see that we are each one of us sure we are doing the right thing to protect Nora.

'Fine.' It has taken her a moment to decide what to tell me. 'But I'll be coming back here to talk to my great-grandmother this afternoon. Amelia! We're leaving.'

SIX

Seventeen days more

Afternoon

Mrs Levene and her daughter are gone and the flat is quiet until I hear the small bell I left next to my bed a little after two o'clock. Nora has slept for many hours. I go quickly to her room.

'So you are awake, Nora. How are you feeling today? I think you slept well.'

She nods and points at the glass on the table by the bed. I pass it to her and she slips the teeth into her mouth.

'Ach, that's better,' she says. 'Good morning, Arifa.'

'You know it is really good afternoon now,' I say.

'It is? So I did get a good sleep then. You know, I had such a fright when I woke up and found myself in this bed. Your flat doesn't smell much like the Cedars either and that's a blessing.'

She pats the bed covers and I sit down next to her.

'I had a fright too when I came in here and saw you sleeping this morning,' I say, but I don't tell her that I bent down close to the bed to hear that she was still breathing, or that I am surprised to hear she remembers where she is. 'I'm used to seeing you in your bed in your studio and in this big one you look so small, even thinner than before. I will have to cook some good food to fatten you up.'

'Even your spices can't be worse than the mush they feed me at the Cedars,' she says. 'I will teach you some of my recipes – the leek soup, the chicken soup that will be very good for making me strong and healthy. And maybe you can learn to make chopped liver the right way in time for my party.'

I always like to hear her laugh. How can such a thin old woman make this noise like the hoot of a goose? She shakes her head and then she is quieter.

'Thank you, Arifa,' she says.

I take her hand in mine and smile.

'For passing you your teeth? I know you can't reach them from the middle of that big bed. Now I will make you some breakfast. *Labneh* yoghurt with chilli pepper, I think today. Maybe a little spicier than Aleppo pepper, but that is not so easy to find in Stepney.'

'Not too much yoghurt with the pepper, Arifa,' she says, 'and I would like it if you can find me some good soft scrambled egg to go with it.'

'Eggs I can find in Stepney,' I say.

I hand her her remote control so she can listen to her music. As I leave the room the violins and clarinets begin to play, but then stop so I turn back.

'After breakfast I would like to spend a little time with Dovid,' she says. 'Is he at home?'

'I think we should be able to do that, Nora,' I tell her, even though I know that finding her son in Stepney may be more difficult than finding Aleppo pepper.

I take my time clearing up the breakfast things and seeing that Nora is clean and fresh, dressing her and transferring her into her chair. I need time to think about how I can do this, what I can say to Nasir. I wheel her through to the living room and ask her to wait just a little longer but when I knock on Nasir's door I still don't know what I am going to say.

He is lying on his bed watching videos on my phone. I know I should be sending him outside to play with the other boys, but he says he doesn't like the other boys on Cornwood Drive and I have heard that maybe he is right.

'What are you watching, *habibi*?'

'Just a video.'

'OK. Can I watch with you?'

'It's just a bike video, Mama.'

So that means no. Nasir is angry with me about many things and one is his bike left behind in Syria. Of course we left it there; he knows we couldn't bring it, but on his bike he was always outside with the boys if there was no bomb warning or curfew, doing the tricks that scare me when he does let me watch the videos. He knows they scare me, but I never told him that for him to be out on the streets on his bike back home was what frightened me the most. My fear is another thing that makes him angry, and so is money. Here I let him use my phone and I bought a printer because I need to know that some papers are real, but he knows there is no money for a trick bike.

'Did you want something, Mama?'

'I need to ask you a favour.'

'Another one?'

'Yes, another one. Can you put the phone down, please?'

He does.

'And look at me?'

That is more difficult.

'I know you find it hard that Mrs Wojna, ah I can't say it, that Nora has come to live with us for a while.' I think I just have to keep going. 'Well, you know that she is very old and you know that we respect our elders, especially when their life has been difficult, when they have overcome great hardships with great courage. And Nora has a son. He is old too, but now she wants to think of him the way he was when he was a boy like you.' A boy that will not look at his mother? But I continue. 'You know about the war that changed their life. She wants him back the way he was before that – so much that now she thinks that's the way he really is.' I wish he would let me sit with him on the bed, put my hand on his. 'Habibi, she wants to think you are her son, Dovid.'

'Are you kidding me?' Now he is looking at me.

'Nasir, show some respect, if not for me then for Nora.'

'But you told me she hadn't lost it.' He taps his forehead.

'She isn't senile, if that's what you mean. Not most of the time. That's a wonder that even her doctors don't understand. And I don't think they would understand why she wants her young son back. That's why she's here.'

'Because she thinks I'm her son?'

'It's part of it, habibi, but she's also here to be with people who understand.'

'Well, I don't understand her and I don't understand why you had to go and bring her here.'

'I know. I don't ask you to understand, just to help a little.'

'Come on, Mama, I played with that kid for hours this morning.'

'Yes, you did.' Maybe not for hours, but yes, he played with her. 'And now I have something more to ask you. You will need to think of how much you loved and respected your nanna back home.'

He picks up the phone again.

'Nasir, will you listen to me? You won't find the people we left behind in my phone!'

I put my hand out and he gives me the phone, but he turns his head to look out at Cornwood Drive. I try again.

'*Habibi*, Nora doesn't have much time left. She has her whole family that wants to have a big party and make her into a kind of celebrity, but maybe she won't even make it that far. She could live another year, who knows, but she could leave us in her sleep tonight or tomorrow. While she is with us, if she calls you Dovid, if she believes you are her son, I want you to say yes, to be him.'

So I have said it. Now Nasir is looking at me again, but I don't like what I see in his eyes.

'You know something,' he says. 'You are as crazy as that weird old woman.'

'Nasir.'

'Look, Mum, I'm sixteen years old. I'm stuck in this tiny bedroom in a stupid flat in a neighbourhood where all they do is hang out and smoke and call after girls and even if I wanted to go out it rains all the f—, all the time. And now you want me to pretend to be some dead Jewish kid?'

'He's not dead, Nasir.'

'He might as well be.'

'*Habibi*, it is Nora's last wish. I know it's hard for you to understand but think, you are the only person in the world who can do this. You are something special.'

'Great, like Stepney's Got Talent.'

I actually laugh.

'Well maybe more like Nasir's Got Talent. Please?'

'No.'

'It won't be so often, just a few times a day maybe, at mealtimes.'

'Forget it.'

I sigh. Why does it have to be this way? How is it that now our children can make us do things in a way that is not what we believe in. I want to think that it's because Nasir left the old ways behind with his bike and his nanna, but I know he began to let go of them before that. Maybe it was the war or maybe not. So, my last weapon.

'*Habibi*, I am earning a little more money now that I am with Nora all the time. Maybe I will be able to save a little more too. And she is old, she is grateful to us for helping her and soon she will be gone.' God forgive me. 'She is a mother; she likes to treat her son. Maybe there will be money for a trick bike.'

In the living room, Nora has wheeled her chair over to the window. There is not much to see. The flats at the back have small gardens, but on this side there is just the road and the garages. Cars. Two big trees a little further. But her eyes are bad and anyway I think she is not looking at the view. She hears me.

'Is that you, Dovid?'

'No, it's Arifa.'

'Ah. I thought… When is he coming?'

'Soon I think. Right now he's doing his homework. He has so much work even though it's the holidays and he's a serious boy, isn't he?'

Is this the right thing to tell her? What will I explain if his homework is never finished?

'He is. So I will wait. Waiting I am used to.' She turns her wheelchair away from the window. 'In that case we have time to play a hand, Arifa.'

Nora keeps her playing cards in a bag that travels with her on her chair. One pocket for the cards and another for the chips. She has told me about the Saturday nights she played with Henry, once the Sabbath was over and Dovid was in bed. Sometimes with friends from the neighbourhood and a little of their music with the violins, not too loud. They maybe didn't know each other in the old days in Poland, but I think they liked to remember how it used to be to get together. Cards are a good way of tricking time and sparking some laughter. Instead of fear you have the excitement of who will win even if you are only playing for matchsticks.

I always shuffle and Nora always deals. *Alte kacker* cards, she calls them, for the old people, with numbers and suits and letters big enough for her worn-out old eyes to see. I didn't tell her that in my old days gambling was not allowed. I told myself that if Allah did exist he would have to forgive me for worse things than playing cards to make an old woman happy. It took me a long time to understand that maybe the way she loves her cards so much is part of what helps her mind stay so sharp. And longer to understand the flushes and the straights and why a number one card was stronger than a number ten. But now I understand the fun of it and sometimes I even beat her.

We face each other across the living room table. Two cards for her and two for me. I bet five matchsticks out of my small pile of thirty. Nora raises me five. I call that and am happy that she can hardly see my face because although I have practised, I do not have a poker face. Still, I only ever play with this almost blind old lady so never mind. She calls me. I knew she would and now I have to think. I fold my hand and she shows me hers. She has a flush.

'Oy!' she shouts and starts to hum a tune. I know it now: she hums it every time she wins with diamonds and it always makes me laugh. She has played it for me on her iPod. Marilyn Monroe sings it, the beautiful, sad blonde woman that probably everyone in the whole world knows. 'Diamonds are a Girl's Best Friend.'

'I know you're after my diamonds,' she says, shaking her fist at me.

'But you have my matchsticks,' I say.

She deals again and bets ten. (I don't mind that the rules say the dealer shouldn't play first. Nora just likes to deal.) I am planning my strategy when she turns her head towards the door.

'Is that you, Dovid?' she says.

I put my hand on hers. Personally, I would not bet that this boy who has come into the room so quietly is her son.

'Have you finished all your schoolwork now?'

'Yes,' he says, 'I'm all done.'

Now I put my hand on my heart, where he can see it.

'Good,' she says. 'Come over here. It's time you learned how to play a hand of poker.'

SEVEN

Seventeen days and counting

Evening

C all eight arrives as I turn the key in the lock of the front door. I'm more Coldplay than classical, but even I can tell the Vivaldi violins I've set for Mummy are crescendo on call nine by the time I have poured some juice and organised some kitchen table colouring for Amelia (one emergency phone bribe is enough for today). I shut myself in the downstairs loo, away from five-year-old ears, and pick up.

'Surely you realise this is no time to refuse to return calls, Deborah. Your father and I are tortured with worry.'

'Hello, Mummy. I'm sorry.' Almost always the right thing to say at the beginning of a phone call with my mother. 'Amelia was in the back of the car and I thought it might make it worse just to say "Bubby's staying in Stepney and I'll call you back".' Whether she would have let me get as far as my offer to call back is doubtful.

'She's staying? What do you mean, she's staying?'

'I mean she doesn't want to go back to the Cedars.'

57

'Oh, for goodness' sake, we all know that. It was your job to make her change her mind and take her back there.'

'I know, Mummy, I'm sorry.'

'Sorry? Sorry?'

Ok, so it's one of her repeat-everything-I-say-but-in-a-shrill-accusatory-voice phone calls, is it?

'Well, sorry just won't do on this occasion, Deborah. Your great-grandmother needs twenty-four-hour nursing care, seven days a week.'

Yep, told her that.

'And a doctor ready to mobilise at all times.'

That too.

'Bubby needs to be in her own studio, surrounded by medical care and eating a sensible diet. Imagine if anything happened to her before the World Record—'

'Mummy!'

'Oh for goodness' sake, you know what I mean. Imagine if anything happened to her at all – in that awful little flat with that Aretha woman cooking her all sorts of spicy food. We need her where her own people can keep an eye on her. Daddy and I are coming over.'

And that was that. I consider avoidance strategies, like popping in next door, taking Amelia to the cinema, or setting fire to the house, but facts must be faced. I had failed in my mission today as badly as Mummy had in her proper plan yesterday. Also, there are suppers to be made, baths to be run, stories to be read and wine to be drunk, all before James gets home from work and Batmum and Robin ring the doorbell. The thought of my parents in mask, cape and opaque tights politely waiting on the doorstep triggers the only real laugh I have had all day, energising enough to carry me out of my hidey-hole and back through to the kitchen to prepare

Amelia's lightly breaded cod goujons (waitrose.com) with oven chips and peas.

———————

'What do you think, James?'

Amelia is tucked up safe with Froodle after goodnight kisses from everyone including the caped crusaders. I love my husband dearly, but I can't help wondering if, at this point, my father might not be better off asking the opinion of the real Dark Knight rather than an orthopaedic surgeon from Northwood Hills. Or, given Bubby's age, the Ghostbusters. Although maybe that's the wine talking, especially since I had only made goujons for one and all I've managed to rustle up since then is a bowl of garlic and jalapeño stuffed olives (also waitrose.com).

'To be honest, I'm not sure what to do about Bubby, but I think Debs has gone above and beyond today,' my hero husband ventures. 'I think we should be asking her what she thinks about this whole mess, I mean, situation.'

Some archaic reflex makes me look across the table at my mother, but the spice from the olives seems to be keeping her quiet for now, so I have a moment to think about what it actually is that I do think.

'I think Bubby should stay with Arifa.'

There, I've said it and I can see from their faces that everyone else around the table is just as surprised as I am. Olives notwithstanding, my mother is the first to recover (no surprise there, then).

'Have you gone out of your mind, Deborah? Where are the nurses, the doctors, the rabbi, for heaven's sake? A 122-year-old Holocaust survivor can't just spend her final days eating halal pork with some Arab woman who arrived on the last boat. Do we know where she's from? Do we know her family? What's in it for her? I wouldn't put it past her and that son of hers to have had a new will drawn up already.

'Sylvia, I do think we should hear Debs out.' James squeezes my hand under the table. 'And incidentally, Muslims don't actually eat pork, halal or otherwise. At least we have that in common.'

His attempt to defuse the situation is sweet, but I am the only one who smiles. I squeeze his hand back.

'I mean, I don't think we have much choice right now. You know how stubborn Bubby is. And somehow she seems less anxious, maybe even less confused. More in touch with her old life.'

'I should think that's another reason to get her back to the Cedars as soon as possible. After all, raking up the memories of all those terrifying things she lived through—'

'Sylvia, please.' Daddy almost never interrupts Mummy and he's done it at least twice in the last two days. 'Go on, Debbie.'

'I don't mean the war. I think Bubby's the only one who knows how to cope with those memories. I mean here, in London. We all know that the grocery is the holy place of Wojnawski family history, well, now she wants to go back and see it. I don't know if she remembers that it stopped being Henry's Fruit long before the Cedars, but there was something in her voice when she was talking about it this afternoon.'

'But couldn't we organise a visit from the Cedars?' Daddy says.

'Yes, I suppose we could, but she kept saying she wanted to be in the old neighbourhood. And then there's Arifa's son. You all heard Bubby last night. She keeps calling him Dovid, confusing him with Grandpa, but it doesn't seem to distress her. You know how angry she can get about him never coming to visit her, even when we remind her that he's an old man now and not well enough for visits, even if they do live in the same care home. Well, there he is, at home with her.'

'Deborah, that's just odd. Michael, we can't allow this kind of freak show. Your grandmother deserves better than some gold-digging immigrants masquerading as her family.'

'Your mother has a point, Debbie. Doesn't she, James?'

'I do want to hear what Debs has to say. I've hardly met them.'

'Thank you, darling,' I say and squeeze his hand again. But with good old Mummy reminding me that sentimentality and financial considerations rarely mix, I really don't know what I do have to say now. Trying to keep the Wojnawski-Levene peace can leave me baffled at the best of times and this is definitely not one of those. Escaping back into the kitchen to rustle up some more olives is one option. Well, it would be if we had any left. And there are three pairs of expectant eyes looking at me from various angles around the table.

'Yes, Mummy does have a point, I do agree on that,' I manage. 'I mean, I hardly know these people either.' It's true, what was I thinking? 'Look, I know I said we should humour Bubby for now, but that doesn't mean we shouldn't plan to get her back to the Cedars once she's enjoyed a quick East London nostalgia trip.' Better, Debs, don't confuse the whole Jewish heritage thing with what's best for Bubby and the family long-term. 'In fact,' and now I arrange my face into my best shocked expression and look my mother straight in the eye, 'Arifa admitted to me that she is being paid to take care of Bubby in her home, but I don't know if that means she still has her salary from the Cedars or if Bubby's paying her directly now.'

'You see?' Mummy is suitably outraged. 'Gold-diggers of the worst kind. I say, let's get her back to the Cedars.' Mummy sits up straight and bangs her fist on the table like an auctioneer when the bidding is over. 'It's early in America. If you won't listen to me, I say we call Adam right now to find out how we can press charges against that so-called carer, have her sacked. And press charges against the Cedars too if they won't co-operate.'

'Look, I really don't think we need to be pressing the legal panic button just yet, Sylvia. The money is one thing, but what my grandmother wants is quite another. Perhaps we should be thinking more about that.' Oh. Daddy seems to have reopened the bidding. 'She has been living in that home for over fifteen years and I, for one, remember the battle we had getting her to agree to leave her flat and she must have been, what, a hundred and five, a hundred and six, at the time?'

Daddy drains his glass of wine and raps that down on the table. He has our attention.

'One thing we don't have to worry about in this family is a shortage of lawyers. Bubby's will is lodged with Dinnelman, Tate and Wojnawski. So is my father's, so is mine and so is Sylvia's. And if you and Debbie haven't instructed them yet, James, I strongly advise you to do so. Paul Dinnelman is my nephew, after all. We spend every other Sunday catching trout together and I hardly think he would fail to mention a request for a change to his great-grandmother's will. Unless of course she was suggesting making him her sole beneficiary.'

'That is not funny, Michael.' My mother rarely finds my father funny.

'Perhaps not, but you see my point. Call Adam if you like. I know he's concerned about Bubby too, but let's not launch him into courtroom drama mode just yet. I'll dot the Is and cross the Ts with Paul tomorrow. I'll check with the bank about any unusual payments coming out of Bubby's account and I'll talk to the Cedars about her room.'

'Good, so she is going back then.'

'Actually, I find I agree with Debbie.'

'But Michael, this is reckless, nothing short of irrespon—'

'She is my grandmother, Sylvia.' Three times. In two days! Bubby's disappearing trick seems to have reset Daddy's peace and quiet preferences. 'She is the world's oldest living person, despite the best attempts of some in that same world to get rid of her.'

He gets up and walks over to the baby grand that has been waiting for generations for a member of the Levene-Wojnawski family to become a concert pianist on it. I stifle an urge to run to him as I see the smallest quiver in his shoulders, and he turns to face us.

'Dinora Wojnawski is a bona fide miracle. Shouldn't that be enough for us to let her decide how she wants to spend the next few weeks? How she wants to celebrate becoming the world's oldest person ever? That's if she wants to celebrate it at all.'

Daddy looks at me and, I'm sorry, I try to concentrate on that shake in his shoulders, but I can't help it. All those emails and invitation designs and kosher menu options flash before my eyes. And so does the joy on Bubby's face that I've conjured up in my mind.

'But we can still have the party, can't we, Daddy?'

'I think you'd better ask Bubby about that, darling.'

'But the caterer, the hotels, the rabbi…' I hope no one else has noticed that the quiver has shifted to my voice. 'I will ask Bubby about it. We could have it here, couldn't we, James? After all, she only said she didn't want it at the Cedars.' The party is secondary, Debs. Daddy's right, we need to think about what Bubby wants. These are *her* last eighteen days – I mean before her world record. Right, I need to focus. 'In any case,' I say, 'we need to keep an eye on her. Paul may be your nephew, Daddy, I may agree with you on bona fide miracles, and Bubby may think Arifa's a *feyne meydel*, but who knows what could happen.' And who knows what I think about it all now between the shake in Daddy's shoulders, Mummy and her lawyers and the empty bottle of wine on the table. I stare down into my equally empty glass and focus. After all, Amelia's half term playdates at the Princess Diana Memorial Playground can bloody well wait. 'If Arifa and Nasir – or Dovid, or whatever Bubby says his name is – are going on the Henry's Fruit pilgrimage tomorrow, then so is Amelia and so am I. It's half term and I'll be needing some activities to keep her busy.' And out of my hair and off my phone. 'This week has just been renamed Trip Down Family Memory Lane Week and it will be a chance for Amelia to learn all about her heritage, because she and I will be spending it with Bubby.'

I feel rather pleased with myself and cross my fingers under the table that my mother's schedule of hair appointments and lunches with ladies will prevent her from signing up.

'Family Memory Lane Week. That's not a bad way of putting it,' says Daddy, and I should feel pleased with myself because the quiver has gone. 'Do you know, I think I'll join you.'

EIGHT

Sixteen days more

Afternoon

Nora is riding in the front, next to Mrs Levene. I would like to see what her face is showing now that we are pulling into a space not too far from the café that used to be her store, but I am right at the back of this big car, next to Nasir and behind Mr Wojnawski and little Amelia swallowed up in her purple car seat. Quaker Street Café it says in fat, coloured letters. They look like someone has drawn them onto the wide blind that would shelter the metal chairs and tables from the sun if one day it stopped raining. There is no one sitting there.

'So, here we are, Bubby.'

Mrs Levene switches off the engine and takes Nora's hand.

'Where's that?' she answers.

'On Quaker Street, at the shop. I mean it's a café now, but, you remember, it used to be Henry's Fruit.'

'I can't seem to recognise anything. What does it say on that sign?'

'It's the name of the café, Quaker Street.'

'This is a name for a café? They don't like their own name? Henry always says, you put your name on your shop, then the people know they can trust you. We have our regulars, many, many regulars. They trust us, they know we have the good prices, the fruit is fresh, good quality. Always good quality, we're proud to sell this fruit.'

'I wish I had been old enough to remember the shop before it shut down,' Mrs Levene says and I think Nora is going to say more about how maybe she thinks it still is today, but Mr Wojnawski has been in the car long enough.

'Perhaps we should go in and see how it looks. Quite a few changes from what I can tell from here. Now, let's get you out of this contraption, Amelia.'

He starts to unbuckle the car seat and I would like to go and arrange the wheelchair, but Nasir and I must wait for the others to get out first. Mrs Levene has already opened up the back and maybe she knows how to unfold it. Mr Wojnawski has helped Amelia down and tilts the seat forward for Nasir and me. I can see that Mrs Levene is still standing at the back of the car. Now she bends into it. Which is the right thing to do? Go and show her where to lift it, which lever to pull to open it, or let her keep her pride? Nora decides for me.

'Arifa! Where is my chair? What do I need to do to get someone to come over here and take me to the shop?'

'Excuse me,' I say and move in front of Mrs Levene to lift out the chair. The mechanisms are simple these days and soon it is ready.

'Who knew folding electric wheelchairs were even a thing?' she says, with a small laugh.

I knew, but I also know a small smile back is best. I wheel the chair round to the front of the car. Nora seems almost as agitated as the day we left the Cedars, and I am glad when I have her safely in her chair. I want to tie her silk scarf around her neck better because even in the spring I like to be careful, but she flaps at me with her hand.

'*Genug*, Arifa, that's enough,' she says and her voice is thin; we should hurry. She has her handbag on her knees, and she is rubbing her thumbs up and down the leather.

'Here we are. This is the door,' I tell her.

She reaches up to pat her wig and now she arranges her scarf herself.

'Allow me.'

Mr Wojnawski holds the door open and I remember I didn't check if Nasir was following. I turn to see and there he is. He is holding Amelia's hand although from his face I think it was her idea. Good.

What a bright place it is, this café. One whole wall is covered with a painting of a woman, her face, very big. Her eyes are shut because she is breathing in the smell of her coffee in a yellow cup. The painter has made it delicious. She is wearing a lot of make-up, with blue on her eyelids and red on her cheeks. She is so big I can't stop looking at her. Mrs Levene chooses a table right underneath her and I wheel Nora in with her back to the wall because maybe the colours are too bright and anyway, I know she wants to be facing out at the shop, even if she can't see so much.

'Dovid,' she says, 'come and sit next to your mother.'

Nasir doesn't look up, not at me, not at Nora. He sits and scrapes his chair as close in to the table as he can get, but Nora reaches over and pats his arm.

'So you see, here we are back at the shop. Oy, I can't even tell you how many years it has been.'

It must be many, many years, maybe almost as many as I

have been alive if Mrs Levene doesn't remember coming here. These times away from what you know are long.

'Now, *bubbeleh*, tell me what you see. I want to know about everything.'

'Bubby, we've only just got here,' Mrs Levene says. 'Perhaps we should order first and then we can all have a look around.' She turns to me. 'Are you going to sit down, Arifa? They generally come and take your order in this sort of place.'

Yes, of course I was going to sit, I was just waiting to know if Nora needed any help. Mrs Levene waves me to the empty chair opposite the giant lady with all her colours. The only other people I have seen so big on a wall were men and they were not drinking coffee. Their eyes were open and staring straight at me. Before the war, it was best to say how much you liked them and after it started it was best not to see the paintings, or what was left of them, at all. Here, I know I may think what I like about this coffee woman. I can buy the same make-up or get angry about her shiny red lips, whichever I like. But I don't know how much time I will need to be living here in this country before I can decide.

Except Nasir, now everyone around the table is staring at me.

'Well, Arifa?' So Mrs Levene has been waiting. She waves her menu at me.

'Don't worry, Arifa, we're not in a hurry,' says her father. 'Take your time.'

'I'll just have a glass of water, please,' I say.

'You're sure?' he says. 'These lattes they have sound rather good. Do you see? Chocolate and berry as well as coffee.'

'She wants water, let her have water,' Nora says. 'They serve berries with the coffee here now?'

'Thank you, but water is fine, really,' I say. I'm thirsty and this café is expensive, I think. They will not let me pay for my own drink, but some of them may be thinking that I should.

'So, Bubby,' Mr Wojnawski raises his glass of milky coffee. 'Here's to Henry's Fruit and to you and Zeyde.'

'*L'chaim*,' she says. It means 'to life' in Hebrew. This I know.

'*L'chaim*,' he answers and so does his daughter. Amelia picks up her milkshake. I pick up my glass too, water for life, and I try to look at Nasir to get him to do what he should do.

'Dovid, you don't drink to life for me and your father?'

I feel the blood in Nasir's cheeks at the snap in Nora's voice, but then she laughs.

'Ah, Henry is already gone and I have such a long life, so long. Why should you ask for more of this life for me? I have enough, it is enough to come back here with my boy.' She pats him on the arm again. 'But if Henry was here, he would like these new colours, I think. We didn't have so many colours, so many pictures.' So now she has remembered the old shop is gone. 'But so many things you could buy on many, many shelves, covering the walls and going almost right up to the top. What is it, the top?'

'The ceiling, Bubby,' Mrs Levene says.

'The ceiling, yes, that is right. So up to the ceiling, the shelves, and Henry with his big wooden ladder when the customer needed a special spice or maybe some shoe polish. We knew which shelf for everything, the customer just had to ask. Everything.'

She pulls the knob on the arm of her wheelchair towards her. It moves backwards and Mrs Levene and I both jump up, but she waves a hand in our direction.

'Am I a child? So let me be, I know how to drive this thing.'

She steers it towards the other side of the café and stops next to an empty table. She tilts her head back. I know she can see that wooden ladder inside her head.

'Henry, what's taking you so long up there? You tell me you know every place where every single thing is on the shelf. So why when we have a customer waiting you can't find what you're looking for? You're hiding something up there? It's where you keep your secret cash box?'

I turned back to Mrs Rosen.

'Oy, what should we do with these men? I should climb that ladder, maybe? Let all the customers see my legs up there?'

We were still laughing when Henry came over to the counter holding that little square box like it was a diploma from law school and he just graduated. He pinched my cheek and laid it down on a sheet of brown wrapping paper.

'Nobody else is seeing your legs, Nora. That's a treasure I keep just for me.'

And the shine in his eyes as he winked at Mrs Rosen was my own small piece of treasure.

'I pack the shelves,' he said. 'I know where to find the ladies' articles. So I'm the one that goes up the ladder. Here you have it, Mrs Rosen, Copper Gold. London's finest.'

'London's finest? You know, your husband is a born salesman, Mrs Wojnawski, such a sweet talker. No wonder business is so good for the two of you.' Her cheeks shone with a copper gold blush. 'You think I don't know I can find this in all the other shops around the area, Mr Wojnawski? With the same picture on the front to show me how good my hair is going to look for the wedding? But I keep coming back here for the sweet talk.'

'That skinny little girl on the label could look as good as you,

Mrs Rosen?' Henry answered. 'Not possible. Copper Gold is the perfect shade for your complexion, I'm telling you. You'll be the belle of the ball on Sunday.'

'You see what I mean? As if he could know something about my complexion!' She laughed the kind of laugh that I knew would keep her coming back to Henry's Fruit for her groceries and her ladies' articles.

'So Sunday is the wedding already?' I said. 'The days go so fast.'

'The days and the years, Mrs Wojnawski. Hannah will be turning twenty-two a month from now.'

'Oy! Is that a fact?' I hardly knew the Rosen girl, but I felt my throat tighten to think of her so grown.

'Twenty-two?' said Henry. 'And I think she must be a beautiful girl when I see her mother.'

'You don't have any deliveries to prepare, any shelves to fill, Henry?' I asked him. 'You think Mrs Rosen wants to hear what you have to say about her daughter? Maybe you know where we keep all the ladies' articles, but wedding talk is ladies' talk.' And scolding him away from the counter gave me a moment to clear my throat.

'And your new son-in-law is from a good family, you told me?'

'Oh yes, oh yes.' Mrs Rosen nodded in case two times 'oh yes' were not enough to convince me. 'He works with his father in leather goods. They have a warehouse down by the docks.'

'The Milbergs?'

'That's right. So you know them?'

'I know their business. Beautiful gloves.'

'They are. Jonathan gave me a lovely pair in chocolate brown when he and Hannah got engaged.' She glanced down at her hands as if maybe she was wearing them, but June is too warm for leather gloves. 'A good family, but a small one these days,' she said. 'His father lost a brother and two sisters. And his own father. His wife too. Only his mother and a cousin came back.'

The list was not short, not long, but it came with a pause, like all the lists.

I nodded and gave her a quick, sad smile and then wrapped her Copper Gold hair dye.

'Is there anything else I can get you, Mrs Rosen?'

'You must come to the wedding, Mrs Wojnawski. And Mr Wojnawski and David too. Come and see my Hannah under the chuppah.'

She put her hand on mine and I just stopped myself from pulling it away.

'Such a kind invitation,' I heard myself say. 'We would so like to share your happiness, but we have no one to mind the shop and we open every day. You know that, I think. Except for the New Year and Yom Kippur.' And at weddings no one can take their eyes away from the beautiful young woman in the finest dress she will ever wear. But I did not say that.

'Such a pity, Mrs Wojnawski. Are you sure you can't make an exception? Just for one or two hours maybe?'

She really did seem sorry that we could not come.

The bell over the door of the shop rang before I could tell her that 'no, I didn't think so', and it was David, in a tangle from running down the street from school.

'Dovid, come and say hello to Mrs Rosen,' I said. 'Her daughter is getting married on Sunday.'

'Hello, Mrs Rosen, mazel tov,' he said and, 'Mama, I told Andrew and Jake that we could play football.'

'Well I think the football will be waiting for you for quite a little while,' I said. 'I need you here behind the counter while I help your father with the delivery boxes.'

'But I—'

'Dovid,' I said in the voice that he knew was to be obeyed or risk his father hearing about it. Because Mrs Rosen didn't need to hear

him say that he didn't understand, that the boxes were always his job.

'Here, Mrs Rosen,' I said before turning away to some peace in the back room, 'please take the Copper Gold as a small gift. Mazel tov *to you and your family.'*

'You used to pack the boxes out in the back, you remember, Dovid? Over there right at the back. There used to be a doorway and we put up that curtain with the wooden beads. They used to click when we walked through.'

Nora shuts her eyes for a moment and then points to the back of the café, where there are tall stools against the wall now and lamps shining on photographs of more walls painted with blue and yellow shapes. Stars. I think there are tears in her eyes, but not in her voice.

'And the counter was just by the doorway with the cash till. In the old days we had that big, big book right next to the cash. Everything we sell, it was written down in the book. Henry called it his Bible. Ach, that man, he had no god left after the war. So, the Bible, counting all our prayers for the future, very careful, no mistakes, because when you arrive at someplace and you get some luck, you want to be careful not to spill it. It's the way my mother used to say: the cow fills up your pail, you will carry the milk gently.' She swivels her wheelchair in my direction. 'Arifa, your mother too she tells you that I think.'

I nod and wish Nasir would look at me.

'And then one day – who can say how many years ago? Maybe fifty, sixty, Henry and me were not so young. So one day a man – this one is young of course – comes to the shop, smart with his suit and his tie and he has a big, huge box, so big I can hardly see his face. Just his eyes staring round the box, like this.'

She laughs to herself now and I see that her grandson and great-granddaughter are nodding at her and smiling. For a moment I feel their happiness in my chest.

'Henry tells me here is a surprise for me, but what a surprise! It was not my birthday, not a *yom tov*; this careful man was never buying me a present. Should I need presents? This was a present for Henry's Fruit, to make us modern and up to the date. In that box it was a new cash till, big and white and made of plastic. So ugly, but up to the date. And so many noises it made and so many lights. Dovid, you used to run home from school, so much you loved to help in the shop with the new machine. But your father made one rule for you, one rule!'

Nora waves her finger in the air with those nails that are still neat and filed. Always polished in pale pink, the way she likes it, as if taking care of her nails will open up the knots in her joints.

'We turned off the switch that counts out the change for you. Mental arithmetic! Count it out in your head, Dovid, that's what he told you. Children who know mental arithmetic are the ones with the good brains, the ones with the proud mother and father. With our customers – they are careful, the people who like to come to Henry's Fruit – you don't make so many mistakes with the change. They count it, you can be sure. Ach, mental arithmetic. But he kept his Bible, my Henry, even after the big new till, and everything was in there, every sale, every prayer. Do you still have it, Machel, is it still in my boxes?'

It takes a moment for Mr Wojnawski to find a voice to answer. 'I think so, Bubby. I'm sure it must be.'

'You should take a look and find it. Bring it one day. I would like to turn the pages. Ach, now you have your telephones and your world of the web, but I would like to turn the pages.'

Nora is still shaking her head as she steers her wheelchair back over to the table.

'You know, Dovid, your father didn't have any god left, but books are important. You need to know about the books. Tomorrow we will go to the *shul*.'

Sixteen days and counting

Evening

'A glass of water, seriously? No, but who does she think she's kidding? I bet she won't be ordering glasses of water when she's spending Bubby's money back in Cairo or wherever it is she comes from.'

'I thought you told me she was from Aleppo, Debs. Syria. Anyway, it's a war zone so I doubt she'll be heading back there any time soon, with or without the cash.'

Adam always has to be right. Always the smart one, shooting down my family-dinner-table attempts at wit and wisdom when we were kids and making Mummy practically gleam with *naches*.

'Yes, I *know* it's a war zone, Adam,' I say and even I can hear the fossilised teenage huff in my voice. I half expect Daddy to come on the line and say 'That's enough, you two. Your mother spent half the day preparing this casserole and I expect you to have enough respect for her to eat it while it's hot'. Half the day. I ask you. 'It was a manner of speaking. You should have seen her with her perfect manners and her way of being right there, you know, hovering around the wheelchair, ready to take care of Bubby's every whim, every time you just wanted to give your own great-grandmother a bit of TLC. And that son of hers—'

'Debs, I didn't call you just to hear you bitch about Arifa pushing you out of the limelight. It's one in the afternoon here and I've got a couple of big cases I need to work on.'

'Oh, right, sorry to keep you away from your *cases* for a couple of minutes.' He really did want my huff to unfossilise into thousands of fragments of grown-up Deborah anger, did he? 'This is just *family* business. Put the clock on if you like; I think we can still just about afford your hourly rate.'

'Oh, come on Debbie.'

'Don't you Debbie me, Adam Wojnawski.' I am an adult, with adult indignation. And only Daddy gets to call me Debbie. 'Bubby has been in her new guardian angel's flat for over forty-eight hours now and this is the first moment you could spare to call me and give me your expert New York lawyer opinion? And you choose that same moment to tell me how to behave? I'm the one who's been charging around the East End trying to make sure she doesn't tip her out of her wheelchair. I'm the one who's had to put all of Amelia's half-term plans on hold.' Oh my God, was there really a touch of the Sylvia Wojnawski in full martyr mode in my voice just then?

'Look, Debs, let's cut to the chase. Are we planning to sue Arifa or not?'

'Well, I…' The part of me that wanted to be the one to help Bubby into her wheelchair this morning and hold her hand when she cried, wants to set the whole of Scotland Yard on Arifa, and if Bubby won't go back to the Cedars, it wants to have her come and live here, with people who love her. But then there's the part that knows that she needs expert care and that Arifa does seem to know what she's doing.

'So?'

'I don't know,' is the best that I can offer. 'Mummy thinks she should already be behind bars, but Daddy is being... Look, you know how Daddy would usually go fishing rather than stand up to Mummy, well, now he seems to have switched sides.'

'Well, I for one think he should wise up. Sue her?' Now it sounds like Adam is revving up into serious attorney-at-law mode. 'We could throw the entire book at her and probably have her deported. Undue influence, breach of duty, intentional infliction of emotional distress, take your pick. We might even be able to stretch it to false imprisonment. And if anything happens to Bubby while in her care we can throw in some recklessness or criminal negligence... And all that with an aged Holocaust survivor. About to become the world's oldest person ever. The tabloids would have a field day. They'll be wheeling out the veterans that fought for her freedom. And the families of the 7/7 victims. Remind me what religion she is?'

I've never seen him in action, but this sounds like Adam is in full flow in the courthouse and it's reminding me of some of those childhood dinner-table battles.

'Adam,' I say, and I try to remember some of the mitigation tactics that occasionally worked back then, 'I think we should keep the tabloids out of this. And the war. I mean, we all agree on looking after Bubby's best interests and those are probably not in a council flat with Arifa, but terrorism? I mean, false imprisonment and all that?'

'When did I say we would go for terrorism charges, Debs?

I'm trying to paint the bigger picture here.' And I'm trying not to let my older brother push my buttons. 'And you know, we could go after the Cedars too. The guy that signed the release document – what did you say his name was?'

'Simpkins,' I sigh.

'Right, well, Simpkins will soon be feeling like he's been simmered in boiling oil. By the time Dinnelman, Tate and Wojnawski have negotiated the out of court settlement, Bubby will be getting free residential care for the rest of her natural life and so will Grandpa David. And we'll still have some change out of a couple of million.'

'A couple of million? Are you serious?' I know I need to keep my mind on what's best for Bubby, but seriously! This is new kitchen, even eternity ring ahead of our tenth anniversary, territory.

'Well, it's been a while since I've handled cases in the UK, so I might be going over the top a bit. You'd have to ask Paul. But basically, it's an open and shut case, Debs.'

I am swiping between family photos of Bubby and Pinterest pictures of open and shut eternity ring cases when James gets home.

'How did it go at the café, my love?' he asks and kisses the top of my head.

He is such a darling. All those surreptitious texts I sent under the table. All those emojis and exclamation marks, and he still asks the right question after his long day at the clinic. Think he told me he had four hip replacements scheduled. Or was it five? I pour Chardonnay into the extra glass that was ready on the coffee table and top mine up. My fourth.

Definitely not my fifth. Because he may have got blood on his scrubs, but I was the one who spent the day with a bunch of total brain replacement candidates and, although I'm keeping it under medically supervised (James) control, all of the latest family peacekeeping challenges are definitely upping my alcohol intake.

'Oh, it was marvellous,' I chirp and raise my glass. 'They must have known we were coming because they had *klezmer* music on, and Daddy and Arifa danced the *hora*. For a minute, I thought Daddy was going to bust a gut trying to hoist Bubby's wheelchair up on his shoulders. I had tears in my eyes thinking of you and me up there on our chairs at our wedding, darling.' I raise my glass again.

'Come on, Debs. It can't have been that bad.'

'Well, it wasn't that good.' I reach over and give him a hug. 'Listen, darling, I'm sorry. Wine o'clock arrived before Amelia even had supper today, I'm afraid.' And now my glass is empty again. 'Tell me about your day.'

'A bit like yours, I think. Blood everywhere.'

I snort.

'And since when are you interested in post-op outcome assessment and *protrusio acetabuli* diagnosis, anyway? How did it go?'

'Sure you don't want to eat first, darling? I've made your favourite cod goujons for you. With peas.'

'I know you're stalling, Debs. Shoot.'

I clear my throat.

'Well, the place has completely changed, obviously. Street art and fancy lighting instead of the weekly shop and those old wooden shelves they had. There's an exhibition on with all these vaguely star-shaped spray-paint scrawls. Jewish artist if the stars are anything to go by – not to mention the prices.

Didn't see anything that looked like a Banksy, though, so if he does own it, he must be going even lower profile these days. And there's one wall with a huge painting of a multi-coloured woman drinking coffee. Amelia loved that.'

'OK. And?'

Knows me so well, my husband.

'In fact, I don't know if it was such a good idea after all.'

'So what happened?'

'Nostalgia happened. Bubby sort of went off into a trance at one point. She went wheeling herself around the place muttering about ladies' articles and a wedding. And then she started talking about when they got a new cash till and asking Daddy to find their old cashbook. She called it the Bible.'

'And what's wrong with that?'

'She was crying, James.' Yes, and so was I. And so was Daddy. 'She should have peace at her age, and quiet. And then there's that boy.' Luckily my glass is full again, though not for long. 'It's just weird. Bubby keeps calling him Dovid and he just keeps looking at her as though he hates her.'

'Come on, darling. He's a kid. He just didn't want to be there. I think he deserves a pat on the back for playing along with the whole thing.'

'Of course you do.' My James is always looking for the best in people. Sometimes even my mother. 'But you weren't there. He looked as if he hated her, I'm telling you. As if he hated all of us. Even Amelia. And that mother of his. Such a bloody saint. "I'll just have a glass of water, please."' Is it me or am I actually slurring my words now? 'Well, I've got her number, I'm telling you. OK, so she knows how to unfold an electric wheelchair in three seconds flat, and she's first on the draw with the paper tissues when Bubby starts blubbing, but I can see right through her game. And what makes it worse is I'm not so sure that Bubby can, even though I'm the one that's family!' I blow my nose to try and hide the green-eyed monster. 'Mummy was right.' Did I say that? 'Gravedigger! I mean gold-digger! And if she thinks I'm going to give up on the Guinness and the rabbi, she's got another think coming. There's only sixteen days to go now.' My voice seems to have gone up an octave. 'What was it Adam said? Undue influence, that's it – reckless driving under the influence. Or something like that. Anyway, maybe I was wrong, James. Maybe Bubby should be back at the Cedars. And maybe Adam is right and we should throw the book at bloody Saint Arifa.'

I look over at James and blow my nose again, loudly.

'Come on, darling,' he says, 'you know you don't mean that.'

Don't I?

'No, I suppose I don't. But if Arifa thinks that she and that son of hers will be the stars of the show when we go to *shul* on the next leg of distracting Bubby from the World Record she can … she can bloody well piss off!'

TEN

Fifteen days more

Morning

'So how is Mrs Wojnawski getting on now that she's back in the East End?'

Mr Simpkins is good at smiling when smiling is the right thing to do, but mostly just with his mouth. Sometimes I see his eyes smiling when's he's chatting with the nurses in the staff kitchen, especially the young ones, but not always with the residents. Now it's just his mouth. I think he is hoping that Mrs Wojnawski is getting on fine, because that way maybe there will be no trouble from her family.

'She's getting on fine,' I say. 'Even a little less confused when we are in my home, and we are visiting the places she used to know and she is remembering many memories.'

'That's good, Arifa, lovely,' he smiles.

'It is,' I smile back. I don't tell him about the tears at the café. 'And she has her appetite back. She tells me my *labneh* yoghurt with chilli pepper for breakfast is delicious.'

'Chilli?' His smile has gone. 'But the doctors don't recommend that for the elderly, Arifa.'

'It is a joke, Mr Simpkins, don't worry. I cook good fresh eggs for Mrs Wojnawski in the morning and we laugh together about my terrible Syrian food.'

'Eggs! Ah, oh ho!'

Mr Simpkin's mouth doesn't seem to know how it should laugh right now.

'Well, Arifa, that's good. Lovely for Mrs Wojnawski to enjoy a joke now and then.' His smile is back. 'Anyway, here, this is the box she was asking for.'

'Lovely. Thank you.' Should I say sorry for the chilli joke? 'Mrs Wojnawski will be happy to have it.'

'I'm sure she will, lovely. And has she mentioned when she will be sending for the rest of her things? Not so much storage space here at the Cedars, I'm afraid.'

'I will ask her, of course. Perhaps Mrs Levene will come after the half-term holidays.'

'Yes, I expect she's busy with the little one this week. Emily, isn't it?'

'Amelia.'

'Amelia.' I see that Mr Simpkins thinks it is a lovely name because he is still smiling.

I do not hear a sound when I open the front door to the flat, so I am careful to shut it quietly behind me. Nora was impatient for her box, so she asked me to get her up early, but maybe she has dozed off in her chair. Nasir must be in bed still, sleeping or playing through his favourite bike tricks in his head. Before, I sometimes left him the phone, but now I have it with me when I am out in case Nora needs me. This also makes him angry. I will give it to him when he wakes up. I hang up my coat and smooth it out on the hook. Smiling back at Mr Simpkins has made my mouth stiff and I would like a cup of sweet tea to help smooth that out too, but the kettle will make too much noise. So I will make *kibbeh*. Chopping the onions and grinding the meat with the dough by hand will feel good and when I serve them for supper and Nora asks me what they are and tells me they smell terrible it will make me laugh. Even now I smile to think of it. I will need the big glass bowl that I keep in the living room because there is not enough room in the kitchen cupboards. It is not beautiful like the earthenware one with the green spiral shapes my mother gave me when I married, but I am glad. When I pound the bulgur and the meat together, I will see through the glass to the plastic-topped kitchen table and so it will make me remember that I live here in Stepney instead of thinking back to my wedding day. And that will smooth things out.

'Hey, Mama, what are you doing?'

I jump. I was thinking about his father's eyes in mine and the music. Perhaps I was humming. Nasir is sitting at the living-room table and Nora is opposite him. She has dealt the cards and they both have a small pile of matchsticks in front of them.

'You're staring, Mum.'

Of course I am staring.

'Nasir, *habibi*, you know how to play now?'

'The boy is trying to beat me. This I did not teach him.'

Nora has put her wig on and a little lipstick too. Nasir has stopped staring back at me and is looking down at his cards. Yes, he has a poker face that must be hard to beat.

'So, you have the box, Arifa?'

'Yes, I do. Just a minute.'

I go back into the hallway and breathe for a moment, not too long.

'Here, I think this is the one.'

'Yes, let me have it.'

She wheels her chair away from the table and reaches out with both arms. I lay it on her lap and she lifts the lid. Her hands are shaking, but she is old – they shake. She first lifts out a folded piece of fabric. It is blue and white and silky with stripes. I know this, it is a Jewish prayer shawl, with long tassels. Nora leaves it folded and hands it to me. Next an envelope and a long black box, the kind that expensive pens came in before fingers tapped on screens and when ink was permanent. Like so many things. Then a smaller square box. Nora moves her fingers across the lid as if they could help her read something written there, but the cardboard is white, blank.

'You thought maybe I lost this, Dovid?' she says.

Nasir is still wearing his poker face, but at least he looks up at her.

'I didn't keep so many things, but the precious things I make sure I have them with me. Thank you, Arifa, I am happier now I have it here.'

Her fingers are still smoothing across the lid. Should I ask her what this thing that makes her so restless is?

'You are welcome. I was happy to get it for you. And Mr Simpkins sends you his best wishes.'

'Oy! That Simpkins can keep his wishes for those youngsters at the Cedars. Does he think maybe I'm missing the place? When I have your cooking and my son with me here?'

I smile at her and I would like to put my hand on hers, but it is still fussing with the box.

'You must be hungry, Nora. I will start cooking our lunch. I was thinking of making *kibbeh*. Do you know them? They're like...'

'Can I have the phone, Mama?'

'*Habibi*, I...' What is the power of this phone that it makes him forget the way to talk, the way to act around elders? 'You know better—'

'I've been waiting for you to get back for hours.'

'But you and Nora haven't finished your game.'

'The game we can finish later, but I have something to show you, Dovid.' She holds the box out to him. 'I think *kibbeh* will be good for lunch, Arifa. Will you make them with mint?'

The bowl is made of glass and the table has a plastic top, but even so I am thinking of home. I wish it was Tarek and our wedding day for the joy of it, but it is my mother. I know her eyes when they open so big that her eyebrows disappear under her hijab. I know what comes next. Until I was old enough to know better, it was an hour or so in my room and I had better not touch my toys or my books (and I never did. I didn't know then that mothers have no superpowers). Later, a list of my faults and how they stained her honour, my father's honour and my own, in a voice that told me that this was the truth and the only truth. Nasir may think he is lucky that she refused to leave her home until it was just a mass of broken stones and that even then she refused to leave her country. He will not hear her tell him how a man of his age must respect his mother when she speaks, must respect his elders when his elders speak. But I cannot escape her eyes and her voice, no matter how deep I look into my glass *kibbeh* bowl. I cannot escape the truth that my modern son with his western ways is a stain on my honour and a mark of my failure. That phone is my only connection with my family, with my mother and her laughter and her truths. Now it is also the knife that cuts the thread and carves my life into a new shape. It means I can see what is left of my family every week, more when there is good news to share, or bad. It lets me tell my mother where I find my spices here in Stepney and what a good boy Nasir is, but it cannot put her arms around me. I try to see only the glass bowl and the plastic table. Chopping onions always makes me cry so I am quick to stir them into the meat and bulgur to soften the aroma.

Nora and Nasir are up, so there is no need for quiet, I know that, but I decide to pound the *kibbeh* by hand. The force will be soothing. An ache in my arms will push out the hum of my mother's voice in my head and, if that doesn't work, I will hum a Syrian wedding song, louder.

'Mama!'

I jump at Nasir's voice so close. I didn't hear him come into the kitchen.

'I won't do it! You've gone too far this time. This whole crazy thing has gone way too far, I'm telling you! I won't wear it.'

'*Habibi*, what's wrong? What are you talking about?'

'I'm not wearing that thing. I'm not her son. I'm not a good Jewish boy. I'm Moslem and you can keep your bloody trick bike! I've had it.'

I try to catch his arm, but he is too quick, out of the kitchen, out of the flat before I can even catch my breath, and when I do say his name, my voice is much too quiet. My mother begins scolding both of us again and I hurry into the living room. Nora has turned her wheelchair to the window, but I don't think she is seeing the two tall trees or the cars. There is a small round piece of cloth on the floor by the table. I pick it up and I see it is a skullcap, a *kippah* I think they call it. White soft fabric with a shine and some letters sewn into it that I cannot read.

'Nora?' I say.

'The boy is spirited. Dovid says he will not wear his bar mitzvah *kippah*. What will I tell his father? That he will calm down and listen to his mother? Yes. Because he will, I'm sure. He is a good boy.'

Today is the day that we will go to the synagogue. The others will be here soon, for lunch and for our trip. They will be angry. I put the cap on the table and go over to the window. Nora is still looking at the view, the two trees and the cars, but she must have smelled the onions because her cheeks are wet with tears.

ELEVEN

Fifteen days and counting

Afternoon

I'd forgotten all the gold and painted wood and complicated sculpting. If the place ever comes up for sale (unlikely, I know) the new owners will have a lot of de-cluttering work on their hands if they want to get their synagogue-conversion featured on Grand Designs. And the windows aren't a patch on the kind you get in one of those sympathetically repurposed neo-Gothic Anglican places of worship offering three and a half bedrooms and majestic proportions. No awe-inspiring multi-coloured patterns, no saints with gleaming halos, no shepherds. And no messiah on a cross. Obviously.

'And you must be Deborah.'

I must, must I?

'Yes. Yes, I am. Deborah Levene.'

And he must be the rabbi, judging from his beard and his cheery uncle body language. I suppose the open arms are meant to be welcoming, but they're borderline #metoo imo.

'Levene, of course,' he chuckles. 'But you were still a Wojnawski when I last saw you here. Probably not much older than this little one.'

Amelia gets an age-appropriate hair ruffle, thankfully.

'Ha, ha,' I manage. 'This is my daughter, Amelia. Mrs Wojnawski's great-great-grandaughter.'

I still don't recognise him from way back when I was not much older than Amelia, but I do recognise the guilty flush on my cheeks from reminders that the Wojnawskis haven't been seen at *shul* for a while. Wait a minute, how does he know we're not Saturday morning regulars at Harrow & Wembley Progressive anyway? And furthermore, we only used to come to the East End for weddings and bar mitzvahs and… Where is Bubby anyway?

'Lovely to be back, Rabbi,' I put out my hand to be shaken, not hugged. 'So many happy memories. Especially for my great-grandmother. Daddy, don't you think we should see how she's getting on?'

'I'm sure she's doing fine with Arifa' is all my father can muster in what is quite possibly one of Bubby's hours of need. 'It is lovely to be back, isn't it?' Oh, the hypocrisy that can be induced by rabbis, especially the old-fashioned ones with beards. 'Seems like only yesterday that I was under the *chuppah* crushing that glass with my foot.' He actually gives a little hop and a stamp. 'Such a pity Mummy couldn't make it, isn't it, Debbie?' What? Has some kind of guilty 'my-wife-made-me-switch-to-progressive-Judaism' conscience sent him completely mad?

'Rabbi!'

God bless Bubby. Her voice may be faltering but it's wriggled me out of that one – and given me an excuse to check up on whether Saint Arifa really is being as well-behaved as she should be on her first visit to a synagogue.

'Is everything alright, Bubby? Anything I can get you?'

I glance at Arifa with a tight smile, instead of the daggers I would have used in other circumstances.

'I was calling for the Rabbi, not for you, Deborah.'

Ah, right.

'Of course, Bubby.'

I give Amelia's hand a tight squeeze because at least I know I'm still *her* go-to source of help and support.

'What is it, Mrs Wojnawski?'

The Rabbi is at hand.

'I was trying to remember some of the history of this place, to tell my friend Arifa. She has come from Syria not so long ago and she is not a Jew.' Possibly something our spiritual leader might have guessed for himself. 'She doesn't know much about a synagogue.'

'Of course. At least I don't suppose she knows much about this one.' A cough to underline his tact. 'The history of our place of worship is long, ancient,' he says, and I pray (LOL!) that this isn't the beginning of a sermon as he starts to rock back and forth on his feet. 'Our community here is a young whippersnapper in comparison, but it has been welcoming the faithful for over 150 years.'

He smiles at each one of us in turn and I start to pray harder, holding tight to Amelia's hand in case I'm tempted to run away.

'This very building, still home to a vibrant congregation despite the pressures of the modern world, was first consecrated as a synagogue by Dutch Jews, Ashkenazis. They came to escape poverty in their homeland and build a better life in the nineteenth century, and they created their *shul* within the walls of a chapel that dates back as far as the seventeenth century. The chapel itself was built by Huguenots, Protestants who were fleeing religious persecution in France. Hundreds of years after the Huguenots, came more Ashkenazis, this time from eastern Europe, seeking safety from pogroms in their turn. And of course, since then, its walls have provided some moments of comfort for those, like you, Mrs Wojnawski, who lost so much and so many to the crimes of the Shoah. Our synagogue, here in the East End, is a sanctuary that has always welcomed the exiled, whoever they may be, whenever they come in peace.'

My father blows his nose and I realise that I have stopped praying. And that I've used up quite a few tissues. Although Bubby seems to be less moved by the history lesson; I suppose she's heard it all before. Less moved emotionally, anyway, because I see that she and Arifa have moved physically. They've headed further down to some of the rows of wooden benches. Bubby's electric wheelchair has quite a bit of speed on it when she feels like it, and Amelia and I have to step up the pace to find out what the fun is all about. It's tricky squeezing between the two peace-loving exiles, but as close relatives, it's understandable that we should want to lap up every drop of family lore, even if it does mean sticking my elbow out.

'Ach, here it is.'

Good, I'm in time for the big reveal.

'Deborah, you are right in the front of it. Arifa cannot see, so you will move over.'

I do not give my great-grandmother's carer the pleasure of another tight smile, or a roll of the eyes, but I move over. A millimetre or two.

'Ouch!'

That jump must have shifted me at least six inches. How

are her bony old fingers strong enough to pinch that hard? I'm not sure whether Amelia's lips are twitching or wobbling, but I am well practised in the art of glares just stony enough to stifle both giggles and tears.

'There. You see? Presented by Mr and Mrs Henry Wojnawski. This is where Henry would sit on the *Shabbas*, the times we had someone to mind the shop, not so many, and at the New Year and Yom Kippur. I took the stairs to sit with the women.' The shine on the brass plaque on the bench seems to be firing up Bubby's memories. 'All of us together, upstairs. The old way. Not like in that new-fangled place of your wife's in Harrow, Machel.' Bubby's fondness for my mother has never needed much to fire it up.

'We have a lift now, Mrs Wojnawski. Would you like to go up and see?'

I don't think Bubby heard the rabbi.

'I don't like these *shuls* where the men and women pray together. It is not the old way. In my day we kept the traditions, we respected the word of God. But I think you know how the young generations are losing their respect, Arifa.'

Well, if she does, the idea of respecting *other* people's families doesn't seem to bother her.

'Bubby, I think the Rabbi was trying…'

'When I was your age, we kept quiet up here. The women and the girls, we listened to what the rabbi was saying and the songs the cantor was singing.'

No, she definitely didn't hear what this rabbi was saying.

'But with the war over, even in a *shul* like this, with the men downstairs and the women upstairs, they have to do their chattering. What's that lovely hat you're wearing, Rivka? Did you hear about Leah expecting her sixth little one? Oy! They say it's going to be another girl and that her Arnold is already going around planning number seven so he will finally have a boy. They are organising wedding lists up there and trading recipes for *cholent*. On the *Shabbas!* I tell you, so many times I want to reach out and pinch them so they would keep quiet and listen. All I have is my Dovid, but if I had a daughter, she would have been quiet alongside me, none of this chattering and recipes. She would know what respect is about in a synagogue. Ach, my God.'

Bubby shakes her head, as if she is coming back from those days. But her glare is still so full of boulders I realise I do have some memories of Friday evenings at *shul* when Zeyde Henry was alive and I wasn't allowed to play hand games with the other girls up in the women's gallery. I move another six inches out of the way of her pinching fingers.

'Arifa,' she snaps. And after all there's no reason not to let her carer have some of the glory. 'I think I will take the lift to get another look to see all the things they've changed.'

Daddy presses the button before Arifa can steal the whole of the show.

'Perhaps we should go with them, Rabbi, given my grandmother's... I mean, the circumstances,' he says.

The Rabbi strokes his beard (because they do, don't they?) before pronouncing on the Word according to Moses or similar on whether thou, the male of the species, shalt go unto the women's gallery or not.

'I see no reason not to, under the circumstances,' is his learned opinion and I for one am not going to ask him which chapter of the Torah he got it from.

If Bubby's glare has softened at the news that her grandson will be taking his first tour of the women's gallery it doesn't show, and the ride up in the lift is silent. When the doors open,

Arifa begins to push the wheelchair onto the balcony, but Bubby waves her away and scoots over to the balustrade electrically. Amelia tugs at my sleeve and pulls at me to follow the wheelchair. I swipe my mobile onto silent and slip it into her sticky hand, shushing her with a finger to my lips. I'll find a moment to brief her later on the fact that this outright breach of Mummy and Daddy's rules is our little secret. And thank God – I mean goodness in here, of course – there are phone rules to break, because I am sure we have been wandering the desert for at least forty days when the Rabbi starts to rock on his feet again.

'The women's gallery was added to the main part of the synagogue in the time of—'

'Rabbi, my friend Arifa is very interested in the history of our *shul*, but she will come back another time. I would like some quiet to look and remember if you could be so kind.'

Hard to tell if he could be so kind or if he is just shocked into silence, but I note with no little admiration (and for possible future reference) that a firm word from Bubby even works on rabbis. She is still looking down into the main *shul* and I try to catch Daddy's eye to see if he can stop her going off into one of those trances. I can tell he's avoiding looking at me, but if Bubby can keep a rabbi quiet, I don't suppose her grandson is going to dare to chip in with his knowledge (or lack thereof) of the history of our former family place of worship – or anything else for that matter.

Ahron Schiffer. Son of Frayda and Yankel, so often at Henry's Fruit that we had no choice, we had to shut it for his bar mitzvah *day. Thirteen years old, but looking so small up on the* bimah *in the suit he borrowed from an uncle or a brother, with the Torah spread out on its scroll before him. His voice was small too. Only one week before,*

Frayda was in the shop to buy herring for his brain, for his concentration. A bag of nerves, and even Henry couldn't comfort her with the shine in his eyes and the laugh that always kept the ladies coming back. Ach, too many nerves for a boy who was one of the lucky ones to read his haftorah *in the* shul, *wearing his prayer shawl and his* tefillin. *And now he was on the* bimah *and here was Frayda in her good hat, up with the other women and their secrets for the best* mandelbrot *or the right* cholent *and I wanted to pinch them to make them keep quiet and respect the Torah and know their good luck to be here and see Ahron become a man in peace.*

'Ssssh!' I hissed at them and one or two turned round and put their fingers on their lips to tell their friends to be quiet, but I knew the recipes and the gossip would soon start again.

The boy's haftorah *portion told of the prophet Elijah and this was worth hearing much more than two ounces of raisins or the way to grind almonds, even though it was not as beautiful as the portion that my Dovid prepared for so many weeks before his own turn to read. How God told the Israelites in the wilderness to bring oil to light the lamps in the Tabernacle and bake the bread every Sabbath.*

'And thou shalt command the children of Israel, that they bring unto thee pure olive oil beaten for the light, to cause a lamp to burn continually.' Dovid read it and read it with his father until he knew it perfectly and until his eyes were stinging, because there were no more lamps burning continually in our home, just pieces of candle that were only alight when they must be. When I needed to cook an onion or some potato for our supper or bathe the sores on my father's skin. When Dovid read his haftorah. *There were only five days to go and everything was ready. There was no* shul *left in this city where we were born and where the German soldiers had made a prison, but Henry's prayer shawl was ready in a box under the floorboards, folded over the* tefillin *that Dovid would strap to his arm and his forehead for the first time and become a man. There would be no*

challah *baked with sweet wheat or wine to say the* kiddush *prayer, but the handfuls of dried chickpeas or barley that our neighbours had brought in their pockets to add to our small store were ready.*

Dovid's voice was still chanting, 'And they shall take the gold, and the blue, and the purple, and the scarlet, and the fine linen', as I dried my hands on my skirt and threaded my needle. The rainbow of his words filled my eyes as the thread made its way through the split seam of a shirt that no longer had any colour at all. And I tried to make the rich sound of those words fill my belly, the way I knew Henry was doing, because he had added a little more of his potatoes to the children's plates as well. I tried to make them shut off the sound in my head of my father telling me, no, I will not take any, you and Henry must eat, the children must eat. The way he told me that evening and the evening before and the evening before.

'Gut, Dovid! You have it now and your Zeyde will be as proud as I am.' Henry banged the book shut and clapped the boy on his shoulder.

'Please God that his Zeyde will still be with us to hear him read his haftorah,*' I thought, but I said nothing and smiled as Dovid went to put the book back in its place under the floor and spend a while listening to his grandfather tell him about his own bar* mitzvah, *the way he had on so many evenings before.*

'I will try and persuade him, Nora. Tell him how hard Dovid is praying for him to be there to hear him read.'

I nodded and smiled again, because it was still sweet to me that Henry knew what I was thinking and because he loved my father too.

'I know you will, mein Liebe,*' I told him. 'Perhaps he will listen to you.' I wanted to tell him that if anybody could do it, he could, and that I loved him, but Dovid burst back into the room. It couldn't be, but it felt like it was at the exact moment that the banging at the door began.*

'Juden! Raus! Kommen da raus!' I heard them shouting and I

pulled Dovid to me. I knew then, in that moment, that no matter what we had made ready, no matter how well we had hidden his tefillin *under the floor, Dovid would not be reading his* haftorah *on the next Sabbath morning and he would not hear his Zeyde's* bar mitzvah *stories again.*

Bubby is still looking down at the men's section, but God (and yes, this time I do mean God), only knows what she is seeing.

'We must set the date for Dovid, Rabbi. The years are passing and we have enough of worrying about thinking back at the war and the boys who never read their *haftorahs*. We need to find a date and I will make Henry agree to shut the shop.'

'But Mrs Wojnawski, David celebrated his bar mitzvah decades ago,' now the rabbi is scratching his head, not his beard. 'Your husband is—'

Daddy puts a hand on his arm and the less than tactful reminder that Zeyde Henry no longer has any say in anything tails off. Bubby spins round from the railing so fast that we all rush towards her, but she bats us away with the hand that's not controlling the steering knob on her wheelchair.

'Which one of you is hiding Dovid? Where is he? I said he must come today to talk with the rabbi and now what have you done to him? Is he downstairs somewhere?'

'Bubby, David is at the Cedars, he's too old for a bar mitzvah, don't you remember? We can go and see him tomorrow if you like.'

Daddy's voice is kind, but much too wide of the mark for her to hear him.

'I want to see him here, now! Is he run away down there somewhere, too scared of reading his *haftorah*? Just wait until his father catches him. That's something to be scared of, not some words of old Hebrew.'

Amelia's eyes are round and scared and this time her lips are definitely wobbling. I pull her into my arms and that leaves Arifa to bend over the wheelchair. She looks scared too. She should be scared. Where is that son of hers who may never have heard of a *haftorah*, but who should know that well-brought up young men show kindness to old ladies? But Arifa has quietened Bubby. She has her hand on hers and, as much as I want to pull it away, to tell her to go back to Cornwood Drive and fetch her good-for-nothing son, right now, even I know that that isn't the right thing to do in a house of God.

TWELVE

Fourteen days more

Morning

'It's alright darlin' leave it to me. Been helping old ladies up this ramp since before you were born. Though not since before 'er Majesty was born by the look of it.'

For a moment Nora is quiet. I am expecting an angry shout back and I think that she must not have heard, but then I see the taxi driver wink and then comes one of her hooting goose laughs. The driver is not so young, but smiling and with big, broad arms. I am happy that some stranger can still make her laugh the way maybe she did when she was a girl.

These famous London cabs have so much room. The driver can turn Nora round so she can see where we are heading. I sit next to her and Nasir will be opposite me when he has finished smoothing the blanket over Nora's knees and checking that she is comfortable.

You are surprised? Of course you are. It is a joke! Nasir will still not talk to both of us and he will only look out of the window at the ugly flats and houses and shops full of plastic, or food that can maybe make a Bengali housewife feel a little like she's back home even though the rain is grey here, but not a Syrian boy who wants to ride his bike and win the trick competition with his friends in the shade from the roasting sun. He is only here in this taxi with us because of the computer. I tried to tell Nora no, he does not deserve it, but she is stubborn the way her family says it and she will not let the gift go. The gift for his bar mitzvah. For David's bar mitzvah. She waited and waited for him to come home last night, after the synagogue. And it was so late when he came. I wanted to send him to his room even though I know that this is no punishment for him, and not a place that will make him think of respect and of what his own grandmother would say to him, or even his father, but Nora wanted to tell him what she was planning right away.

'Arifa, why do they call it an apple store? We want fruit, we can find it in the shops next to your flat.'

Nora has already made this joke many times since Nasir told her last night that this was the best place to buy a computer in the whole of London. It is getting harder to laugh at it, but I see that she is growing more excited as the taxi brings us closer to the big shopping centre that they built when they were having the Olympics, so I try.

'Ha! You are right, Nora. These modern people they try to turn things on their head to fool us old-fashioned people out of our money. But maybe I can find some Aleppo pepper there for your eggs.'

'Pepper, yes. And some raisins so you can make me some challah.'

'It's called Apple because Steve Jobs only ate fruit when he invented it and he wanted it to come before Atari in the phone book because that's how things worked back then.'

It is the first time that Nasir has answered Nora's joke. I turn to look at her and then at my son. He is still looking out of the window, but she is smiling at him the way my heart still feels, even through all the sadness and anger and shame he brings me.

'And who is this Steve Jobs and why was he only eating fruit? He wanted to be so skinny?' she says.

Now Nasir smiles and he looks straight at Nora for the first time since their poker game.

'You've been around for over a hundred years and you've never heard of Steve Jobs, Nora?'

'Jobs I know,' she says. 'Yours will be a doctor or a lawyer, God willing. But this Steve who only eats fruit? This is not a serious man who can make a good career for himself.'

Nasir bursts out laughing and Nora hoots with him. Her tired old eyes have a small shine in them and I wonder if this old woman doesn't know exactly who Steve Jobs was and what he did for a living.

'Nora, Steve Jobs created Apple. It's a company and they make the best computers in the world, I told you that. They invented iPads and iPhones and they make the most money out of all the companies, anywhere, because they're just the best, that's it. So I don't think you need to worry about his career. Anyway, he's dead now.'

'He's dead? That's what eating fruit did for him. I'm telling you, you need good balanced food, like my good chicken soup. And why all this just eating fruit, anyway?'

'I don't know. He was a genius. Geniuses do crazy things, that's why they're so creative. You know, like Picasso or Mozart.'

'Genius? Sounds more like a *shlemazel* to me. Now, Albert Einstein, this was a genius – invented the physics theories, knew all kinds of mathematics and mental arithmetic and even got out of Germany before the Nazis arrived,' she hoots. 'And your Stephen Jobs wants us to buy his computers in a fruit store. Oy, Arifa, these are the times I wish Henry was here to see this world we have today. We had a fruit store. We sold the things people need and here I am still today. You think I was eating only fruit back in that store, Dovid?'

And now we all laugh, with a mix-up of fruit and chicken soup, geniuses and the crazy world that has put the three of us here in this famous black cab somewhere in London.

'Alright back there? Here we are, Stratford Westfield. I'll be round with that ramp in a jiffy, Yer Majesty.'

I think of that laughter when I see the two of them there at the table, Nasir sitting right at the side of Nora and looking at the screen with her, and my heart feels full. I can't pretend that part of the fullness isn't jealousy and I ask my own mother to help me take the selfish mother feeling away and just enjoy the pride in my boy. The computer is very pretty, Nasir is right. Silver and smooth and with that lit-up apple and a bite taken out to remind me that I am a weak woman, the way it says in Nora's holy book and in mine. I go back into the kitchen. My mother is right: I will only feel pride for my boy helping this old lady to live her last days happy.

I have five missed calls from Mrs Levene and one from her father. He will be kind, I think, and understand that his grandmother wanted to go with Nasir to choose the gift quickly, but she will surely not. He will ask Nora how she liked the bright shops and if now she wants her very own iPhone, or maybe one of those big watches they had there that light up and ping and would make her wrist so heavy she couldn't drive her wheelchair anymore. Mrs Levene would love that idea. She will tell me again how I have no respect, how it is wrong for Mrs Wojnawski to be living here, especially if I am taking her out on trips without asking for permission and without taking her and her own little daughter along – don't I think Amelia would have enjoyed a trip to the Apple Store, doesn't she deserve time with her family? She will threaten me with her brother, the one who is a lawyer and says that I am risking the life of the woman who should be the oldest in the world. She will not call me a sinner, but that is what she will think. My head is spinning from those bright lights and all the inventions that made that Stephen so rich before he died. I will make tea before I listen to the shouting on the messages.

I make the tray nice with a piece of my embroidered cloth from home. Milk in the cup for Nora and plenty of sugar for all three of us. They are still sitting close together staring into the screen and they have the look on their faces of a moment they might remember for a long time. I fetch my sewing from the bookshelf. I was planning stuffed aubergine for lunch, but I would like to steal a piece of this moment. If I just sew quietly, Nasir won't notice that I'm at the table with them, and *mezze* from the fridge will be nice too. I make a few stitches, but that lit-up apple is too tempting. So I look and they both still have their noses in the screen and I wish I had brought my phone from the kitchen to take a picture.

'You see, it's just like a real card table and you can decide how many people you want to play against and even where they are in the world. I think it's better than the first site we looked at.'

'But how can they be somewhere else in the world?'

'It's like I told you, Nora. It's the internet. The worldwide web, remember?'

This is my Nasir? He is explaining something he already told her before, without that big sigh of his? Without his eyes shooting up to the ceiling? This Steve Jobs really is a genius. I would give all the apples in the garden of Eden to have Nasir talk that way to me.

'We need to sign you up and put in your payment details and give you a password. Have you got an email address?'

'A what?'

'An address on the internet.'

'Arifa has my address. It's at The Cedars, but I don't want people from all over the world writing to me about poker games.'

'It's OK, Nora, they won't, don't worry.'

'So you give them the address here.'

Still no big sigh?

'Fine, so you haven't got an email address. Not a problem, we'll make one for you and we'll give you your own password.'

'That's what I said, this address, here.'

'Yes, if you like, only it's a special one. I'll show you how it works and then write it down on a piece of paper with your password in case you want to log on when I'm not around.'

'You want me to keep a log now, Dovid? What are you, a *meshuggeneh*? I am too old for diaries, my eyes are no good,' she rubs the heel of her hand against her forehead. 'I like this Stephen Jobs machine, but I think maybe we should stick to the real poker, with my *alte kacker* cards, on the table.'

Nasir laughs and I think maybe the apple has moved this flat in Stepney Green to Eden.

'You'll see, Nora,' he says. 'Don't worry. Trust me.'

And I have to stop myself asking them to please don't talk anymore when she puts that crumpled hand with its pink fingernails to his cheek and says, 'Trust you? Because I wouldn't trust my own son? Now show me where I need to sit my *tuchas* at this poker table.'

Nasir blushes and he looks so much like his father that I half wish he would lift his head and see me staring. But he will not while that screen is pulling him in. So I go back to my sewing and make each stitch for Tarek, as if they were flowers on a silk headscarf and tomorrow was our wedding day again.

'Mum!'

I jump and suck my finger where I pricked it.

'Nasir!' Did they finish their game already? 'What is it?'

'The door, didn't you hear it? Can't you see we're busy?'

The door? Is it so late already and Mrs Levene and her father are here to take Nora out again? The clock on the bookshelf says 11:30 and nobody asked them to come for lunch today, but I see through the shapes in the glass on the door that they are here anyway. That must have been what those messages wanted to tell me. What I want is a little *mezze* with my son and that other ancient mother of his, but I breathe in and open the door.

'Arifa, where on earth were you? I left you at least three messages. You have the care of my aged relative! Don't you think it might have been more polite, not to mention professional, to call me back?'

'Mrs Levene.' I would like to be polite and say come in, but she already has.

'Good morning, Arifa. I'm sorry to barge in on you like this, but we did try to warn you.'

'Yes, I'm sorry, Mr Wojnawski. We were out and I only saw there were messages a few minutes ago.'

Mr Wojnawski is holding Amelia in one arm and a big package in the other.

'The Bible,' he says, 'from the shop. I found it and we thought Bubby would be so happy to see it.'

'Of course,' I say. 'Come in.'

In the living room, Mrs Levene is standing next to the table with her jacket on, her back straight. Too polite to sit without being asked.

'Please, have a seat, Mrs Levene,' I say.

She takes the place next to Nora and puts her handbag on the table, unbuttons her jacket. She doesn't seem to know what to do with it.

'Shall I take your coat?' I say.

'Oh, stop fussing, Arifa,' she answers.

'Debbie!'

Mr Wojnawski did not bring up his daughter to forget to be polite in another person's home.

'Oh, sorry, Daddy, sorry, Arifa. But all those messages. I do think you could have returned one of my calls.'

I smile and I want to offer tea, but again she is too quick.

'Anyway, we're here now. To see Bubby. How are you today, Bubby?'

There is no answer and she reaches out a hand. Nora slaps it back with her eyes still on the screen.

'Oh!'

Mrs Levene takes her handbag from the table and puts it on her lap. She runs her hand through her hair.

'Bubby?'

This time it is Mr Wojnawski.

'What do you want? You can't see that I'm busy?'

'I see you're on a computer. That must be a first! It belongs to Nasir, does it? Hello, Nasir, how are you? Good of you to take the time to show my grandmother how these things work.'

'Hello. I'm fine and it's no problem.'

Nasir gives a quick smile.

'I bought this computer,' says Nora and her voice is firm. 'We went this morning to one of these new kinds of fruit store. I taught Dovid how to play poker with the cards and now he is trying to tell me that cards are the old way, that the modern way is to play on the line. This *meshuggeh* boy says we can even play with people on another line in Las Vegas if we want to.' She pats Nasir's arm and hoots. 'You know, Las Vegas, where they have the biggest casinos in the world. Oy! I am 122 years old, so they tell me, and I tell this boy I don't need to be modern and go on the line and keep a log. I tell *you*, this boy and his fruit machine make no sense to me, but I never went to Las Vegas in all my long life, so maybe my son will take me there with his world on the line!' Now she looks straight at the relatives who've come to see her so early. 'So you think I am too old to understand how it works. And maybe you are right, but why should this be a worry to any of you? This is Dovid's computer. A present for the bar mitzvah boy from his mother. He just wants to show it off to me. Does one of you have a problem with that?'

Mrs Levene looks like she definitely does have a problem with that, a big one, but her father speaks before she can.

'That sounds like a wonderful present, Bubby. You know, Debbie and I have come to see you a bit sooner than we planned because we have a present for you.'

'For me? You think I need presents at my age?'

'I think you'll like this one.'

He puts the big package on the table and lifts the lid and then the paper from the inside.

'Look, Bubby. From the shop. It's your Bible.'

THIRTEEN

Fourteen days and counting

Afternoon

S uch a relief to be outside in the spring sunshine after hours cooped up in that poky little flat. And *mezze* for lunch. Honestly. It's all very well apologising and saying she wasn't expecting us. I mean, how many messages does she need? So, *mezze*. A dab of hummus and a stuffed vine leaf. Perhaps not quite wholesome enough for an exceptionally elderly lady who is more used to a nourishing bowl of chicken soup or some salt beef from Selfridges, especially when she's been out all morning spending her money on expensive gadgets for some badly-brought-up-son-impersonator...

'Mummy!'

'What is it, darling?'

'Come on, everybody's waiting for you.'

That's a relief, then; I wasn't saying it out loud. But she's right, they do seem to be waiting.

'Oh dear, sorry, sweetie. I was just, erm, smelling the blossoms. I mean, seeing if there was any blossom to smell yet.'

Amelia has her hand on her hip and that 'oh, Mummy' look on her little face.

'Come on then, I'll race you to the gate. There's nothing as jolly as a visit to a cemetery, is there?'

And I put a spurt on, fast enough not to find out whether an unusually bright five-year-old girl with attitude even knows what the word cemetery means. Amelia's face when I let her win just before we reach the gate is pure suddenly-lost-my-attitude five-year-old joy. I scoop her up and swing her round and plant a suddenly-everything's-right with-the-world kiss on the tip of her freckled nose. Bubby may be bad tempered, Mummy may think Arifa is a gold-snatching body-digger, and I may think she's angling to out-stick me as the family glue, but a half-term outing on a sunny day with a daughter as adorable as this one really is a wonderful thing.

'Oh, you are such a fast runner, my Meelie. If you keep practising, you're going to win all the medals on Sports Day this summer. And then Mummy and Daddy will be so proud of you we'll just have to eat you.' And she squirms and screams as I gobble her under the chin. No freckles there, just warm skin and the beat of her excitement underneath. I breathe in one deep breath and swing her back down on her feet, but she keeps her hand curled in mine.

'Another race, Mummy,' she says.

'Oh goodness, darling, not just yet. Mummy's much too out of breath and I know you're just going to win again.'

I smile down at her and don't add that I've just noticed the look on Bubby's face.

'So, Bubby, which headstone do you want to show us first?' I say, in what I hope is a jaunty tone. After all, this is London's oldest Jewish cemetery (founded in 1696 by the first Ashkenazis to arrive and full up by 1852 – Daddy briefed me on the drive over) so it's bound to be our cheeriest memory-lane trip so far. No answer from the grumpy super-centenarian. She must be having one of those days. First, she didn't glance through a single page of the Bible that Daddy decided he needed to deliver so fast that Amelia didn't even have time to finish her daily over-the-garden-fence chat with Amelia B., bless her, and now she's off down the cemetery path in her wheelchair without so much as a second cantankerous-old-lady look back at me over her shoulder.

I give Amelia's hand a squeeze and pick up the pace. Daddy is striding along next to the wheelchair on one side and Bubby's two new nearest and dearest are on the other. At least I won't miss out on any gems about eighteenth-century rabbis and their legacy if I keep up with them.

'Sorry if we kept you waiting back there, Bubby,' I say as Amelia and I catch up with the posse. Still no answer. Bubby's scowl has morphed into a determined glare and I hope she finds the deceased person she's looking for before Amelia reckons it's time for her afternoon snack, because I think my great-grandmother might have something to say about stopping for a bag of seedless grapes and a handy pack of Oreos.

'To the left, here,' she suddenly orders and steers her chair so sharply that Daddy has to hop out of the way.

This side path is narrow and stonier and I spot Arifa's reflex to grab the wheelchair out of the corner of my eye before she can even reach a hand out. I manoeuvre myself into position faster than you can say Moishe Robertson, tugging Amelia with me.

'Here you go, Bubby. A bit bumpy just here, isn't it?'

No elbow work necessary, Miss Home Care 2018 has got

the message and I give her one of my sweetest smiles as a bonus. She can pop that in her halo and smoke it.

Protecting Bubby's old bones from too much of a shaking means letting go of Amelia's hand, but she's soon busy making sure the lions and tigers around here don't eat her by jumping from one stone to another. The jolts up my arms almost have me regretting my decision to drive the chair and I'm about to offer to hand over to Daddy when Bubby barks another order.

'Here. Stop! This is where I am heading.' And she points.

We all look (except Amelia who is still stone hopping, just now more or less on the spot) and there, covered with blotches of green and yellow that my school-day memories tell me must be moss and some other similar yellow stuff, is a very old, very small headstone.

'Take me closer,' is the third order.

Well, I would, but the thing is there is quite a lot of muddy grass and yet more stones between Bubby and her intended destination. James is my go-to saviour for all things mechanical, but even I know that electric wheelchair wheels and mud probably don't mix.

'I said take me closer!' she says.

I look at Daddy. After all, he was my saviour before James, wasn't he?

'Oh dear, Bubby,' he says, in his best smoothing things over voice, 'this is going to be tricky. How do you feel about just having a look at it from here?'

'At the grave of the oldest Wojnawski we can find? From here? And you don't understand that this will be the last time I will be looking at it before I die? I am asking my Wojnawski family today to take me closer!'

So that's a no then. If I try hard enough, I can see the

thought bubble hovering over Daddy's head. It says FFS, or it would if he was on Twitter.

'I could pop over there and come back and tell you what it says?' he tries. The defences Daddy built around growing up in a family of survivors have always been a mix of peacekeeping and denial (yes, I know that might be where I get it from) but really?

'I know what it says on it, you idiot boy! I want to sit next to it, touch it.'

'Yes. So a photo on my phone wouldn't work, then?'

He is brave, my father.

'I can sit next to a photo? Touch a photo? I was coming to this grave with my husband every year – twice a year, for the birthday on the stone and at Sukkot – and now my own family wants me to look at a photo. A photo I can see in my bed in the Cedars. I didn't need for Arifa to bring me back to the old part of town to look at a photo.'

Bubby's face wears the look of exasperation that we have all come to know and dread, but underneath it is her paper skin, with the hollows where her cheeks used to be and pain in their shadows. And we know how far back that pain goes and where it came from. How hard she has fought to keep it hidden. I can see the same pain in Daddy's defences and in his eyes as we look at each other across the last resting places of some of the other Jews who also knew pain and exile.

'OK, Bubby, we'll find a way,' he says.

What feels like hours later but, judging by Bubby's lack of scolding is probably only minutes, Daddy and Arifa have given up on the idea of carrying an electric wheelchair containing an aged woman and are instead unfolding it empty next to the Holy Grail of headstones. Amelia has gone hopping off with Nasir, after shouting something about boredom and please, and Nasir has gone hopping off with Amelia much to my surprise and displeasure (but I suppose this is not the time to make a fuss). I am left holding the baby. I mean, the Bubby. Like a baby in my arms, or almost. She feels as light as a baby, but bonier and I am terrified I might drop her. I consider asking Arifa to carry her over for safety's sake, but no, this is family business. Deborah Levene née Wojnawski is woman enough to ensure her great-grandmother reaches her destination without causing the kind of incident that would put an end to any hope of world-record-beating celebrations, in the Cedars' function room or anywhere else. In any case, I would protect Bubby with my life. You've got this, Debs. I step forward, back straight, head up, chin up (don't tell my mother that her oft-repeated mantra from my teenage days has finally come in handy) and my feet feel for a way around the stones and other obstacles that are daring each other to trip me up. Bubby is invincible and so am I. I take a deep breath as I reach the chair and unfold my bony bundle into it.

'So *finally* I can see this grave,' it says.

Laughter is one way of gulping down the sudden jolt of love pouring into the gap where I was holding her.

'Yes, you can, Bubby,' I say, and laugh some more to stop the jolt turning into tears. 'I'm just going to see where Amelia is.'

I know where she is. I can hear her and her new best buddy hopping and ghostbusting in and around the graves. No respect for their elders. I should go and get her, that Nasir-Dovid is all sorts of bad influence, but I find I'm too tired to think of anything except whether it's nearly time for wine o'clock at home with James. I turn to Daddy—he'll know what time it is—and see that Bubby's tired too. She could look at what's left of the Hebrew on that grave all she likes now, but her eyes are closed. Darling bloody old crone.

I leaned back against my Henry and he leaned against the stone that marked the bits of dust that were all that were left of Jakov Krigsman now.

'He lost one war anyway,' he said and I nodded into his chest. 'Jakov Krigsman. Born 10th of Sh'vat 5515, died 7th of Iyyar 5578.'

Henry knew the inscription on the headstone with its Hebrew dates by heart. The way I knew the rest of the story.

'Krigsman comes from the Yiddish for warrior. They say first the forefathers changed it to Wojneman, from wojna *for 'war' in Polish, and then Wojnawski, so they sounded more like Polish warriors when the pogroms began maybe two hundred years ago. The Krigsman side of the family were already out of there, already over here in England. These were not stupid people.'*

'I know, Henry,' I said. And I knew without picking my head up from his chest that he was tapping his finger to his forehead because that's what he did at this point in the story.

7th of Iyyar 5715. 29th April 1955. Our wedding anniversary. Dovid was minding the shop and here we were at Jakov's grave. The way we were every year. Henry telling me the family history, because that was his thread with heaven, and me saying, 'Yes, I know, uh-huh,' and looking up at the green and yellow light filtering through the new leaves and feeling his chest rise and fall, because that was mine. I knew the story well enough to say the right words and make the right noises even when my thoughts were up in that speckled light, peeking through the leaves to the pieces of sky behind them. Some years there was thick grey cloud, some years there were tufts and shreds of white like the beards of the forefathers and sometimes all the pieces fitted together into a wide blue puzzle that gave no clue about whether there was anything or anybody up

there. Dead forefathers, dead yiddisher mamas skinny from starvation and with numbers on their arms, unborn babies waiting on stars to know who their parents would be, or even God. It had never rained on 29th April in Stepney, not once in eight years. Today was a forefathers' beard day. My favourite kind, because they reminded me of lying on the grass on summer's days with Perl and Raysel and Klara and looking for shapes and our future husbands in the clouds, the way all girls everywhere did. Before the war came.

'Some people say there were Wojnawskis who came to England after the Germans lost the first time around, but nobody has been able to trace them. There were more Krigmans though, ones who followed from Jakov's line and ones that must have been his cousins, his great-grandchildren's people and way further down the family line, from all over Poland.'

'Yes, Henry,' I said and turned onto my side, my cheek pressing against his silk anniversary tie and my chin still tipped up to heaven.

Blue mixed with yellow has always made green and the leaves in this cemetery on a day bright like today were so green they must have been drunk on sunlight. They danced and bobbed the way Raysel and me danced on Shabbas afternoons when nobody was looking. First she took the lead and pretended to be the handsome fiancé and then it was my turn. And today the polka the trees were dancing to was lively enough to give me a good look at the clouds hanging over Henry and me in our new country. Every 29th April for eight years, next to the gravestones, he gave me a small piece of jewellery — a silver brooch, a ring with coloured glass for a stone — something to begin to replace the few treasures passed down from our families that went to German families, or for melting in the war. And every 29th April after I thanked him, I looked for the shape of a girl child up in those clouds. Once I even thought I saw her, with her sky-blue eyes, but the leaves bowed to each other at the end of a tune *and when the next one started up again, she was gone. Or maybe I imagined her in the first place.*

'In any case, now we know for sure there are Wojnawskis in Stepney, because here we are, mein tayer einer,*' Henry said, 'mein Zieskeit, mein Liebe. And Dovid is grown now, so soon there will be more who will be safe like him and make our little store bigger and open more and more stores and make more and more Wojnawskis. Maybe even a doctor or a lawyer to make you happy,* mein Liebe.*'*

And this was always the end of his anniversary tale and always the moment he gave me my new piece of treasure and kissed me as I searched the clouds in my mind.

'Ach, I think it is time you went home to your husband, Deborah. And I am ready for a game of poker with Dovid.'

I jump as the clump of clouds that I have been looking at through the trees turns from an extraordinarily round diamond eternity ring back into a pumpkin. James. Yes, it would be lovely to get back home and have a snuggle on the sofa before Amelia's bath time.

'Well, if you're ready, Bubby, I'm ready,' I say and pull myself onto my feet, stretching. I look round for Amelia, but whatever game she's been playing with that good-for-nothing teenager must have been good because they're still playing it. And I can't hear them.

'Amelia,' I call. 'Meelieeeeee! Time for grapes! Time to go home and see Daddy!'

Nothing.

'Time for Oreos!'

I wait a little longer this time because Oreos should get a reaction.

'Oh for goodness' sake,' I say, because of course Amelia playing with Nasir was never going to be a good idea, 'I suppose I'm going to have to go and look for them, aren't I? Did you see which way they went, Daddy?'

'I'm not sure I did, darling,' was all my former knight in shining armour can muster. No wonder I replaced him with a younger model.

'Perhaps we can both look, each one in a different direction, and your father can stay with your great-grandmother,' is Arifa's attempt.

'I think you and your family have already done enough damage,' I begin to say, but stop in my tracks as Nasir comes running towards us out of nowhere.

'Mama, Mama, quick, Amelia's fallen,' he shouts. 'And she won't get up!'

'What? Amelia? Where is she? Oh my God! Daddy, stay with Bubby!' and I am running after Nasir and Arifa, catching them up, grabbing Nasir's hand, overtaking him, pulling him. 'Where is she? AMELIA!'

FOURTEEN

Fourteen days more

Evening

Mrs Levene is crouching on the ground, her back round over her daughter's body. Nasir is standing next to them, his head hanging down; I see how he is hurting. I don't wait. I don't ask. There is no time. I pull at the mother's shoulder.

'Mrs Levene, please, move aside, let me see her.'

'Arifa! How dare you? This is my daughter! What do you think you're doing? Call an ambulance for God's sake!'

I pull harder.

'Move aside. I'm a doctor. Move aside. Nasir, call the ambulance. Dial 999.'

She hears me and jumps away from her daughter as fast as if I had a gun. The girl is on her back and her eyes are closed. One leg is at a wrong angle. No blood I can see. I check for breathing and pulse and turn her on her side, taking care of the injured leg. I hope she will cry out with pain, but she does not.

I look up and see we are close to the cemetery wall. Did they climb it?

'The ambulance is coming, Mama.'

I nod and stay beside Amelia.

'Amelia, can you hear me? Amelia, I'm Arifa, can you tell me your name? Can you tell me how old you are?' Her breathing is good, but there is no answer. 'Mrs Levene, please, come now. Talk to her.'

Mrs Levene drops to her knees, heavy. Her face is grey like the dust in our bombed-out houses in Aleppo, like the faces of the people there. My chest is tight like hers, I know.

'Take her hand,' I say. 'Talk to her.'

'Amelia,' she says, 'darling Amelia, talk to me, it's Mummy. Tell me your name, you remember.' She presses the little hand against her cheek. 'Talk to me, Meelie, shall we sing the Froodle song?' Her question catches on a sound from her throat that has no name. 'Arifa, what's wrong with her? Why won't she answer me? Meelie, Meelie darling, Mummy's here. Everything's going to be fine and Daddy's going to make you better.'

She looks up at me. 'James. I have to call James. Arifa...?'

'It's alright, Mrs Levene,' I tell her. 'I will call him as soon as you're in the ambulance with the child. He is a doctor. He will be calm. He will know where to go.'

'But he needs to come here. He needs to make her better.'

I take her hand. She lets me make a link with her daughter.

'He will make her better. With the doctors at the hospital.'

'But is she going to be alright? What's wrong with her? You said you're a doctor, didn't you?'

'Yes, I am. I was, in Syria. But we have to wait...'

My words are stopped by the sound of a siren close to the wall.

'Nasir, go and tell them where we are. Run!'

He does and I hold a mother's hand as her child lies quiet as death by her side and the bombs explode in my head.

I make Nora comfortable on the sofa after a hurried supper. Nobody talked, just pass the salt, the *muhammara*. Nora has her music and her remote control and a small glass of the vodka she had me buy for her. Nasir is in his room with the new computer. The tricks must look even more frightening on a bigger screen, or maybe he is talking to his friends and telling them what happened. Will they care? They are used to small children being rushed to hospital or dying in front of their eyes. Children or parents or great-grandmothers or best friends. The loved ones lost or damaged. So, Nasir has his computer, and I have my phone. I think it is too late to call my mother now, but her voice would be like honey on a throat dried out from crying.

First I will try a message.

Marhaba Mama. Are you still awake?

I start to wash the dishes as I wait. These telephones with their apps and their high-speed connections make us forget that it takes time to travel thousands of miles, especially for the older ones. My mother is younger than Nora, but for her a fruit store is still a place to buy fruit, not machines that bring genies out of pretty silver bottles. And when I was a girl and she showed me how to sew, her careful stitches taught me that to be patient is necessary and will bring good things, but it was a hard lesson to learn back then and now life in London has been unpicking the seams. There is not much to wash after a simple supper for three and there is no message from Mama; she must have gone to bed. There is no message from the hospital either and I must wait until tomorrow to know how the child is and to hear my mother soothe me and tell me everything will be alright. So. I will see if Nora is ready now.

I am untying my apron when the phone rings.

'*Marhaba Mama!*'

'*Marhabtain habibti.* What is it?'

'Nothing special, I just wanted to hear your voice.'

'And I am always happy to hear yours, but we spoke yesterday, didn't we? So, what is it?'

Of course she would know this is not an ordinary call.

'I wanted to tell you that next week Nasir and I will be able to see you on a bigger screen. He has a computer now, so when we call you on video, we'll be able to see you better. He's very happy.'

'A computer now? Like the one he had at home?'

'Even better. With a faster connection and a great screen, like I said, so he can watch his bike videos.'

'And frighten his mother even more with all those tricks he used to do.'

My throat feels smooth again and I laugh.

'Frightened? Me? When he gets a new bike, I will ask him to teach me to do the trick where he turns it around in the air.'

'I hope to see that one day. I will try not to be frightened watching you.'

I breathe in the sweetness of her voice.

'I hope the computer wasn't too expensive, Arifa. And a new bike will cost money too.'

'Don't worry, Mama, he's happy with the computer now, so the bike will wait. And I save a little, here and there. He is my son and you taught me that a child's happiness is a mother's happiness, didn't you?'

And she taught me to always tell the truth. I don't know if she can feel that I am stitching sentences so that the embroidery hides the plain fabric underneath. I think she can, because she was the one who taught me my needlework.

'And a grandmother's happiness too,' she says. Of course she can see through the pretty patterns. 'But he shouldn't stay on that screen too much. You are safe over there; he should be outside with boys of his age, getting air into his lungs.'

'I know, you're right, but the air is not so clean in London. And he's learning to play old-fashioned games on it with Nora. You remember? I told you about the old, old lady that I'm looking after, the one that's going to be the oldest person in the world. You see, he still respects the elders, even though he can't come to see you, help you with the shopping, your plants.'

'So I'm an old lady now, am I?'

I laugh again.

'Of course not, Mama, but you are Nasir's elder and he loves and respects you. I don't want him to forget how that goes.'

'I know, I'm teasing you. But how is it he can play on the computer with this Nora? I thought you told me he wouldn't go when you asked him to come to help you cheer up the people at the care home.'

Oh! I must be careful, I'm dropping my stitches and my mother's memory is sharper than needles.

'Yes, I know, but he said he would come if he could bring the computer,' so now I have given up on embroidery, but a daughter's quiet life is a mother's peace of mind and Allah will forgive me, surely. 'And today he brought a little happiness to one very old lady.' There, I have managed to tidy up my stitches again.

'That is a good thing. Nasir is a good boy, *habibti*, these times are hard for us all. It's late. Ask Nasir to talk to me on his computer tomorrow.'

'I will, Mama. I love you. *Lailah sa'idah.*'

'*Lailah sa'idah, habibti.*'

My mother is right, it is late, even here in London, and Nora must be waiting for me to wish her a good night too and settle her in bed. I fill a glass with fresh water for her teeth and take it through to the living room. I am expecting to find her with her eyes closed, asleep or listening to her music, but Nasir is with her on the sofa and he has the computer on his knees with its apple lit up, pulling them in.

'I raise you five,' she says.

'I call that and raise you ten,' Nasir answers.

Nora is quiet for a moment, her eyes fixed on the screen and her hands folded still. I wait there with the glass, like an idiot, and don't dare move.

'I raise you ten,' she says.

Nasir laughs and turns his head to look at her.

'You're bluffing,' he says.

Nora says nothing. Her eyes may be too old to tell whether Nasir or anyone else is wearing a poker face, but she has had decades of experience at staying still and holding on to her feelings from the inside. The card table has been her way of practising and staying in shape, but I know it isn't where she learned her own poker face.

'I'm out,' Nasir says and Nora hoots.

'Oy, my Dovid, you maybe have the new fruit machine poker, and I maybe don't know which buttons to push and where to click and how the log works, but I have the old-fashioned tricks. Your flush beats my three of a kind – I know that, you know that. But my bluffs beat your excited young *kop* any time. You need to slow down a little, Dovid, think with that *kop* of yours and read the game, read the game.'

And she hoots again and Nasir laughs too and I am happy for them that they can get caught up in the apple's web and stop thinking about what happened in the cemetery this afternoon.

'*Mazel tov*, Nora,' I say. 'I think it will be a long time until the boy can bluff the way you can.'

'You could be right, Arifa,' she says, 'but he's a bright boy; he wants to learn. He has understood that what he learns in poker he can take with him in his life. And he has a good teacher, don't you, Dovid?'

Nasir smiles. 'The best,' he says.

'You want me to try to beat you again?'

Nora's smile is full of all the times she has won at poker, but I know that her days for playing until the early morning are over.

'I think your student needs to get some sleep,' I tell her. 'How is he going to have the energy to battle with you tomorrow? And you told me you wanted to go to the hospital in the morning.'

'The hospital? Why should I need the hospital? I am just a little tired from the cards and the walk in the cemetery.'

I look at Nasir, but he has opened the computer again and all I can see on his face are the colours from the screen.

'You said you wanted to see Amelia, see how she was doing after she fell.'

Nora puts her hand to her forehead, the way she does sometimes when her still-sharp brain clouds over.

'Somebody fell?'

'Yes, in the cemetery. You remember?'

'I remember the cemetery. I remember sitting by Jakov's grave with Henry, the way we do it every year, but I don't remember falling.'

'Never mind, Nora, it's late,' I say. 'We can decide about the hospital in the morning.'

'Wait a minute, just a minute,' she says. 'There was a girl, that's right. You told me she fell. Who was she again?'

'Amelia. Do you remember? Your great-granddaughter's girl.'

'I have a great-granddaughter?' Nora shakes her head. 'But I do remember now, there was a girl, she was playing with Dovid. A light-haired girl, a pretty thing, she made me think of... Dovid, who was she?'

Now she has pressed both her hands to her forehead. It is late, I must get her to bed. I haven't seen her agitated this way since she left the Cedars.

'Come, Nora, let me get you into your wheelchair and into bed. Look, it's past midnight.'

'But I want to know who she was, where she came from. How old was this girl? Did she have blue eyes, eyes that were light like her hair? Dovid, did you know her? Will she be alright?'

Now Nasir has shut the computer and his face is as closed as the lid, as blank as it ever could be playing poker. He looks up at me, then at Nora and runs from the room.

FIFTEEN

Thirteen days and counting

Morning

Our four hands, clasped on the bed sheet, remind me of a picture book Amelia used to love. *Let's hold hands with Mummy, let's hold hands with Daddy,* it says. I can't remember what it's called. Amelia used to call it the hand book. She would ask for it sometimes at bedtime. I mean she still does, of course she does; it's still one of her bedtime favourites. I hold her hand a little tighter, but I don't dare squeeze. Amelia's small hand in mine, Amelia's small hand in Daddy's. Is every single thing going to make me think of the days before yesterday and whether Amelia loved something, played with something, still does, might do again? I look up and across at James and find he is looking at me. I reach over with my other hand and he takes it. Six hands now in a ring, like a nursery rhyme, like the ones Amelia loved, loves, might love, will love again. She will, she will, won't she?

'We should bring in some of her books from home. Read to

her, like they said, shouldn't we?' I say. 'She loves her picture books.'

'Yes, we should. She does love them.'

'Yes, she does. I'm sure she still does.'

'There's that one about Mummy's hand and Daddy's hand.'

'You thought of that one too?' I thought my heart was too full of fear, too broken to have room for James, but I was wrong and now I squeeze his hand tight to see if that might block some of the panic. 'Her hands are so small, aren't they? Can she feel we're holding them?'

'I don't know. They don't know. Do you remember what they said? But it's like the books, maybe it will help.'

Can it be right that even doctors don't know, even the one who is her father and is sitting with her here by the bed?

'Amelia. Amelia, darling, I hope you can hear me. It's Mummy, I'm right here and Daddy too. We're not going to leave you; we're going to stay, so we'll be right here when you're ready and Grandpa and Grandma are going to bring Froodle and lots of stories, so we want you to be strong and try your best to come back.'

Now I am squeezing James's hand so tight I think I must be pushing all his blood back up his arm and through his body and down into Amelia so that she can have his strength and I can feel that my face is wet, but I don't care, I will not let go and break the ring. We will give her everything that she might be able to feel or hear, anything that maybe will turn into the smallest tap on the shoulder and make her turn round and laugh up into our faces again so we can swing her round and round and never let her go.

The hospital café is painted in cheery colours that probably lift some people's spirits. It's nearly empty. Mummy and Daddy are waiting for me at a table by the window. Why did they sit so far away? It will take me ages to walk over there and I need to get back upstairs as soon as I can. As I get closer, I see that Mummy's face is pale under her make-up and Daddy's eyes are dull, but they are both hiding it behind a smile.

'Debbie,' they say and pull me into their arms, so I feel like the day I was ten and my cousins were going to live in Canada for ever. Daddy's chest smells of pepper and lemon through my tears and Mummy is softer than she has been since I can remember. I need to get back to Amelia—I can't stay with them —but my arms burrow me into their circle and I breathe long breaths that hook themselves round their necks. I feel hands rubbing against my back and lips on my hair and then sobs, but I don't know if the sobs are mine or not.

'We've brought the things you asked for,' Mummy says, once the sobs are over. 'Her books and Froodle and some clean pyjamas. And Amelia from next door and her mother came round with a drawing.'

'And I had Judy on the phone,' says Daddy. 'She's asked me to tell you that Amelia is in their thoughts—that all the family over there are thinking of all of you.'

My throat tightens even more and I have to concentrate to breathe properly.

'And there's another bag with a couple of changes of clothes for you and your toiletries. I popped in one or two good lipsticks,' Mummy lowers her voice, 'and a small bottle of gin and some tonic. You need to look after yourself too, darling.'

I nod and burst into tears again and my awful, snobbish,

self-centred suddenly-tower-of-strength of a mother folds me back into her arms.

'How is she?' they both say together when I am calm enough to hear them.

'Stable,' I say, 'still unconscious. They say the scan showed some swelling to the brain and that's why she's…' I press my knuckles to my mouth. 'James can tell you more about that I think.'

'Of course, darling,' says Daddy.

I nod and try to think.

'They don't know what's going to happen. But they told us she opened her eyes just for a second or so while they were examining her and that's probably really, really good, they told us.' And I have to believe that something so frighteningly bad might, just might, be really good. 'And they say we should ask them any questions we have, but when we do they mostly say they don't know. I mean, they don't say it like that, but they don't know. They say we should talk to her, touch her, hold her.'

'Of course you must,' Daddy says, 'and we will too, just as soon as you think we can see her. Whatever we can do, you know that, don't you, darling?'

I nod, my hand over my mouth again.

'Do you know how it happened, darling, how she fell, how high she was?' he asks.

This time I shake my head.

'And have you talked to Nasir? Asked Arifa what he's told her?'

I squeeze my eyes tight and force myself not to scream.

'I'm sorry, James will be… I can't, I mean, I have to get back to Amelia,' I say.

The inside of the lift is blank and I try to turn it into a time machine that will take me back to a place where there is no Nasir and no day trips with Bubby. But then the doors open. Into a space that is so alien my body feels weightless. I would float and bump around under the ceiling if I wasn't holding these bags, full of the basics you never knew you would need when you are heading to a critical care unit to sit with your own five-year-old daughter and hope she will regain consciousness. Soon. Now. Bags that are full of stimuli. Picture books, drawings, photos probably. A favourite cuddly toy that smells just right. Hard alcohol.

More cheery colours along the corridor. For children who are wheeled along it with their eyes shut and parents who would rather be exactly anywhere else on earth. I mean, rainbows! Sun-fucking-beams! All I can focus on is a little girl lying at the other end of these bloody rainbows with wires all over her, and a man who promised me he would always take care of her.

There they are. Bed eight. Thank God I have these bags to keep me walking.

'Any change?'

James shakes his head and then stands and stretches. Amelia does not. James takes the bags from me and puts them on the ground. He puts his arms around me so I don't float up over the bed, and I remember that nobody can always take care of somebody all of the time. Not even this man, with his muscles, his medical degrees, his money, and his laugh that can cure me and Amelia of almost anything.

'I've got Froodle,' I say, 'and the books and things.'

'That's good,' he says. 'We should give them to her.'

'You should laugh, James. You know how she loves it when you laugh, when you tickle her.'

The words sound crazy out loud, in this ward full of wires and beeps, next to our sleeping daughter, but they are true, and not knowing if James or I or Amelia will ever laugh again is even crazier.

'I know,' he whispers. 'I would if I could.'

And I trace his laugh lines with my finger.

'I had a text from Arifa,' he says.

'No. I need to talk to Amelia,' I say.

'But Debs, darling...'

'Let me talk to Amelia. She needs me with her and I've been gone for ages.'

I sit down by the bed.

'Hello, my angel,' I say. 'I just saw Grandma and Grandpa and they said to send you the biggest kiss. They're going to come and see you soon, so I bet you can't wait for one of Grandpa's stories.' I give her her grandparents' kiss. 'Which one shall we ask him to tell you first? The one about the boy that ate the orange pips and had trees growing out of his ears?' I pause, just in case the silly orange tree story she loves can make her answer me. 'You do love that one, don't you, Meelie? He used to tell me that one too and it made me laugh even more than you, I think.'

I aim for a laugh now, but it comes out more like a gasp.

'And they brought you Froodle. Isn't that lovely? Daddy, can we have Froodle?'

He opens the case and brings Froodle up from under the side of the bed, like a puppet in a show, the way he's done so many times before at home, peeking out from behind Amelia's pillows, surprising her by scurrying along the bedhead. It always makes her squirm and squeal and reach

134

out for her own fluffy green piece of security. I mean, it used to.

James lays the frog against Amelia's cheek, its velvet just under her nose. Only Froodle smells like Froodle and only Amelia knows how he got that way and I'm holding my breath and now I'm squeezing James's hand and we are both staring at our daughter.

There is a shrill noise and I jump and try to work out where it's coming from. Is it one of Amelia's machines? Is that a nurse running over here? James puts his hand on my arm and shows me my phone. It's screaming at me. 'Arifa' it says in bold letters on the screen and I stab at it to make her go away and switch the ringer off, which is what I will do now every time I step out of the lift here on Amelia's floor. James puts his arm round my shoulder.

'We should speak to her, Debs. I'll talk to her.'

I can't seem to answer him.

'We should at least let her know that Amelia is stable, that we'll be in touch with any news.'

All I can see is Amelia's head against the pillow.

'I can't have that woman near me. Why won't she leave us alone?'

'Debbie, Arifa may have saved Amelia's life. We owe her our gratitude.'

'Gratitude? For putting our whole family in danger? First Bubby, now this. And what about her son?' I know I let Amelia go with him. I know a stronger mother would have said no, she stays where I can see her, but now I have no strength left to face it. 'Without Nasir, Amelia would be at home now, playing, drawing. She would be Amelia.'

'Darling, we don't know what happened. Talking to Arifa could help us understand.'

I turn my face into his chest as my own chest shakes.

'Not today, of course not, darling. When you feel ready.'

I wonder if I will ever find enough new strength in myself or in his arms.

'She said in her text that Bubby would like to come and see Amelia. I know it feels too soon, but we need to give her every chance we can to get better. You know how she loves Bubby. Maybe that connection could be the one that wakes her. And she's been having so much fun with Nasir too. The neurologists think that sometimes recent triggers can be the ones that get through.'

He tries to lift my chin, but I can't get my face out of his chest.

'Debs? Darling?'

How can my own husband turn against me? How can any of the doctors think that that boy, the boy that put our daughter in this bed, could come here and be the one to wake her like some kind of prince charming in a horror story? I will be the dragon. I will breathe fire to stop him. I pound my fists on James's chest until he catches them in his and pulls me into the goodness of his heart.

SIXTEEN

Thirteen days and counting

Afternoon

First, I remember the lipsticks that Mummy said she'd put in the bag with my clean underwear and my toiletries. Then I remember the gin.

'Meelie, my angel,' I say, 'I'll come back and read you another story in a minute. I'm just going for a wee.'

I kiss her forehead and hover just a few inches above her face for a moment, in case an eyelid flickers or she says my name. James is asleep in the chair next to her bed. Amelia has thick blonde hair like straw that doesn't come from anyone on either side of the family, but they have the same nose, long, Jewish, with beautiful flared nostrils. I think I can leave them for a minute.

My face in the mirror is grey. Part shock, despair, panic, terror, part unkind lighting, as if being in the visitors' toilet of a paediatric intensive care ward wasn't unkind enough. I rummage round for one of the lipsticks and put it next to the sink in case someone comes in. Mummy has thought of everything except a glass, but I wasn't intending to add tonic anyway. The gin burns and I shut my eyes. When I open them again, I am still grey. I take another gulp. Not much change in my colour but no more need for lipstick. I will do whatever it takes if it might make a difference to Amelia. I run the tap icy cold and splash water on my face. I was born a Wojnawski. I can do this.

James is in the corridor when I come out. Pacing.

'What's wrong? Why aren't you with Amelia? What's happened?'

I want to hit him – one of us has to be with her all the time, and if they've sent him out then that means something has changed, I know it. I clench my fists, but the gin helps me keep them by my sides.

'It's OK, darling,' he says. 'It's a new shift. The nurses are handing over and doing their notes. You know, like this morning after the night shift.'

It's true; I'd forgotten.

'And I couldn't find you. I went to the parents' room, but I couldn't find you.'

'I'm sorry,' I say. 'I didn't want to wake you and I thought you and Amelia would be OK just for a couple of minutes.'

I point to the toilet door and he nods. He looks crushed. I reach up to take him into my arms for what I realise is the first time since he stopped me falling when the ambulance arrived at the hospital and they took Amelia into surgery. James doesn't cry. He's a rugby man, a surgeon who saws bones and screws metal into hip joints; he was named after the world's most unshakeable spy, but now his tears are hot and he needs me to hold him.

'Mrs Levene? Mr Levene? Excuse me.'

The voice is quiet, but unmistakable, and I'm not sure now

if the gin will be enough. I turn in James's arms and pull them across me.

'Hello, Arifa,' he says, and the tears are gone; he is my armour again. 'Hello, Bubby.'

'Thank you for letting us come so soon,' Arifa says. 'Mrs Wojnawski has been very upset about your daughter. I think she needs a moment with her, but I know this is hard for you so soon.'

Same old Arifa. Always knows what's best for everyone. Always so bloody thoughtful. I bite hard on the inside of my lips and nod.

'Deborah, I wanted to come before, but I am too old to make my own decisions they tell me and they wouldn't let me come.' Bubby's eyes are clearer than I have ever seen them and I try to swallow back the lump they have brought into my throat. 'I know a mother's pain, *mamme sheyne*, I know. If you let me, I will talk to her and ask her to come back to you.'

I nod again.

'I will wait here,' says Arifa, 'until you are ready.'

'No,' James says, 'please come with us, Arifa. Debbie and I want to thank you for what you did yesterday. We think you might be able to help Amelia again now.'

I hang on to James's arms with all my strength and keep nodding because that is all I can do.

It is difficult for Bubby to get close to Amelia between her wheelchair and the machines around the bed. Seeing her bony hand reach out to pat Amelia's arm is almost unbearable. In my head, I beg Meelie to find even an ounce of the steel hidden in her great-great-grandmother's bones and grab onto it and pull as hard as she can.

'Amelia, darling,' I say. 'Look, Bubby has come to see you.

You know how much she loves it when you come and visit her. Can you say hello to Bubby, my angel?'

I hold my breath, praying that the presence of the matriarch does what Amelia's doctors, her parents and her machines have failed to do. It doesn't and another crack opens in my heart.

'Amelia,' Bubby says, 'I know you can hear me. I know it. I want you to listen to me because I was once a little girl like you. Oy! I think you don't believe that a crinkled old lady like me could be pretty and cheerful like you, but I'm telling you, I was. I had brothers and my sister and every day we played and ran and laughed. We had work in the house too; we listened to what our parents told us and when they told us we were finished, off we ran so fast and so happy.'

Bubby laughs and shakes her head, taking us with her all those years back to Lodz. Maybe Amelia is with her too. Maybe Bubby can do this.

'I had my best friend Raysel to play with and we played some games you could not believe, Amelia. I think you have your best friend too, don't you? You know, she wants to play more games with you too, I think she is waiting for you to come home so you can be back playing together and making your mama crazy! Ach, the mamas, we love our little ones so much, even though they make us crazy.'

Now she has taken my baby's hand in both of hers and I am crying again.

'But you know, my little one, I know the dark place where you are now too and how much you want to come back to us, how hard you are fighting inside. When I was younger, a woman already, but still a girl inside, I went to a dark place. The people wanted to stop me laughing, being happy. They wanted to stop me loving my family, my friends and make me just a body, a shell. My body could still move—yes, this is true —but to me it felt stuck, heavy, I think a little the way yours feels. But I stayed inside it, Amelia, just the way you are staying inside yours now. I laughed inside. I played inside. I played with my Dovid, with Raysel and my brothers, even though they were gone. I made myself happy, every day when I woke up in that dark place, because, if not, how could I come back? I took a little song I used to hear into my head, a little joke with my brothers, maybe even a little quarrel with my mama.'

The silence around the bed is thick. None of us has heard this before.

'Is that what you are doing, Amelia? I think so. And if you didn't yet, OK, so try it. You will see how it makes you feel a *bisl* better, a *bisl* stronger. This funny frog of yours will help you find the tunes again and whisper you some stories. And I have a funny little brooch–it has a butterfly–that your Zeyde Henry gave me, and the frog and the butterfly they will play games for you too. I will give it to your mother for when they have helped make you stronger. You know, you are lucky, you have your parents with you. Here they are, right here, you see them? They are waiting for you to come back out. We are all waiting for you and then you will have your butterfly and we will have such a party! You and I will make the cake together, a good, sweet honey cake to celebrate that you came back and that I got so old, so old. And we will invite your best friend—we will invite all of your friends.'

She cups Amelia's cheek in her hand.

'I did not have the party when I came back, *mamme sheyne*. So I want you to do this for me, for your Bubby, for Raysel and my brothers. Come back for us.'

I pull James's arm closer around me for a moment and then release it and go to Bubby. I lean in until our heads touch.

'Thank you, Bubby,' I say.

'Deborah, I know your daughter is still in there. She will come back, I believe it. But you must believe it, you and her father. Tell her you believe it, that you know it. Make her come back with this truth.'

'I will. We will, Bubby.'

'And there will be this butterfly and honey cake. And dancing. And vodka.'

I hold the brooch, that now I remember from special family suppers, tight in my fist. If Bubby can find the strength to whisper her secret memories to Amelia and take me back to my own childhood, that must mean we can bring the child we both love so much back to us, doesn't it? I kiss her beautiful old cheek.

'Yes, there will be honey cake. And vodka,' I say. I turn to Arifa.

'Arifa,' I say, 'thank you for what you did yesterday. I was too panicked to know, to understand. You helped. Very much.'

'Mrs Levene, of course. I just did what I could.'

'Call me Deborah, please.'

She nods. I breathe in deep, hoping there may be some gin left for me to lean on.

'It must have been very hard for you to come here, to leave your country, your husband,' I say, knowing the words are not enough.

'It was, yes,' she says. 'My husband is gone, but he speaks to me, jokes with me inside me, the way your great-grandmother said. Deborah. And your country has been good to me.'

'I think it has been good to my great-grandmother too. To

all of us,' I say. 'We didn't know you were a doctor, Arifa. You must miss that too.'

She shrugs.

'Being a doctor is hard in my country these days. Here, I am taking care of Mrs Wojnawski.'

'And Amelia too, yesterday.' I swallow but I need to ask her. 'You must have experience caring for children in accidents. I mean, bombs and so on, I'm sorry.'

'Debs, darling, Arifa might not want to think back to all of that and Bubby must be getting tired. You must be tired.'

James is all goodness, but Arifa is a doctor too and, so far, the other doctors, James included, haven't given me any answers.

'I'm sorry, darling. I'm sorry, Arifa, but I need to know.' Now I do wish I had more gin. 'Arifa, do you think she will come back to us? Amelia. From what you know from your country. From what you saw yesterday. Today. Do you think you could have a look at her now?'

Arifa clears her throat and looks up at James. He looks at me and nods and she goes over to the bed. She picks up Amelia's wrist and takes her pulse. She leans over and I can't see, but she must be looking at her eyes. She scans the machines and James hands her the notes from the end of the bed. She clears her throat again.

'It is difficult for me to give you a prognosis without a full examination and I think the doctors here have told you what has happened to Amelia, what her injuries are,' she says.

'Yes,' I say, 'they have, James has, but none of them can tell me whether she will wake up again, whether we can have her back. Please, Arifa, can't you tell me?'

'Deborah, I am sorry, I can't say anything for sure, I think you know that. But Amelia, she is a Wojnawski. She has

Dinora's blood in her body and yours. I do know that she will be fighting this inside her, the way her Bubby told her. I think she heard what she was saying and there is one more thing I can tell you. Sometimes, after the bombs, in the hospitals where the doctors can only dream of being able to do what the ones here can do for Amelia, there are children who seem to hear nothing. Their people come—they talk to them the way your Bubby talked to Amelia—they leave the hospital crying because no answer comes. But their child is a fighter, like Amelia, and their child did hear; they are playing inside with their best friend or their brothers, and two days later, maybe, or one week later, they come back from inside themselves and they call for their mother. And soon after that they are dancing and eating cake with honey. This is what I know.'

I look at Arifa, searching for those brave children in her eyes. I believe Bubby and I believe her.

SEVENTEEN

Twelve days more

Morning

Nora is sleeping late this morning and Nasir too, although for him that is nothing new at the weekend. For her, not so much. She is exhausted. After the trips to the café and the synagogue she was a little tired, but happy, and wanting to tell me more stories over supper. But last night, after the hospital, I was beginning to worry with her face so pale and her voice quiet. She slept in the taxi coming back to the flat and then told me she wanted to go straight to bed. Just a cup of warm milk. Nasir was still in his room. I put my head round his door yesterday afternoon to tell him we were leaving and he must have come out because the *kibbeh* I left him were gone when we came home. He wouldn't eat them with us at lunchtime, before we went to the hospital. Told me he had schoolwork to do before Monday.

Amelia. I still don't know exactly what happened, but this was not a fall from tripping over a shoelace the way Nasir told me once the ambulance was gone. I thought Mrs Levene and her husband might have more questions yesterday, but it is too soon. But they will have questions and they will be right to ask them. I will leave Nasir a little more time, for his schoolwork and his fear, but I will ask him and I will not let him hide inside his new computer, even if his father is not here to pull him out the way he pulled Ranim out of the rubble.

I thought I was heading to the kitchen to make tea and check we had enough eggs to scramble, the way Nora likes it when her breakfast is late, but I find I have sat down on the sofa where I just folded my sheets and blankets. I have some photos of Ranim in the folder that I managed to keep with me when I came here, but I don't need them to see her. She is always in my eyes and always eight. So pretty with her smile with the tooth gaps and that little dip in her left cheek. I forget how they say it here. Pretty like a sunny day and very clever at making her papa do anything she wanted him to, just with that smile and maybe an extra kiss. So it was even harder that it was Tarek who tore away the bricks and pieces of plaster that covered her. His hands bled, but nothing would stop him. And when he finally had her in his arms, we both knew that no doctor would ever bring her back, not even her mother. When we cleaned the dust from her face, she still had gaps between her teeth, but we knew we would not see her smile or that little hole in her cheek—her dimple, yes, that is the word—we knew we would not see them again. This, I did not say to Mrs Levene yesterday, even though Ranim and Tarek were with me as I took that poor child's pulse and wished that I was a better doctor who could make all of the children live and smile and run. For now, Nasir and I are the only people in England who know that there was once an eight-year-old Ranim who sang songs and drove her brother crazy and ate and slept and woke up again. Nasir will never speak of her; she is his deepest war wound. I choose to keep her inside me where she can keep singing, play with her friends and joke with her brother, the way Nora said. I don't know if one day I can bring her back out. I wish Nora would wake up. Scrambling eggs and making sure she is ready for the day will stop me thinking.

I finally make it to the kitchen. We have eggs so I have no excuse for a quick trip to the shops before Nora's bell rings. The papers are still on the table. It seems I didn't tear them up and put them in the bin the way I planned to after I took them out of the folder last night. I can feel the gentle push from Tarek inside and his necklace on my skin. He understands what it is that's been stopping me and that yesterday something changed.

Evidence of Fitness to Practice. An acceptable primary medical qualification. Primary Source Verification. I keep looking at the first form in case I can make the words say something else, but they stay the way they were. Evidence. Source Verification. These are things that were once in a locked drawer in my desk at home in Aleppo. But now that home is gone and the pieces of smashed desk have probably been taken for firewood by somebody who stayed. The second form seems kinder. Help for Refugee Doctors, it says. I think of Ranim and Amelia and their closed eyes. I took Amelia's pulse yesterday and I helped one mother start to fight through the wait instead of just sitting and crying. But Tarek has been telling me that I could do more again, that I am ready. I tick Refugee Status and then fill in Doctor of Medicine and University of Aleppo. There is a buzz in my fingers where they hold the pen. The country and the date of qualification. Then my area of medical specialisation, but Nora's bell rings. Today my specialisation is to make eggs for a very old woman, wash her, dress her, maybe play a game of poker with her. I am happy to do it and have a place in the life of a woman who has turned the struggles of so many years into iron that gives her the wisdom to speak simple words to a sick child. She is ringing her bell again. My next specialisation will wait.

———————

'I think I will wear the green silk blouse today, the one that Henry gave me. I used to wear it with a butterfly pinned on.'

Nora is looking at me in the mirror as I soap her shoulders at the bathroom sink.

'I like that one,' I say. 'It matches the colour of your eyes. So, you would like to go out today? Where should we go?'

'I want to invite Deborah and her husband to the Luncheon Club. The kosher one, next to the little synagogue, where Sadie and Morris go. I forget the name, but it's not so far from the shop. They have good fish there, nice barley soup.'

'That sounds delicious,' I say, although I think this lunch club has changed into a vegan café or a cocktail bar, the way her grocery changed too.

'They need a little pick-me-up right now,' Nora continues, 'with the shock from the little one. A good, thick barley soup can calm the nerves just like a chicken soup.'

I nod into the mirror. So she hasn't forgotten about the accident again.

'I'm not sure that Mr and Mrs Levene will be able to leave the hospital today,' I say. 'But if it's barley soup you want, you can give me your best recipe and I will buy the ingredients. We can make it together.'

'Arifa, I tell you the best barley soup is at the Kosher Luncheon Club.'

Her voice is sharp and she looks down at her hands and

then again at me in the mirror.

'You are right, I was mixing things up. They must stay at the hospital with the girl.'

Now her voice is quieter. I nod and smile at her and give her shoulder a soft squeeze.

'You tell me what you would like for lunch, Nora, and I will make it for you.'

'What has Dovid told you? He was with her when she fell, wasn't he? Did he say anything about what happened? You know he is a good boy, my Dovid. He is not the kind to hurt even a fly.'

'No, I know. Of course he wouldn't hurt Amelia. Accidents happen, the way they say.' We are both this boy's mother now. How can we help him tell us the truth? 'But for now he hasn't told me anything. Has he said something to you?'

Nora sighs, but she does not answer. I keep soaping, now down her arms to where the numbers are tattooed, on the left side. I don't look there. I don't want to see these numbers or learn them by heart, the way she has.

'It's time to remove the towel now, Nora. Is that OK?'

I always ask, out of respect, and she always removes it with no comment, no waiting. I wash her chest, her back, these parts of her body that no one except carers and nurses and doctors have seen for many years, tens of years. She is so bony, her skin is thin and delicate, with folds that I must be careful to clean and dry. I hope my touch tells her that I care. Today she is quiet, but some days she chats or even hums one of the tunes with the violins that she loves. I always half expect her to tell me to hurry or clutch the towel back round her chest as soon as I reach her back, but there is no shame or shyness. I hope this she has learned through a lover's trust and not through the cruelty of what she lived through in her war.

'I will ask him, Arifa. This is a thing a mother must do,' she says.

I know she is right. But I don't know how it is that, after Tarek, after Ranim, after all the broken furniture, it may be easier for a different mother to ask my son to tell the truth.

'So, Dovid, are you busy learning ways to beat me later?'

Nora's wheelchair is so quiet that Nasir's shoulders jerk back at the sound of her voice, and I only just stop myself ironing my fingers instead of one of her blouses.

'You shouldn't creep up on people like that,' he says. 'You almost gave me a heart attack!'

'A heart attack?' Nora says, and hoots with laughter. 'I'm the one with the worn-out heart that we must be careful with. So, what are the tricks you have up your sleeve for me?'

'Actually, I'm doing my homework. Back to school on Monday.'

Nasir's voice is almost as empty as when he talks to me and I want to tell him to have more respect, but Nora is too quick.

'This is your homework? It looks like something more entertaining than when I was a schoolgirl. Let me have a look.' She turns the screen towards her and I am relieved to see Nasir remembers his manners at least enough not to snatch it back.

'A bicycle,' she says. 'Look at that, going so fast. This is not mathematics or poetry class. What are they teaching you with that?'

I can't hear Nasir's answer and nor can Nora.

'What is it you say? You forgot how old I am again? You need to speak up a little.'

'I said I'm on a break. Gonna get back to my homework in a couple of minutes.'

'A break is good, Dovid,' Nora says. 'We all need to take a break now and then.' She leans into the screen. 'I like the look of this one. Is that you on the bike there?'

'Kind of,' he says. 'It's an avatar.'

'You have a what?' she says.

'No, an a-va-tar. It means like an icon.'

Nora raises what's left of her eyebrows.

'I mean a picture that's meant to be me. Like, I can change the hair colour or the helmet so it looks like me. And then I can race the bike against the clock or against another player.'

'Racing I like,' says Nora. 'Henry and I used to lay a bet twice a year, on the Grand National and the Derby. I remember once we even had a winner and he bought me a bottle of my favourite scent. The number five. Ha! But that was the horses. I don't know about the bicycles and I don't know how you can get to race them inside that machine. Why don't you show me how it goes?'

'Sure. I can do that.'

Now he has his smiling voice back. The one I used to hear, the one he has with his friends.

'I'll go against the clock first, that way you'll be able to see the tricks better.'

He switches up the sound and all I can hear is the music, rock and roll with loud guitars, until Nora shouts.

'Oy, Dovid! This is too fast! You're going to fall off that track and break something.'

Nasir laughs.

'It's OK, it's just a video game, you can see that. If I fall, I'll lose some points, but I can start again, don't worry.'

'But I don't like to see you fall.'

'OK, I'll slow down a bit so you can see the tricks. Look, here we go, a 180, OK. So then I ride backwards, that's a fakie. Another 180 and I'm gonna pick up a bit more speed so we can go for a … back flip.'

'Oy! Dovid!'

'Don't worry, I've got this. Look, see this gap coming up, that means I can try for a 360. Yes!'

'No! Dovid, stop this. You're frightening me. I don't want to see it.'

'It's OK. It's just a game, I told you. Here we go for a tail whip. And … shit, missed it. I mean, sorry, I missed it.'

'And look at you, all smashed on the ground!' Nora puts her hand to her heart. 'I don't care if this is just your what-have-you on the screen that you were telling me about; we don't need another one in the hospital after the little one.'

Now her voice is weak. I wonder if I should go over and see if she needs me, but in this she is a stronger mother than me.

'Dovid, you didn't forget Amelia is in the hospital, did you? And you know she hasn't woken up yet,' she says, 'but you never ask how she is doing.'

Nasir is still staring into the screen but now his fingers are quiet on the keyboard.

'Why is that? Is it that you are scared of something?'

Will he keep his eyes fixed on the screen or will he turn and run?

'What is it that happened when she fell? How did it happen? Dovid, you will have to tell us some day soon. Maybe you can be the one to help Amelia.'

The smell of scorched cotton tells me I have been staring at my son too long. But I cannot see what is inside his head or what he is still staring at on his screen.

EIGHTEEN

Twelve days and counting

Evening

Amelia with a Cheshire cat grin. Amelia with a chocolate ice cream cone as big as her head and a brown blob on her nose. Amelia asleep, with Froodle tucked under her chin. Amelia laughing up into her daddy's face with sea-soaked hair and a bright blue sky behind them. Amelia in a school-uniformed portrait with her hair in bunches and almost a smile. Amelia at home in the garden, holding hands with Amelia B.

Our room in the hospital's special Robinson House facility, with fully equipped kitchenette for fully heartbroken parents, just minutes' walk from the beeping machines and rainbow paint (as the brochure the senior nurse gave us doesn't say) has been designed for rest, with its calm colours and easy-on-the-eye artwork. But rest would be too simple and my thumb keeps swiping across the photos on my phone. If I go fast enough, it almost looks as though Amelia is racing from the seaside to school and back again, gobbling chocolate ice cream on the way and always smiling, even in her sleep.

It's been more than forty-eight hours now. The doctors say the first few days are crucial and we need to tell them about any signs. Movement, blinking, yawning. I keep thinking I've seen her blinking, but it's like the trick in the photos, she hasn't, not yet.

I put the phone face down on the bedside table (light wood, neutral, no sharp edges) and flick on the TV. It would be easier to rest with James's shoulder to lie on, but he has sent me here for a bit of shut-eye (the first time I've ever heard him use that phrase, but then it's the first time our daughter has been in a coma) while he keeps watching for yawns and blinks. It's the *Antiques Roadshow*. I love the *Antiques Roadshow*. I flick to the next channel. *Dragons Den*. James loves that. The next channel has the Hairy Bikers cooking something that looks delicious. My phone rings when I get to a report about some people shouting on Sky News and I almost drop it as I grab it from the table.

'Adam!'

'Hey, Debs, how are you doing?'

'I'm…' I can't speak. I can't catch a breath. I can feel the sobs rising again.

'Debs, I'm here, downstairs. How do I get in here? Can you let me in?'

Can I? How does he get in? I switch off the news and make myself think.

'Adam, yes. I'm in room eight. Buzz number eight.'

He buzzes and I have to find the intercom. It's by the door. Of course it is. I press the button. I stand by the door in case I can't get up again if I sit back down on the bed. Adam is coming, but he's in New York, isn't he? Why is he taking so long? The doorbell rings and I am howling into his chest. He feels like I am six and he is ten and all of our pets have died.

'Debs, I'm so sorry,' he says when my noise is over.

I keep my nose pressed into his chest and nod.

'Look, let me shut the door so we can go and sit down,' he says. He takes the intercom receiver out of my hand and hangs it up again and when the pieces of the room are in the right order again, he takes my arm and leads me back inside.

'Mummy left me some gin,' I say. 'I think there are some glasses.'

'That's OK,' he answers. 'It's a bit early for me. Jetlag.'

'I didn't know you were coming. Thank you.'

'Are you kidding? I got the first flight I could. I called James when I couldn't get hold of you. Didn't he tell you?'

'Did he?' I look down at my phone to see if it can remember. 'Yes, he probably did. I'm glad you're here.'

He squeezes my hand.

'So, how is she?'

'She's still sleeping. She's peaceful and not in any pain. They say there's some swelling in the brain so they made a little hole in her skull to ease the pressure.'

Adam squeezes my hand tighter and I squeeze back, even though by now the telling has become easier. It's the waiting.

'But they don't know what will happen next or when.' I push the lump back down my throat. 'She's fighting, though, I know it. I know she's coming back to us. Bubby says so and so does Arifa.'

'Arifa? What's she got to do with this?'

'She's a doctor, Adam. Turns out she was a doctor in Syria before she came here. In the war. So she knows about trauma and head injuries.'

'Right. Well, that's a surprise. And reassuring, I suppose.'

He runs his hand across the stubble from his jetlag. 'But none of this would have happened if she hadn't agreed to let Bubby come and live with her, would it? I mean, you were on one of those outings with Bubby and her when it happened, weren't you?'

'Yes, with her son too. Nasir. And Daddy.'

'And do you know what happened yet? How Amelia fell?'

'Not exactly. We were at one of those old Jewish cemeteries in the East End. Bubby wanted to see the old Wojnawski grave that she used to go to with Zeyde. I was so tired when we finally got her there that I let Amelia go off playing with Nasir. And now look.'

I look down at my phone again, but the Amelia photos aren't smiling up at me anymore.

'It's not your fault, Debs.'

'I'm her mother, Adam.'

'And since when do mothers have to keep their children in eyeshot 24/7? He's a teenager, isn't he, this Nasir?'

I nod.

'So letting your daughter play with a teenager who at least should be responsible does not make you a bad mother. This is not your fault.'

I try to look up at him, but my eyes won't make contact with his. They might show through to all the feelings of guilt that are pulsating behind them. So I shrug and shake my head.

'Has he told anyone how it happened?'

'No. I don't think so. We haven't seen him and when Arifa came to the hospital yesterday, I didn't ask her.'

'But don't the doctors need to know how high the fall was?'

'I don't know. They're treating her injuries.'

'And what does James say?'

'James is her father. He's as scared as I am. He's stopped being a doctor for now.'

Adam puts his arm round my shoulders and stops being a lawyer. The quiet is better, but it doesn't last long.

'Debs, don't you think we should find out how she really fell? I mean, if it was Nasir's fault, he should at least face up to it. And maybe we should think about, you know, looking at the legal side of things.'

My head is screaming at me. My big brother is here. Opening the door to him was like stepping back through a wardrobe into a time when I wasn't any kind of mother and the two of us were the ones on the photos with ice creams and school uniforms. A time when we played cops and robbers and built hideouts in our bedrooms. And tore up each other's paintings and hated each other and fought.

'Arifa might have helped save Amelia's life, Adam,' I say, and I know he can hear the hair-pulling, eye-gouging girl behind my flat voice. 'I haven't got the energy for lawyers now and I need the little I have left at all for my daughter and my husband. You have no idea how glad I am you came, but I need you to be my big brother, not some Manhattan attorney in a suit putting a case together, and if you can't give me that, you might as well get the next flight back to New York.'

Now I am looking straight at him, but it takes him a while to lift his eyes to meet mine.

'You're right, Debs. I'm sorry,' he says. 'Maybe I do need that gin after all.'

The brother who fought me and squabbled, but always ended up on my side when it mattered tries for a smile.

'It's OK, Adam,' I say. 'Please don't leave.'

'No, of course I won't. I know you and James need to concentrate on helping Amelia to get better and trying to get some rest every now and then. And I'll help you. I know Mum and Dad are here too, but I've taken a room in a hotel just down the road, so I'm your man. Your chauffeur or your grocery shopper, whatever you need.' This time, his Adam-through-the-wardrobe smile works. 'Your big brother, basically.'

'That sounds good,' I say and smile back at him. 'I'll get us that gin.'

Adam is flat out when I wake up. He's sprawled on the bed next to me and the empty crisp packets from the hospitality welcome hamper are scrunched up in clumps on the covers. When my eyes adjust to the dark, I realise we both still have our clothes on. I reach for my phone. Nothing since my last call to James and then his emoji text with heart eyes and a not-exactly-appropriate thumbs up. Better than a thumbs down though. It feels like it's the middle of the night, but it's only quarter to eleven. Doesn't that mean some time in the afternoon for Adam? I can never quite remember which way the clocks go east or west, so maybe it's much later in New York. Or maybe it's the gin.

I should call James, tell him that I didn't ring before because I fell asleep really early, but I don't want to disturb Amelia. I text him and add that Adam's here, that that's fantastic, that I love him, but he shouldn't call because Adam's sleeping. Plus the pink heart wrapped in a ribbon emoji that I only ever send to him.

He texts me back straightaway.

Don't worry I was hoping you were asleep. How's A?

Glad he got there safely. Must make you feel a BIT
better. Amelia still sleeping and all good. I love you too.
See you at shift changeover. Sleep darling.

And another emoji, this time blowing a kiss. I do feel a BIT
better, but only a BIT. I flick to the photo of Amelia and James
at the beach. The sun was behind me so you can just see my
shadow on the sand between them, but I'm there in their eyes,
I can feel it, so hard that I shove the phone away into my
pocket. It snags against something. The little silver butterfly
with purple wings. Amelia's favourite colour. Bubby never had
much jewellery, but even so she couldn't have known that this
was the one thing I remember her telling me was a precious
gift from Zeyde. I wasn't much older than Meelie and I didn't
understand why my family didn't have furniture or gold or
knick-knacks that were passed down from one generation to
the next. Just a few stories about the old days in Lodz that
mostly tailed off into silence. But now I do understand and
now Amelia has her own piece of what will have to do as
family heirloom. Or she will when she wakes up. I'll take a
picture of her wearing it and put in a frame for Bubby. My
hand almost goes for the phone again and more torture by
photo, but I make it stay down by my side. I close my eyes and
open them again. But all I can see behind my eyelids is more
torture: Amelia, with or without ice cream, Daddy or Froodle,
jumping around the garden, dancing with me in the kitchen or
lying still in her hospital bed, surrounded by beeping
machines. Maybe if I took my clothes off and got more
comfortable, I could get back to sleep and be in better shape for
her in the morning. Take my make-up off, clean my teeth, even
have a shower.

I know it's a cliché, but the water does feel good. Hot,

stinging and then massaging some of the fear out of my shoulders. They really have thought of everything at Robinson House, this—what? Hotel? Guest house? Loony bin? Even lavender scented shower gel. I'm more Molton Brown Orange & Bergamot at home, but all the wellbeing articles say that lavender is soothing, meant to help you sleep. I tip my head back and turn my face into the shower jet, closing my eyes until it washes the pictures of Amelia from under my lids. Then I switch off the water and take a deep balloon of breath. It's warm and quiet in here, and wet, like a tile covered womb. I don't know if I want to curl up and suck my thumb or flail around and kick at its shiny walls. I let myself sink to the floor and rest my head against the side. I won't stay long like this—I can hear Mummy telling me I'll catch my death and then what good would I be to Amelia—but it does feel good to let go. The shower head is dripping, each bead of water popping in my ears in a lullaby beat that has my head bobbing. And then my phone rings. I have the volume turned way up to make it impossible to miss anything and I am clambering out of the shower and racing back into the room and stabbing at the phone with wet fingers that won't let me answer it. Adam grabs it out of my hand and presses the green button and hands it back to me.

'It's James,' he says.

'James? James? What is it?'

'She's opened her eyes, darling! She's closed them again, but they were open for—I don't know how long, but I held her hand and talked to her and asked her if she could talk to me. She hasn't, not yet, but Amelia opened her eyes, Debs.'

NINETEEN

Eleven days and counting

Morning

The doctor's mouth is moving and her fingers are pointing to charts, but I can't hear her because the big swollen thing pumping in my chest is too loud. It started banging when she said there was no change in Amelia's brain activity. I'm sure she said no change. But how can that be? Aren't her eyes connected to her brain? And she opened them, so something must have happened? Why doesn't that show up on the charts?

Now I can see that James is talking too and he's looking at me. Am I supposed to answer him? I swallow hard and shake my head to see if that will stop the blood rushing in my ears.

'Darling?' he says.

'I'm sorry, darling,' I say. 'Sorry, doctor. I wasn't quite following. Um, I got confused about the part about her brain activity not changing. Surely that's not right, is it? I mean, she opened her eyes, so that must mean she's getting better, mustn't it?'

The doctor smiles at me, one of those smiles that you know is a cover-up, and I grit my teeth and hope that my heart will keep quiet.

'Well, Mrs Levene, you're right in thinking that the kinds of signs we've been asking you and Dr Levene to be on the lookout for are very important and that they can be signifiers of a modification in cerebral response.' She must have noticed that I am having trouble computing this because she adds, 'I mean that sometimes we really can confirm that there has been a change in brain activity.' I grab James's hand. 'But that's not always the case and I'm afraid that this time, for Amelia, we are going to have to put her eye movements down to reflex rather than any indication of a return to consciousness or awareness.' Now I nod yes, over and over again, even though my own brain is shouting *no* at me inside my head. 'You can see that on this chart, here.' She tracks a line with the pen from her breast pocket, and I can see that, the line and the pen, but I can't see what she means—I really can't.

'Are you sure?' I beg. 'I mean, really sure that there was nothing?'

'Well, there is still an awful lot that we can't be really sure of in coma patients, Mrs Levene, but we are able to monitor brain activity by EEG. That's what we call electroencephalographic monitoring.' She pauses to check that I'm still following. 'And I'm afraid that in Amelia's case, as of now, there has been no change. But that doesn't mean that she won't respond or that she won't open her eyes more often and for longer periods. It's a good sign, really it is, it's just that I cannot say, as things stand this morning, that there *will* be an improvement.'

I shut my eyes and tighten my grip on James.

'Thank you, doctor,' he says. 'We do understand how

difficult it is to give us any sort of prognosis. It's just that any little glimpse gives us so much hope, that we...'

He grips me back.

'Of course it does, Dr Levene. And you must keep hold of that hope. Amelia needs it. She needs both of you to keep doing exactly what you've been doing so far. Try to keep rested, but stay with her as much as you can. The next forty-eight hours are really crucial.'

'But she will wake up, won't she?' I say. 'I mean, James is right about the prognosis and all that, but we do need to know. I need to know.'

'We're doing everything we can to help her,' she answers, 'and I know you and your husband are too.'

This time, her smile is the one from the bedside manner empathy training that James has been on too and I am glad she doesn't try to reach out to put her hand on mine because I think I would have slapped it away.

'When can we see Amelia's consultant?' I say.

Their training must be good, because she is still smiling.

'Well, it's Sunday, so the consultancy rounds will begin again tomorrow, but you can talk to the duty registrar later this morning,' she says, 'although I think he may not be able to tell you much more than I have.' Still that smile. 'And of course, we'll contact Dr Mirza immediately to let her know if Amelia shows any significant change.'

'Yes,' I say.

'I know how hard this is for you and your husband.' *No, you don't; no, you don't*, I wish I could scream at her. 'But you can put your trust in all of our team here. We are all experienced professionals and will do everything we can for you and Amelia.'

'Then you have to bring her back to us,' I shout inside my head.

'Of course,' James says, out loud. 'We know that, Dr Kalraiya. Thank you for all that you and your colleagues are doing.' He puts his arm round my shoulder. 'I think it's time for us to get back to Amelia, don't you, darling?'

Dr Diplomacy has left for his sleep shift at the Heartbreak Hotel when Mummy rings. I don't pick up and I don't listen to her message. I text.

> On my own with A. Can't leave her. No change. x

I will tell her about Amelia's eyes when she can use them to see, cry and laugh again, because otherwise Mummy will be here as fast as she can get Daddy to drive her and if he's gone Sunday fishing, she will jump in a cab and I can't deal with her this morning. I can't.

> I'm sorry darling. Soon, I'm sure. Isn't Adam with you? xxx

As if being sure changed anything.

> No. He's sleeping. Jetlag. Soon, I'm sure.

No, I won't send that. Be nice, Debs. Take two:

> No. He's sleeping. Jetlag. Good to see him last night. Expect he'll—

Another text comes through as I'm typing. From Arifa.

Hello Mrs Levene. How's Amelia?

That's it? How's Amelia? And if calling me Mrs Levene again is her way of— Oh, there's another one.

I'm so sorry about what happened. It was an accident I promise. I think u must hate me but pls pls I want to come n see her. Try n talk to her. Pls. Nasir

I look down at my baby with all her wires and her freckles and her silence and I see Nasir running at me in the cemetery, his face pale with fear and shouting that Amelia won't get up. Then I see her hopping around the graves with him and showing me the cat picture with all the wool that he helped her print out a hundred and fifty million years ago. And I see that my precious, sensitive, funny, comatose daughter is smiling and laughing at this boy, at an almost big brother who I know in my heart would never have deliberately harmed her. My heart starts thumping in my ears again.

Ok. Yes. Come to the hospital.

I press send.

TWENTY

Eleven days and counting

Afternoon

The song swirls through my head, connecting me to Amelia through the wire of our EarPods. My left ear and her right ear. Nothing on the charts to tell me if she's hearing anything, at least not that I can see, and I know I shouldn't think this, but I'm glad Dr Kalraiya isn't here to explain. Amelia loves Billie Eilish. Loved her as soon as I put Spotify on in the car and there she was with that spell in her voice. The words aren't for five-year-olds, but neither of us really listen to them; we just get caught up in her melodies. Sometimes Amelia chirps up with 'I don't wanna be you' completely out of tune or 'a bad guy really really rough guy' and always has me laughing out loud. Now it's the ocean eyes, blue like Amelia's that Bubby always tells me are a throwback to someone in her family before the war. That stubborn blue gene digging its heels in behind the brown ones and refusing to be beaten, so that it pops up every few generations. I can't remember which great-great-uncle/third-cousin-five-hundred-

and-twenty-nine-times-removed was the last blue-eyed Polish Jew because I never really listen. But now I wish I had and I wish, wish, wish that Amelia's stubborn gene would force her eyelids to open so I can fall into her ocean eyes again the way Billie sings it.

I close my own eyes because I'm tired and hum along because nobody can hear me except maybe Amelia and she's used to it. She might even wake up just to laugh at me and tell me 'be quiet Mummy, I can't hear Billie.' When it gets to the part about diamond minds and being lonely, there's a mermaid behind my eyelids, blonde, beautiful, with ocean eyes, obviously. I hope Amelia can't see her in case she lures her in, just like Billie Eilish and her songs, down under the waves and away from me. I take her hand in mine and put my head on her chest. I can just hear her heart, slow, in time with the song in our ears. I know I'm not allowed to, but I climb up onto the bed and lie down next to her, looping the wires and the tubes that I can out of the way. I have no tears left today and I'm glad, because otherwise Amelia and her bed would be drowning in them and the mermaid would pull everything, bed eight, Amelia, wires and all, down into her cave so she and Amelia can play together. Maybe if I shut my eyes again and hold on tight I could make her pull me down with them.

A hand on my shoulder brings me back to the surface. There's a pair of trainers on the floor next to Amelia's bed and a pair of jeans above them. It's that time already? Shit! My entire body burns with the thought of being draped over the bed when I should have been sitting neatly, primed with gin and lipstick, on the chair next to it when he arrived. And my mind can't seem to focus. The hand shakes my shoulder again.

'Yes, OK, just a second,' is what I try to say, but it comes out as a grunt.

I swing my legs off the bed and the hand grabs my forearm to steady me.

'No, but what do you think you're … get off me,' I say and pull my arm away.

'Debs, it's OK, it's me,' says the hand's voice.

What? Who?

'Adam?'

'I told you I was coming in as soon as I could. Guess you were tired too.'

He takes the earpod out of my ear and helps me down from the bed.

'Right, sorry. I thought you were Nasir.'

'Nasir?'

'He wants to come. I've told him to come. He texted me this morning and when I saw your trainers, I thought they were his.'

'Oh. Wow. So, you think he's going to tell you his side of the story and everything?

'I think so. I don't know. I hope I don't hit him.'

He pulls me into a hug.

'You won't. I won't let you. And nor will James. We came over together and I left him talking to one of the doctors over there. He'll be here in a minute.'

'OK, thanks.'

It's like the tears. I don't have anything left to say. I can't talk to Adam about mermaids.

'So how is she?' he says.

'About the same,' I say. 'The last doctor said that the fact that she opened her eyes again was important, only it wasn't and basically she didn't have a bloody clue about anything. And we have to keep looking for brain signatures or something and wait to talk to the consultant tomorrow.'

Adam bends over my sleeping beauty and kisses her on the forehead.

'Hey, Amelia,' he says, 'it's Uncle Adam. I came all the way from New York to see you and all I brought you was this t-shirt.'

Their favourite private joke doesn't make Amelia laugh this time, but it does snag on some primitive smiling mechanism deep in my brain, so maybe it has in hers too.

He unfolds the t-shirt. Classic I love NY. She has one for every visit in every colour you can think of, plus baby bibs, a piggy bank and socks. Right through to a baseball cap and matching mitt, because she loves baseball as much as Adam does—not. Uncles, I ask you.

'I hope I've bought the right size this time, babes,' he says. 'You look like you've grown. Although it's hard to tell while you're lying down.' He leans in close. 'Amelia, darling, I need to see you standing up so I can see if it fits you when you try it on. What do you say? Can you give it a try? For your Uncle Adam?'

His voice is quiet and steady, but when I look for any signs that maybe Amelia has heard and wants to come and hang out with the uncle she worships, all I see are the tears running down his cheeks. He reaches for my hand and I realise that somehow I have a new stock of tears too.

'She's so beautiful,' he says.

'She is,' I say.

'Hard to believe she's—'

'I know, Adam,' I say quickly, because it is hard, hard as

diamonds and I would give all of mine, all of them, every one of all of my family's non-heirloom jewels, to make it stop.

'Sorry, Debs,' he says.

I shake my head. 'I'm sorry too. It's just ... well, it's been three days of hard now, but I get it, this is the first time you've seen her. I know how that feels—it hits me every time I walk in here. Like a documentary I once saw about a man with some kind of weird amnesia who forgot everything he'd seen like ten minutes before, and every time his wife came back into a room he thought he hadn't seen her for years and he just hugged her and cried. Every time he saw her. The way every time I get to this bed, I feel like I'm falling because in my head she's running around the garden or riding on James's back or driving me mad because she's making us late for school.'

He squeezes my hand.

'I can't believe I used to shout at her because she couldn't find the toy she wanted and we were going to get to school five minutes late. Telling her off while I buttoned her coat, rushing her into the car seat, not letting her listen to the music she wanted in the car because that would teach her.'

'Debs, you're her mother. All mothers do that.'

'Do they?'

'Of course they do, Deborah. You will please not add guilt and self-pity to the list of things you need to worry about. You have enough to eat on your plate already.'

Bubby? How did she get here? First Adam and now Bubby. Should I be adding going deaf or crazy to my list of things to worry about? I shake my head in case I've still got the EarPod in, but it's true that her wheelchair is very quiet. Bubby being here somehow makes things feel softer. I don't know if it's the way she talked to Amelia last time or because she's cheated death so many times that it seems impossible for it to reach us when she's around. Or just because I love her so much. I go to kiss her and see she has almost given her minders the slip. Arifa is just coming into the ward with James. And Nasir.

I play for time.

'You're right, Bubby, thank you. How are you today? Look, did you see? Adam is here. He arrived from New York last night.'

'And who is Alan?'

'Adam, Bubby. My brother. The one you used to say would be the death of you because he once had a *goyische* girlfriend.

'*Mein Gott!* This I never had in my family!'

I need a different tack to jolting her memory.

'You know, Bubby, the clever one. The New York lawyer.'

'Ach! The lawyer, why didn't you say so?'

She swivels her wheelchair.

'So you don't have a kiss for your great-grandmother?'

He does and while Bubby is in his arms, the posse makes it to Amelia's bedside. James has a kiss for me and one for Amelia and then the kind of big smile for Arifa and Nasir that only my big-hearted husband could manage in the circumstances.

'So, Arifa and Nasir have come,' he says.

'Yes,' I say as I dig for a small smile myself.

'Hello, Deborah,' says Arifa.

'Hello, Arifa, how are you?' I say.

Nasir's hands are balled together and he is looking down at them hard, as if he is trying to understand how it is that paper beats stone.

'Hello, Nasir,' I say.

'Mrs Levene,' he whispers.

I look up at James for help, but I needn't have worried.

'Oy, you people!' Bubby's hands fly up in the air. 'It's not enough for you to have one person with no voice? Amelia is the one sleeping here. You are here to talk to each other, to talk to her. Help to wake her up. But if you are all going to stand around making this small-talking you may as well go home and leave her with her Bubby. I will talk to her if you won't.'

She glares at us with those boulders back in her eyes.

'Dovid? Didn't you have something you wanted to say to Amelia? And her parents?'

'Yes, um, I…' He is still looking at the rocks in his hands.

'It's OK, Nasir. This must be very difficult for you.'

I will never know where James gets his endless supplies of empathy from, but I have to pinch myself so I don't scream.

'Would it be easier if it was just the three of us?'

He puts his arm round me and I do not move. I am superhuman.

Nasir finally looks up from his hands and his eyes are still shouting at me to 'come quickly, there's been an accident, Amelia won't get up.' He needs to stop the noise in his head and so do I.

'Nasir, please, it would help us all if you told us what happened. Maybe it would help Amelia,' I say.

His hands are shaking and now he presses them together, like a prayer.

'Could I talk to her first? Please? Amelia?'

James looks at me and now there is a prayer in his eyes.

I am superhuman.

'Yes,' I say.

Someone cranks the volume up on the beeping of Amelia's machines as Nasir leans close to her. Billie Eilish and the mermaid have morphed into trash metal banging at my brain. James is still holding me, and Bubby has caught on to my arm.

Will my superpowers be enough to keep her sitting straight in her wheelchair?

Nasir straightens up and comes over to face us. The beeping and banging stops.

'I told her I was sorry,' he says.

'Thank you.'

James and I echo each other.

'And I am. It's the worst... I don't know how... I can't sleep since she fell.'

James puts his hand on his shoulder.

'Nasir. Tell us what happened, please.'

The only silence that has ever been longer was waiting to hear my baby cry after that last agonising push. James is crushing my fingers this time too.

Nasir presses his hands together again and his eyes seem almost to be looking in on themselves. He closes them.

'We were playing. I was carrying her on my back and whirling round and round. She was laughing and telling me she loved it; it was the way Daddy twirled her round too. And she wanted to go higher, so I tried, but I'm not as tall as you, I'm sorry. I nearly dropped her, so I said we had to stop, but she wanted to go higher and ... I don't know... She was so pretty and happy, laughing like that and then she pointed at a tree and said she wanted to be a bird because I couldn't fly her high enough.'

Nasir puts his face in his hands and I stay where I am because, yes, I am superhuman.

'I told her no,' he says. 'No climbing trees. No birds. But she begged and begged; she wanted to be a bird, but she promised she wouldn't let go, she knew that, and she was so pretty when she was laughing, so I found a small branch and she climbed and I was right next to her all the time, right underneath her to catch her if she fell, but she kept climbing even though I told her no, come back and then she was too far above me and I told her no birds, I told her 'come down I will twirl you higher.' And she started to come down—she's a good girl; she listened to me. But her foot caught a dead branch.' His voice snaps. 'And she fell. And I'm sorry, so sorry, *iinaa asif katir*, and all I can think about is Amelia and Ranim and what you should do to me because I failed them. Both of them. And I know you can't forgive me.'

TWENTY-ONE

Ten days more

Morning

Nasir's uniform is clean and neat when he comes into the kitchen. Even his tie is knotted right, up under his collar with his top button closed. But there are creases in his forehead and smudges under his eyes from getting up early for the first time after the holiday or from not sleeping, or both, I don't know.

'Ach, this is how a boy should look when he is at school, Dovid,' Nora says. 'Tidy man, tidy mind, your Zeyde used to say, but I think you don't remember; it was before the war. So you are ready? You have all your books? You have your *kop* straight like your tie?'

I laugh and put his bowl in front of him quickly because I can see that, no, his head is not so straight, but we all need a quiet breakfast this morning.

'I think he is nearly ready. All he needs is a hot cup of tea and a little *mamouniyeh*, good and sweet and made fresh this morning. Would you like to try some, Nora?'

175

'This is the porridge with the nuts?'

'It is a little like a porridge, yes. We make it with some semolina and plenty of *samneh*. This is butter that has been melted to separate. Cinnamon on the top and nuts.'

'So the porridge is part of your scheme to get rid of me with all this butter? No need to worry about the world's record if my veins are all clogged up and bursting from your cooking, Arifa,' she says and pushes her bowl across the table. 'Cinnamon I like.'

'Me too, Nora,' I say and serve her a portion, with an extra pinch of the spice our cultures share on top. Out of the corner of my eye I see that Nasir has almost finished his.

'A little more, *habibi*?'

I reach for his bowl without waiting for an answer. For Nasir, this is a breakfast for second, maybe third servings and it is early, he still has time.

'I have to go, Mama. I'm going to be late.'

'Late? But it's only…'

'Gotta go. Got an early class today. See you later, Mama. Bye Nora.'

And he's gone. I don't know about an early class when the school gates don't open still for half an hour, but I see he wants to be gone.

'In such a rush today, that one,' says Nora, 'but that is a good thing. School is the most important. It's where they make proud mothers. Am I right, Arifa?'

She has learned to know me so well already that her old eyes don't need to see the way I looked after him as he left.

'Stop worrying about him. He is still feeling the shame from yesterday, even if you and I know he should be feeling proud for speaking out. The school is the best place for him now, with his friends, his studies, somewhere that nobody knows about the hospital. He will come around with a little time. The same way Deborah will.'

I want to say, that's if he really has gone to school this morning, but I don't.

'You're right, Nora. They will work it out.'

I pile up the bowls. There's no hurrying away to school for me, but I can keep busy.

'I see you liked my porridge,' I say.

'Your *mamouniyeh* was delicious,' she says, 'especially with the extra cinnamon.' She puts a hand on my arm. 'Arifa, who is Ranim? Dovid mentioned her at the hospital yesterday. I think he said he failed her and Amelia.'

My hands tighten around the breakfast bowls and my throat seals up, but I know I have to give her an answer.

'Oh, Ranim was a young girl we knew when we lived in Syria. We knew her well.' I will not lie to my own mother and I will not lie to Nora, but I cannot tell her all the truth. 'She died in the war, like so many children.' How can I care for Nora and Nasir, how can I try to be a doctor again, try to help Amelia and her parents and keep Ranim playing inside my head if I have collapsed from bringing her out into the world a second time? They say that the pain from giving birth is the worst a human can feel, but it is not true. The pain of losing a child that grew inside you is sharper, longer and has no anaesthetic. 'Nasir feels responsibility for her. He was her hero and he often played with her after school, but not on that day. He was out with his friends on their bikes, far from the houses where the bombs fell, *alhamdulillah* for him, but that day the bombs did fall and nobody could save her.'

'Ach, Arifa, these wars,' says Nora, 'and these children, so many of them have died.'

I nod because I do not trust my throat to let me speak.

'Thank God we have our son,' she says.

I nod again and she steers her wheelchair over to me.

'You know, our Dovid did look so smart this morning.' Her smile is a proud mother smile and maybe she is right. 'I would like to go out again today. I am missing those trips we have been having. Maybe I can get a new blouse, something smart for when I am the oldest of the world. I think it is soon now.'

This is the present and the future. If Nora can pull herself away from the past then so can I.

'It is. Just ten more days. I am so happy you have decided to have your celebration and share it with the little one when she is better. So maybe you should rest in case my *samneh* is too much for you.'

'For me? Oy! You think a little butter can do what all these years and those Germans haven't finished off yet?'

Her hoot is much louder than my laugh, but she doesn't notice. I keep moving forward.

'But it's my job to look after you, Nora, and you already had me wake you up early today to see Nasir off to school.'

'This is a *mitzvah*. A mother with a son like that gets even more life in her bones. And so I am up and we have plenty of time for shopping and seeing the old places. I will rest later, maybe see if my old *kop* can learn how to open up a game of poker on the fruit machine so I can beat that boy again when he gets home.' Another hoot. 'But don't worry, Arifa, it will be only after he has finished his homework.'

It is still early, but the traffic on Commercial Road is already angry and loud, with the cars honking the lorries that stop to unload and the brakes of the buses screeching. Nora asked to go in her wheelchair so she could see how the neighbourhood has changed up close. It's only a few minutes to walk, so I suppose the pollution won't kill her either and the noise gives me a chance to think some more about the silence at the hospital yesterday after Nasir said he was sorry. It's true that he waited three days after Amelia fell and it's true that they thanked him and I understand that they needed time to be alone together, just the parents and their child, to think, to process, the way they say, but he is my son and he has nobody to take him in their arms. His father and his sister are gone, his bike friends are back in Aleppo, or dead or both. Or somewhere in Greece or Germany, or maybe just around the corner in this city where no one knows their neighbours. Me he will not allow, in case I squeeze all of Syria up to the surface. I hope he is at school with his tie still on, but I also hope he has undone his top button.

'Here. This is it.'

I think that's what Nora said. In any case, she has stopped her wheelchair.

'Look, you see it?'

I bend down to hear her better and see where she's pointing.

'There's something you like there, Nora?' To me, these fashions look cheap and not good enough to wear for her party, if she ever has one. 'I think this is one of those places where they only sell to other shops. You want me to try?'

'They call it wholesale, Arifa; this I know about because we Jews invented it. Most of these shops around here were Jewish in the old days, but that's not what I meant. Look.' She points again, up. 'You see that little arch over the door? Made of stone?'

'Yes, I see it.'

'That was the Grand Palais theatre. This stone is all we have left now. They took it down and made it into a *shmatte* shop, like they wanted to make some kind of Jewish history joke, but before, it was the most famous Yiddish theatre in the whole of London, I think maybe even Europe.' This time her laugh is quick like a flash of memory. 'They put so many plays on, even after the war. The funny ones, the classy ones, they even did Shakespeare in Yiddish sometimes. You can't imagine Hamlet saying "*tsu sein oder nicht tsu sein*", can you?' And now she hoots. 'But he did, I promise you, and we all said it with him and cried with that poor *meshuggeh* Ophelia in the river.'

'Shakespeare. I once saw Romeo and Juliet played in Arabic,' I say, but I'm not sure that she is listening.

'*Tsu sein oder nicht tsu sein,*' she says, '*dos is die frage.* You know, Arifa, I think I would like to go inside, see if they kept anything. The curtains maybe.'

I press the buzzer because the shop is called Soho Wholesale, like Nora said, with a small sign saying 'Trade Only. Closed to the Public' and a phone number for appointments. The window advertises Italian fashion, but the person who comes to the door is wearing a sari. I always thought saris were from India, but in Stepney I have learned that most of the women who wear them here are from Bangladesh, even though I am ashamed that I knew nothing about this country before I came here.

'Can I help you?' she says, looking at me.

'I hope so,' I say. 'We were wondering—'

'Yes, you can help us. It is windy and noisy out here and we would like to come in and look around your shop.' Nora has no use for scene-setting.

'Right. Well, the thing is, we're not open to the public, my love.'

'That is a beautiful dress you are wearing.' Although she knows that flattery can sometimes get you everywhere. 'And I think you will agree that I am not the public. I am soon becoming the oldest of the world, the oldest ever, and I have been living round about here for more years than all of your family added up together.' She gives the lady in the beautiful sari what I know is a friendly smile. 'In fact, I used to go to the theatre right here in your shop. Did you know that?'

'I didn't, no, my love. Very interesting.'

Her nod pretends to be polite, like so many nods in London.

'It is, yes, very interesting. And I'm sure you would like to know more about the inside of your shop. And not leave such an old woman out here in the wind to shiver when I tell you I will soon be the oldest in the world. I think you are not looking for this kind of publicity.'

I cannot tell if the nod is softer or just hoping to avoid publicity, or maybe it is because this other woman was not born in London either.

'Listen, why don't you come in, my love?' she says.

'Thank you, we will. Good morning. My name is Dinora Wojnawski and this is my friend, Mrs Arifa Hashmi. And, for your information, I am not your love. I have many people in my family who love me and frankly I am too old to add any more.'

'Right, of course my— I mean, Mrs Donasky. Is that right?'

'Wojnawski.'

'Right. How can I help you?'

'I would like to look around. So I was telling you, that right here, for many, many years there was a theatre. A Jewish theatre where we sang and shouted in Yiddish and cried and listened quietly. They called it the Grand Palais, oy, very fancy! It was right here. Where you are selling the *shmatte.*'

'Oh, I've heard of that, *shmatte.* That's clothes, isn't it? Everyone in Stepney knows that there were all sorts of Jewish shops here before, but I didn't know about the theatre. You're right, my love, very fancy.'

Nora is steering her wheelchair away from the shopkeeper towards a rack of Italian fashion suits, but she is not deaf, at least not always.

'The name is Wojnawski. From Poland. These suits are not so fancy.' She sweetens her words with another attempted smile for the shop assistant. 'My Henry always wore a suit, come the rain, come the shine, although in our shop he would take off the jacket and put on his apron. We had our grocery shop over there on Quaker Street. A bit further up near the Spitalfields Market. Do you know it?'

'Oh. Yes, I do know it. There's a lovely café down there, with exhibitions. Very arty.'

'Oy! This café is where I had my shop and all my life after the war. Mrs Hashmi and me were taking a coffee over there just the other day. It's a beautiful place. You can buy anything you need there, anything. You just ask, we will find it for you. The apples, the bananas, the eau de cologne for your husband to smell good at *shul* on a Friday. Ach, we didn't have so much time to go to *shul*, Henry and I. We were trying to make a good living for our children; we kept the shop open on the *Shabbas*, God forgive me. But he smelled good, my Henry, plenty of eau de cologne for when we went to the theatre. Not so often, maybe not even once a year, but he smelled good and he always wore a smart suit, and a rose in his buttonhole to the Grand Palais.'

I never told anybody, but my favourite part of going to the theatre was when the lights went down just before the curtain went up. This was the thrill of being about to see the beautiful sets and the actors in their costumes and make-up, and also of Henry putting his hand on my leg in public. In the dark, of course, so no one could see, but still a small thrill after all those years. I put my hand on his and held my breath as some other invisible people pulled the thick velvet curtain away from our life with all the other immigrants in the East End of London and took us back home to the old country.

There she was, the yiddisher mama, washing the clothes and telling everybody about her wonderful son, her Shmendrik, her darling, gentle child the way our Goldfaden, the most famous Yiddish writer of all, our yiddisher Shakespeare, had her say it, just like all the yiddisher mamas back then and still today. Just like my yiddisher mama who never knew, thanks to God, that only her goose of a daughter would come all the way through the war with her own son and husband and live to run a fine grocery store in another country, a fine country, and watch the actors on the stage pull back time. Henry laughed loud as this mother on the stage cursed the villagers that called her boy a fool, and even louder when the rabbis tried to knock his lessons into him at the yeshivah. I gasped when the beautiful Roze almost fainted. Her own father told her she had to marry Shmendrik, that idiot! And what about her true love, her Dovid (such a fine name), the one she had secretly promised herself to and who would not give her up?

Ach, what a lucky woman I was to be safe here in the dark, snuggled up to my own true love and with no worry about matchmakers or marrying a foolish man who cannot add the numbers in his head or read the holy book. No worry any more about the snow blowing its way through the wooden huts or the barking of the dogs and the guards, or being so hungry that an old piece of bread tasted better than my own mother's challah and was never enough so I would have eaten the grass if there was any. No more worry, just the small hole inside that never closed, where the old country and my own family used to be. Where I kept the ghosts. Mamme and Tatte, Hershel, Josef, Yankel and Divorah and my Miriam.

Henry clapped and sang and now he was up on his feet with half of the theatre. Roze and her Dovid were hand in hand on stage and Dovid stamped on the glass so that everybody in the audience cheered and shouted mazel tov! *I shouted with them and the happy couple looked so fine, Roze in her dress with the lace and Dovid in his wedding suit, with their families all around them, and the tears poured down my face.*

Nora strokes the fabric of a suit jacket and pulls it to her face as if she wants to see if it smells of men's perfume. I see that her eyes are wet before she hides them from us. Every time we take one of these journeys to her past it shows me the strength of this old woman. Could I go to the souk, to the hospital where I had my clinic before the war, to the beautiful park where the Queiq river runs without breaking into pieces?

'I would like to see a blouse,' she says and now her eyes are back to being calm and pale, tired from spending so long seeing so many things. 'Do you have silk? I want it for a special occasion.'

'Certainly we have silk, my— madam,' the shop assistant says. 'A whole section with some lovely blouses just over here.'

She shows Nora to another rack, full of bright colours, shiny.

'Here you go. You can feel the quality.'

'This is rayon, I think. I am looking for silk.'

'Well, this is very popular these days. Sells all over the West End. Art silk, we like to call it. It's … erm … short for artificial.'

'Yes, I can feel that.'

Nora reverses her wheelchair away from the arty blouses and almost runs into the sales assistant. Almost, but not quite and I have to force my laughter back down into my throat as she jumps out of the way because I know that Nora is an excellent driver.

'Thank you so much for letting us come in and see your quality *shmatte, mein liebe Dame*,' she says. 'Arifa, I would like to go home now. I think I will wear my green blouse, from when silk was silk and Henry loved me, for when Amelia wakes up and we have our party.'

TWENTY-TWO

Ten days and counting

Afternoon

'I know you told me on the phone, Deborah darling, and Adam filled me in a little bit when he came home for supper, but what exactly did he say? I mean things are clearer face to face, aren't they?' My mother always likes to have her story straight, usually for when she gives her lunch friends their blow by blow. And today, even though I know that this time she needs to know because she loves Amelia too, her questions feel too big for the little family room at the side of the ward where we're waiting for Amelia's nurses to change shift. 'Did he actually offer an apology, as such?'

I look over at James, but there has to come a time when I stop relying on him to field every question that might make me cry when I answer it. Every question, basically.

'He did. He said he was sorry. He even said it in Arabic, I think. And he was crying. And I wanted to be able to tell him we forgave him—I forgave him—but I couldn't. Because I don't know if I can. And James couldn't say anything either, could you darling?' No, no he couldn't, because my rock of a husband, had dissolved into tears. 'So Nasir told us what happened and asked for forgiveness and nobody said anything. There was just silence and then he ran.'

'But it was an accident, that's what Nasir said?'

'Yes, Mummy, he said it was an accident. Do I have to go through all of it again?'

'No, of course you don't, darling, forgive me. I mean, I'm sorry. I mean, oh God, no, please, you've already told me what he said and that's enough, of course. It was an accident. It's just, wasn't he looking after Amelia at that point? Wasn't he responsible for her safety?'

'Mummy, all this is hard enough as it is. I mean it was hard enough to listen to what Nasir had to say. I'm Amelia's mother and I was there with them. Have you got any idea how that feels? And what about you, Daddy? My five-year-old daughter is still in that bed over there in a coma!'

'No, darling, of course we can't imagine how you're feeling, and you know we are with you and James every step of the way,' says Daddy. 'We just want to be sure about what Nasir's told you.'

'Well, the way things stand, it looks like we might be waiting quite a while to hear Amelia's version,' I snap. 'If ever.'

I stare at them and I hate myself because how will I live with myself, live at all, if that happens? James takes my hand in both of his and presses it against his lips.

'It's alright, darling,' he says. 'I think your parents are just trying to understand.'

'Yes,' I say. 'I know. I'm sorry.'

'We're all sorry, Debs,' says Adam. 'Listen, maybe both you and James want to go back to the hostel to have a bit of time together. We can stay with Amelia and call you if there's any change. Anything at all.'

'Thanks, Adam, but no,' James says, and he's just ahead of me. 'One of us has to be here all the time with Amelia. All the time. She'll need her parents, at least one of them, to be there when she wakes up.' He stands up and stretches.

'Will you go, darling?' I say. 'I just want to talk quickly to Mummy and Daddy and then I'll be over.'

'What is it, Deborah?' Mummy jumps in as soon as James leaves the room, followed by Adam.

'It's nothing important. It's just the caterer keeps calling and I don't know what to do. I don't pick up and I probably haven't listened to all the messages, but they want to know what's going on and they're beginning to sound pretty cross.'

'When did you last talk to Bubby about it?' says Daddy. 'Has she said anything about changing her mind?'

'We haven't talked about it for ages, even before Amelia. The only thing she's mentioned since, was the first time she came here. She told Amelia that when she wakes up, she wants to have a party with her, make a honey cake, invite all her little friends.'

'Well, that sounds excellent. A double party. Even better.'

Daddy's glass is nearly always half full and especially at parties.

'Yes, but it's not just the caterers. There are hotel bookings and the rabbi and all the people we were expecting to come. My phone is full of them.'

'Deborah, you are not to worry your head about any of that for a moment longer. I will take care of the rabbi and your father will look after the rest. Won't you, Michael?'

'Consider it done, Sylvia dear. Just point me in the right direction.'

I do love this pair when Mummy is in gin and lipsticks mode and Daddy is just Daddy.

'Thank you,' I say.

'Nonsense,' says Mummy. 'You need all of your energy right here.' Mummy with empathy really is quite lovely. 'But, there is just one other thing I wanted to talk to you about.'

Ah. Not quite all of my energy then.

'I went to see Grandpa David yesterday. I think we'd agreed it was your turn again, but obviously I went, given the circumstances. I didn't want him to miss his weekly visit.'

'I don't think Grandpa David would have noticed if we'd skipped an entire month, Mummy.'

'No, of course not. And of course I wouldn't have expected you to go, that's not what I meant. It's just that he's been asking for you.'

'Asking for me?'

'Apparently. He didn't say anything while I was there, but his weekend carer said he'd been singing that "Oom-pah-pah" song and calling for Debbie. Loudly and very out of tune. The song, I mean. He's been disturbing some of the other residents and apparently one of the nurses says he keeps singing it every time she comes into his room and looking at her in an odd way.'

I burst out laughing and, oh, it feels so good, such a relief to discover that I can still find something funny. Mummy starts laughing too—another discovery—and sets off Daddy and the three of us cling to each other, our shoulders shaking.

'Anyway,' Mummy manages to pull herself together, 'the carer wanted to know if you could come and see him— Grandpa, I mean—and try to calm him down. I told him you couldn't, explained everything, but he said that one of the other resident's families was threatening a formal complaint and that if they did the Cedars might not be able to keep him.'

'A formal oom-pah-pah complaint, I ask you,' says Daddy and pushes us over the edge again.

'Well, you can take him home with you, Daddy. You're the nearest next of kin anyway and you can teach him the rest of the words. I bet *Oliver!*'s on Netflix.'

Now that I'm laughing, I don't know if I'll be able to stop, how I'll be able to pull myself together to go back to Amelia, whether I should pull myself together or if a mummy howling with laughter might be the memory trigger that brings her and her own beautiful laugh back to us.

'Is everything alright?'

Adam sounds more than a little confused.

'Yes, oh, sorry, honestly. It's just something that Mummy said.'

'Mum?'

Adam's confusion is growing. Like me, he probably can't remember the last time she ever said anything that made us laugh this much.

'Yes, don't worry, just something about Grandpa David singing musicals.'

'Oh, right. Well, I guess I can see how that must have been pretty funny.'

'It was, it was.' And I just can't stop giggling.

'It's good to see you laugh, Debs, about musicals or anything else. It's just that James thinks you should come.'

'What? Why didn't you say so?' I've stopped laughing. 'What is it? What's happened?'

'Nothing. I mean Amelia hasn't... Look, Nasir's back.'

I don't know exactly how I got from the family room to Amelia's bed, but yes, Nasir is back. He looks so different in school uniform. Even a blazer, although I don't know why that should surprise me. He's talking to James and by the look of it, neither of them are crying. So far.

'Hello, Nasir. You're back.'

'Erm, hi, Mrs Levene. Yes, I am.'

'Nasir wanted to tell us again how sorry he was, darling. Explain a bit more. He was hoping it would be just the two of us.'

James. James and his bedside manner. Always finds a way of breaking the ice.

'OK. Of course. Adam, can you head off with Mum and Dad? Mummy was saying something about shopping, or the rabbi or something.'

He does and so now it's just the two of us. Three with Amelia. Four with Nasir.

'Thanks for coming back, Nasir,' says James. 'Debbie and I understand how hard it must be for you.'

I nod. As hard as I can so he knows that the two of us really are on his side now.

'And we're sorry that we couldn't find the words after what you told us yesterday. It's hard for us too, you know that.'

Now Nasir is nodding and he's even looking James in the eye.

'Has there been any change, with Amelia?' he says.

'No, she's stable,' James answers, 'but the doctors say it's still soon enough for her to come round without too many after-effects. Maybe none at all.'

'I'd like to try and talk to her again. I've brought the picture of her cat that we made on my mum's phone, so maybe I could show her that. She really liked making it.'

'Maybe we could just chat things through first. What do you think, darling?'

I try to keep my voice light, but laughing with my parents feels like a lifetime away.

'I think that makes sense.'

Silence.

Broken by James.

'So you were telling us that Amelia kept wanting to climb higher? On the tree.'

'Yes, that's right. But I know I should never have let her start climbing the tree in the first place. I tried to stop her, like I told you. I really did.'

'I'm sure you did, Nasir.' And I am. How many times has Amelia wriggled out of my arms? How often has that I-love-you-Mummy smile charmed me into submission? 'I know how hard it can be to keep saying no.'

I'm talking to Nasir, but I'm looking at James and I hope he can see how sorry I am.

'I'm so sorry,' Nasir says.

'I know,' I say.

I am still looking at James and there's still a part of me that wants to scream and pound my fists on his chest, but I know I can't turn all my fear and guilt into blaming Nasir.

'And I'm sorry too, Nasir. It was an accident. I know that.' And I also know that Nasir is hurting and that, with Bubby, he could be one of the only people to bring Amelia back to us. 'I believe you. We believe you, don't we, James?' I don't wait for an answer because this is James, he believes him. 'But forgiving is so hard. I don't even know how to forgive myself. I'm sorry, Nasir. I know that's hard, but Amelia is our baby, our future. She's what makes us into a family and for now all that has gone.'

I find I'm in James's arms again. Nasir has his head down and his eyes closed.

'We do believe you,' James says and puts a hand on Nasir's shoulder. 'And you can come and see Amelia whenever you want to, can't he, darling?'

'Yes, of course he can,' I say.

'We need as many of the people she loves here with her to try to bring her back.'

Nasir lifts his head and looks at both of us. 'I love her too,' he says.

'I can tell,' says James. 'Now go and show her that picture.'

TWENTY-THREE

Ten days more

Evening

Every time I look out of the window, the same cars are there, the same trees, sometimes a neighbour walking their dog and even a couple of the boys that hang around the street, but not Nasir. He doesn't even have a phone for me to try and call. I'm earning some more money now, why didn't I buy him one at that Apple Store? Maybe he came back to the flats and one of those boys asked him for his phone and when he said he didn't have one they got into a fight and maybe beat him up or even knifed him. There are always stories about boys being knifed on the boards outside the newspaper shop. And they are usually dead. I keep asking myself what my mother would do and I hear her voice telling me that this is not Syria, that he will come home, not to worry, have patience, in my day there were none of these phones and the children always come home, *habibti*, make yourself a good hot cup of *zouhourat*, can you find the hibiscus flowers in London? it will calm you, soothe your stomach, *habibti*. And yes, I have the

194

dried flowers for *zouhourat*, but no, I have not made it. The knot in my stomach can only be soothed by one thing and it is not tea and in any case the kettle is not by the window in the living room where I am sitting with my sewing, unsewn. I would go out and look for him, but I cannot leave Nora even though for now she is having a nap. It is not a criticism; it is just a fact. The way my feeling that Nasir didn't go to school this morning is a fact, I'm sure of it now, because if he had gone to school he would have come home from school, wouldn't he? Unless the boys that knifed him were waiting for him outside the school gate.

Nora's bell rings and my sewing falls on the floor. So the nap is over. I was right not to leave her, of course I was. I take one more look out of the window before I go through to help her back into her chair. Cars, trees, dogs crouching and making dirt in the grass and no Nasir.

'I'm coming, Nora!'

'Thank you, Arifa,' she says after she has put her teeth back in.

'You are welcome,' I say. 'How was your nap?'

'Very restful, very restful. I have been sleeping so much better since I have been staying with you and Dovid.'

'I'm glad,' I say. 'So, shall we get you up and into your chair?'

Nora is as weightless as a hibiscus flower and I soon have her sitting comfortably with a light blanket over her knees.

'Would you like a cup of *zouhourat*? I was just going to make some for myself.'

'That is the flower tea, isn't it? This one you usually make before bed, not after it. So the boy is not back then?'

I will never know how Nora can switch between mixing things up and understanding everything, unless she decides to leave her brain to the scientists. But then she would have to die first and so far, that is not part of her plans.

'No, still not home, but I think he must have had study after school or maybe gone back to a friend's house.'

'He doesn't ring his mother to let her know about that, with these phones the children all have these days?'

'He doesn't have one yet, but sometimes he can borrow one from a friend and sometimes not,' I half lie. 'Now, how about the *zouhourat*?'

'*Zou-hou-rat*,' she says, 'sounds like a very good idea for your nerves. I will get the poker game ready for Dovid while you're making it.'

I take a quick look out of the window on my way to the kitchen. No Nasir. I wish I could magic a phone into his pocket while the kettle boils, but I have no wand. The dried hibiscus flowers smell beautiful even before I pour on the water and I try to breathe their calm in deep, but there is no result. I put a couple of sesame biscuits on the tray for Nora. Supper looks like it will be late tonight and she will be getting hungry.

'Hi, Mama.'

Oh! *Alhamdulillah*, I hadn't picked the tray up yet and dropped boiling tea all over my feet!

'Nasir! Oh my days! Where have you been? Why are you so late?'

He is in the kitchen. It must have been the noise from the kettle. I force myself not to try to take him in my arms.

'Sorry. I lost track of time.'

'But where were you? Did you go to school? I was worried this morning; you were in such a hurry.'

'Of course I went to school, don't worry. But I went to the hospital on the way home.'

'Amelia's hospital?'

'Yes.'

'Oh, Nasir.'

'It's OK. I would have asked a friend to let me phone you, but I wasn't planning to go. I was walking home and I just turned off towards the hospital without thinking about it.'

'It doesn't matter. You're home now. Come on, take your jacket off and sit down. I've made some *zouhourat*.' I take his blazer. 'How was she?'

'About the same. I showed her the picture we made on your phone. She liked playing with it when she came here that time.'

'That was kind of you, *habibi*. And her parents were there?'

He nods.

'And?'

'It was OK.'

'*Habibi*, I'm worried about you. This is too much for you to carry on your own. Did you talk to them again?'

'Yeah. It was better. They were alright. They know it was an accident. They said I could go back and see her whenever I want.'

'*Alhamdulillah, alhamdulillah!*' I don't care if he sees that I'm crying. 'I am proud of your courage,' I say. 'Now take this tray through to Nora; she's been waiting for you to play a round of poker.'

I sit at the kitchen table with my own cup of *zouhourat* and no need for its powers to do more than make the air around me fragrant. Nasir is not waiting for me to come and identify him in a morgue. He will not go to jail for putting a five-year-old girl in a coma. He went to his London school this morning with his hair brushed and his tie straight. And now he is playing poker with a 122-year-old woman who likes to think he is her son, on a computer that she bought for him. I think her people call this feeling *naches*. In any case, I like it. I take a sip of my tea and remember how she spoke about her husband this morning, with his perfume and his flower in his suit at their theatre that is now selling cheap suits made who knows where by who knows who. I wonder if one day when I'm old (but not 122) I will be back visiting places near Cornwood Drive that became part of my new life here and that have been given a new life of their own. I don't know. The way I don't know if I will be able to go back to Aleppo one day to see what has been rebuilt, rearranged, turned into something new, left to rot with the bodies underneath it. I know that Nora has never been able to return to Poland because of her own war. It is too soon for me to decide about mine.

I go into the living room to be with the living. Two heads, one with black hair, one with a bright scarf covering bald skin, staring into the screen in silence. I can see that they are still alive because Nasir is rubbing his finger up and down his nose and Nora is rocking gently backwards and forwards in her chair. I sit on the sofa and pick up my sewing. Supper just needs to be reheated. It can wait, I want to be with them, the people who are my connections with both my countries and who stop me from swimming back across the Mediterranean to dig up graves.

The computer plays a fanfare.

'You did it again, Nora, high five,' Nasir says. 'I don't stand a chance against you, even on the computer now.'

'Don't underestimate yourself,' says Nora. 'You're learning. It's only been a week or so and I can see where you have improved. But you go too fast sometimes, too bold.'

'And you're learning too, for sure. How did you manage to find your way around the computer so quickly? We only picked it up the other day and you told me you swore by your cards.'

'Ach, Dovid, practice makes perfect. I like this fruit machine. I wasn't so sure, but now I like it, so I've been spending some time now and then, learning how to use it, a *bisl* every day. I played with Igor in Russia this evening before you came home and Mustapha in Turkey. I beat them both,' she hoots.

'You've been playing online? How did you manage that?'

'You think old means *meshuggeh*? You showed me how to open up the game three times, or four, maybe even five. You gave me a piece of paper with the password and I typed it in. You set it up with my banking card. Where's the difficult part?'

'Ha!' Nasir laughs more than I've heard him laugh for many, many months, maybe years. 'Did you hear that, Mama? Nora's learned her way round the fruit machine. She's not just going to be the world's oldest woman; she's going to be the world's oldest online poker champion!'

'She's a woman of many talents,' I say, 'and she has a good teacher.'

'This is right.' Nora's grin is as wide as a watermelon. 'I have plenty of tricks up the sleeve of my blouses, and you and that Stephen Jobs have kept the fruit machine nice and simple for me.'

'I love it!' Nasir says. 'Next thing we know she'll have her own YouTube channel. Poker Night with Nora or something.'

'What is this YouTube?'

'It's a video app, like a TV station and anyone can start up their own shows. We'll get you an agent, Nora, a hair and make-up artist and you'll have special guest stars playing against you every week.'

'Nasir, stop teasing her,' I begin, but I needn't have worried.

'Dovid you are the *meshuggeneh*!' Nora is trying to hide the way he makes her laugh too, but it's not working. 'I already have plenty of tubes and nobody wants to see them, let me tell you. You can keep your apples and your hair stylist. The poker on the fruit machine is enough for me and anyway I wear a wig.'

'Have it your way, Nora,' says Nasir and he is still laughing. 'I was just looking to the future, seeing if we could kill two birds with one stone, between the world record and the poker, and make you a star.'

'Thank you, you are very kind, but I like keeping things with a low profile. I think we can carry on the way we have it, a game with the cards here, a game on the machine over there. We teach each other and so it will be winner and winner—isn't that the way they say it? And maybe sometimes when you're out at school, I will see what is happening in the world of the web.'

'Well, Igor and the others had better watch out is all I can say,' says Nasir. 'Shall we start another game?'

'Don't you have homework to do?' I ask. I don't want to be the one to always stop the fun, but somebody has to remind him that real life doesn't happen inside a computer.

'Come on, Mama. I'll do it after supper. Nora will be tired then. I'll do it then, I promise.'

'But we're already late, *habibi*.'

'Please, just this once, Mama.'

And he comes over and bends to kiss me on the cheek. Game over, like they say on his video games.

'*Habibi*. OK, just this once. So I will go and get supper ready.'

And this wins me another kiss and a feeling that something has changed in this tiny home in Cornwood Drive in rainy Stepney, so I leave them to their pairs and their straights and their flushes.

The table is almost ready. Rice with a little thin noodle and nuts and some chicken soaked in lemon that smells almost as good as the *zouhourat*. The tea has done its job, with a little help from Nasir and Amelia's parents, and I hum as I set the table. Then the doorbell rings, a long time and then again. I have no idea who this could be.

'Nasir, will you answer that? Supper is almost ready.'

Who is it? Could it be that Nasir wasn't at school after all and the head teacher has come to tell me? Or he made up the things about the hospital and got into a fight and this is the other parents?

'Mama, Mama, leave the supper. It's Amelia's granddad.'

I wipe my hands on my apron and think of my mother. The humming feeling has turned into a stone in my chest.

'Mr Wojnawski, how are you? Is everything OK? Did you need something?'

'Arifa, Bubby, I'm fine, yes, I'm well, very, very well. Bubby, I came as fast as I could. I wanted to tell you – all of you – in person. It's Amelia.'

I hold tight to Nasir's hand.

'She's back with us. Amelia's back! She's come round, she's going to be alright.'

Nora reaches for my other hand.

'Machel, are you sure of what you're saying?'

'It's true. I'm sure, I really am. She's coming out of the coma. She opened her eyes a few times this evening and then they stayed open. She moved them when Debbie talked to her. She didn't quite look at her, but she moved her eyes and she moved her fingers when her mother held her hand. When I left the hospital, she was still awake, still with her eyes open. It's not over yet, they're doing lots of tests, but the doctors say they think she's coming back to us!'

TWENTY-FOUR

Nine days and counting

Morning

Even unfocused, her eyes are magnificent. A blue that can't be compared to flowers or skies or some kind of semi-precious stone. They are Amelia blue and when you look closely, and I have never looked so closely, there are lots of little flecks of brown as if the gene pool wanted pieces of my eyes and James's and our ancestors' to be in hers. Levene-Wojnawski brown. And the most important thing is that her blue eyes are open, nearly all the time now, and the doctors say that's a very good sign, really a very good sign. They won't make us any promises, but they say it's a very good sign. They are monitoring, they are testing, but this is a good sign. And so are her hand movements. Responsive hand movements they call them. When I took her hand yesterday, after she opened her eyes, after Nasir left and James and I were alone with Amelia, she moved her thumb, tapped it on my hand as if she wanted to squeeze back and now she's doing it more often, sometimes her thumbs, sometimes her fingers, both hands. When we talk to her, her eyes move and a few times I thought she was looking at me. It was during the night. The nurses wanted me to sleep, but I have never felt more awake. The only time that comes close is when she was born, the monkey. She kept me waiting and panting and guzzling gas and air for hours and then arrived just past midnight and I was exhausted, but wired, wired so there was no hope of any sleep on that first night that I spent staring through the perspex side of her cot at those dark blue eyes that all babies have when they're born. And now she's done it again. Coming back to us in the evening and pulling me into her eyes. No need for anaesthetic, but a monster hit of adrenaline and purest love that had me clinging to James and crying and laughing and unable to take my eyes off her and unable to sleep and not tired and not for one second being able to imagine being anywhere else but next to this bed with Amelia in it until it's time for us to take her home. Because the doctors aren't making any promises, but the signs are there, that's what they say.

'OK, Mrs Levene, Mr Levene, if you could just give us a bit of room, we're going to help Amelia sit up against her pillows. It's important to start getting her upright as soon as we can, but gently, so we can make sure her blood pressure doesn't drop. And we also need to make sure her body's balance organs can start working again. We're not sure yet if there's any problem with her inner ear, so we want to monitor that and, we hope, get her balance working again by itself.'

I'm glad Philomina is on duty today. Of all the nurses we've seen, she's the one who finds a way of treating us all like people, Amelia too, and telling us what we need to know without making me feel like an idiot. I haven't seen the other two before. James and I are pressed into each other. I'm beginning to get used to feeling my surgeon husband tremble.

'Try not to worry if you see her head flop. It's only been a few days, but she hasn't been using her neck muscles and they can lose strength quite quickly. Sitting up will start to help that too, before she begins physio, but we'll make sure Amelia's supported properly, so there's no need to feel anxious about that.'

I don't dare nod in case my own neck muscles have lost their strength too.

'We know you're doing everything you can for Amelia,' says James. 'Thank you.'

'OK, Amelia, we're going to sit you up now.' Philomina is completely focused on Meelie and I am holding my breath. 'It's something new that you haven't done for a few days, but Elsie and I are here to help you, and Carlos is going to tuck some pillows round you. We know it might feel strange for you, so try not to worry. If you feel any pain, just move one of your hands, doesn't matter which one, and we'll stop. Alright, honey?'

She looks deep into Amelia's blue eyes and then quickly at Elsie.

'One, two, three, here we go. That's great, Amelia. You're doing great. We're almost there.'

Her eyes are still open and I don't think she's moved her hands. Please, don't let her be in pain.

'There you go, honey. Look at you sitting up, that's wonderful. Your mum and dad are just here and they're so proud of you. They'll come and sit with you in a minute. Carlos is just making sure the pillows are all where they should be so you're comfortable.'

Philomina is stroking Meelie's arm and she is still looking

into her eyes. All three nurses are smiling at her. The depth of their kindness is what makes my eyes sting.

'OK, Amelia, you're doing great. Now, if you're feeling dizzy, if there's anything uncomfortable, try to move one of your hands.'

Nothing.

'OK, good. Now, Amelia, if you can hear me, try to move one of your hands.'

Amelia's hands are flat on the sheet. Philomina is still holding one of her arms. Amelia raises the fingers of her left hand, all of them.

'She can hear, James, she can hear and she's not in pain!' I whisper. 'Oh God, Amelia, we love you.'

One of the other nurses has her hand on my shoulder.

'I think it's time for you and Amelia's dad to take over. The doctor will be here soon for a full assessment and to talk about what happens next, but for now what your daughter needs most is you.'

I don't know if it was the relief or the information overload that triggered my sleep mechanisms. The joy of a day that began with Amelia responding to her nurse's questions, hearing them, was overwhelming and it took all my strength to listen to Dr Mirza explaining that she might have lost some of her memory, that it might come back, that she might not recognise us, that she might start to shout or cry or lose consciousness again. Or not. That she might start to speak and remember who we are, what happened, her name, that she has a next-door neighbour called Amelia too, that she's five years old and why aren't I at school? that she had to work with her team now on a whole series of tests and she would go through all of that as soon as possible, but that right now they needed Amelia to themselves and we needed to get some rest. So here we are, James and I, sharing the same bed for the first time since I gave him a blow-by-blow account of Bubby's trip to the synagogue and the brass plaque with the Wojnawski name on it and how a pinch from her bony fingers got me jumping out of the way for Arifa to have a better look. That time we were at home and his eyes were wet from laughing. This time we're in the Heartbreak Hotel and they're dry from emotional power surge.

My phone says it's 11:30 and it's the morning, so I've only been asleep for a couple of hours and it feels like I could sleep at least until 11:30 tonight. But I check for messages. Dr Mirza couldn't say exactly how long she and her team would need with Amelia—God knows how many hours, days, weeks, it will be before we stop hearing 'can't say exactly', 'can't be sure', 'promising, but there's no certainty as yet', 'we'll let you know as soon as we can.' In any case, there is no message from Dr Mirza yet. There are a lot of messages from Mummy, one from Adam and one from Nasir. The one James sent everybody when we got here will have to do for now.

He is sleeping on his back and the snuffle from his nose is almost a snore, but not quite. I suppose if it was somebody else, I would call it a snore, but this is James and everything he does is adorable. Well, almost, and today I'm not getting into that. His white t-shirt smells of Eau Sauvage (a tip from Daddy) and adorable sweat, and his beautiful biceps curve up and round where the sleeves end. I snuggle up and run my fingers along the dark hairs frizzing out of the neckline. James catches a breath and then goes back to an easy rhythm. I try again and pull at one of the hairs. Now he turns onto his side, eyes closed, easy breathing. So I close my own eyes and start to follow the rhythm of his chest rising and falling. His hand grabs my wrist.

'You're awake then,' he says.

'Yes,' I say.

'What time is it?'

'Not far off twelve last time I looked.'

'Any news from the hospital?'

'No, just family. And Nasir.'

'Good. So how come you're not sleeping?'

'I was. And I was about to go back to sleep when you grabbed me.'

'Right. That wasn't you messing with my chest then?'

'It might have been. I was half asleep.'

'Of course you were.'

'What are you trying to say, darling?'

'What do you think, babes? You usually know what I'm about to say before I do.'

'That I should go back to sleep and save my energy for later.'

'That's what I should say, but I was thinking of something else.'

'That it feels good when I mess with your chest.'

'Something like that.'

'That you've missed us being together like this.'

'Now you're getting closer.'

'That you love me and you always will.'

'Oh God, yes, I love you, Deborah Levene. I love you and our daughter.'

His grabs my other wrist and his kiss takes adorable to a whole new level. If there's one thing that I am sure of, it's that I want to be smelling Eau Sauvage and my husband's irresistibly adorable sweat until death us do part.

TWENTY-FIVE

Nine days and counting

Evening

'Amelia's recovery so far really is very encouraging,' says Dr Mirza, and James and I look at her like nodding dogs. 'Of course, we can't be sure,'—we know, we know—'but people who come out of a coma within days rather than weeks and whose progress is rapid tend to have the best outcomes, particularly in young children.' If James and I had them, our tails would be wagging. 'They will often recover completely— full brain function, including speech and cognitive function— although the timescale varies and Amelia will need a lot of support, both from you and your family, the team here at the hospital and therapists, once she's back at home.'

'She will come back home, won't she?'

'I think we can be confident of that, Mrs Levene, although I can't rule out any relapse yet, and I can't give you much help on timing for now.'

'No, we understand that. It's just so wonderful to know that we'll be able to bring her back home, isn't it, darling?'

'It's the best possible news, thank you, Dr Mirza. Thank you to you and all of your team.'

'It's the outcome we aim for for all our patients, and their parents. I think you know that, Dr Levene. We've been able to confirm that the swelling to the brain is negligible now and the fact that Amelia has been able to recognise you both and say her name, even though there is some mechanical speech impairment, which may be due to the tubes we've had to use, as I say, really is very encouraging. I still need to consult with my colleagues on exactly the right recovery plan for her for the next couple of days, but we should be able to walk you through that tomorrow.'

I am dumbfounded. James and I are both back to nodding again.

'Take your time to take it in and spend as much time with Amelia as you can, as long as you stay rested, especially you, Mrs Levene. She's going to need you. And visitors she knows well can start to come back again now to help her stimulation, but just for short periods. Take it steady. Your daughter is going to be alright.'

The look on Bubby's face as she wheels towards the bed tells me what people must see when they look at me. Behind her wrinkles (I have less than her, but more than I did four days ago), there is elation, pride, relief of course, but also something rigid as if she's wearing a bright, shiny party mask that she can hide behind if one of the other guests sets fire to the curtains. Arifa is walking as if she had wings for feet, but if she has a smile it's covered over by the fear that all this might be an illusion. I walk over to meet them.

'Bubby, I'm so happy you're here!'

I bend down and take her feeble skin, bone and steel in my arms.

'And you too, Arifa. I'm not sure that Amelia would have come back to us if it wasn't for the way you both talked to her. Come and see her, see if she recognises you.'

'She can see who people are now?' Bubby's mask cracks just a little.

'Some people. She knows who James and I are, and her grandparents, but not the nurses, but I think that must be logical. You're the only other people who've been allowed to come and see her so far since she's woken up.'

I wheel her next to the bed and she stares into Amelia's face as if she was looking for a map to find the way out of a maze.

'She is sitting up,' she whispers. 'This is a miracle. *Mamme sheyne*, I am your old, old Bubby, can you hear me?'

'It's OK, Bubby, you can talk a little louder.'

'But I don't want to scare her.'

'I know, don't worry. You shouldn't talk *too* loud, but she needs to be able to hear you.'

'You are right, I am a foolish old woman.' I cross my fingers. 'Amelia, *mamme sheyne*, this is your Bubby.' Thank all the Jewish saints, she didn't bellow into Meelie's ear. 'I hear your parents are very proud of you today, *bubbeleh*.' Her voice starts to crack as Amelia turns her eyes towards her. 'Ach, thanks God, you can hear me, can't you? I knew you would find a way back to us, that you would keep playing and singing inside. Soon you will be playing and singing again with all of us. I am sure of it, Amelia; you have the strength.'

My beautiful daughter looks at me now.

'Mummy,' she says, dragging the word along her tongue. 'It's Bubby.'

'Yes, my angel, it is. It's Bubby. You are so clever, so clever. She's come to see you because she loves you and she's so happy and proud that you're getting better.'

'Proud? Yes, I can say I am proud of this child who has been fighting so hard. You can hear that, *mamme sheyne*, I think? And you remember who I am? Of course you do, you had a good *kop* then, you have a good *kop* now. And these doctors are going to help you make it even better so you will be ready in time for our party.' She reaches out to stroke Amelia's hair. 'Do you remember that I made you a promise, Amelia? That we would eat honey cake together to make the party even sweeter? Well, you know what? I made one for you and I have it with me. Arifa has it in her bag.'

And now I have a lump in my throat from her honey cake.

'Oh, Bubby, you foolish old woman, I love you so much. But Amelia can't eat chicken soup yet, let alone honey cake, you know that.'

'Then you will share it with your husband, and Arifa and I will make another one for when this little *meydl* is ready. It will give you strength while you are waiting.'

'That sounds wonderful, Bubby. Will you make us some chicken soup too?'

'Chicken soup, always. Once a day keeps the doctor away,' she says. 'Although these days I have to eat more of the hot pepper and spices, that's right isn't it, Arifa? You know, maybe you should tell the little one about some of your recipes, maybe tempt her to get better a *bisl* faster?'

Arifa looks at me with some of her old wariness in her eyes.

'Please, Arifa. But easy on the pepper.'

Arifa takes off her coat, smooths down her hair and clears her throat before going over to the bed. She takes Amelia's hand and starts to hum, slowly and peacefully. Amelia's fingers close round her hand and she begins to sing, still quietly and with words that I don't understand, but that seem to have a call in them. Amelia looks across at me and then back at Arifa, and the focus in her eyes is steady. She loosens her fingers with the sway of the song and picks up her ugly green Froodle, pulling him to her face and putting her thumb in her mouth, the way she knows she's not supposed to, but always does. I have to flex every muscle in my body to stop myself from climbing onto the bed and holding her the way I do for bedtime stories and instead I watch her listening to Arifa and her spells.

'This was a gift my mother sent for you, Amelia,' she says when the song is over. 'It's something she used to sing to me when I was your age and much, much older. If you like, I can teach it to you when you're feeling a little stronger.'

'Yes please, Rifa,' my miraculous daughter says. 'I like it.'

'Then you must try and get strong quickly so I can teach you in time for your Bubby's party.'

First Bubby, now Arifa. Maybe the party really is going to happen. It's one miracle after another in this hospital.

'Rifa?'

'Yes, Amelia.'

'Where's Nasir?'

Arifa shuts her eyes for a moment and presses her lips together. Then she smiles at Amelia.

'Nasir sends you lots of love, *habibti*.'

'Where?'

Now Arifa looks at me and I nod.

'He's downstairs waiting for me because, you know, you mustn't have too many visitors at the same time or for too long. We don't want to make you tired; you need to rest to get strong.'

'I want Nasir.'

Dr Mirza said to take it steady. Can it be steady for Amelia to see the person she was with when she fell? I wish Dr Mirza was here to ask. I wish James was here. I even wish Mummy was here to ask or to bring me some gin. But they're not and I'm Amelia's mummy and she's asking for Nasir and I have to make the decision. Now. Couldn't telling her she can't see him be just as upsetting as remembering what happened? And she may not remember. And Nasir is down in the café, waiting. Now, Debs, you have to decide now.

'Well, in that case, I think we should ask him to come up and see you.'

I know I was right when I see the size of the smile on Nasir's face when he arrives. He is in school uniform again, looking smart, and the picture of Amelia with her bunches and her smile is back in my head, fighting for space with questions on how long it will be before she can wear her school uniform again.

'Hello, Nasir, thanks for coming to see Amelia. Did your mum tell you she was asking for you?'

'Hi, Mrs Levene,' he blushes as red as the stripe in his tie and nods like he'll never stop. 'I know. I couldn't believe it. It's so amazing that she's woken up.'

'Look, Meelie, here's Nasir. Do you remember, you asked him to come and see you and here he is.'

'Hi, Amelia,' he says and turns to look at Arifa.

'It's OK, *habibi*,' she says. 'Just try and talk the way you usually do, normal. Not too loud, not too quiet. She'll be able to hear you and maybe she'll answer you.'

'OK.'

'Yes,' I say, 'and try and ask Amelia about things you think she might be able to remember.' Now I whisper. 'But I think it's best if you don't talk about what happened in the cemetery unless she does, OK?'

'OK.'

He turns and gives Arifa a quick hug and then goes back to Amelia.

'Hi again, Amelia, it's Nasir,' he says.

'Nasir,' she says.

'It's good to see you with your eyes open again. I was really hoping you would be awake again soon and now you are, so that's awesome.'

He looks over at Arifa and she gives him a you-can-do-it smile.

'I went back to school yesterday. Half term's over, so, you know, back to school. I bet you can't wait to go back to school and see your friends, can you?'

'School.'

'Do you like school?'

Amelia nods.

'That's good. I don't really, but I did when I was your age, cos you just get to play and stuff, don't you? Colouring and singing and playing with your friends. What do you like best at school, Amelia?'

She looks at him and I know it must be wishful thinking, but I can see something in her eyes that's trying to remember.

'Amber,' she says slowly. 'Oliv … Olivia, Mae.' A pause. 'Lucy. And Amelia B.'

I clap my hand over my mouth. These are the names of her friends from school, and the other Amelia, her bestie from the other side of the fence.

'Are they your schoolfriends?' Nasir asks.

'Yes,' she says, 'and next door.'

I go over to Nasir and squeeze his shoulder.

'They are your lovely friends, aren't they, my angel? You know, I think you're going to be seeing them all again very soon!'

TWENTY-SIX

Eight days more

Afternoon

I f Nora could still walk, she would be pacing up and down the living room. I have told her I would fetch her book as soon as she asked me for it, but she is still wheeling her chair around when I arrive with it. I don't know what the trouble is and she is making me nervous.

'Ach, here it is, let me see it, Arifa.'

'But it's heavy, Nora, you'll break your wrist. Let me put it on the table for you.'

'So. Henry's Bible from the shop. This is what I need to look at. I thought it was lost.'

'I kept it safe for you in the cupboard in my bedroom—your bedroom. Mr Wojnawski brought it last week, do you remember?'

'Remember? I should remember? What I need to remember is in this book.' She taps it with a perfect pink nail. 'I don't need these machines you have. These phones, the fruit machine Dovid keeps showing me with the poker games all lit up with colours and music. I like my cards made of cardboard, with the big numbers and the Kings and Queens, and I like my memories inside this book.'

'Of course, Nora, I understand that.'

'The memories are important. You heard the little one with her memories, her friends. She is young, her *kop* is good even with the fall she had, but I need to go through the pages to find my memories. You see that, Arifa?'

'I do. So many things fade,' I say. 'Would you like me to bring you something while you're looking at it? A glass of water or a nice cup of milky coffee? Or a *zouhourat*? You liked that yesterday.'

'A vodka. I will take a vodka.'

'But isn't a bit early for vodka, Nora? It's only three o'clock.'

'Oy, what does she think she's telling me? I am not some little child at school with her school friends. I am a grown woman—much too grown and too old for somebody to tell me it's too early for vodka. So, vodka in the small glass with no ice please, and if you don't have herring, a nice biscuit.'

Now we are both at the table, Nora with her Bible and her vodka, and me with my forms. I didn't tell her, but I thought about adding a little water to the glass. Then I said to myself that maybe some things she doesn't remember, but I'm sure the taste of plain vodka isn't one of them. And she's right, 122 is old enough to make your own decisions. Probably none of the Wojnawski-Levenes will be popping in to check up on us this afternoon.

I have reached 'Area of Specialisation'. Nora is still looking at the first page, inside the cover. She is wearing the glasses she puts on for playing cards. She runs her finger down a list, sometimes stopping for a moment to tap the page. I leave her to her past and go back to filling in my future. They need to know many things: Date of Basic Medical Qualification, Area of Specialisation, Date of Specialist Medical Qualification, Title of Specialist Medical Qualification, and then more. I remember very well the day I passed my medical degree and the celebrations with the other students and then at home with my parents, but I don't remember the date. I have no Bible and no Quran to help me and my diaries were long gone even before the bombs could tear them up. Tarek would say, don't worry, you think they're going to check the date for every refugee who wants to be a doctor in the new country? It must be true, but I would like my form to have the right information. It feels like the right way to start my future.

'Ach! Here is the first day that Dovid went to school. I remember how he looked with his suit and his *kippah*. So smart and so clever.'

'I'm sure he did. It must have been a big change, going to school in England.'

'This is not England. This is the first day he went to school, the way I said. In Lodz.'

'You have the dates for the times before you came to England?'

'Of course! In my Bible. That is what it is for. The numbers for the shop to make the business right, this I worked on with Henry, and the days and times for our life, sometimes before the war, sometimes after. This was my part. Henry said I looked back to the past too much, but I didn't look so much, I just liked to have it there. To remember.'

She takes off her glasses and taps the page and I wonder

which times she is thinking of and whether she has written down the days and times for her war times too.

'You have lived in war, Arifa. You know that we have no choice about remembering those times. And that they are not days to write down in a diary.'

She puts her hand on mine. She is another mother who has lived through war. Of course she knows what I am thinking.

'I know you know where I went in the war and who put me there and I know you know that this is a time of my life that I cannot forget. You have washed and dried the skin and the numbers they wrote there enough times. You have put that itching wig on my head that I have to wear to be respectable, but maybe you didn't know how I got this way with a head plain like an egg. You are old, Mrs Wojnawski, they tell me. So old and that means so bald. *Neyn* is what I am telling you, Arifa. *Neyn!*'

I have seen the numbers on her arm, I have seen her bald head, but now I am seeing a dark anger on her face that must have been written on the inside of her body.

'Fear, Arifa, terror. This is what cost me my hair, such beautiful dark hair that my Henry told me shone like silk. Silk that was fit for a cloak.' Her voice is quieter and she puts her hand to her forehead as if she dare not touch the part where her hair once grew. 'Fear of their guns and their dogs and, yes, of their gas that killed us. They shaved away all the silk, but it was my terror for my family that made it first grow white again and then fall out. In clumps of straw, white like the cliffs of this new country we came to. Where you came too, Arifa. Did you see the cliffs when you came?'

'No, Nora,' I say, but I think she didn't hear me.

She puts her glasses on again, turns a few pages and stops at another list. Even with her glasses she has her nose up close to the page. I see this is a way to cover over her fear, the way her prickling wig can protect her eggshell head. I have Tarek's pendant to hold my fears and I know these safe places hold them tight when we need to lock them. Nora has gone back to her Bible and I go back to my forms. Maybe Mama has kept our dates. I will ask her.

The mountains rising out of the water were a sight to see. Bright white in the morning sun that had risen in the east and was lighting our way west. Henry held me round the waist with one arm and the other held Dovid tight against the railings of the boat, even though I told him he was meshuggeh, *the boy was much too big and heavy for him now, he could fall and drown.*

'The White Cliffs of Dover, they call them,' he said. 'This I learned from one of the sailors, so you see, taking a stroll for a smoke after supper is not so useless after all. We need to learn about our new country.'

'We will learn plenty when we get there,' I said. 'For now, I want to keep the memory of our life before, at home. I don't remember any sailors there.'

Although, I agree, these white cliffs are very beautiful.

'1st of June 1946. Remember this date, Dovid,' his father said. 'It may not be easy, but it is the start of our future, in a new place, so you need to remember this journey and these cliffs that have a name almost the same as yours. You don't think that's a good sign, Nora?'

'I hope it is, but you are right, the future may not be so easy.'

He pulled me closer to him and spoke into my ear.

'Maybe not, but we have been through much worse, all three of us. We have left too much behind to stop trying to make our future.'

And then he spoke aloud, with the part for Dovid to hear, the part for the son who had his own memories of the worst that he could ever suffer, but who must not hear about his parents' memories.

'And here we are, the three of us, together and looking at something more beautiful than maybe we have ever seen.'

But in my head, the fields that stretched away from my own small house, my mother's face, my brothers and sisters, and Raysel, Perl, Klara and especially Miriam, were even more beautiful.

'It is magnificent,' I said. 'Don't you think so, Dovid? Don't you think we will be happy in this new place, where you will have new friends and a new school, and a home again for the three of us?'

Dovid turned to look at me and I saw the shine from the white of the cliffs and his father's face in his eyes. So I made a promise to him in my heart to remember this date, to write it down in a special book, with all the dates and the moments of our new life together. I made a promise to myself to write down the other dates from our old life, together and apart, and keep them in a place where only Henry and I could see them so that I would only share those memories with mein ein Lieb. And I made another promise to Miriam that I would keep her safe in that same book and tell Henry and Dovid to promise too that they would keep her safe with me. So safe that now only the three of us would be able to find her, and so quiet that only we could talk about her and know her name. The past would stay in the past and for the future, for Dovid, I would look at the cliffs and help Henry build a new happiness, with more dates to look forward to and more places to go to.

'When we get off the boat, we will take a train. We will have seats and somewhere to eat our sandwiches,' I told him. I would make myself leave behind my terror of trains that comes from the trains with no windows and no water and hundreds of frightened people packed together, some sick, some already dead. I would make myself leave it back in the past if it helped Dovid forget his own terror.

'I want you to look out of the window and tell me what you can see in our new country. They say England is very green with small hills and lots of farms, a bit like the ones near Lodz. But we will go to

London. You will see, it's a fine, big city where we will have to stay together so we don't lose each other.'

'Come on, Mama,' Dovid said. 'I'm not a baby anymore. I won't need the two of you to show me round.'

'You have no idea. You've never seen a city big like this one, where they speak another language. You might not be a baby, but you're my son and you will be staying with me and your father.'

'Don't scare your mother, Dovid,' said Henry. 'She wants to keep you safe. Did you ever know a mother who didn't want to have her son stay with her?' He ruffles Dovid's hair. 'Now, let's enjoy this view because we won't be seeing it again. This is a day for all of us to remember.'

'Arifa, I would like another vodka. This is something from the old days that we can still enjoy today. Will you take one with me?'

'No, thank you, Nora, I don't drink alcohol.'

'Ach, yes, I was forgetting; you have even more rules in your religion than we do. Did you ever taste a vodka?'

'No,' I laugh, 'and not beer or wine or whisky either.'

'I know, you like to keep to the rules, that's true. I see it when you play cards,' she says. 'Sometimes I wish I didn't keep to the rules so much, but it was hard in the old times. The rabbis with all their rules, then the Germans with more, much more and much worse. Then I couldn't break the rules or they would break me.' She takes off her glasses and closes the book. 'It's all in my Bible, Arifa, I will show you some day.'

'Would you like me to bring you something with your vodka?' I ask.

'You know I like the herring with a vodka, but you never bring me any.'

'I'm sorry, Nora, but the herring you like is not so easy to find around here these days.'

'So much has gone from those times, that is why it is good to have my book back. It has been too long since I looked at it. But it is hard to read about the things that sometimes you remember, sometimes you forget. You forget because you have to; it is too heavy to live with these things inside your head all the time.' She rubs a hand across her forehead. 'It makes me think of the little girl in the hospital. All those things she has to remember. Those friends of hers, the way she talks, even how to move her fingers. Who is she again, Arifa? I know I should know her, but reading my Bible mixes me up.'

'She's Amelia, Deborah's daughter. Your great-great-granddaughter. Do you remember, she had a fall when we were at the Jewish cemetery?'

'Amelia? Deborah? This is the Hebrew word for bee. So busy, buzzing around. There is something buzzing round my head about that child. She reminds me of a little girl I knew in the old days, one of the ones in my book that sometimes I want to remember and sometimes to forget. Like the bee searching in the flowers for the pollen. One day it brings honey and one day it stings. This sting swells too much in my head, this girl is too much memory for me.'

I have been getting to know that the way Nora thinks can change and that sometimes she even chooses what she wants to understand and see, the way she does with Nasir, her Dovid. The agitation from The Cedars has mostly gone since she came here to my home and her memory has been stronger, but now the accident, the hospital, seem to be muddling her.

'But Nora, you were so happy yesterday when Amelia was awake and we went to see her,' I try to choose my words to make things simple. 'When she knew who you were. You brought her honey cake.'

'Stop with the honey. I don't want it.' She covers her eyes with her hands. 'I don't want the cake, and the girl in the hospital with her blue eyes and her wires and her school friends is making the bees sting inside my head. She needs to stay inside the Bible with Raysel and Hershel and the others, so the buzzing stops in my head.'

Now she is running both of her hands back and forth across her forehead and her eyes are shut tight. I wish it was the too-early glass of vodka, but I can see that the stinging is stronger than that.

'Nora, please, let me give you a cup of *zouhourat*. Let me play you some of your music.'

I try to put my hand on hers, but she pushes it away.

'This buzzing is too much for me, Arifa,' she says and she stares at me with blank eyes. 'The girl is bringing me too much pain. I tell you I won't go to the hospital to see her again.'

TWENTY-SEVEN

Eight days and counting

Evening

I do miss being at home, but in the end the not-quite-so-Heartbreak Hotel is not so bad, especially when your daughter is doing well enough for you to feel a little bit less guilty about spending some time there with your husband. After all, the hospital is literally a three-minute walk away and my phone is always on, ringer turned right up, 24/7 and beyond if necessary. Alright, I do feel guilty, and scared that I'm going to miss something, but the doctors say it's best for everybody. Amelia needs time for her therapies, and James and I need to rest, especially at night. A good night's sleep is such a tonic, as Mummy used to say. Well, she didn't actually; her tonic has always come mixed with gin, but everybody knows that eight hours a night helps you feel happy and bright. Or was that the gin?

James should be back from the hospital any minute. I almost wish he'd say, 'Hi, honey, I'm home' when he gets here, so it would almost feel like we were back to normal. But then we'd be wondering why Amelia wasn't coming flying down the hallway to climb up his legs and that would feel horrible. So a kiss and a hug will be just perfect. Pretty much anyway.

I locate cutlery, salt and pepper, napkins, plates and bottle opener. Glasses I already have covered thanks to the gin I shared with Adam what feels like years ago in this very room. Setting the table is almost a thrill because before tonight it's either been burgers in a bag, crisps from the welcome hamper or an empty stomach. Dinner tonight is one notch up, with Nando's peri peri chicken on actual plates, with chips for me, corn on the cob for James and coleslaw to share. I don't think they do cod goujons, but that's probably a good thing. Plus a bottle of Cabernet Sauvignon, but I will make James promise to make me promise to stick to just one glass. For the same reason that my phone is on 24/7, obvs. I would like to add candles, but I couldn't find any in any of the cupboards. The faux floral arrangement from on top of the chest of drawers in the bedroom will be fine, even if it is in tones of peach.

One buzz on the intercom and one bound up the stairs and James is home. I mean back. I melt into his arms and stay there until he whispers 'I'm hungry' into my ear. Turning back into solid wax with a heartbeat is not easy, but it's true, the peri peri does smell good.

'I have just the thing for hungry,' I say. 'Nando's and all the trimmings. Come and see.'

James looks at the table and laughs.

'Debs, you are incredible. The day your culinary skills catch up with your flair for home design you will be unstoppable.'

I don't know whether to laugh back or hit him over the head with the Cabernet, but that would be a waste, so I just say, 'I'm glad you know good taste when you see it. House

Beautiful has fake orange flowers down as this season's big thing, as I'm sure you've heard.'

And it feels so good to be bantering with my darling husband again, almost as if Amelia was tucked up in bed upstairs with Froodle instead of wired up in hospital with Froodle and a team of intensive care night nurses. But she isn't —upstairs, I mean—and the banter can only paste over so many cracks. I pour us both a glass of wine.

'How was Amelia when you left, darling?'

'She was getting tired, but doing great. I saw the speech therapist and he said that she was making really good progress. He thinks the way she slurs her words will hardly be noticeable in a couple of days and that her sentences are getting more complex. She told me to give Mummy a kiss when I got back here.'

'That's fantastic! Why didn't you tell me when you arrived?' And I move in for an Amelia kiss via Daddy with added Cabernet Sauvignon flavour. 'That's better. And great news on her speech too. The physio told me they were starting to work on strengthening her muscles too, except for her broken leg of course. I can't believe how quickly things seem to be moving, when she was still in a coma forty-eight hours ago.'

'I know,' James says, 'but she's a fighter, our daughter. Stubborn or determined, depending on whether she got it from you or me.'

'Definitely determined, darling, and that definitely comes from the Wojnawski side. Nobody has ever accused me or my mother, or even Bubby come to that, of being stubborn.'

I wink and reach for the wine bottle, but James catches my wrist.

'Just the one we said, didn't we? Save the drinking for Bubby's party, unless she's still being stubborn about that.'

'Do you know, I'm not sure. She's made a few comments about having a party with Amelia when she comes out of hospital. You remember? She said it that first time she came in with Arifa, but I thought it was just part of trying to reach her and get her to come back to us. But then she talked about it the other day again. Wouldn't it be wonderful if she did decide to go ahead, darling? A celebration of life for the oldest and the youngest—as long as Meelie's well enough.' And as long as everybody gives me the time and space I need to help make sure she does get well again. 'In any case, Mummy and Daddy are dealing with all the caterers and things now, so if they've cancelled all that and if Bubby does change her mind, they'll just have to deal with uncancelling it. I can't.'

'Oh shit!'

'What?' James never swears. 'You don't think they can handle it?'

'It's not that. I'm so sorry, darling, I completely forgot that your dad texted me this afternoon to ask if he could come over tonight. I told him I'd check with you and then I forgot, sorry.'

'Don't worry about it. It's not as if it's Mummy—she would have just turned up if we didn't answer. Just text him back and say tomorrow would be better. Tonight's date night, darling.' And I stretch over the table for another kiss. After all, it's only the wine that's on ration.

'Mmm, you're right darling.' James stretches over for his turn. 'He would have said if it was urgent. Now let's eat this chicken. Pass the peri peri.'

'Of course. I got your favourite. Extra hot.'

I know it's not very sophisticated, but James and I do like a bit of sexy innuendo on a date night.

'I got a medium for me in case yours was *too* hot for me to handle, but,' and here I lick my fingers, 'I think I might need you to spice it up for me, darling.'

'You just say the word, babes, and I will be on it.' James takes a bite of his chicken and runs his tongue over his lips. 'Sizzling,' he says. 'Now I just need you to check if my corn is piping hot too. Can't have corn on the cob if it's not dripping with melted butter.'

Now I dissolve into a fit of the giggles. Not exactly sexy, but God, does it feel good. James looks at me with mock irritation and then plants another kiss on my lips. Peri peri flavour this time. That feels good too, until my maximum volume phone butts in. I scramble for it because it must be the hospital.

'Hello, Debbie. I hope I'm not disturbing you.'

It's Daddy, I mouth to James and shoot my eyebrows up in the air.

'Hi, Daddy,' I say. 'James and I were just eating, but don't worry, we can always heat it up again.'

James clamps his napkin over his mouth so I'm pretty sure only I can hear his howl of laughter.

'Oh, I'm sorry, darling, it's just that I left quite a few messages on James's phone and he didn't answer.'

'Oh right, sorry. He probably forgot to switch the volume up when he left the hospital. Is everything alright?'

'Yes, fine. Well, it's just…'

'Just what, Daddy? Is this about Amelia?'

'No! No, not Amelia, not at all, don't worry darling, no, I mean you have more news there than we do. Look, it's a bit complicated. And important. It's about Bubby and I'd rather talk to you and James in person. Do you think I could come over?'

'Come over? Now?'

'That's what I was thinking, yes.'

'Oh. Right. But isn't it going to be a bit late by the time you get here? I mean we must be at least an hour from Harrow.'

I give James my best oh-for-God's-sake grimace.

'Right. Thing is I'm just down the road from you at the Hoop and Grapes. With Adam.'

I cover the phone and whisper loudly, 'He's just down the road and he's with Adam. I think they've been drinking.'

James shrugs. I shrug back with added raised eyebrows.

'OK, Daddy. Come over.'

The hot sauce is still on the table, but James and I have cooled off by the time Daddy and Adam arrive. I don't like the look of the former's distinctly uncombed hair or the fact that the latter is wearing a suit.

'Sorry, darling. Sorry, James. We really wouldn't have disturbed you. It's just that… How can I put it?'

'It's OK, Daddy, I'm sure you wouldn't have come if it wasn't important. We'll finish supper later.' But if he could get to the point quickly, that would be nice.

'Yes, well, it is rather important.' He runs his hand through his hair. I knew his new dishevelled look was fishy. 'Look, I know things have been going well with Arifa and Nasir. I mean, she's a doctor and they've both been wonderful about helping Amelia get better.'

'And?' I say, the pull of the hot sauce still not quite gone cold.

'Well, it's just…' Now he clears his throat.

'Look, we think one or both of them may be embezzling Bubby.' Adam the New York attorney steps in.

'Em-whattling?' I venture.

'Embezzling. Stealing if you want a blunter word,' he says.

All of Arifa's saintliness, her preferences for glasses of water and her ability to be exactly where Bubby needs her exactly when she needs her, come back to hit me like a blunt instrument. Plus the thought that—just when we've begun to trust him again—maybe Nasir really could be playing fast and loose with Bubby.

'Stealing?' says James.

'From Bubby?' I say and sink onto the sofa.

'Well, I've been checking Bubby's account every few days,' says Daddy. 'I mean, I trusted Arifa, but we agreed we should keep an eye on things seeing as she's being paid directly. And everything has been fine, until a few days ago.' His hand goes to his hair again. 'The thing is, I started seeing new charges on her debit card. Some of them are quite big ones. You know how she loves a game of poker, well, now she—or somebody else— is playing online.'

'That computer!' I say.

'Yes,' says Daddy.

'There are debits to GG Poker, Party Poker and bet365.' Adam has the details, as ever. 'I'm hoping that Nasir—I mean it's obviously Nasir—isn't planning to get his game on every day of the year because we're already a couple of thousand down.'

'It can't be,' I say. 'I mean I wasn't sure about Nasir at the beginning, but the way he's been with Amelia at the hospital. The way she asked for him after she came back to us. He couldn't be stealing from Bubby, could he?'

I reach for the wine bottle, but James gets there first.

'Darling, I know you're upset. I'm upset, I mean I think we all are, but let's try to keep a clear head. We don't know for sure it's him, do we, Adam? I mean there must be hackers targeting that kind of site.'

'I've been clicking around them,' says Adam, 'and they look pretty secure to me.'

James looks like he's just heard that Robin Hood has switched sides.

'And we're already talking thousands then?' he asks.

'Well, we've cancelled the card, so he won't be going any further. But it's hard to tell whether he's been losing or if he's been raking in the chips and holding onto the cash. These gambling sites all run more or less the same system. You deposit your stake on one card, but you can scoop your winnings on another one or straight into a bank account. Whatever works.'

'So, he could be leaving Bubby high and dry on one side and sitting pretty on the other.' James's metaphors are not exactly original, but they do seem to be hitting the nail on the head.

'Exactly,' says Adam.

'They do say there's no smoke without fire,' I say, and pour myself a glass of red.

TWENTY-EIGHT

Seven days more

Morning

I hesitate, but then knock again on Nora's door. I don't remember if this is the third or the fourth time this morning. Again, no answer and yesterday I didn't like the sound of what she was saying about memories swelling in her head and bees that sting. I pray for courage and go in. She is lying on her back with her eyes open and the noise of my heart sets bombs off in my ears.

'Nora?' I say, 'Nora, can you hear me?'

I am next to the bed, close to her, but there is no answer. I go over to the window to pull the curtains so I can do a visual check for breathing instead of feeling for a pulse right away and scaring her. Another short prayer and I turn back to the bed.

'Nora?' I try again. She is still silent but now a ringing *zahgrouta* of joyful women fills my ears as I see her chest rise and fall. Slowly, but enough. I take her hand and stroke it. Her thin skin is warm and I move my fingers up to her wrist and

235

count. Fifty. Slow, but she is resting, maybe just woken up. I wait for a moment and start to count again.

'I am not dead yet, Arifa.'

Her voice is Nora's voice, strong and sharp with a tease in its tail and her teeth in her mouth and I have to stop myself from lifting my tongue in my own *zahgrouta* to the heavens.

'I see that, Nora,' I say, 'but I am here to take care of you as a friend and a doctor. And you know that it's my job. Imagine what your family would say about me if anything happened to you.'

This should make her laugh, smile at least, but she keeps looking at the ceiling, or maybe at something inside her head.

'How are you feeling today? It's past ten o'clock and you have slept a long time. Any pain or discomfort?'

She shuts her eyes.

'Nora?'

Nothing.

'I just need to know a little about how you are feeling. Most days you are so bright, you want me to get you out of bed so fast and take me to your old places. So I need to know if I have to call in another doctor.'

This has her eyes open.

'So? Any pain or discomfort?'

'Of course I have pain. This is my life, pain and heartache. What is this you call discomfort? This is for people who only know a good life, so when they catch a little flu, have a little trouble with their boss at the office, they complain about their troubles. This is what they call discomfort. I know this and you know this, Arifa. No, I have no discomfort.'

Yes, I do know. Part of me breathes a sigh of relief that Nora does not need a doctor. Part of me wants to weep with her.

'I understand, Nora, but I still need you to tell me if you are feeling any physical pain today. In your chest, maybe, or your head, your stomach, anywhere. Do you feel breathless or have a feeling that something is pressing down on your chest?'

'I feel old, that is all. Old people should be allowed to feel the pain of their life and their losses.'

'Of course. But we must try to make sure that physical pain doesn't make it worse.'

'That is discomfort, Arifa. In this I am comfortable.'

'I'm glad, Nora.' I am still holding her hand and I squeeze it. 'Shall I get you up? Make you some breakfast? I have eggs with pepper if you like.'

'No. I am comfortable.'

'But you need to eat. We cannot have you wasting away.'

'I'm not hungry.'

'I see. Well, at least let me turn you. Perhaps you have been lying on your back for a long time. You know that pressure sores can be very dangerous.'

And I know that Nora is capable of turning herself, but she is stubborn and at least this way she has no choice about saying yes to something.

'Yes. If you must. I will be comfortable lying on either side.'

I reach for her bedpan as quickly as I can and then turn this tough, wise, angry woman, my friend, to face the bedside table.

'That's it,' I say. 'Don't forget to ring the bell if you need anything.'

'I know,' she says. 'Arifa, wait. A little scrambled egg, please, but no pepper.'

I find the special tray with the legs that fold in the back of a kitchen cupboard. This is the first time that I have needed to use it, the first time since the Cedars that Nora has asked to eat in bed. What was in the list of the names of Amelia's friends? What is in the Bible? I have no reason to ask her; she has already told me. Pain and heartache. But why now, when we were all so happy that the little one was awake again and beginning to come back to us? Why did she say she wanted to keep her inside the book? I have caught myself, a few times, painting Ranim's face on Amelia's in my thoughts, waking from a dream where she was in the next bed in the hospital with the doctors telling me, Dr Hashmi, have you seen? your daughter is going to be alright. There is pain in those moments and part of it is the pain of holding her inside me. Should I tell Nora? Share my pain to see if hers is the pain of holding the ones lost in her own war inside her too?

I knock on Nora's door again and this time go straight in. Nora is flat on her back again, with her eyes closed and her chest rising. So far, so good.

'Your eggs are ready, Nora, and I've made you some tea. Strong and sweet, the way you like it.'

She opens her eyes.

'Thank you. I'm tired, but I suppose I must eat.'

I help her up onto the pillows and set the tray in place.

'Enjoy your eggs,' I say, 'and ring if you would like anything else.'

'I would like you to sit with me.'

'Of course, Nora. It's a pleasure.'

'Ach, don't overdo it, Arifa. I know you have other things to do. The pleasure is for me because today I am already tired of my own company.'

'If you say so,' I say and start tidying the few bits and pieces in the room that don't really need it.

'I asked you to sit with me, not do the housework,' she says.

'You did, that's true,' I say and pull the chair by the window over to the bed. 'How are the eggs? Still hot enough?'

'They are good,' she says, 'fluffy. You are a good cook, Arifa.'

'You were a good cook too from what I hear. I'm still waiting for you to make me some of your chicken soup.'

'*Oy vay is mir!* I tell her I'm tired of my own company and she talks about me. You don't have anything else to tell me?'

My life is so small these days. What can I tell her that isn't part of her own life?

'I wonder how Amelia is getting on today,' I say. 'It's more than two days now since she came out of the coma and she was already speaking so well when we saw her. I'm surprised we have no news from your grandson or Deborah, but then they say that no news is good news, don't they?'

Nora grunts.

'It took me so long to understand what that meant. How could news never be good? English can be so strange. Did you find it difficult when you first came here?'

'A little.'

'Anyway, Amelia seemed to be making good progress the last time we were at the hospital. Shall I send a message and say we would like to visit again later? If you're not feeling too tired.'

'I told you I wouldn't go back to the hospital. I don't want to see her. It gives me a pain in the head and one in the chest.'

'But she is getting better and I'm sure she would be happy to see you again. She loves you.'

'What's wrong with you today, Arifa? Have you gone deaf? Maybe you are the one who needs to go to the hospital. She is doing well, so I am happy for her and her family, but I will not go anymore.'

'I see.' With a woman this old and this stubborn, what can I do to make her change her mind? If I didn't think it might help Amelia to see her, I wouldn't even try. 'Well, maybe I will send a message to Deborah to see how the little one is doing. I would like to know.'

'So send a message. That's your business. But *genug*. I don't want to hear about her anymore.' She puts her knife and fork on the plate and folds her napkin. 'I would like another cup of tea. And to look at my Bible.'

An hour or more goes by, time for me to tidy my tidy kitchen, check that I already made Nasir's bed, clean all the windows and change my mind a few times about sending off my medical forms. Nora's bell has still not rung, but it is my job to look after her, isn't it? Of course, I knock again.

'Arifa,' she says when I open the door just a crack, 'I am still reading my Bible and I don't want any more tea.'

'I was wondering what you might like for lunch,' I say, even though I know that an early lunch after a late breakfast is no excuse.

'I have just had my breakfast. You will have to try harder than that.'

'Would you like to listen to some music?'

'Music can be good. I like the violins. But I don't need you for that, Arifa.'

I knew it. She is very old and today she is very bad tempered, but she is not stupid.

'Goodbye,' she says, 'leave me with my dates and my lists and my people.'

'Fine,' I say and shut the door.

My phone pings with a message. Mr Levene wants to pop by, he says, this afternoon with his father-in-law and Adam. Deborah's brother, I think. He doesn't say why. It seems a strange combination, but I suppose Deborah will stay at the hospital with the little one and I am happy that the mother is not on the list. I should go and tell Nora. No, she will either bite my head off or tell me to tell them not to come and this I cannot do. I will tell her at lunchtime, maybe she will be in a better mood.

Now I have a choice: sewing or applying to become a doctor in the United Kingdom. One reminds me of the family I have left behind in Syria but is soothing. The other reminds me of all that I achieved and all that I failed at in Syria and is frightening. And in the other room is an old woman who is not afraid to open the pages to her demons. I kiss Tarek's pendant and pick up a pen. Now I must tell them about some tests I have taken. PLAB is one, and IELTS. But I have never heard of them so of course I haven't taken them. And if I tick the 'no' box will they tell me I'm not fit to be a doctor? My phone will tell me what they are. Or Nasir's fruit machine. And then there is a small space for Any Other Information? Why the question mark? Could it be that people who need the Refugee Doctor Initiative have no other information? We are a list of qualifications and dates and tests and maybe any other information or maybe not. Tarek would say this is my anger speaking and that will get us nowhere. My mother would say it is my fear and that Nasir and I are safe now that we are in England and able to take this Doctor Initiative. The question mark wraps itself round my pen so I don't know what to write. I bite at the plastic end and pull out the stopper to see if the answer will swirl out like a genie in a bottle.

For the first time today, Nora's bell rings. So far, no genie and I hope she has changed her mind and wants to get up and go somewhere. I would love to check on Amelia, but anywhere would do. Just like her, I am already tired of myself today.

'Ach, here you are,' she says as I go back into her bedroom. 'I thought you were never coming.'

'I'm never so far away, Nora,' I say with a smile. 'What can I do for you?'

'Is Dovid at home?'

'No, he won't be home for quite a while. Today is a school day.'

'In that case, I will stay in bed. I have had enough of the past for today. Now I would like you to bring me the fruit machine. If I can't play with my son, I will go to the world of the web and find Igor or a Yulia and maybe one or two Antonios.'

'If that's what you want, Nora, but I thought you said you wanted to play the old way again, with your cards.'

'I said that? When? I have a machine with pictures and music and people all over the world and I told you I liked the cards better? I don't think so.'

I smile because how can I ask her to remember what she said two, maybe three days ago when she is more interested in the memories in her Bible? But I would like to stay with her and see if I can make her laugh when I make too many mistakes with the flushes and the straights and she knows however hard I try, she will always win.

'You're right, Nora, the computer is fun, but I miss our games with the matchsticks.'

'Matchsticks are for the old days, Arifa. Please bring me the fruit machine and stop with the fussing. You need to try to be a little more like me and start living in the modern world.'

TWENTY-NINE

Seven days more

Afternoon

Now Nora's bell doesn't stop ringing. I have never heard her shake it so loud and so long before and I am praying it is just more of today's bad temper as I push open her door.

'Nora, what is it?'

'This is how long it takes you when I ring for you? I am ringing and ringing and waiting and waiting.'

Good. A temper is easier to deal with than telling her family about illness or more accidents.

'I am sorry. I am here now. What can I do for you?'

'You? You can do nothing. It's Dovid I need. I asked you for him before. Where is he?'

'He's still at school, Nora, but he should be back quite soon.'

'But I need him now. Quite soon is too late, I am telling you. You think my nerves can take this aggravation at my age?'

She lies back against the pillows and closes her eyes. I have heard her angry before, of course, but there is a sour woman in her voice that I haven't known before.

'I'm sure he will be here in just a few minutes and I'll tell him to come straight through to see you.' What is the best way to try to soothe her? 'Or would you like me to help you out of bed and freshen up so you can be in the living room when he comes home?'

'I am tired, Arifa, you don't know that? You think I want to pull myself out of bed, get washed, get dressed when I am exhausted—*oysgematert* with my old bones? And this is how she wants to help me?'

'I will leave you to rest until Nasir comes. Unless you think there is something I can do while we are waiting.'

Her eyes stay closed.

'A glass of water? A shoulder rub?'

Still closed. I try to shut the door quietly behind me.

'Arifa!'

So. Maybe there is a way through the temper.

'Yes, Nora?'

'It's the computer. The poker. It won't let me play.'

'That's strange. I will have a look if you like.'

'Of course I like! You think I'm telling you this to make you happy?'

I laugh and go over to the bed.

'Here. I tried the Party Poker place and the other one. I don't remember the name. All of them and they say I can't get in. Dovid told me this world of the web is on all of the time. They don't want my money anymore?'

'I'm sure they are very happy to have your money. It could be there is a problem with the Wi-Fi.'

'The wire? I don't see any wires.'

'No, you're right, there are no wires. Wi-Fi is a kind of connection to the internet with no wires. Let me have a look.'

I click on the Wi-Fi symbol and I can see Nora is folding and unfolding a piece of paper in the corner of my eye. She is right, Nasir would be better at understanding the problem, but I can check the Wi-Fi and maybe a couple of other things. I don't like this new agitation. You hear about the teenagers getting addicted to their screens and I know Nora loves her poker, but there has been something wrong since I gave her her Bible yesterday.

'No, the Wi-Fi is working fine. See, I can open web pages no problem.'

'No problem, she tells me! What good is it to me when you can open the pages if they don't let me into the game?'

I cough and try to think of this computer like my sewing. Like my mama taught me, you need patience to get the stitches right and I have been lucky with Nora so far. This is the first time her famous bad temper has been pointed right at me.

'What did you say the first site is called? Poker Party?'

'Something like that. *Meshuggeh* name. They think it's a party when you have a poker face and money on the table?'

Google comes up with partypoker.com and I click to open it.

'Yes, that's the one,' Nora says. 'Here.' And she passes me the paper she has been worrying in her fingers.

Nasir had the good idea of making her DinoraN, so I won't mix up the Js and the Ws from Wojnawski, and I smile when I see the password: fruitNora122!

'OK. Let's see. It looks like your account is working.'

'So what's the problem? Why are they blocking me out?'

'I think I just need to try to start a game and then we'll see.'

'And what are you waiting for?'

I imagine myself patiently making a nice, curved stitch that will turn into a colourful flower with a little time and try to find the place to open up a new game.

'They want to know how many players.'

'What does it matter? Tell them five. It's trickier that way and most of these Vladimirs don't have my patience.'

My flower stitch gets tangled up laughing as I type and click.

'Oh. Here it is. 'You are not authorised for play. "Please consult your card issuer." So it's a problem with your card.'

'With my card? What are you talking about, Arifa? They won't let me play so of course I don't have any cards yet! *Meshuggeneh*.'

'No, I think they mean your credit card.'

'But why is there a problem with that? I gave the details to Dovid.'

'I don't know, Nora. I think we will have to wait for him to come home. Or we can ring your bank if you like and ask them.'

'*Gott in Himmel!* The woman is a *shlemazel!* I thought you said you were a doctor. You are a doctor and you don't know to make this fruit machine work? And now you want to bring in the bank when all I want to do is play a quiet game of poker to make the time pass while I wait to see my Henry again. With my aching bones. You have any idea how long 122 years feels like? I never complain, I never shout and now I don't have even a simple card game to keep me company.'

'I'm sorry, Nora. Would you like me to get the real cards for you?'

'No! I want some peace and quiet. Just get out and leave me with my Henry and my bones.'

This is a way of speaking that I would not accept from

anybody else, but it's true, I have no idea what 122 years feels like. And maybe it feels even longer when your mind mostly stays sharp as a sewing needle.

I nod. 'I will come back when supper is ready.'

I shut the door and lean back against it. It must nearly be time for Nasir to come home, but I don't know if I can send him in to see Nora in today's mood. I check my watch. Yes, not long now, a little less than an hour. Maybe he will manage to make her laugh, cheer her up. But now I would like to go out for a walk, smell some smells that are not inside this flat even if there's no fresh air anywhere around here. I could buy some spices, talk to the Bangladeshi grocer about the way they use them in his country, the way they cut their vegetables and cook their rice. But this is not possible. They say that London is one of the biggest, most beautiful cities in the world, full of different places to go and things to see. The bridge that lifts up its arms to let the ships sail through, Buckingham Palace and the flag that says whether the royals are at home, museums full of art and old things that somebody brought back from a country in the east for the people in the west to treasure. And here I am in Cornwood Drive with nothing more than sewing, sewing, sewing. Soon I will end up tearing out all of my careful stitches and embroidering a picture of my face with steam coming out of my ears onto a headscarf.

I go into the living room and open the window. The sky is quite bright and the air is beginning to feel warmer, but the same two trees are still there, and the cars. A couple of English flags hanging out of some windows, but the royals are not at home here. There are lots of people who have come from countries in the east on Cornwood Drive, but we don't hang our flags out. I lean out of the window, close my eyes and breathe in the air. Keeping them closed lets me turn the smell of tyres and petrol into something from a much hotter street for a moment. With cars too, but also some cooking oil and spices if I try hard enough. I open my eyes because I have been in London for so long now that I am not even sure if these memories of hot, spicy streets far away ever really happened. I look at my watch again. Still more than forty minutes before Nasir comes home. I don't want to call my mother because I want my thoughts to stay here in London, and Allah plus every god from every religion in the world knows that I don't want to do any more bloody sewing or fill in any forms. But there is nothing to see here except cars and trees and flags belonging to people who might find out that they liked me if they agreed to speak to me. They would let me save their children's lives anyway if they had to. One of them comes round the corner with a dog on a lead. It stops at the bollard outside number seventy-one and lifts its leg. Then it sniffs at the scruffy patch of grass in front of the flats and crouches down to finish things off. The man watches and waits and then calls at it to come on. I want to shout down to him to find a bag and take the mess away, but he would just shout back at me and tell me he knows where I live. Maybe I should just go and do some sewing after all. Now there is a smart grey car coming round the corner and slowing down like it's looking for somewhere to park. I can see a space a little further on, but I won't shout down for that either. Anyway, now they have found it. Three men get out and one points back down the road towards number seventy-one. Of course! It is Mr Levene and his family. He sent me a message this morning and I forgot it with all of Nora's temper and her poker problems. So now it is a good thing that I couldn't go for a walk and spent most of my day tidying things that were already tidy. And it is probably also good that I forgot, so I didn't keep turning my mind over with ideas about what they want to talk about, this time. I don't want them to see me hanging out of the window like a woman with washing to dry so I pull it shut and hope that they are here for a medical question and not something about where I come from or who my son is or why I should not be trusted with the angry old lady in my bed. But the brother is with them and Nora told me he is a lawyer in America, so I suppose they are not coming to see an ex-Syrian doctor. I put *barazek* biscuits on a plate and switch on the kettle. The doorbell rings.

'Hello, Arifa, I hope we're not disturbing you.'

Mr Levene is always kind and polite. I like him.

'Not at all, please come in, all of you.'

'Hello there. Nice to see you again.'

His father-in-law is always respectful too. I show them through to the living room.

'Please, have a seat,' I say.

'Thank you,' says Nora's grandson. 'This is Adam, my son. I think you might have met at the hospital.'

'Yes, we did see each other there. Hello, Mr Wojnawski.'

'Hi, Arifa.'

He puts his hand out for me to shake. I don't know if this is more politeness or the beginning of a meeting.

'I am happy to see you, Mr Levene,' I say. 'How is Amelia doing today?'

'Good to see you too, Arifa. She's really doing much better. Improving every day, especially her speech, which her doctors say is a great sign of things getting back to normal.'

'I'm so glad. I have been hoping to go back and see her, but Mrs Wojnawski has been a little tired.' I give them all the biggest smile I can manage. 'Can I bring you something to eat or drink? I have some homemade *barazek* biscuits with the sesame. A cup of tea or a coffee?'

'No, thanks, Arifa,' the grandson says, 'just had a cuppa before coming over. I think James mentioned there was something we wanted to have a chat about.'

'Yes,' I say. I think waiting for him to tell me more is better.

'My grandmother isn't up just now?'

'No. She's been tired today, as I was saying. Should I go and see if she would like to join us?'

'No, no, we should let her rest if she's tired. She's not ill, is she?'

'I don't think so, no, just tired. I'm keeping an eye on her, of course, though, and if there is any change I will make sure she sees a doctor. A doctor from here, I mean. I will tell you.'

'Good, that's good,' says Mr Levene. 'And I can always take a look at her of course. If necessary.'

He smiles. I smile back. There is a silence. His father-in-law takes an old-fashioned handkerchief out of his pocket and blows his nose. The brother leans over to him and nods.

'Yes. The thing is, Arifa, that Adam and I—well, our family —think there is a problem. We're grateful to you for looking after my grandmother, but it's just…'

This is the first I've heard of gratitude and it sounds like the kind that comes before a complaint. The way some residents at the Cedars liked my soft hands but not their colour.

'Sure you don't want me to outline all of this, Dad?'

So the lawyer wants to take over.

'No, no. In any case, I'm sure Arifa will have some kind of explanation. Look, Arifa, it's quite simple.'

I hope it is, but he is snuffling his nose with his handkerchief again, so I am not too sure.

'As I think you know, I have access to my grandmother's

bank account. Practically standard practice for a woman of her age. Well, I mean, if there were other women of her age of course. In any case, standard practice for the very elderly. Nothing untoward as far as your payments are concerned, Arifa, let me reassure you on that.'

Untoward? What is that? I will look it up later but for now I smile and nod.

'Good. But you see, there have been quite a lot of unusual debits over the last few days. Quite a few big ones actually. To online poker websites.'

Alhamdulillah! This I can explain. If he ever gives me a moment to say something.

'And of course, I know you know that Mrs Wojnawski decided to buy a rather expensive new computer for your son recently.'

'What my father is trying to say is that we believe your son has been stealing from my great-grandmother.'

So the lawyer brother does not care if he interrupts his father. I suppose this is a man who has never learned to sew. Well, I am still not in the mood for sewing either.

'I'm sorry that you think that my son could do this,' I say. 'I assure you that he is a good boy who would never steal from anybody, whatever you may think of him or my family.'

Now the older Mr Wojnawski blows his nose again, but the younger one keeps his eyes on mine. Mr Levene's cheeks are red.

'And I am sorry to tell you that I have an explanation that I think you will not like.'

'Of course you do,' says the lawyer with a TV show courtroom in his voice that *I* do not like. 'We're listening.'

'I am glad, Mr Wojnawski,' I say because I think in this country they say we are innocent until they prove we are guilty. 'I think you and your family all know that Mrs Wojnawski, Nora, loves to play poker. She teaches it to everybody and she has taught it to my son.'

'Exactly,' he says. 'To your son who you say would never steal from anyone. Go on.'

I am still not in the mood for sewing, but I will if I have to and I will keep my stitches neat and tidy.

'She taught him to play with cards, but when she bought the computer, he showed her how she could play on the internet, to have a little fun. She may be old, but she likes to learn new things and have fun.'

'So you say my great-grandmother is the one having the fun?'

'I do. And I am trying to explain.' Sewing in the imagination is useful, even when my own living room is being turned into a courtroom. 'Nasir enjoys playing poker with her too. And he even showed her one of the trick bike video games he loves. But he never goes on the poker sites without her.'

'That's what you think.'

'I know my son, Mr Wojnawski. And I also know that he showed Mrs Wojnawski how to log into these sites by herself and add in her card details. Even this morning she tried and she was very upset when she found she was blocked out.'

'Of course she was blocked out, as you put it. My father had the card cancelled as soon as we saw that the money was missing. But that's not the point.' He stands up, puts his fist onto the table and then turns to look at me even harder, just the way they do on TV. 'Come on, Arifa, do you really expect us to believe that a 122-year-old woman can work her way round a Mac well enough to play online poker by herself? I don't think she'd ever seen a laptop before you and Nasir took her down to the Apple Store, let alone logged into one.'

'Adam, listen, let's keep things civil, shall we?'

'Thank you, Mr Levene, but it's alright, I will speak for myself and my family.' I count to three in the most complicated stitches I can think of. 'I come from Syria, Mr Wojnawski. I think you know that my country has a dictator who decides on the laws. But it is different here and in America, isn't it? So why, in your way, do you decide who has done what without even asking them? Without checking on anything?'

'Are you saying you want me to question my great-grandmother? Tell her I don't trust her and risk putting a fragile old lady under severe stress?'

'I am not. She is tired and prefers to stay in bed today. We should respect her and leave her to...'

The front door slams shut—I didn't hear it open—and Nasir comes into the room.

'Oh. What are these...? I mean, hello. Mama?'

'Here is my son, gentlemen. As I was saying, we should leave Mrs Wojnawski in peace, to rest. But I think now you will be able to ask Nasir all the questions that you think are required.'

THIRTY

Six days and counting

Morning

I t looks as though spring has properly sprung when we pull into the driveway. Daddy is the soil under the fingernails branch of the family, and James is happy leaning on a shovel and chatting to him while he does the weeding and prunes the roses, but even I know that the yellow ones are daffodils and there is blossom on the tree next to the living room window. The sky is properly blue too and the only cloud on this particular Northwood Hills horizon is that the doctors aren't letting Amelia come home yet. But they are letting me get things ready for her, so here I am.

'The garden is looking lovely, darling, but admiring it from inside the car isn't going to help us get Amelia's bedroom organised now, is it?'

And here is Mummy too. Ready, as ever, with one of her helpful hints. It was six of one and half a dozen of the other. Come home to sort things out solo and run the risk of dissolving onto Meelie's bed with nobody to wipe my tears away for me. Or come home to sort things out with Mummy and run the risk of dissolving onto Meelie's bed with her telling me to pull myself together. I've already used up all my taking-decisions-about-complicated-dilemmas on Amelia, and James is back up to his elbows in blood in the operating theatre. He told me worrying about me coming home alone could be grounds for a slipped scalpel, so here we are, Mummy and me. Hints about gardens and cars notwithstanding, I'm hoping she might just be in gin and lipsticks mode after all.

'No, I suppose it isn't. But Daddy's done a wonderful job of keeping everything trim, hasn't he?' I say, because it's the only sayable thing I can think of under the circumstances.

'Ah, Daddy and his green fingers. So good of him to do *his* bit to help out every now and then.'

That's a no on the gin and lipsticks then. Still, we make it to the front doorstep and I fumble in my bag for my keys, wishing I'd thought of slipping in a miniature Gordon's of my own.

'Home, sweet home,' I say, and hope Mummy doesn't notice that I'm hanging onto the *mezuzah* for dear, sweet life. If she does, she is unusually quiet about it and I manage to wobble through into the kitchen, dump my handbag on the counter-top and run myself a glass of water. A gin substitute in appearance only, but cold enough to turn the ignition on in my brain. Not very many revs per minute, but at least enough to simultaneously get me up the stairs into Meelie's room and fend off any more maternal helpful hints.

Farrow & Ball Cinder Rose on the walls and pink flamingos from John Lewis (where else?) staking out the curtains. Her bedroom is just the way it was before our trip down cemetery lane. I mean, of course it is, I knew it would be; I just didn't know how that would feel. There's a sparkly denim skirt and a pair of stripy tights draped over her chair from making our minds up about what she wanted to wear that morning and an Elsa from *Frozen* crown on the floor. The only thing missing is Froodle on her pillow. And Amelia. I reach for the doorframe, but it's turned into my mother's arms and she puts them round me and we cling on to each other, both squeezing so tight that we have to stop to breathe.

'She'll be here soon, darling, that's what we need to get into our silly heads.'

Mummy's hand cups my cheek and I see in her eyes that her helpful hints and digs about Daddy were just the only way she knew of getting herself through this door. I put my hand on hers.

'You're right, I know.' I pick the crown up off the floor and that ridiculous 'Let It Go' song starts up in my brain. 'But it's so hard to stop thinking about how close we came. I don't know if I'm ever going to be able to let her out of my sight again once she's back here.'

Mummy takes my arm and we sit down on Amelia's bed. Fluffy heart shaped cushions and more flamingos that used to peck at Froodle or eat up Amelia's toes or gobble her tummy, depending on how hungry they were at bedtime. I run my finger up and down a spindly leg and try to stop my eyes blurring it with tears.

'Kids are tough, darling,' says Mummy. 'Look how hard Amelia's been fighting. She's talking so well again now and you said the physio is very pleased with her. She'll fall again, you know that, in the playground or the back garden, but I'm sure she'll get back up and then she'll have us all in stitches when she dresses up in her costumes or sings those funny Billie Irish songs.'

I nod, but now I can't see any of the flamingos.

'You make it sound so easy.'

'It won't be, I know. But it will get easier. She'll keep surprising us, the way she has at the hospital. And I'll keep playing the bad cop and bullying you if I see you crying too much and letting yourself go.'

The fingers wiping away my tears for me don't feel like they belong to a bully and I wish it hadn't always been so hard to get to the gin and lipstick behind the perfectly styled hair and fake Chanel. That it didn't have to take a five-year-old's brush with death or the disappearance of the world's oldest woman to peel away the pearls and get at the soft skin underneath, even if it is a bit wrinkled now. She hands me a tissue and I blow, and then another one that comes up black with the mascara that I was Debs enough to even think about putting on this morning. I shake my head at myself and make a sound that's half-way between a laugh and a hiccup.

'I promise I'll dial 999 if I need to.'

'Good. And I promise I'll get here before the boys in blue.'

'Thanks, Mummy.' I smooth the flamingos on Amelia's pillowcase and arrange one of the heart cushions so it's right in the middle and neat enough for me to think about something else. 'Have you had any news about Bubby? Does she know about all that business with Nasir and her money?'

'I'm not sure. Daddy went to talk to them about it—Arifa and Nasir, I mean—yesterday afternoon, with James and Adam, but Bubby was in bed and they didn't want to disturb her.'

'Yes, James told me. He said Arifa told them Bubby had been playing poker on the computer on her own. Which sounds pretty outlandish given she'd never even seen one until last week. I just thought Daddy might have heard something more.'

'I don't know, darling. And anyway, you know I didn't trust Arifa when she ran off with Bubby in the first place. And I don't trust her now to tell us anything that might point a finger at her precious son. Daddy will just have to go back and insist on talking to Bubby. That's if we allow her to stay there. Do you know, I think this is the proverbial straw. We should be demanding that Bubby goes back to the Cedars after all, even if we do have to get her there on a camel!'

This time I do laugh, regardless of thieving sons, bullying mothers and mascara-soaked tissues.

'I think that Mr Simpkins has already rented out her room, Mummy. And I agree, we totally have to get to the bottom of this poker thing, but do any of us have the energy right now to take on a fight with Bubby about leaving the East End?'

'Oh, I don't think the Cedars will have any problem finding a space for her once they see the colour of her money.' She worries the pearls around her neck. 'But you're probably right about her digging her heels in. Anyway, we've got bigger fish on our plates these days, haven't we?'

Now she goes over to Amelia's chair and folds her skirt and tights into a neat pile, with no fish or camels or other not-quite-idiomatic animals in sight.

'We need to get Amelia's room ready for her and organise the things she needs for leaving the hospital.' I know that, but I am also beginning to know that even Mummy flails around for things to hold on to when she can't quite see which way to turn next. 'And we need to think about the party. Just six days to go now and lots of decisions to be taken.'

'Did you talk to the rabbi?'

'I did. And he's holding the date for the time being.'

'That's good.'

'Yes. And Daddy's made a couple of phone calls to the caterers and at least one of the hotels. We're not quite sure where they stand on cancellation fees and so on, but we've already told you you're not to worry about that.'

'Thanks, Mummy,' I say and I actually mean it. 'Amelia told me about going to the party again yesterday. She said Bubby was going to make honey cake and it was going to be her party too. I hope she doesn't change her mind again; Bubby, I mean. Meelie's excited. And when I think of the way Bubby talked to her in hospital, I'm sure she helped bring her back. I mean, it just makes the idea of them being together for the celebrations even more special, don't you think?'

'I do, darling and we'll do our best, but you know how donkey-headed Bubby can be. We'll have a special party for Amelia here if needs be and make sure there's at least three kinds of honey cake.'

'And what about Arifa and Nasir?'

'Well, Adam's looking into legal action.'

'No, I mean at the party. Do we still invite them?'

'No, of course not, darling! How could we? First the kidnapping, then the accident, if it was one, and now theft. Adam has even been talking about embezzlehood and coercion and all sorts of unspeakable behaviour.'

'I know, but I just don't know what to think, Mummy.'

I pick up the cushion and pull it into my arms, stroking the fluffy plush into a maze of roads we could turn down. Or not.

'And Meelie would be so disappointed.'

'We'll invite all her friends from school. And Amelia B. I know the boy has been with her at the hospital, but you can't want him near her now she's better, surely?'

'But Amelia will.' I look down at the cushion and see that

I've started pulling the fluff out of it. 'You know, Mummy, I do think Nasir really helped bring Amelia back and I'm sure now it was an accident. He wasn't to blame and if anything, maybe I was.'

Now the mother who has always been so ready to blame me for anything has screwed Amelia's skirt and tights up into a ball, and I'm wondering whether blaming daughters ran in her family too.

'You know what? I think those clothes will be perfect for her to come home in,' I say. 'And, honestly, her room is perfect too. Let's just grab a t-shirt and a couple of pairs of knickers. I'd like to get back to the hospital.'

THIRTY-ONE

Six days and counting

Afternoon

Every time I walk into Ladybird Ward, I feel like I could fly. Yes, there are children here with all sorts of body parts in casts and some have traction contraptions or drips in their arms, but they are awake. They can talk. Some of them can walk. And here, the sunbeams and rainbows on the walls, the dozens of ladybirds flying home and even the street-art-style insects on the teens section feel like friends who've been waiting for me to arrive. Just like Amelia. Who will either be in her bed playing on James's old iPhone 8, or chatting to Heather in the bed next door (chatting soon anyway, talking slowly for now), or off somewhere with a physio or her speech therapist. But not wired up to a machine and not tangled in tubes and not unconscious. I've always loved ladybirds.

A little lamb called Cain (I'm all for Biblical, but really?) waves at me from his bed. He's three and he's told me all about jumping too high on a bouncy castle last weekend, both legs, poor thing. I wave back, but I'll have to get the next instalment when I leave (fingers crossed he wasn't trying to jump up and down on his brother), because after this morning's cocktail of tears and animal proverbs shaken and stirred, what I need now is to see and feel Amelia.

'Look, sweetie, I've brought your suitcase!'

I hold her Peppa Pig on wheels up high and then snuggle in for a hug that feels like I will never need any kind of cocktail, or even gin, again, ever.

'Mummy, you're squashing me.'

Amelia's voice is muffled, but it's a complete sentence and I have to force myself to unswaddle her instead of squeezing even harder, because, well, I mean, a complete sentence!

'Sorry, darling, it's just that you are so very delicious. Much tastier than the boring old chicken sandwich I had for lunch.' I put Peppa down by the bedside table and perch next to Meelie on her cleaner-than-clean bed. 'What did you have?'

'Sausage and mash.' She pauses. 'And peas. Hard.'

I know that calling hospital food food is pushing it, but hard peas?

'They roll. Too hard.'

'Oh, you mean it was too hard to eat them. With a knife and fork?'

She nods.

'Aha,' I say and look around the ward in all directions. 'I've got a secret for you, Meelie, but you have to promise not to tell anybody. Not the nurses, or the doctors and especially not Grandma.'

She nods again.

'Tell me!'

I look around again and lean in to whisper in her ear.

'You can eat the peas with your fingers; just don't tell them I told you. In fact, you can eat anything you like with your fingers, especially the chocolate ice cream. OK?'

She cracks up and I crack up and for a moment the laughter is all there is. We could be anywhere and the joke could be any one of the hundreds we've ever giggled and howled over together. But I never did get round to signing up for those mindfulness-for-mums classes and my mascara is soon running again. I just hope Amelia is laughing too hard to see the relief and the fear that have punched a hole in my fun.

'Silly Mummy.'

She's calmed down again, but there's still a smile pulling at her lips, so I think I'm safe for now.

'Silly? Me?'

I make the face she calls my nutty noodle and she's off again. I pull her onto my lap and her giggles send little waves into my chest that feel way better than any of those endolphin rushes or whatever they call them (Mummy would know).

'Yes, silly. Ice cream's too cold.'

'I suppose so. But it would taste good if you licked your fingers.' And I nibble at one of her thumbs. 'Anyway, I've brought you some clothes, because the doctors say you'll be able to come home soon.'

'Soon? When?'

'I'm not too sure, darling, but soon is good, isn't it? And I brought you your Elsa crown too. You can be the Ladybird Ward Snow Queen and everything you touch will turn into ice cream, even your medicine.'

'What kind?'

'Chocolate. Or Strawberry. Whatever flavour you like. Do you want to give it a go?'

She plants a kiss on my lips, so I take it that's a yes and unzip the suitcase.

'Your Majesty.'

I'm a sucker for a Disney Princess and especially one as adorable as Miss Amelia Eve Levene biting her bottom lip as she lowers the crown onto her head and adjusts it to make sure the blue plastic diamond is front centre.

'There,' she says. 'Pretty like Elsa.'

'Beautiful, my angel,' I say. 'Just don't turn me into a ball of Cookie Dough.'

She immediately begins to prod me in as many places as possible, obvs, and just as I think we're about to collapse into another fit of the giggles, she starts to sing. And now she *sounds* just like Elsa too.

I force myself not to gape at her and make a vow to sign up for a degree in neuroscience as soon as Meelie is safe back home. She keeps belting out the theme from *Frozen* and none of those *Inside My Brain* documentaries on the BBC have ever felt this unfathomable. My beautiful princess of a daughter is still singing and waving her arms around when I feel a hand take mine.

'She can remember the words.'

James's voice can't believe it either.

'I know.'

'And the tune.'

'I know.'

We both sit and watch until Amelia notices that her prince has arrived and throws her arms around him.

'Daddy!'

'Good afternoon, Your Majesty.' He bows his head to her. 'Beautiful song you were singing.'

'I love Elsa and, look, Mummy brought my crown.'

Another complete sentence and this one is even in two different parts.

Amelia tweaks James's nose.

'Now you're made of vanilla ice cream.'

'I am?'

'Yes. I can make it when I'm Elsa. Mummy said so.'

'I see.' He rubs his nose and licks his finger. 'Tastes delicious. You won't eat me, though, will you?'

'Not sure.' Now she moves in for an Eskimo kiss. 'And Mummy said I can eat with fingers. Even ice cream.'

'Shhh!' I hiss. 'That was supposed to be our secret. Daddy might tell Grandma.'

Amelia claps her hand over her mouth, but her eyes are shining, and the idea of ice cream and Grandma tips us over the edge again, bringing James with us. Now the laughter stays caught in our circle, as mysterious as all those complete sentences and the Elsa song and just as beautiful and I can't imagine how I will ever feel like crying again.

'Hello, I wonder if you can help me. I'm looking for Amelia Levene on Ladybird Ward,' the nurse turns her head towards me and James and winks, 'but I must have got the wrong bed.'

'Oh. Amelia Levene? Let me think,' says James. 'I think you've got the right ward, but this is Queen Elsa's bed. Perhaps you'd better ask the ward Sister.'

'Yes, I thought it sounded like Queen Elsa,' says the nurse. 'Oh well, I'll check up on Amelia when I find her. Will you tell her I was looking for her if you see her?'

'But it's me! I'm here! I'm Amelia.' Amelia's eye roll is cuter than any eye roll that I (and I expect anybody else) have ever seen. 'Daddy, you're silly too. You know Elsa isn't real.'

'That was really you singing, was it?' the nurse says. 'It

sounded lovely. A little bit loud maybe,' she winks again, 'but lovely. Dr Mirza will be very pleased to hear about it. Do you know all the words?'

'I know most of them. I love Elsa and Anna and I've seen it about seven times.'

'Have you?'

'Yes. Or maybe eight.'

James and I look at each other. I can tell that he can't believe how much progress she's made since yesterday either.

'And when I was four, I had a *Frozen* birthday party. With Olaf cake.'

'Did you? That must have been delicious.'

Amelia nods.

'Why don't you tell me some more about it while I do your checks?'

'Well, Elsa is the queen, but she's sad because she makes ice everywhere. And Mummy said I could make ice cream if I was Elsa.'

'Did she? Have you got any chocolate for me?'

'That's my favourite.'

'Mine too. Or salted caramel.'

'But Anna wants to help her because she's alone in the ice castle. It's sad to live all alone. My Bubby lived on her own before Rifa came.'

'That's my great-grandmother,' I say. 'Meelie, that's fantastic. You can remember so many things.'

'Of course I can remember Bubby, silly,' she says. 'And Rifa. I like Rifa, and Nasir.'

'They sound very nice.' The nurse lets go of Amelia's wrist and lays her arm back down on the bed. 'Next time you can tell me more about them, but for now I need to go and check

267

up on some of the other children—see if I can catch any of them singing.'

Amelia smiles up at her.

'Your doctors are going to be so proud of you when they hear about all the stories you've been telling me.'

'Oh no, not the ice cream! It's a secret.'

'I promise, cross my heart. Anyway, now the best thing is for you to keep telling your mum and dad about Elsa, or maybe ask them when your bubby—is that it?—will be coming to see you.'

She squeezes my arm as she turns away from the bed.

'I'm not a doctor, Mr and Mrs Levene, but this is good, really.'

My eyes sting even though I'm never going to cry again.

'Let her sing if she wants to, but don't forget she still needs to rest.'

'Of course, thank you so much, we won't. Forget, I mean.'

James gives her one of his best 'I can't thank you enough' looks and sits with Amelia on the bed.

'Will you tell me the bit about when Anna meets Kristoff and his reindeer. What's its name?'

'Sven, Daddy. Don't you remember?'

'Sven! Of course.'

Of course, he doesn't remember. It's Mummy's job to watch cartoons on a loop with a test on all the names of all the main characters and their best friends afterwards. I even caught him with his eyes shut at the cinema the first time round.

'Sven is the reindeer and Olaf is the snowman that Elsa makes by mistake, doesn't she, Meelie?' I say. 'I'm going to let you tell Daddy the rest of the story while I go and powder my nose.'

'I know what that means,' says my astonishing daughter

who can even recognise a cover-up when she hears one, and I stick my tongue out and leave them to their Disney fest. My head feels so light as I fly along the ward with the other ladybirds that I hardly begin to worry about what she might ask Daddy about Bubby and Arifa and I float right into the sticky trap laid by Cain and his ridiculously heart-wrenching three-year-old plaster casts.

'Will you sign them for me now?' he chirps.

'Oh, Cain. Gosh, haven't you got a lot of signatures already!' I babble.

'Please?'

'Of course I will, sweetie. Have you got a brother?'

Oh Debs, stop babbling.

'No. Why?'

'Oh. No reason, I meant, do they still hurt?'

'Not really. They itch.'

'Poor you, that must be horrible. Now, what shall I write?'

He hands me an orange felt-tip and I nibble at the lid before realising I could turn it into a carrot nose. I'm actually starting to feel quite pleased with my rendition of Olaf when I feel an arm around me that I hope can only be James.

'Debs, darling, I think you'd better get back to Amelia.'

'Why? What is it? What's wrong?'

'It's not her, don't worry, she's fine. I mean she's really getting there, told me the whole Elsa story, but then I got a message from Arifa.'

'And?'

'Well, you know I told you Arifa said Bubby was tired? I said I would take a look at her if she was worried. And now she's sent me a message. She says Bubby hasn't got out of bed since the last time she came to see Amelia at the hospital and now she's hardly eating. She says she's examined her and hasn't found anything, but I think she thinks she'd better get a second opinion.'

'Sounds like you'd better go then, darling.'

I give half-finished Olaf one last swirl and Cain a pat on the plaster cast and head back over the rainbow to Amelia's bed, nose unpowdered, as Dr Levene hightails it out of the hospital.

THIRTY-TWO

Six days more

Evening

I t is true that Mr Levene has a very nice bedside manner. This is something I learned about at the Cedars. They said a good bedside manner was important, but I didn't see it so often. The old people there were too grumpy, or senile or old to need it, I suppose. In Syria, we don't have a name for it and some of the doctors have it, and some of them don't. Anyway, Mrs Wojnawski is his great-grandmother-in-law, so it is normal that he is kind to her, but today he is here as Dr Levene, not Mr, so his way of talking is different, but it is still kind. Mrs Levene is a lucky woman. Maybe she talks in a different way with him, too.

I see that the examination is the same as I would do it and I will try to remember that for when I decide to finish filling in the forms. Pulse, blood pressure, a little talking to hear the voice and see how the cognitive response is. All the ear, nose and throat checks and the lumps that could be in the neck and under the arms. The ganglions, they are called. He uses a

271

forehead thermometer for her temperature, which I don't like, but I can see that it is practical and less unpleasant for Nora. Next will be the abdomen.

'I'm just going to have a look at your stomach area, Bubby. Is that OK?'

'You're asking me if that's OK? You're the doctor. Henry, he never wanted the doctor in the house, but I say with a doctor you listen to what he tells you.'

'Glad to hear it,' he says. 'Alright, let's have a look then. I want you to let me know if you feel any pain where I'm pressing. Here?'

'No.'

'And here?'

'Not either.'

The same no-pain ping-pong passes from one to another a little longer until Dr Levene smooths the bedcover back over.

'And what about any other pain, Bubby? Does anything else hurt? Anything at all?'

'Does anything else hurt, he asks me. *Oy vay is mir!*'

And she hoots her goose laugh. It's a little quieter than usual, but it's the first time I have heard it since we were at the hospital with Amelia.

'My legs are hurting; my back is hurting; my head is hurting; my heart has been hurting since long before your grandparents were born. You think you get this old without something hurting? I let you have a poke at me because this *meshuggeh* woman here says I need to see the doctor and you're the doctor. So, you poke. Did you finish your poking already?'

'I think I've seen everything I need to for now.'

Dr Levene looks like his bedside manner means he mustn't laugh. I know how he is feeling.

'And what's the verdict, doctor? You think I'm going to

drop down and *shtarben* before the party so everyone can get their hands on my money a *bisl* quicker?'

Now he is torn between laughing and the polite shock that the people in this country use, but I am just happy to hear Nora hooting and complaining again.

'Bubby, of course not. From what I've seen, you are in good physical health. I'm just a little worried about what Arifa has been telling me.'

'Arifa? What has she been saying about me? Has she been meddling where she's not wanted?'

'I wouldn't call it meddling. She's just told me she's worried about you. Seems to think you're upset about Amelia and something to do with playing poker.'

'Now you're telling me you're one of those head shrinker doctors? I would like it if you stick to what's going on in my body.'

'Whatever you say, Bubby, although just so you know, Amelia really has been doing much better these last few days. And she'd love it if you felt up to coming to see her.'

'I am glad,' she says, 'but I don't.'

He waits for more, but these days the child and the poker are things that turn Nora's face as blank as when she's playing cards.

'Which brings me back to the physical things that Arifa is worrying about.'

So, he is almost as stubborn as she is.

'She tells me you've been refusing to get out of bed for days and now you're hardly eating.'

'Ach, how should I eat with all the spice she puts in my food?'

Now I am the one not to know if I should laugh or not.

'But she told me she's been making you scrambled egg and chicken soup.'

'She calls that chicken soup?'

'I followed your recipe, Nora,' I say. 'Next time you can come into the kitchen and show me where I'm going wrong, if you like.'

'Arifa's right, Bubby. It would do you good to get out of bed.'

'And now the two of you think you know what's good for me?'

'We say that as doctors, Bubby.'

'Ach, yes. You are both doctors. I forgot it for a moment. You know, sometimes my head is hazy.'

Dr Levene looks over at me with a smile.

'And so, tell me, what do the doctors order?'

'Well, Bubby, as I was saying, staying in bed for long periods isn't going to do you any good. I know Arifa has been making sure you turn regularly, but you're going to lose muscle tone and it will be harder for you to feel comfortable once you're back in your wheelchair. Not to mention good bowel and bladder function.'

'So don't mention it then!'

This time he cannot help himself and he chuckles. I have to bite my cheek.

'Quite,' he says. 'And I don't need to explain to you what will happen if you don't eat a little more. I'm sure Arifa will go easy on the spices.'

'I eat when I feel hungry. I have gone without food for many weeks in my life before, I think you know that. So long that even the bits of grass we could find tasted good. And as you can see, even back then they couldn't kill me.'

Now nobody is chuckling.

'Bubby, your strength is legendary, and we all thank God that you are still here with us. But I would be in breach of my Hippocratic Oath if I didn't find a way of making sure you stay well for as long as possible.'

He takes her hand and looks at her in a way that is more than a bedside manner.

'If I can't count on you to listen to Arifa, I'll have to see if we can move you somewhere else. Perhaps you could stay with my parents-in-law or we could look into booking you back into the Cedars.'

Now he looks over at me again and this time he winks.

'And if we don't see any improvement after that, we'll need to look into running some further tests in hospital.'

'No,' says Nora.

'No?' says Dr Levene.

'No, I will not stay with the wife of my grandson and no, I will not go back to the Cedars or to the hospital. This is not a negotiating matter.'

'Ah,' he says. 'And do you think you will be able to follow my advice while you're here at Arifa's?'

Nora says something that is too quiet to hear.

'Sorry?' he says. 'I didn't catch what you were saying.'

'No matter,' she answers. 'Arifa, I think you forgot the secret ingredient from my chicken soup. I told you about it, remember?'

'That's right, now I do remember you said there was a secret ingredient, but I am foolish, I don't remember what it was.'

'The dill. You must chop a *bisl* dill and add it at the end of the cooking. This is why your soup tastes wrong.' She puts her hand to her forehead. 'It's so simple, *mein Gott*. If you put the dill in your soup, I will eat it.'

Now I look over at Mr Levene with a smile.

'Dill, of course, Nora. I have some soup in the fridge that I can heat up for you if you're hungry.'

'Well, I am a little hungry. Just a small bowl though. Boiling hot. But only if it has the dill with it.'

I am lucky to live around the corner from Commercial Road where so many people have come from other countries to make their living from grocery shops, the way Nora did with her Henry. When I get back to the flat, I have learned that the name for dill is *sholpa* in Bangladesh and that the cooks there add it to rice and the lentil curry they call *daal*. I am also lucky that Mr Levene was not in a hurry and agreed to wait with Nora while I went for the dill, because Nasir is refusing to come out of his bedroom except to eat and wash and go to school since the Wojnawski family visit the other day. And he won't listen to me when I try to say that I told them how Nora learned to use the computer to play her poker, that she won't talk about it and how she is too weak now for me to try to make her. Only now Nasir is in the kitchen, with Mr Levene, and I almost drop my bag of *sholpa*.

'*Habibi*, I didn't expect to see you until supper time.'

'I was hungry. I wanted a snack.'

'We were just having a quick chat. About Nasir's bike.'

Both of them talk at once, like children who have been caught with their fingers in their mother's bag. I don't know if they were talking about the poker and what the lawyer brother said, but I will let them have their secrets. There is nothing to steal in my purse.

'I'm about to make some good soup for Nora,' I say, 'and

there is plenty for both of you. Or I have some lamb *shakriya* in the fridge if you would like to stay to eat, Mr Levene.'

'That's kind of you, Arifa, but I need to be getting back to the hospital.'

'Of course, I am sorry to have made you wait. *Habibi*, will you have some soup? I found Nora's secret ingredient at the grocery.'

Nasir's eyes have returned to the look of blame he used to give me before Nora began to make him laugh with the fruit machine and the poker.

'What's that then?' he says, with a smile that makes him ugly. 'Something as past its sell-by date as she is?'

'Nasir!'

Who is this boy? Where is my son? The one that wears a uniform with a tie and a blazer. The one who used to laugh with his sister when she sang her songs. And where is his father to tell him that this is no way to talk?

'Nasir, that is no way to talk about Mrs Wojnawski.'

My breath catches in my throat. Tarek is gone, but here is another father who can maybe make Nasir think and talk straight.

'Says who? You're not my father. Who gave you the right to tell me how I should talk in my own home?'

So then, maybe not. I will have to keep trying to be my son's mother and his father.

'That's enough, Nasir! Nora and Mr Levene are guests in our home and I will not have you showing them such disrespect. What do you think your father would have to say?'

'What difference does that make? He's dead! There's a war in the place that used to be our home, remember, and it killed my father and my sister. And now I'm supposed to just be polite and quiet and behave the way the elders like it, because that old woman didn't get killed in her war, is that it? Well, I'm a war survivor too, you know, and I don't think the things she and her family have to say about me is any way to talk either!'

Now his eyes are full of the shaking of the ground as the shells and the walls of the houses hit it, and they are full of the stench of dark smoke in the air and the sweet laughter of his father and his sister. I know, because all of those things fill my eyes too.

'Habibi.'

I let my half-empty purse and my small bag of dill fall onto the table and go to embrace my son, my family, but my arms set off another bomb inside him and he pushes them away.

'Don't touch me! I don't know who you are anymore with your chicken soup and your hypocrisy and sleeping on the sofa and running when her bell rings. How many mothers would make their child pretend to be somebody else's son?'

'Habibi, I...'

'I don't want to hear it. If it hadn't been for Amelia, I would have been long gone. Tell her, who knows, maybe I'll see her around.'

And I hold on to the table with all my strength as the slam of the front door turns the kitchen into rubble. The silence is exactly the way I remember it in the one or two moments before the shouting and the calls for safety used to start, and the people who still had houses and family ran to help or sat and stared at the dust in the air.

'Arifa, I'm sorry.'

I turn my head to where the words came from. It can't be Tarek, can it? The voice is not right.

'He'll be back soon, I'm sure of it. He just needs to cool off a little.'

When my eyes focus, I see it is Mr Levene, the doctor, with his good bombside manner.

'I hope you are right, doctor,' I say.

'He mentioned a sister. I'm sorry, I didn't know.'

I shake my head to keep the dust out and he puts his hand on my shoulder. I shrug it away and take the bunch of dill out of its plastic wrapper.

'Perhaps you should go now, Mr Levene. Mrs Levene and Amelia will be waiting for you. Please send them my kindest thoughts.'

THIRTY-THREE

Five days and counting

Afternoon

I did think about asking Bubby to do the online shopping honours now that some are saying she's a silver surfer, but then I remembered I had a previous order all set up on waitrose.com and that a selection of oven-ready goujons, thin & crispy quattro formaggi and olives would do. So now, the delivery boy has left and I have unpacked the bags, switched on the oven and sampled a glass or two of the Chardonnay that has recently become a fixture of said previous orders. I'm about as ready as I'll ever be for a Wojnawski/Levene family lunch—aka negotiations on what to do about Nasir—that are likely to degenerate into unarmed combat, and God knows why I let James talk me into this. It probably had something to do with what he told me about Nasir shouting at his mother about once having a sister, before slamming his way out of the flat. He said Arifa wouldn't talk about it, but I can't think about that with Amelia still in the hospital. Mummy did try to persuade me to let her host today's hostilities, but honestly, now that they say I can sleep at the hospital again, the Ladybird Ward and our own home are the only places I'm prepared to put on my radar. I'm sure James will help wash up and clear away the wreckage before we get back to Amelia and the nurses have promised she'll be fine on her own. *She's doing so well and she coped without you yesterday morning, didn't she?*

One more sip of wine and I will pop the pizza in the oven and polish the plates. Well, I will just take them out of the cupboard, but I do find a little alliteration is lovely when you're looking forward to a lively lunch. Or maybe the tiniest bit tipsy. After all, this is the first bottle I've opened (and half emptied, or half filled, depending on what happens later) since that one or two glasses I had with James back on date night at the Heartbreak Hotel. And now I come to think of it, this whole naughty Nasir nicking off Nora scenario saw that little soirée to a sad and sorry end too. I'd better have another glass of wine.

I'm not quite sure how they got there, but now Mummy and Daddy and James and Adam are all sitting round the kitchen table. The plates are in the right places and the pizza is piping hot. *No, pull yourself together, Debs!* They are here on serious business and Adam is already talking, about something.

'Nice bottle, James. Napa Valley is always a good choice with a simple lunch like this.'

That's a relief then. Although, hang on, what does he think he's on about? I'll give him simple with his hint of an American twang. Probably wouldn't even be able to pronounce half of the French stuff we've got in the wine fridge.

'It is good, isn't it?' I say. 'Perfect with pizza. And sweet of you to understand that we didn't go for the whole five-course tasting menu this time, what with having to pop back to the hospital later.'

He smiles at me and raises his glass.

'Sorry, Debs. That's not what I meant. I just... Look, it's good of you to have us.'

'You're forgiven,' I say and wish I could kick him under the table, the way I would have done in the good(ish) old days. It really is all too simple to slip back into those age-old family roles sometimes. Let's hope we can get back to the kid-sister big-brother solidarity phase too.

'It really is good of you to have us,' says Daddy, 'and I know you'll be wanting to get back to Amelia as soon as you can, so what do you think about getting started? On the Nasir situation.'

I think I'd rather eat an entire jar of maximum strength jalapeños, given that I prefer to avoid bloodshed at the kitchen table whenever possible, but I also think I'd better not say so. There is a nanosecond of silence when nobody seems willing to be the first to go over the top, but Adam soon has his tin hat on.

'OK,' he says in brilliant New York lawyer fashion. 'I think you all know that if it was up to me, we'd have started proceedings against Arifa and her, erm, son long ago. We already discussed undue influence and maybe even false imprisonment when Bubby let herself get talked into leaving the Cedars.' He takes a sip of water, which I imagine means he means business, and proceeds. 'But no, nobody wanted to go there. And you know what the first rule of negotiations is with people like this? If you give them your hand, they'll cut off your arm, and that's about where we stand today.'

Now there are quite a lot more nanoseconds of silence.

Daddy gulps. Mummy's pearls suddenly seem too tight around her neck. James has turned an odd shade of puce. I take a small, but simple, swallow of Napa Valley.

'Adam, I really don't think that kind of metaphor is appropriate—and especially when we're talking about people who may have helped save Amelia's life, whatever did or didn't happen with the poker,' I say and give my brother a look that I hope could kick him all the way to the Napa Valley.

'Debbie is right, Adam. I think we get your drift.' Now I give Daddy an I-love-you-Daddy look. 'I think we all agree that we need to get to the bottom of this latest incident,' he continues, 'but let's try to keep things in proportion.'

'If you say so, Dad.' Adam seems disappointed that he can't invoke the Counter Terrorism Act. 'But let's not forget where Syria stands on the State of Israel.'

'Adam!'

The volume is so un-Daddy-like that everyone stares at him.

'This is not the International Court of Human Rights and we are not on CNN. And nobody is asking you to play Sean Penn as the hotshot lawyer out to save the world. We are simply trying to decide on the best steps to take if, and I say *if*, we need to prevent this boy from taking further advantage of my grandmother - and your great-grandmother. So, as I was saying, a bit of proportion, please.'

'OK, you're right, I got a bit carried away. But I hate to see how these people are cheating Bubby out of her hard-earned savings.'

'Daddy's right though, darling, we do need to be sure first. But if that is what they're up to, what line of action would you be leaning towards, legally?'

Is it the wine, or does Mummy's recent entente cordiale with Daddy even extend to family meetings now?

'Well, we've tried getting a confession out of him,' says the legal eagle.

'You mean talking to him,' says Daddy.

'Exactly. And that didn't get us very far. Now, Dinnelman, Tate and Wojnawski do a pretty good line in negotiating out of court, so I'd suggest that that's our first port of call.' Another sip of water. 'And if all else fails, we go to the police.'

Now, the nanoseconds seem to be turning into eons. We've all aired our views about theft and kidnapping and legal action since Bubby left the Cedars, but this is the first time anyone has seriously—Adam was serious, wasn't he?—mentioned bringing in the police. Even as a last resort.

'I sincerely hope that won't be necessary.' Thank goodness for Daddy and his sense of proportion. 'But I do agree with Adam that we should talk this through with our lawyers.'

But if Daddy isn't sure Nasir did anything wrong, why do we need the family lawyers? I can't help seeing images of Arifa singing to Amelia at the hospital, and then Nasir in his uniform, and Amelia telling him the names of her friends at school.

'I'm not sure that I go along with all of this,' I say. 'I've listened to you and Adam, Daddy. James has told me he's seen Bubby's accounts on the poker sites and yes, the money has been moved, but Bubby trusts Nasir and Arifa. And there's one thing nobody has mentioned from what James told me about your conversation with them the other night. Darling?'

Adam is about to raise an objection, but the way James cuts through the air with his long surgeon's finger makes him think again.

'Quite, darling. It's simple. We all know how much Bubby

loves playing poker. She taught most of us to play herself. Well, Arifa and Nasir both say that when she decided to buy him a computer, Nasir taught her to play online and that she's the one pouring the money into these gambling sites. Brightening up her life a little.'

'Come on, James. *She* decided to buy him the Mac? *She's* a whizz with the trackpad? OK, so that's the line the two of them tried to sell us, but you're not saying that means we should believe them, are you?'

Adam is not going to let his argument drop without a fight.

'All I'm saying is innocent until proven guilty, Adam. British legal system 101.'

Exactly. No more made-up Hollywood law at *my* kitchen table!

'I know most of you think it's ridiculous, if not impossible. How could this incredibly old lady get her not-so-addled head round the internet?' continues my fact-based physician husband. 'Well, I say the real question is, how has she managed to live this long? And stay about as sharp as any of us round this table?'

More nanoseconds. None of us have the answer to James's questions. Obviously.

'I examined Nora yesterday and I'm happy to say that she is still in surprisingly good physical health.' Yes, James *is* a doctor and a fine one at that. And he's my husband and pretty good at that too and I know who I'd trust with the carving knife at the family table at Christmas, I mean Chanukah. 'Having said that, she does seem out of sorts about something, quite possibly the fact that we've taken away her new poker toy. I tried to ask her about it last night, but it was late and she was tired.' He pours himself the last drop of Napa. 'Look, if I'm wrong, I'll be happy to go along with whatever legal action is needed, but before we start talking about Dinnelman, Tate and Wojnawski and calling in the police, I think we should remember that Bubby trusts Arifa and she trusts her own family.' He takes my hand. 'Debbie, Bubby loves you. I think you should go and ask her what really happened.'

THIRTY-FOUR

Four days more

Morning

Tarek has told me that today is the day. His words were clear in my head when I woke up. Finish the forms, *habibti*, it is time for you to show them who you are. This was the heart of our marriage, showing each other who we were. I keep trying to let him know that I am still who I am, but it is getting harder. He is right, it is time to be me again. I don't care if this form wants to know the colour of my skin and if I am bisexual or not, because this is not who I am. I am a woman, a wife, a mother, a daughter, a doctor and I deserve some respect! I know I cannot go back to Aleppo. My home is gone and my country does not want doctors who treat everybody—the demonstrators, the fighters, the old men with nothing left in their eyes, the babies with their arms torn off, and even the dictators. So I will continue to cook and clean and care for this ancient Jewish woman, my friend, but one day I will be a doctor here, in the place where I hope in time I will have a home that does not feel like a box of bricks with a sofa to sleep on. Because I, Arifa Hashmi, am the woman that Tarek knew and not the person that Nora's family accuse of theft and dishonesty and worse. Not the mother that sees anger in her son's heart and maybe deserves his disrespect.

I check my phone, but of course there is nothing. My own mother has told me to leave him be, that he will come round, come home, that at least he has sent me a message to tell me he is staying with Farid from school for a while. From Farid's phone because Nasir left mine behind where it can mock me. Do I know this Farid? Can I find where he lives or call his parents to tell them to send my son back to me? No. So I will fill in my form to see if I can find myself again and stop myself from screaming out of the window onto Cornwood Drive and its flags and its shitting dogs. Whether I will have the strength not to go to Nasir's school tomorrow to plead with him to come back I do not know. But I do know that I don't have the strength to make him.

I push back the blankets because Tarek's voice in my head reminds me that I still have the strength for that, even though my own voice is telling me that I may as well lie here on the sofa until Nora's bell rings. The Arifa he knew only stayed a long time in bed when he had his arms around her. Otherwise, there were children to send to school, a clinic to go to or a paper to finish. But not here. Still, I rise and begin the clockwork of every day since Nora came. Fold sheets and blankets. Check my phone. Bathroom. Check my phone. Dress. Check my phone. Start to make breakfast for me and Na—. For me. Today I will make *mamouniyeh* because it was Tarek's favourite as well as Nasir's. Perhaps Nora will be feeling well enough to share some with me. I check my phone and then take the folder with the forms down from the bookshelf before going to the bathroom.

I, Arifa Hashmi, future M.D., am Other, Arab, tick. My sexual orientation is Heterosexual/straight, tick and *alhamdulillah*, because life as a woman in Aleppo, and sometimes even here in London, is already difficult enough. No, I do not consider myself to have a disability unless they count several holes in the heart that will not heal, and maybe a new one just starting. I will not let them open up this hole. I will care for Nora as long as she needs me, but then I will be a doctor again and heal real holes in the bodies of real people. I will sign the form and then moisten the glue strip and fold and seal exactly the way it says, and then I am sure Nasir will come home and I will promise him that I will be who I am again, the way it is right to be. I sign. I moisten with my tongue to add a little of my DNA and fold and seal. I hold the piece of cardboard to my breast. Nora's bell rings, the way I knew it would, to end this small ceremony. She and I will celebrate with tea, even though she will not know what we are toasting, and I will do what she needs me to do, even if she doesn't ask me kindly, but I will not keep quiet when her people insult me and my people. I check my phone and go through to the kitchen to warm the *mamouniyeh*.

'What do you have planned for me today, Arifa? I have been too many days in this bed.'

Nora has drunk two cups of tea and eaten all of her *mamouniyeh* and a soft pear that I cut into quarters for her. Her cheeks are still hollow, as she nods with the sound of the violins and clarinets she has at last brought back into her room, but I find her skin is a little brighter this morning.

'This, I agree with, Nora,' I say. 'I was beginning to think we would never get you out of this bedroom again.' I tidy her dishes and pick up the tray. 'But first, how about a shower? There's nothing like running water on your skin when you've been shut up in bed for too long.'

'A shower is good,' she says, 'but I want to go outside. How is the weather?'

I tweak the net curtains, but I am worried that it is too soon, that she is too weak.

'The sun is out, but I see quite a lot of clouds. I think it will rain.'

'Then we should hurry. I would like to go with Dovid to see his school.'

I wish I had a hand free to check my phone again, even though I know there will be no message and that Dovid will not be coming with us. And Nasir neither. I turn myself into Dr Hashmi to make my voice stay still.

'I will have to have a quick look at you first to make sure you are well enough to go out today,' I say, 'but in any case, Dovid will not come with us. He is with a friend. Homework, I think.'

'So you tell him to come back.'

'I would like to.' I would like to think I could tell him to do anything and have him listen to me. 'But he doesn't have a phone with him and this boy, Farid, his friend, is somebody he just met. I don't have his number.'

'Ach, these boys, they think the friends are more important than the mothers. But I suppose a boy this age needs some freedom. So, we will go together, you and I. It is not far from here. And not so far from my shop either. We can go there for lunch.'

This is a woman who knows who she is. Maybe not always exactly where or when or in which order, but who. I am sure she fought her own war hard to make sure she would not lose herself in those camps that she will not talk about and, in this way at least, she has won. I allow myself a squeeze of her shoulder and she puts her hand on mine. Again, the surprise of soft, warm skin in the middle of the wrinkles and the fighting.

I have been to Stepney Green many times before Nora came. I thought she wanted Nasir to show her where he is learning to be like the other new English students with the uniforms that only hide a part of where they or their parents have come from. His school is quite a walk from Cornwood Drive, but we could have done it with Nora wrapped warm in her chair. But I should have known, she would want to go there with Nasir on a school day, with his blazer and his tie neat and close to his collar. Today we are coming to her own son's school and she is right, it is even closer, and it is a good place to visit on a Sunday morning before the spring rain comes. There are benches close to the clock tower where I would sometimes sit with a *kibbeh* warmed at home or a pita bread filled with falafel. Some of the trees are bare today and some already have new leaves. I didn't know there was a Jewish school here once, or any school at all.

'Look, see the gate, Arifa? With those big iron letters. The big S and the J and the small S. The Stepney Jewish School, they called it. They shut it down years ago, but Dovid came here with his good jacket and his shirt. They didn't have the uniform back then and some of the children had only a knitted sweater, but Henry and I made sure that he came in clothes that were tidy, and clean of course. When he grew, we would save his clothes for the younger boys. He knew to take care and not put holes in them, but the times he behaved like a fool too much with the other boys, I mended them.'

'Most of the mothers around here have forgotten how to sew now,' I say. 'I am happy that I still have the mending and making things beautiful to keep me attached to my own mother.' And I think that Nora and I are not the only ones in Stepney holding on to threads that lead back in time.

'The S, the J and the s.' She runs her fingers along the metal letters. 'This is where Dovid learned again to work and study, so he could grow and earn his living in freedom after all those years when we lost each other.'

'It is such a blessing that you found each other after those terrible years. Were you separated for all of the war?' I look at her to see if this is, at last, the time she will talk about those times, here outside her son's school. 'I'm sure he was a good student,' I say, because maybe this is a better way for her to start, 'and I know how much you and his father supported him and worked to give his life the best start.'

But no, she is not listening to me. She is holding tight to the curled metal and looking for her boy in the empty courtyard that must once have been full of the shouts of children.

I was as proud as any mother could be when Mr Feldman stopped me at the school gate.

'Go on, David,' he said. 'Your friends are waiting and I have something to discuss with your mother.'

All I had from my son that day was a wave, but he already told me that my kisses had to stay inside the flat over the store. The teacher's smile broke up the worries that were starting in my head, even though Henry always told me Dovid was a good boy, serious, and I gave him a smile back.

'Good morning, Mr Feldman, did you and Mrs Feldman enjoy a restful Sabbath?'

'We did, Mrs Wojnawski, thank you. I think you and Mr Wojnawski did not have too much time for yourselves with all your work in the shop.'

I smiled again.

'We try to give a good service to the community. Many people need a spice or a couple of onions or a pot of cream cheese when they don't expect it,' I said.

'Of course,' he said, 'and we are grateful to you.'

Because this was a Jewish school that kept the traditions, but left the laws to the English judges, I knew that. We had moved a long way from our Polish city, Henry and I.

'I wanted to have a quick word with you about David. His English really has improved tremendously. We are very happy with his progress.'

'Then so are we, Mr Feldman, thank you. That is fine news.'

'But, in fact, what I wanted to talk to you about is his mathematics.' Now his smile grew wider. 'He really is a first-class student. I don't think I've ever seen a boy quicker with his mental arithmetic and now that we're moving into algebra and trigonometry, it seems he has something of a gift.'

Algebra, this I knew about, but the other one, with the trick in its name, was something I had never heard.

'Mrs Wojnawski, if you and your husband agree, I would like to offer David some extra classes after school. He doesn't have too many years left ahead of him here and I do believe he is university material, maybe even an Oxford man.'

'Thank you, Mr Feldman, that is a beautiful thing to know.'

Oxford I had heard of—of course I had—and my heart was swelling with *naches*. 'But Dovid knows he must help out at the store after his school day and I am not sure if we will have the money to send him away to university.'

'Of course, Mrs Wojnawski, I understand, but you needn't worry about the money. There are plenty of scholarships for exceptional boys like David. And I wouldn't keep him every day, just one or two, if you agree.'

The school bell burst into my picture of my gifted son with a smile on his face and a flat square hat on his head from the university, and Mr Feldman held his hand out to shake mine.

'Think about it, Mrs Wojnawski, talk it over with David's father. You know where to find me.'

And then he was gone, with his own wave back and his way of walking that meant business, but had the children happy to follow him. Dovid and his friends must have gone inside the school already and Mr Feldman stopped to scoop up a group of small girls still jumping over lines of chalk. Dark dresses and white socks that were mostly round their ankles and had to be pulled quickly up to their knees. Curls pulled into braids down the side of their heads or straight hair cut square across their forehead so they could follow their studies. One, with hair that was lighter than the rest, hung back a little and then turned to look at me, back at the gate, with bright eyes that were lighter too. I raised my hand to wave, but it made her run to catch up with her schoolfriends. They were all beautiful and they were all Miriam, every one of them, and they had all arrived at school that morning with one hand in mine and the other in their brother's. The way they did every day. And they stayed at the gates for a kiss when Dovid ran off waving, stayed for a kiss and even a moment or two in my arms. And I held tight onto those moments because I knew she would grow and the kisses and the moments would soon be gone and I would be left with just a wave, if

294

I was lucky. Then all the Miriams had disappeared. Mr Feldman had done his job and sent them into their classroom to sing their alphabet and trace their fingers around words like cat and mat or aba and ima. Father was at the shop, open early and already busy. Mother was at the school gate, waving goodbye. Her heart was full with pride for her clever son, and empty with a sorrow that was as empty as the hand that I was sure had been holding her clever daughter's. Sorrow that these moments at the school gate would never grow up and become a time to say goodbye with a kiss or a wave to her Miriam.

'Miriam, *mamme sheyne*, forgive me that I didn't come before. But you know that your *aba* and I are as proud of you as we are of Dovid. Our *sheyne meydel* with your nose like my own *mamme* and so brave, always. I know you were brave when you left with all those other children. I felt this. I had to feel it.'

Nora's voice is low and it takes me a moment to understand that she is talking. I turn to her, ready to tell her we should go, she will catch cold, but I see that she is crying, tears spilling down her face as her lips move. Must I listen? Must I stop her? I move a little nearer, but her face stays close to the gate. I lean forward to ask can I help her, but my telephone starts to shout out at me. Can I leave her to cry? Is it Nasir?

'Yes? Nasir?'

'Arifa?'

'Yes?'

'This is Deborah, Mrs Levene.'

'Yes, hello.'

I hear banging in my ears, but I know I must listen. Maybe she knows where he is.

'How are you? How's Bubby?'

'Good, we are well. And you? And Amelia?'

'Oh, Amelia is doing so well, thank you. We hope she will be coming home tomorrow. We are so happy, so excited.'

And so scared, I know.

'That is wonderful news, Deborah. I am happy for you all.'

'Thank you, Arifa.' She is quiet for a moment. 'And Bubby is doing better, is she? James said she was well, but tired.'

'Yes, I think she is feeling better. Today she asked to get out of her bed.' She doesn't need to know we have gone out for a walk.

'Wonderful!' Deborah's voice is happy, but there is something else in it too. 'I was hoping that she is well enough for me to come and see her. It's a while since she's been to the hospital and I won't have much time once Amelia's home.'

'You want to come today?'

'Could I?'

Could she? This is the first time she has asked me and not told. No, she could not.

'I am sorry, Deborah, but you and your family cannot come to my home.' I shut my eyes to feel that Tarek is with me, that he knows who I am and what I will allow. 'I will not accept what you say about my son, about me and my intentions and until you have other things to say, I will ask you not to visit.'

'But, Bubby?' Now her voice has no more wonderful. 'Look, Arifa, that's one of the reasons I want to see Bubby, to ask her what happened. James told me—he told all of us— what you and Nasir said. And I think he's right. He must be right. I mean, I know my family … I know *I* haven't always exactly, well, I haven't always welcomed you.'

Can this angry, kind woman, who maybe doesn't know who she is—who is sometimes sweet, sometimes stinging like the bee Nora told me about—can she want to apologise to me?

'James and I want to believe you, but I do need to talk to Bubby about it all.'

'I see,' I say and I think. What must I do for Nora? Here outside these gates to her son and her memories.

'Arifa?'

I have no right to decide for her, but I have the right for myself.

'It is as I say. I will not allow you and your family to come to my home anymore.' I feel Tarek cup my cheek and smile into my eyes because he knows that I will do what I must to be who I am, for me and for Nasir. 'But your great-grandmother and I have planned to have lunch at the café. The one that used to be her shop. We will be going there soon. If you would like to take a tea with her this afternoon, that is where you will find us.'

297

THIRTY-FIVE

Four days more

Afternoon

Today, the woman on the café wall with her bright make-up and her yellow coffee cup seems friendlier. The pictures of my country's leaders that I saw floating just under the surface of her paint have disappeared and taken their angry eyes with them, and now I know that I will never wear such shiny red lipstick, and I know I will not put on a headscarf either.

'Do you see, Arifa, they have bagels here, and even with lox and cream cheese.' Nora has already picked up the menu and it is good to hear her talk about food; she must be hungry again. 'I like the people in this café,' she says. 'They want to take me back to the old days when all the streets around here were full of Jews.'

I laugh.

'So this lox,' I say, 'that's food from Poland?'

'In Poland we ate the *schmaltz* herring. But the lox is salmon, the pink fish. I never saw it in the old days in Poland, but all the Jewish people around here were crazy for it. Henry, he was crazy for it—the smoked salmon and the *schmear* cheese with a couple of capers and always the raw onions that made his breath terrible!'

Now her hooting goose laugh is back and that is even better to hear, although I am not sure if she can go straight from chicken soup and *mamouniyeh* in bed to raw onions.

'Smoked salmon should be soft enough for your teeth, but the bagels might be a bit chewy, Nora.' I don't want to stop her hooting, but I don't want her choking either. 'Look, they have some good soups too—carrot and coriander, spiced lentil.'

'Ach, soup, soup! It's always soup these days,' she says. 'Yes, I will eat the chicken soup now that you have it right with my dill in it, but except for the chicken, I am sick of soup. Look, I have my false teeth now.' She makes a face to show them to me, even though she knows I know what they look like. I clean them every day. 'They are good enough to chew with and I will have some bagel.'

So bagels it had better be, then. I choose falafel in a pita bread, like the ones I sometimes used to eat for lunch on my days off from the Cedars, sitting on a bench near the old Jewish school that I didn't know was there, but I don't think the ones here are likely to take me back to my old days. I check my phone to see if I can find my own schoolboy, but he is still hiding. When it comes to ordering a drink, I nearly ask for a glass of water, like I did the last time I was here, but then I take another look at the menu.

'I will have a berry latte,' I say, 'with extra blueberries and chopped almonds on top.'

If Nora's family was here they would think, and maybe they would even say, that it is interesting that I have found myself some money somewhere. But they are not here, and in any case, they wouldn't understand what it is that I have found and that it has nothing to do with money. I just hope that it is not too late for me to explain it to Nasir and have him come home again.

'Arifa, there is something I would like to tell you about Nasir.'

How does she do this? Does she know my own mind even better than hers? Has she understood that he has left home? Could it be that what her family says about the poker is true?

'What is it? I hope he hasn't done anything to upset you.'

'No, of course not. Nasir is a good boy. Ach, he's not perfect, the way some people would like it, but a boy should not be perfect, he needs to test things out before he sees how his life is going to be.'

'You're right, Nora, even though it can be hard for a mother to let him test, the way you say.' I stop myself from checking my phone again, another test.

'Yes,' she says, and then, 'you know, I think I am the one that has upset him.' She puts her hand on my arm. 'I feel foolish, Arifa. How can it be that I am so old and yet I feel so foolish, like a girl who has never left her mother's kitchen.'

I put my hand on hers.

'I am sure you haven't upset Nasir, Nora. And I never find you foolish. Funny, strong-headed, maybe, but not foolish.'

'Thank you. I hope you know that for me you are a true friend, not just somebody I pay to cook spicy food for me and clean me up.'

Now I laugh, and press my fingers around hers.

'I know, of course,' I say, 'and you know that you are a great friend for me.'

'But I have been selfish, perhaps even a little cruel. I—'

'So ladies, one smoked salmon bagel—that's for you is it,

love?—and a falafel plate.' The service is excellent in this café, very quick and polite. 'And I'll be back with the drinks in a jiffy. You wait till you taste the berry latte. Great choice, you'll see.' Though this time I would have preferred it a little slower.

'Go on, Nora, what is it you were saying? Or would you like to taste your bagel first?'

'The bagels I have eaten many in my life. What I want to tell you and Nasir is that I am sorry.'

'Sorry? For what?'

'Sorry because I know that Nasir is not my son, my Dovid. Of course I know this. I think always I knew it, even if sometimes with my old *kop* and my tired heart I wanted to go back to when Dovid was a boy. But I am not his mother, the one he tries to test all the time. That is you, you poor, patient woman, and God bless you for it. And you know, I wanted it so much that sometimes I did believe it, truly. He was my boy, the one that I cried out for so many times when we were separated and the one that came back to me and worked so hard with Henry and me to build our life here. Right here, in this shop.'

She looks around her as if she could see everything the way it used to be with her worn-out eyes. And I know that I must listen and wait.

'It was wrong to make him play this game. To ask him to follow a foolish old woman around the places she used to know. And make him feel foolish. The young boys don't like to feel foolish.'

'You mustn't say this. Nasir was able to give you some happiness in these days when you have come back to your home, and that is a privilege for him.'

'Ach, you are always so kind, Arifa, always trying to see the good things. But you think this is my home? I lived here many, many years, it is true, with my husband, my son. We made ourselves a home to live in, but the home that made the shape of our life was gone long before. I saw that again when I was at the school gates just now and I knew I must say goodbye to playing this foolish game of mine with my Dovid.'

The heart shatters when it must say goodbye to a child, and Nora's tears this morning were full of its pieces. But she has more to tell me.

'And I saw those schoolgirls again, the ones with their dark hair and their socks fallen around their ankles. And I thought I saw a light-haired girl in the playground with them. I tried to say goodbye again to Miriam. I have been trying since the day that little one fell in the cemetery. But I find it is impossible. She never left my heart, but now I can feel her in my eyes and ears again, and even my fingers.'

'Do you mean Amelia?' I thought I was used to the way Nora sometimes changes from one part of her thinking to another, but now I am finding her hard to follow.

'Amelia has come back to her parents. She will be strong again, but Miriam? She slipped out of my arms so long ago. I tried to go with her, but they would not... It was not possible.'

Nora's eyes have a shine in them again, but it comes from tears, not the years turning back. Her cheeks have grown hollow from the struggle of so many years holding the tears inside, but now they are falling onto her face for the second time today. I think I am beginning to understand a little about Miriam.

A hand pulls a chair away from our table and a woman sits down without asking if we will let her.

'Bubby, is everything alright? What is it? Who's Miriam?'

I take Nora's hand. Of course, Deborah is here.

'Hello, Deborah,' I say. 'Look, Nora, Amelia's mother,

Deborah, is here. Do you remember, I told you she would be joining us?' I hope she does remember, but I am not sure if she will let this woman who can sting as well as make honey see her tears.

I turn to Deborah. 'Nora and I went to see your grandfather's school this morning. I think you know how our children can bring our tears out.'

She smiles a quick smile.

'Yes, I do, but I heard something about a Miriam. Do I know her? Is she the one upsetting you, Bubby?'

'Deborah, how are you?' Nora has pushed her pain back inside. This is something she has had practice at doing. 'Don't worry about Miriam; it's an old story. Tell me, how is our little Amelia doing?'

Deborah looks at me and then back at Nora.

'Oh, she's much, much better now.' She looks at me again with worry between her eyes, but then she sees that she will not hear about the tears and she takes a deep breath. 'It's been wonderful to see how fast she's been improving since she woke up. Her speech is almost back to normal and she can walk a little way with crutches, even though she mostly uses a wheelchair—a bit like yours, Bubby, but not electric—and she's made so many friends on her new ward. And James and I are so excited, she's coming home tomorrow. We can hardly believe it.'

Nora claps her hands together.

'That is the news I have been waiting for. I'm so sorry I haven't been to see her for a while. I have been missing her.'

I want to tell her I am missing Amelia too, but for now the one I am missing is Nasir.

'She's been missing you too, Bubby. We all have.'

'I have been a little tired, but I hope I will be able to see her soon. I am very, very happy for all of you.'

She claps her hands again, as if she is hoping that the soft noise of her skin can hide the sound of the shake in her voice. It is a small shake, maybe normal for a woman so old, but I hear it. I don't know if her great-granddaughter does too.

'Thank you, Bubby,' she says. 'I don't want to stop you from eating, but there is one other thing I wanted to ask you about.'

So, she didn't notice, or if she did, she thinks her family's business is more important than whether her great-grandmother has her appetite back or whether her questions might take it away again. I draw in the muscles of my belly from the fear of what I know she is about to say and the anger that she still wants to say it.

'Ask,' Nora says. 'I will take the time to eat while I listen.'

And push the pain even further back inside, I think. Deborah takes another deep breath.

'Well, Bubby, I know you haven't been able to play poker on your computer for a few days now, and I know that's been upsetting you. Daddy—Michael—told me that that's because your credit card has been blocked at the bank.'

She stops and looks at Nora to see if she will say something, but her mouth is full of salmon and bagel.

'The thing is—I don't know if Arifa has told you—that it was Daddy that asked the bank to block it. And that's because... Well, the thing is that my father and my brother think that Nasir— that's Arifa's son, you know that, don't you?'

Nora is still chewing.

'That Nasir must have been playing instead of you, using your money. Maybe even stealing your money.'

Now she has stopped chewing. Deborah starts playing with the chain around her neck. I want to speak, but my phone buzzes in my pocket.

'I mean, you've only just started using a computer. We—I mean, they—can't imagine how you'd have been able to learn to go online by yourself. I mean, it's complicated unless you know how. But James and Arifa—and Nasir—well, they all say he didn't do it.'

Deborah is breathing a little fast now and a message from a number I don't know tells me that Nasir will be back to pick up his school things this evening. Should I tell her what she and her family have done to what is left of mine? Nora puts her bagel down on her plate and wipes her mouth with her napkin. For now, I will let her do the talking.

'Oh, they do, do they?' she says.

'Yes, um…'

'And what do you think about all of this, Deborah?'

'I think James must be right, that Nasir's telling the truth. I mean, he is usually a pretty good judge of character, I mean, he is a doctor. And Nasir has been so wonderful with Amelia.' She pulls at her necklace again and I see she reminds me of her mother. 'But then I do know that it takes a while to learn your way around a computer, especially for … well … older people.'

'So you think I'm an idiot?

'Of course I don't, Bubby.'

'You think I am not capable of making a machine work? Of writing down some numbers and a password and—what do they call it—the mail address? After all these years in this shop? Right here, working and noting down the sales and the missing stock and remembering who didn't pay yet!'

Now Nora is like a woman who has never known tears, unless they were tears of anger. I share them, burning behind my eyes, when all I want to do is take my phone and call this new number and tell Farid that Nasir must wait, I will be back soon, I will cook his supper for him, some *kibbeh* to remind him of home.

'And you think that that boy, the one who is like flesh and blood to me, who has sat with me and entertained me, an ugly old woman, you think he would steal from me? That his mother would let him?'

'No, Bubby.'

'No is right! I am telling you he did not and she did not! And you can go and tell that to your father and your brother.' She folds her napkin slowly and lays it down next to her plate. 'Tell them that maybe I am thinking of changing my will to help these people who have been so good to me.'

Deborah's mouth drops open and I feel I am looking in a mirror because so does mine.

'In fact, do you know what?'

Deborah and I both shake our heads with our mouths still open and Nora folds her napkin into an even smaller square.

'It really has been too long since I came to see Amelia. She's coming home from hospital tomorrow, you say? Good. So don't bother telling anybody. I will come and tell them myself.'

THIRTY-SIX

Three days and counting

Morning

'Amelia, Amelia, Amelia, Amelia!'

The little blur of purple jumping up and down on the lawn is also Amelia: Amelia B, next-door neighbour and our Amelia's official BFF at home (as opposed to her sometimes three, sometimes four BFFs at school). Her sign has an extra L in WELLcomE HoMe! and lots of Elsa-and-Anna-style blue snowflakes, plus two little girls holding hands in the middle. Amelia-and-Amelia-style. My Amelia opens her car window and waves at a dangerously horizontal angle and I am relieved to see that Julia B (my own BFF at home and Amelia B's mum) is holding tight to her Amelia's hand, thus avoiding further injury to either or both of our daughters, as well as an entirely unwelcome trip back to the hospital.

'Mummy, look, it's Amelia!' says Amelia. 'Can I invite her to play?'

'It is lovely that she's here to greet you, darling, and what a lovely sign she's made,' I say and deposit a kiss on my angel's head, 'but I think we'd better get you settled in a bit before you have a play date.'

'Please, Mummy?'

Her little forehead scrunches into a frown that I wish I could smooth away instantly, but I shake a no, hating myself for it.

'Daddy? It's not fair. I haven't seen Amelia for ages and I've been really ill in hospital and everything. Please, Daddy?'

James gives Amelia one of his best twisted-round-her-little-finger smiles, but he's been fully trained in united front parenting. I squeeze his knee, just in case.

'Mummy's right, darling. You need to take it easy to begin with, see how you get on with getting up the stairs, getting used to all the things in your bedroom again.' He reaches over to squeeze Amelia's knee as her frown threatens to burst into tears. 'And Froodle will probably need lots of cuddles to help him get used to being at home again.' Now he smiles over at me. 'But I'm sure if Mummy says it's OK and you're doing fine, Amelia could pop in for just a few minutes a bit later.'

Perfect. He is just perfect. Support for Mummy in the face of an impending tantrum and a nimble final flourish that puts the smile back on all of our faces.

'OK, Daddy,' says the princess, just as our very own James in shining armour brings the car to a stop and Amelia B rushes across the driveway, jumping up and down behind her WELLcomE HoMe sign next to the car.

Once the broken leg in its cast has been negotiated out of the car, both Amelias stand and grin at each other until Amelia B grabs Amelia L round the waist in a lop-sided hug, making her laugh so hard she almost drops her crutches.

'It's so good to have you all back,' says Julia, pulling me

into a hug. 'How are you? How is she? Is everything going to be OK?'

I nod back against my own impending tears and wish that I was five again, like the Amelias, with no need for how-are-you and yes-everything-will-be-fine-at-least-I-hope-so, because smiles and giggles and wobbly hugs tell them all they need to know.

'Mummy, Mummy, have you got the pen?'

Amelia B tugs at Julia's arm until she pulls a thick purple marker out of her pocket.

'Thank you!' she shouts and is back at Meelie's side in less time than it takes her mother to say, 'Careful with her leg!'

James props Meelie up so she can hold her cast out and her bestie crouches on the gravel, pen lid off, tongue poking out in concentration. Her skills with a marker are slower than her sprinting, but A + A finally appears on the plaster, followed by = and then, little by little, a shaky purple heart.

'There!' she says, and Meelie says, 'Thanks, Amelia!' She looks up at James, who nods, and then she says, 'Daddy says you can come and play in my room afterwards.' Amelia B says, 'OK, I will.' And then they wave at each other and grin again. 'See you later!'

'Where do you keep your napkin rings, Deborah?'

It took some negotiating, but Mummy finally agreed that she and Daddy would wait a couple of hours before popping over to see the wounded soldier now that she is safe back at home. She has done the delivery and unwrapping ceremony of a full Elsa costume, complete with peroxide blonde wig and new crown boasting dozens of plastic turquoise diamonds. She has done the grandmotherly inquiries about health and being extra careful and doesn't it feel lovely to be back in your own bedroom. (To be fair Amelia was very, very happy to see Grandma and Grandpa and to open her present and have them wrap her up in their arms and sign her leg again.) She has done the sending James and Daddy out to the garden so she can do the concerned mother checking that I will be sure to get my sleep and not overdo it and put my own oxygen mask on first because otherwise I won't be any good to anybody. And now she is doing the helping out in my kitchen routine for the first time in living memory, while I wonder how much longer she is going to spend beating around the bush.

'We don't actually use napkin rings, Mummy,' I say, 'but there are some paper napkins in the cupboard next to the fridge.'

'Really?' she says. 'Should I put some table linen on your birthday list? We could pop to John Lewis to choose some together.'

'That's sweet of you, but we have plenty. It's just that I want to cut down on the washing and ironing at the moment, with Meelie just getting back home.'

'Of course, darling. Have you thought about having Carmela come in for a few more hours than usual?'

(Carmela is my cleaner.)

'Not yet. James and I are just getting organised. We haven't really thought about all that yet.'

'Of course not. And then there are the party preparations. If it's still going ahead, of course.' A-ha, here we go. 'I mean, I know we said I'd take care of that now you've got so much on your plate, but, well, did Bubby say anything about it when you saw her?'

Finally!

'The world record party? No, she didn't, but she looked well and she seems to have her appetite back.' Two can play at the beating around the bush game. 'I went to see her at the café, you know, where the shop was. She was having lunch with Arifa.'

'Was she? How lovely.' I don't think I've ever heard my mother use the word lovely about anything to do with Arifa and something tells me she doesn't mean it this time. 'She must be feeling better then.'

'Yes, I think she really is, although she looked even skinnier than usual. Still, she was tucking into a lox and cheese bagel when I arrived.'

'A bagel?'

'Yes.'

'They do bagels at the café?'

'Well, yes. I think it's a Ye Olde Easte Ende type of thing. Why?'

'Nothing really, just a thought.' Mummy's cat-with-the-cream-cheese smile would suggest that this is quite some thought. 'The thing is that… Well, I didn't want to bother you with it,' she tries to hide her smile and look at me thoughtfully, 'but I cancelled the caterer.'

'You did?'

'I did, yes.'

'Go on.'

'Well, they were getting really rather difficult about the whole thing, brandishing percentages and penalties and full cancellation fees and all manner of things, so I told them that it wasn't terribly wise to be shirty with Sylvia Wojnawski. Mentioned a couple of the people at the *shul* who have contacts at the *Jewish Chronicle*, and something about the fact that I have an awful lot of friends with grandchildren about to reach bar mitzvah age.'

'You didn't!'

'I did. And, none of your concern, but there will be no charge for the last-minute cancellation of the Wojnawski-Levene event. I am actually rather proud of myself.'

If I thought that she would know what to do with it, I'd have given my mother a high five. I go over to the cupboard to find the paper napkins that she's completely forgotten about instead.

'And so you should be,' I say. 'But what if Bubby does finally want to go ahead? I mean, I know Amelia will be heartbroken if the whole thing's called off.' And if I'm honest, I will be too. With Amelia safe and at home again, Bubby's party feels like it would be lox and cheese bagels and chocolate ice cream and honey cake and piri piri chicken and all good things combined. 'There are only a couple of days to go now, aren't there?'

'Well, that's the thing, darling.' Mummy follows me round the table rolling up the napkins, as if willing a set of matching rings to miraculously appear. 'That's what I was having that thought about.'

Mummy's moment of glory is clearly not to be rushed. I'm surprised she's not waiting for the boys to come in from the garden for the big reveal.

'Yes?' I say (do not allow even a trace of the trademark Wojnawski irritation to infiltrate your voice, Debs).

'Well, the thing is, they do bagels. Maybe they know how to make chopped liver and *gefilte* fish. I mean, of course we'll need some proper finger food that people will actually want to eat, but I'm thinking, why don't we see if we can hold the celebrations at the café? In Bubby's very own shop?'

This time, I can't help myself. I hold up my hand for a high five and (wonders will never cease) she does know how to do one!

'That's a great idea, Mummy, really. I mean, the timing might be a bit tricky, but I bet Bubby would love that.' Or rather she would have loved it if she hadn't started threatening to change her will. But the café really is a why-on-earth-didn't-we-think-of-that-before-level idea and the way Mummy's managed to put off talking about Nasir and the great poker heist so spectacularly probably deserves a high five of its own, although there comes a point when there is only so much bush to be beaten. 'We can ask her about it later if you like. She's coming over to see Amelia.'

'Oh, how lovely. Amelia will be so pleased to see her. Arifa's bringing her, is she?'

'Yes, of course.'

'Lovely.'

She's not getting a lovely about Arifa past me twice.

'I thought you'd be pleased. Look, Mummy, I really do think your party at the café idea is genius, but you know as well as I do that I went to talk to Bubby about her version of Nasir pirating her online poker.'

'Pirates? Nasir's a pirate on top of the all the rest of it?'

Ah. And there was me thinking that pirating was in the same territory as high fives.

'Using her information to log into the computer, Mummy. Pretending to be her and pocketing the money she's lined up for her poker games.'

'Oh, of course. And what did she say? I mean, I'm assuming she had no idea he was stealing from her. My goodness, darling, the shock could have killed her!'

And with just two days to go before the world record, I hear her think.

'It would take more than that to finish off Bubby, Mummy, but you're right, she had no idea at all that Nasir was stealing from her.'

'I knew it!'

I have a look at my watch. It is almost lunchtime and I'm pretty sure my resident doctor would agree that a glass of wine would be an excellent cure for the shock I'm about to inflict on my mother. I pour two and hand one over.

'Well, actually, she had no idea because she says Nasir had nothing to do with it. He wrote out all the instructions for playing online—her password and everything—on a piece of paper and she's been gambling away to her wrinkled old heart's content all by her very own self. At least she was until Daddy told the bank to put an end to her latest attempt to fritter away our inheritance.'

'Deborah, I don't believe it.'

Mummy takes one of her carefully rolled napkins and starts to smooth it out with the flat of her hand.

'Well, that's Bubby's story and she says she's coming over to tell you all about it herself. I called Adam and he'll be here after lunch. She wants him to hear it too.'

Mummy reaches for another napkin.

'And there's one more thing. She's threatening to change the terms of her will. In favour of Arifa and Nasir.'

I raise my glass of grape-flavoured smelling salts to her.

'Cheers, Mummy,' I say.

THIRTY-SEVEN

Three days and counting

Afternoon

'122 years, 162 days. Only three more days to go.'

Bubby's writing is a scribble, but she ends with a small flourish and taps her pen on Amelia's cast.

'So, *mamme sheyne*. Now you have a world-record breaking leg. Tell your parents they don't throw it out when the doctors cut it off, it should be worth some money some day.'

The excitement on Amelia's face at this new addition to her collection of doodles and signatures switches to terror and I swoop in in an attempt to switch it back.

'Don't worry, my angel, Bubby didn't mean your actual leg —she was talking about your cast and she's right, it could be worth a lot of money once she becomes the oldest person in the world ever.'

'Could it? Enough to buy a *Frozen* castle? Like the one with the lights you can turn on and off, with lots of colours.'

'Enough to buy a *Frozen* castle for you and one each for all your BFFs, and even then you'd have plenty left over.'

It seems that James is good at swooping in too and Amelia is back in five-year-old heaven.

'Really, Daddy?' She wheels herself even closer to Bubby. 'Bubby, when are you breaking your record? It's soon, isn't it?'

'It's like I said, just three more days. And after that maybe all the fussing will be over.'

'But we will have the party, won't we? With the honey cake like you told me when you came to see me at the hospital?'

'We will have the party if it makes you happy, *mamme sheyne*,' she cups Amelia's face in the skin, bone and nail polish of her hand, 'but you will have to help me to make the cake.'

'I promise. But you have to promise to let me lick the bowl, like Mummy does.'

'Of course. Children must always be allowed to lick the bowl and the mixing spoon when they make a cake. I always used to let my little—I mean, my Dovid—lick the bowl when he was your age, so why not you?'

Did I hear the tiniest tremor in Bubby's voice? Over licking spoons? In any case, Meelie plants a kiss on her cheek and scoots her chair over to the other side of the living room.

'Arifa, Nasir is coming to the party, isn't he? Does he like honey cake? I can make him some cupcakes if he doesn't.'

Because Nasir isn't here. James told me how he slammed out of the flat when he (my husband) dared to mention that it was wrong to be rude about ancient benefactors who've kindly presented you (Nasir, obvs) with the latest in overpriced IT gadgets, free of the proverbial charge. So no, he didn't make it and here is Arifa, sitting in one of my best Conran Shop armchairs opposite my charming brother Adam who is sitting in the other. They look about as comfortable as a pair of six-inch Jimmy Choos, with Arifa failing to hide the fact that she probably intends to make my entire family squirm under her stiletto heel just as soon as the party talk is over.

'Everybody likes honey cake, sweetie,' I say, but to be honest I have no idea whether Nasir has ever even seen one. I just think it might be an idea to delay the death-by-designer-footwear moment as long as realistically possible. 'Bubby, has Mummy told you about her new idea for where we might hold the festivities?' (Of course she hasn't, given that she and her minder only just got here, but see above re. delaying tactics.)

'Of course not.' See! 'She married my grandson maybe, but this doesn't make her a woman who tells me anything. Rumours and gossip about innocent people she will talk about, but ideas to make her Bubby-in-law happy? Forget it.'

Ah. Not quite the tack I was hoping the conversation would take. And unfortunately, my mother never has been one to turn the other cheek (far too New Testament for Sylvia Wojnawski) so before I can whisk the room back to sweetness and honey cake, she has opted for salt in the wound.

'Well, if you hadn't told me that you'd tried to talk Michael out of marrying me on my wedding day,'—and here her smile doesn't even try for a sugar coating—'we might have become better friends, Dinora. As it is, the sense of family that I know you so appreciate in me has led me to admire your—how shall I put it?—tenacity, and to play my part in organising a memorable event to mark your own very special occasion. I was hoping to talk to you about my idea this afternoon, but I know when I'm not wanted.'

Gosh! Sylvia Wojnawski's martyr mode really is shining in all its bitter splendour today. But Bubby still hasn't lost her appetite for the fight.

'My dear Sylvia, I am glad you have remembered that it is *my* special occasion we are talking about, and I remind you I would like to celebrate this *my* way. And since you have decided we will talk honestly, let me tell you that I am quite aware that the only thing you admire about me is the size of my bank balance, and do you know what? I would like to decide what I do with that my own way too, instead of having your husband fiddle around with it.'

So here we are. The poker chips are on the table and Mummy looks like she's been kicked with something sharp. I look at Arifa, but she hasn't so much as opened her mouth yet.

'Bubby, look, let's try not to get upset.' Thank goodness Daddy still has the energy to at least try to sweeten the air, because the honey cake I was handing round has ended up in crumbs. 'I think Sylvia really does have a lovely idea for your world record celebrations.'

'Maybe she does, maybe she doesn't. You think I care? Ach, I have not put my tired old body into a cab to come to this house to talk about the world record, or the party, and not even the *meshuggeh* honey cake.' I gulp and look over at Amelia in case of tears, but luckily she has managed to snaffle my phone and is now plaster-cast-deep in Crushed Candy. '*Mein Gott!* I am here to talk about poker and why all of you nosy people have decided to stop an old woman enjoying one of the last pleasures of her so long life.'

Mummy and Daddy are silent. So are James and Adam and Arifa, and so am I. The only thing stopping a pin drop is the beep of Amelia shifting electronic candy around her screen. That doesn't seem to bother Bubby. She laces her fingers into a triangle and looks over them at us.

'I would also like to talk about how you dare to accuse my friend here—yes, Arifa is my friend. How you dare to accuse her and her son of stealing my money.'

The candy is still shifting around the screen and now the rest of us are shifting in our seats. Except Adam.

'Bubby, I understand that you think of Arifa as your friend, and I understand she has opened her home to you.' He looks across at the woman in the other armchair, and I wonder if, finally, he really is beginning to understand. 'But you haven't known her and her son that long and we are all simply trying to protect you, as an elderly and vulnerable person...'

'Elderly and vulnerable? Vulnerable?' Her voice, with its unshakeable yiddisher accent, sounds anything but. 'I'll give you vulnerable,' she snaps, 'with your shiny shoes and your expensive *shmatte*. You've never been vulnerable in your life, and who should you be thanking? Do you ever think about the hard work your grandfather did in the shop at the age when you were driving around in your father's fancy car? Not to mention thanking me and my Henry.'

She might be right about his youth, but Adam is definitely looking a little vulnerable now.

'But, Bubby...'

'*Genug!*'

She raises her tough old hand and shakes it at him in case he might not have understood that she's had enough, but just as she is about to deliver what may be a blow to crush far more than candy, a car door slams outside and Arifa runs out of the room. Out of the front door in fact. I head over to the bay window. On the street is a not-so-fancy car. On the driveway is Nasir, fresh from school by the look of his uniform. And Arifa. So he will be here to witness Bubby avenge his honour. The car drives away and Nasir takes his mother's arm. They exchange a few words and then she goes in for a hug, or at least she tries, but then realises that hands on arms will have to do. She nods and the two of them head down the drive. I think we may all

319

be about to be crushed underneath their feet, whether they are wearing Jimmy Choos or not.

I almost bump into Mummy as I turn back to the room. She's the only one to have followed me to my observation point (surprise, surprise) and she lets out what I can only describe as a yelp as I brush past her. Adam is sitting as far back in his armchair as he can manage; Bubby is still glaring at him from the sofa, Daddy is pacing up and down the room and I think James must have gone to open the door. Amelia is still crushing her candy and if anyone tells me she's too young to be playing on a smartphone, I will ask Arifa to lend me her Choos.

'Well, everybody, Nasir's here,' says James, prompting Amelia to drop my phone and swivel her wheelchair round to face us all again. She's been listening in all the time, the little wretch.

'Nasir!' she shouts and Nasir wiggles his fingers at her across the room with what is probably the smallest smile I have ever seen.

'Sweetie,' I say, picking up my phone before she can wheel over and open up the whole can of honey cake again, 'why don't you take this and have some fun in the kitchen? There are a couple of things the grown-ups need to talk about with Nasir.'

'You mean I'm allowed to play on your phone for as long as I like?'

'Well, until we've finished our chat with Nasir and Arifa and if you leave the door open so I can keep an eye on you,' I say and I almost see her (undamaged, thank God) brain cells registering this moment for future reference.

'Cool,' she cheers and swivels off towards the kitchen. 'Mummy, can I watch Elsa videos too?'

Who was it that said that rules are made to be broken? I think it might have been me and I shoo her out of the living room with a nod and a kiss.

OK. Now for the final scene. I think about following Amelia out to the kitchen and grabbing a quick class of white wine, but one broken rule is probably enough for now and I confess that there is the itsy-bitsiest part of me that is quite looking forward to seeing the look on my family's faces when Bubby tells them her side of the story.

'Darling, I think Bubby is quite keen to get back to when she was telling us she'd had enough.' James takes my arm and leads me back into the arena.

'She was telling Adam,' I say, those good old sibling reflexes kicking in as usual, 'but you're right, it's time we all heard what she has to say. I don't suppose I should offer everyone a glass of wine, should I?'

James laughs and kisses me on the cheek as he sits me down on the sofa between him and Bubby. Best seat in the house.

Bubby coughs. And begins.

'I am very glad that Nasir has been able to come here.' So, he's Nasir, not Dovid. 'I have said it before, and I will say it again: he is a good boy. He has been kind to a foolish old woman who wanted to dream that her own boy was back, the way he once was.' There is another short silence until she coughs again, a long cough that has me looking at James just in case. But, '*Reboynesheloylem!*' she suddenly shouts, a colourful exclamation that roughly translates as 'Oh Great Rabbi of the Heavens', or similar. 'Here you all are, insulting him, insulting his mother, the only two people who have been wanting to spend my last days with me, the way I want them. And what do I get from all of you? *Bupkis!* Only insulting them and insulting me!' She shakes her head at us. 'I may be a foolish old woman, but I am not a fool. I showed this boy how to play poker; he showed me how to use the fruit machine. The computer!' she says and raises her hand in the air, although how her old eyes spotted that Daddy was about to give us some explanatory context about Apples and Macs I will never know. She must have a sixth sense as well as a science-defying ability to ward off dementia. 'Who says the *alte kacker* can't learn the computers? Those other old crones never had the mental arithmetic training I had with my dear late husband.' Now, the corner of my eyes spot that Daddy's bottom lip has started to tremble. '*I* gambled the money; *I* placed the bets.' She looks around at us and raises her hand for silence again. 'I will now ask you to unblock my card again and I will tell you this. If anybody says one more word about my friends here stealing money from me, I will be taking a taxi to see my great-nephew the lawyer. You might be my *meshpuche,* but if you still want to have a shot at my money, you had better start acting like a family should.'

This time, the silence is so thick I think I can feel it vibrating. But Bubby hasn't finished.

'Arifa, my dear friend, Nasir, my boy,' she says, and her voice is as soft as honey cake. 'I would like to say I'm sorry to both of you in the name of all this foolish *meshpuche* of mine.' My husband's, mother's, father's, brother's eyes (and probably mine) all widen as she points a pink fingernail at each one of us in turn. 'Now, Sylvia, Michael—ach, please don't ask me to remember all of your *meshuggeh* names—I believe it is your turn to apologise.'

With Amelia safe behind her screen in the kitchen, now there is not even an electronic beep to break the silence. I'm expecting Arifa's stiletto heels to look even sharper when I steal a glance across at her, but the deep Conran Shop cushions seem to have relaxed her. Or maybe it's the prospect of my entire family begging her pardon. So far, though, all I can hear is, well, *bupkis*. But Bubby's right, we do all owe Arifa and Nasir an apology. At the very least. And as hostess to these ceasefire negotiations, it looks like I'm expected to make the first peace offering. I clear my throat. That sets off a chorus of small coughs and I look over at Daddy, because surely he knows what to say.

'Arifa, Nasir, Dinora is right. We should have realised that a woman with her strength and resilience, with an intellect that has stood the test of over a century, would be more than capable of learning how to switch on a computer and click on a couple of buttons. We should have respected her wishes from the word go, and that includes accepting that she wanted to leave the Cedars and even that perhaps she didn't want to celebrate her long life in the same way that we did.'

Now the coughs have given way to gasps because nobody —and I mean nobody—expected my mother to get the apology-ball rolling. Sylvia Wojnawski, of all people, admitting she was wrong and—let's face it—that somebody else was right. But hang on a minute, she hasn't apologised yet, so if you ask me, this is really all about the money.

'I know what some of you are thinking,' she says and of course now she is looking straight at me, 'but this is not about the money.' Oh. 'Yes, I have been known to enjoy the finer things in life,' I am still in too much shock to laugh, even at this, 'but I have many of those already and they include my wonderful husband and children and my darling, miraculous granddaughter.' Mummy has reached out to take Daddy's hand and now, with the mention of wonderful children, darling Amelia and miracles, I don't know what to think. By the looks of it, Daddy and Adam don't either. 'The penny finally dropped just now, with all of my family here, together, listening to Dinora and her logic. I'm not sure that I've ever properly listened to her before. Everything we've been through with Amelia has made me begin to see what really matters and today, with everything you've been through, Dinora, and you too, Arifa, I finally understood that I have been too caught up in the way *I* thought things should be, not what really mattered to you. I am sorry not to have respected your wishes, Dinora. Arifa, Nasir, please accept my apologies. If my own mother had lived to be here, she would have told me I should have known better.'

And with that, the person formerly known as Sylvia Wojnawski sits back in her armchair. She looks exhausted, but there is something looser about her jaw, like a reverse facelift, that reminds me of gin and lipstick.

'Mummy's right,' I say, and it actually doesn't feel that strange, 'we do owe you all an apology. You know how much I love you, Bubby, and I'm sorry I didn't trust your judgement. Of course, it's up to you decide how you want to spend your last, I mean where you feel comfortable. And as long as she can celebrate your record with you and some honey cake, Amelia will be happy.' James squeezes my hand, so I know I'm doing OK. 'But mostly I owe an apology to Arifa and Nasir, who have done so much for me and my family. Amelia might not be with us today if it wasn't for you, Arifa. And, Nasir, you already know that we do believe that her fall was an accident, don't we, James?' He nods. 'And I know how much you love Amelia and how much she loves you. I'm sorry I didn't hold on to that. If I had, I would have seen just how much both of you have come to care about my great-grandmother too.'

I look over at Adam, who coughs again, before adding,

'Yes, maybe I've been too hasty, but I've always had Bubby's wellbeing at heart. Maybe I misunderstood and, in that case, well,'—he coughs again—'I'm sorry.' A heartfelt apology is not quite how I'd describe it, but he is still looking vulnerable and straight at Arifa and Nasir, so I, for one, am prepared to go for sibling loyalty this time and believe he means it. Then comes Daddy, adding the loveliest compliments for my mother that I think I have ever heard, and James joins in the remorse-fest too, although frankly I don't think my peace-loving husband has anything to apologise for to anyone.

'Why don't we all raise a glass to all of us,' he says, expertly warding off any kind of awkward hush.

'That's a lovely idea, darling,' I say. 'There's a bottle chilling in the fridge, and plenty of softs for anyone who prefers not to drink alcohol,' I add, proving that my ability to prevent any new culture-slash-religion-based rifts is almost as expert as James's.

I'm on my way to fetch the peace offering when a froth of Elsa blue on wheels fizzes out of the kitchen.

'Mummy, I'm bored of watching the Snow Queen,' it says, in a world first. 'Can't you grown-ups hurry up? I want Bubby to teach me and Nasir to make honey cake for her party.'

THIRTY-EIGHT

Two days more

Afternoon

Nora has wheeled herself over to the other side of the café and Deborah and I unpack the bags from the supermarket. I think she must be looking inside her head to see where she could put the food we have bought on her shelves that go up to the ceiling, the way she said the first time she came back here. Two kinds of pickled cucumbers that I have never tasted, one sweet and sour, one salty. Nora tells me they come from Russia and Poland. Rye bread and salted beef to make sandwiches, carrots and cabbage for a salad, potatoes for pancakes she calls *latkes* and more and more. There is kosher wine that I will not taste and that they both say is terrible and of course some bottles of vodka. These are to go with the herring fish we bought in a jar. The honey cake and the chopped liver we will all make at Deborah's home and bring on the big day. At last, it feels as if the sweet has been stronger than the sour and Nora is almost as excited to celebrate her record as Amelia, although she is still too stubborn to show it on the outside. Finally I am excited too, and happy that I will be here with her and with Nasir.

'So, ladies, how are you getting on? If you put the fruit and veg and the dairy on a separate table, I'll take them out to the cold room for you.'

The waitress is the same one as when I came with Nora for lunch one or two days ago. So polite and friendly.

'That's great,' says Deborah. 'It really is so wonderful that you agreed to let us have my great-grandmother's party here at such short notice. You know you're doing us such a big favour.'

'You're kidding me, love. We're not open in the evening mid-week anyway and I wouldn't miss it for anything. The oldest person in the world ever and this used to be her own shop? I'd call that an honour, not a favour.' She winks at us. 'And then there was what you were saying about the press and the Guinness Book of World Records popping in.'

Deborah laughs one of those laughs that people here use for people they don't know and must be polite with.

'I'd say you deserve all the publicity you get, though I don't know how much that will be,' she says. 'We've had over 122 years to think about how to organise things, but the whole thing has turned out to be a bit last minute.'

Her laugh is a little more relaxed this time. Underneath I know that she is almost as happy as Nora that the party will be here in this café with its painted lady on the wall and its memories.

'Your mother had a good idea to hold the party here,' I tell her.

'Yes, she did,' Deborah says. 'And that's a very rare event, although I'm sure she will draw everyone's attention to it as often as she thinks she can get away with it on the big day.'

'You are hard on your mother,' I say. I could not have said it before what happened at her house yesterday. Deborah throws me a look with hurt in it, but then she lowers her eyes and nods.

'I am, you're right. But then until Amelia's accident she was always hard on me. And Daddy.'

'I think she must have been a difficult woman to grow up with. Maybe her mother was too. And Nora was for sure a hard act to follow. I think that is how you say it?'

She nods.

'In my country, we must respect the parents, the older ones, always, even though it is sometimes not easy. And for my own mother it is hard to understand why I cannot make my own son respect me. For me too.'

Deborah puts her hand on my arm.

'I really am sorry about the way we've all behaved towards you and Nasir. What we thought,' she says. 'It wasn't just empty words yesterday.'

'You weren't just trying to keep hold of the money you will get when Nora dies?'

'Ouch,' she says, but her hand stays on my arm. 'I deserved that. No, I wasn't and, you know, I'm not sure if Bubby ever will die. I think she actually might be indestructible.'

Now we both laugh and, I don't know how it could be possible, but I find we are in each other's arms as we keep laughing.

'It's true,' she says. 'I probably should respect my mother more. Maybe it will be easier now that she's understood that it really is possible to see things from other people's point of view. I thought I was going to have a heart attack when I realised she was actually being sincere about apologising to you and Nasir.'

'Me too,' I say.

We both laugh even harder and when we are done, I see something soft in her eyes.

'Arifa,' she says, 'James told me that Nasir ran away from home because of what we said about the poker.'

'Yes,' I say, 'but he's back now.'

'I know, and I'm glad.'

Deborah seems to be searching for how to continue, but I cannot help her.

'And he told me something else. That Nasir said he used to have a sister.'

I do not want her to go further. 'Deborah, these are private matters. We are here to help your great-grandmother with her celebrations. I would like to keep to happy times.'

'I understand, but…'

'Please, I said this is private.'

She nods and takes more groceries from the bag.

'What was all this laughing about here? You didn't finish unpacking the groceries yet?'

Nora has used that trick again of surprising people in her quiet electric wheelchair.

'You want to share this joke with me?'

I look at Deborah, hoping she has understood and I find a way to laugh again. She laughs too.

'Oh, Bubby, you mustn't tell anybody, but we were talking about the shock of Mummy saying sorry yesterday afternoon. And she really meant it, I'm sure of it. You used some old yiddisher witchcraft on her didn't you, you horrible old lady!'

'Ho! It was one of the finest moments I have enjoyed for at least twenty years,' Nora says and her hoot helps Deborah and me go back into real laughter again. We laugh together for more minutes, until Nora claps her hands to make us stop.

'*Genug, genug.* Oy, that poor Sylvia,' she says, although her eyes are still creased with the thought of it. 'And now I wonder if you two are any better. You need an old woman like me to help you get these groceries ready? We need to get out of here. Have both of you forgotten that we are going to see my Dovid?'

I don't know if Mr Simpkins is on duty today, but I am glad that we don't run into him and his smile that is not a smile on our way up to the fifth floor. The green light is on when we get to Mr Wojnawski's room and Nora touches the little box that the Jewish people hang on their door and kisses her fingers. She wheels herself right up against the side of the bed. Deborah goes with her and I follow, carrying Nora's big Bible from the old shop in a bag.

'Dovid,' she says, 'how is my *bubbeleh* feeling today?'

She runs her fingers along his cheek. If somebody came into this room and saw them together, would they know which one is older? Would they think that this was a wife or a sister come to visit a husband, a brother who has not been as strong in pushing against the years? Mr Wojnawski's eyes are shut and his mouth is open. Sometimes the years are not so kind. How can it feel to be so old and see your child in front of you looking even older? Nora looks towards me.

'Do you have a handkerchief, Arifa?' she says.

I pass one to her and she wipes the wet from the side of his mouth and chin. So many many years, and I see that it still feels like being a mother who loves her son.

'Dovid,' she leans even a little closer. '*Ich hob eppes dir tsu vayzen.*'

I turn to look at Deborah, but she shrugs her shoulders. 'It's Yiddish,' she whispers. 'That's mostly what they spoke together in the old days, Bubby, Zeyde and Grandpa David, but then it got lost being handed down into the modern world. I don't really know any, except the usual words. You know, *meshuggeneh* and *shmatte*, that kind of thing.'

Just a few weeks ago, I wouldn't have known, but now I nod.

Nora is still talking softly to her son, but he seems not to hear or at least he doesn't answer. I was never on duty on Mr Wojnawski's floor here at the Cedars, but the other carers say sometimes it's difficult to know. It's the same for so many of the old people in this world now, where the body won't let go of this life even when the mind has moved on to the next.

'Ach, how much I would like to talk one more time with my boy, hear him call me *Mamme* one more time. It has been so long. Ten years maybe.'

Nora is still looking into her son's face, but now her voice is louder.

'Ten years, and so many more since his father died and my Dovid became the man of the house. "The boss of Henry's Fruit at last," he used to say because he was still angry that we couldn't send him to his university. "Wouldn't," he said, but that shop was our life; we needed him to help us build it. He was counting, always counting, the way his father told him and then later counting his own money to save and send his own son to the university. Your own father, Deborah. And then your father took his turn and made his own money counting other people's money for them. Your grandfather was so proud.'

Deborah puts her arm around her great-grandmother's shoulder.

'And now I am so old that I have to see him this way, so I don't know if he can hear me or see me and feel proud or angry. He can't even count anymore.'

There is pride and anger in her voice, the way there must be for a mother sitting by a son whose life is behind both of them, but then Deborah speaks.

'You know, Bubby,' she says, and her voice has hope in it, 'last time I came to visit Grandpa David, I sang him a song that we used to sing together and he remembered, he really did. He even sang a bit of it with me and then one day when Amelia was in hospital, Mummy told me the carers here said he was singing it again and calling for me.'

Nora looks up at her. 'Please,' she says and reaches for Deborah's hand.

'You're sure? I don't think you liked it when we sang it when I was younger.'

'If Dovid likes it, I like it. The past is in the past, Deborah. Just try to make him sing it for me.'

Deborah leans in close to the thin shape of a man in the bed. I know she loves her Bubby very much.

'Hello, Grandpa, it's Deborah. I'm sorry I haven't been to see you for such a while.' She waits for a moment and then, 'I'm going to sing you our song from *Oliver!* again. You know, the one with the oom-pah-pah. You can sing with me if you like.' Another moment. 'One, two, three… Oom-pah-pah, oom-pah-pah, that's how it goes.'

I don't know this song and I don't know what this oom-pah-pah means, but Deborah carries on, singing louder and louder. I don't think the carers I used to work with here will like it, but it is making Nora smile.

'Oom-pah-pah, everyone knows…'

She starts to sing too in a weak voice that I can hardly hear underneath Deborah's, and she moves her son's hand in time with the tune. Then her voice gets louder and I see that he has opened his eyes. A small slip of a voice like steam rising from hot tea comes out of his mouth, and Nora holds his hand to her face now, still singing this song that now I understand.

'Dovid, *bubbeleh*, it's *Mamme*,' she says, as Deborah keeps singing, a little quieter. 'Look, I brought the Bible from the shop to show you. It has all the dates in it, all the arithmetic that your *tatte* taught you.'

I bring the big book over to the bed and help Nora prop it up where her son can see it. She puts on her glasses and starts to turn the pages.

'See, these are the pages where *Tatte* wrote everything we sold in the shop, every day. You remember? He used to make you go over them with him after you finished your homework, before supper. Ach, you used to hate it; you wanted to go out to kick a ball with those friends of yours and talk about the girls, I know.'

Could he be listening to her? It is difficult to tell, but his eyes are still open and they are looking at his mother's face and the tears that are falling onto their family bible.

'And this is the day we arrived in England, on the boat, see? I know you remember the boat, *bubbeleh*, and those beautiful white cliffs that *Tatte* told you had almost the same name as you.'

This time she uses the handkerchief to wipe her own eyes.

'And here is the day we opened our shop, Henry's Fruit. Look, I even have a photo.'

She holds a small photo close to his face. With their old eyes and the tears, I don't know if either of them can see the couple and their son standing in front of the piles of fruit and vegetables outside the shop. The man that must be Henry is wearing an apron and has his arm around his wife. Even though she looks in her forties, I can tell it is Nora. The teenage boy is smiling a smile that shows all his teeth.

'And, Dovid, here is Miriam.'

Nora turns to the back of the book. She runs her fingers round the face of the small child in the photo before she shows it to her son. How old is the girl? Four, maybe five, like Amelia?

Deborah has stopped singing and is looking at the child in the photo. She is black and white, but we can see that her hair is blonde and her eyes are light and shaped like Deborah's eyes, like Amelia's eyes. Like Nora's eyes must once have been. Deborah puts her hand to her mouth as her grandfather reaches out for the photograph. His hands, with their bunches of purple veins, shake as he holds it close to his face.

'Miriam, *Mamme*,' he says, and a smile like the ones Nora must have seen so many, many years ago smooths the angry shape of his twisted mouth. It lifts a second smile up onto his mother's face. '*Mamme*,' he says, 'she is always our Miriam.'

THIRTY-NINE

Only one day and counting!

'Are you sure we need that many onions for the chopped liver, Bubby? People are going to be crying enough tomorrow as it is.'

I may not be Northwood Hills' best *balaboosta* (that's a housewife and homemaker, not a ball-bus— I mean, frighteningly bossy woman, in case you were wondering), but I do know that the traditional cuisine of my ancestral religion has a tendency to go a little *trop loin* with the raw onions. Hence my decision not to wear mascara for this morning's cook fest, but tomorrow the media will be there and I, Debs Levene, will be in full make-up, mascara and natural finish foundation included. So, easy on the onions, Bubby, although that's easier thought than done.

'Deborah, did your mother teach you nothing in the kitchen?' She doesn't wait for me to answer, but she's right, the only thing Mummy ever taught me to cook was a bowl of Coco Pops. 'I will never know how you came to grab yourself such a good husband!' Bubby's ideas about equality of the sexes are about as traditional as her cooking, and I prefer the latter. 'So.

We cook the onions for the chopped liver in plenty of *schmaltz*,'—that's chicken fat—'and that way they are good and sweet and melting, and nobody will be crying. They will all be gobbling it up and wondering how they never tasted anything so good.' If she says so. Chopped liver has never been my go-to Jewish delicacy, but I'm willing to humour Bubby with just one day to go. 'The cooked onions they are for the liver, the raw onions they go with the herring and the vodka. *Farshteyn*? You know, Deborah, your good husband could start thinking of running away with a real Jewish *balaboosta* if you're not careful.'

Did I say I would humour her?

'I'll give you a real Jewish *balaboosta*, you horrible old lady,' I say and shake my best non-stick spatula at her. 'The only other woman James might think about running away with is you, Bubby. You know how much he loves your chopped liver and your chicken soup.'

'Oy!' she laughs, 'everybody loves the chicken soup and anybody can make it if they have the right recipe, even Arifa. Isn't that right, Arifa?'

'It is, but yours is still better than mine, Nora.' Good old Saint Arifa. 'Although now I know about your secret ingredient, I will be practising. And when your party is over, I think we should have one of those cook-offs they have on the television. I will challenge you to my chicken soup against your *kibbeh*. With Mr Levene as the final judge.'

Oh! Now Arifa is looking at me out of the corner of her eye and with quite the *balaboosta* smile in the corner of her mouth. So she really does have that sense of humour I glimpsed yesterday after all.

'I'm sure James would love that. And no need to go easy on the hot sauce, Arifa. He loves a bit of spice.'

Arifa has the grace to blush and I laugh and squeeze her shoulder to make sure she knows that I got the joke. Not so easy to tell between the two of us, given all the mud, sweat and tears that's been slung over the past couple of weeks.

'Is that chopped liver nearly ready, Bubby?' I ask. 'We've got two different honey cake bases to make and I promised Meelie I would call her when it was time.'

'Call her, call her!' Bubby says. 'By the time she's tied her apron and washed her hands, we will be ready. And if not, she can learn a couple of things about making chopped liver the right way for her future husband.'

'Bubby! I am not having you turn my daughter into a *balaboosta* at the age of five. You are 122 and that means this is the twenty-first century, in case you hadn't noticed.'

Arifa laughs, but I don't know if Bubby heard me over the noise of the blender mixing the liver and onions into a paste at booster speed.

I don't suppose that it matters that Amelia has decided to wear full Elsa dressing-up regalia to bake honey cake with Bubby. She has a non-matching Peppa Pig apron tied round her middle and her silver butterfly brooch pinned to that and I think she actually looks rather fetching.

'Now, *bubbeleh*, we pour in the honey. This is very sticky, so we go good and slow. Yes?'

Meelie nods. Her serious face gets even more serious as she bites her bottom lip and pours. The way she did the day she remembered how to sing in the hospital. Biting her lip, I mean, not pouring honey. I spent so much time staring into her face and wishing she would smile, or cry or bite her lip in the ten days she spent there, and that was the afternoon when we knew she really was coming home. I will always remember every word, every laugh, every lip-bitten-in-concentration scrap of it.

'Mummy, are you listening?'

'Oh, sorry, sweetie. You look so adorable in your costume and I was trying to remember the words to Elsa's song.'

'Well, we haven't got time for that; we're baking.' Now she has her hands on her lacy blue hips. 'I was asking if you wanted a turn to stir the mixture.'

'Of course I do! You don't think I'm going to let you and Bubby tell everybody you made these delicious honey cakes all by yourselves, do you?'

I have my turn to stir, then Arifa has hers and then it's back to the oldest and youngest loves of my life. The honey smells as sweet as it does when we dip apples in it at Rosh Hashanah to conjure up a good year, just in case I needed reminding of what a lucky woman I am.

There are more lip-biting moments as Amelia and Bubby melt butter, sift flour, weigh out dark treacly sugar and finally put the first of the cake tins into the oven.

'Now it is time for you to lick this bowl,' says Bubby. 'A promise must be a promise.'

Amelia licks. Her bowl-licking face is almost as serious as her stirring face and by the time she and her wooden spoon are finished, the bowl looks clean enough to start the whole process again.

'I want to be a baker when I grow up,' she says, giving the spoon one final slurp.

'I thought you wanted to be a doctor with Daddy,' I say.

'I did. But I've changed my mind and I want Bubby to come and work with me in my baker's shop.'

'You do, do you?' Bubby's eyes are a dead giveaway for the laughter that she and Arifa and I are all doing our best to keep to ourselves, but Meelie doesn't seem to have noticed.

'Yes. We will have purple aprons with butterflies like this one and Amelia's Cakes written on them and I know you're very old so if you want you only have to work in the afternoon.'

'Then I will come, *bubbeleh*, and I will teach you to make apple cake and *babka* and *rugelach* and *mandelbrot*. So you will have a fine selection for your customers.'

Bubby presses her lips together out of respect for my daughter's new career plan and cups her cheek in a floury hand.

'Thank you, Bubby!' Meelie's smile is ecstatic, although I'm pretty sure her future colleague's examples of Jewish *haute patisserie* mean as much to her as the rules of French grammar do to me. 'Mummy, are we finished with making the honey cakes?' I try to keep my nod as serious as possible. 'Good. I'm going to go and do a drawing of my baker's shop for Bubby.'

'That sounds like an excellent idea.' I untie her apron strings and kiss the top of her head. 'I'll call you when the first batch is ready to come out of the oven.'

And she's off, crutches swinging and blue lace floating behind her, stirring up that mixture of love, amazement and fear that no amount of bowl-licking can stop me feeling almost every time I look at her.

'She has recovered so well, such a strong child. You must be proud,' says Arifa.

'She has and I am, very proud. And very grateful,' I say.

'That face! So beautiful. She reminds me so much of Miriam,' says Bubby.

Miriam again. Arifa and I both look at Bubby. There is love, amazement and fear on her face too.

'Bubby, who *is* Miriam? You keep mentioning her,' I say, although I think Arifa and I are both beginning to understand.

After the heat of the bodies jammed together and the stink of toilet waste and death, the cold air when they opened the doors tasted as fresh and perfect as freedom. There was so much noise and it took me a moment to see that this was more soldiers shouting and dogs and no freedom, of course. I needed every part of being a mother, every second of every day since giving birth, to understand that my leg was still squeezed up tight because a child who was my daughter was hanging on to it. I reached down and pulled her up onto my hip and locked my eyes onto Henry's. I knew the filthy holes that used to be his cheeks were a mirror for mine and I saw that his filthy hand was locked onto Dovid's. We nodded to each other to promise that we would never stop searching and I jumped down from the train before they could crack my back, or worse Miriam's back, with their rifles or their bullets or their dogs' teeth. I heard more people jumping. I prayed that Henry and Dovid didn't fall, but I only looked into that blurred space in front of my eyes and refused to focus, the way I had learned to do it inside the train.

Even my unfocused eyes could see that the shapes moving one way were women and girls, and the other way men and boys. I moved and sent Henry and Dovid more promises through the locks we had made and pulled Miriam tighter against my chest so that our ribs jabbed and scraped. She did not talk and she did not cry; she only pushed her lips against the skin of my face, panting. Now, the cold was cold again and I ran my hand up and down her arm to warm her heart. We moved, following the line of female shapes holding themselves together and leading the line of other female shapes doing the same. I kept trying to warm my Miriam's heart.

Then I felt hands with leather gloves on my arms, trying to pull it away from me and I gasped and snatched it back. Miriam's lips pressed too hard against my face to make even a sound.

'Die Kleinen kommen mit mir! Lass sie los!'

'Nicht Kleine! Sie ist nicht eine Kleine!' I knew if Miriam was too small this leather monster would swallow her in one bite.

'Dann muss sie runter und gehen. Runter!' The monster pointed at the ground and pulled again. 'Runter, sage ich.'

Runter. Down. Walk. I nodded and dropped my giant, skinny eight-year-old daughter to the ground, keeping my lock on her hand.

'Walk, Zieskeit,' I told her and she walked, tall, grown-up and as fast as the monster pacing beside her, until it gave up and went to look for more babies to eat.

We slowed a little to give her legs some time to grow more and my heart some time to push out the fear of the monster and fill up with anger and hate. Almost to the top, with just a small space left to hold the love for the people I was locked to.

'Mamme, where did Tatte and Dovid go?'

This was a child who had lived half of her life in the ghetto, who had seen her Zeyde starving to death there from giving his food to his family, who came here on a train for cows, with nothing to eat and only water from their hoses the one or two times when it stopped.

'I don't know, Zieskeit. In a line like this one, but with boys and men, I think.'

'Will we see them again?'

'I don't know, Zieskeit.'

She didn't ask any more questions, but our fingers sent messages, tangled together as we walked.

'Halt!'

The shout was far away quiet, at the front of the line where it must have sounded loud in the ears of the first female shapes. We kept walking until we got close to them and I made my eyes stay blurred and my fingers strong. Sometimes the dogs barked, sometimes growled, and the monsters walked around, pulling some shapes out of the line and shaping them into another line a little further away.

'Stand straight, Miriam,' I told her and locked our fingers even tighter. 'You used to be the tallest of your class. Stand tall and then they can think you are ten or twelve, maybe even thirteen, Zieskeit.'

My voice did not fail and I poured iron into her arm through our fingers and pushed it into her backbone so she would grow. I felt her push, stretch, aim high like a cannon. I focused my eyes, straight on the monster that came to our place in the line and I shot it with the guns inside them, but it did not fall.

'Das Mädchen. Wie alt is sie?'

'Dreizehn. Dreizehn Jahre.'

'Liegender Jude!' *The back of a leather hand knocked my jaw, but I felt nothing.* 'Sie ist sieben oder acht, nicht mehr.'

'Nein,' I whispered, 'she is not eight, this is my big girl.' I pulled at Miriam's shoulders. 'She is not eight, she is thirteen, soon fourteen.' I pushed more iron into her back and begged her. 'Stand up straight, Miriam, stand up straight.'

But the gun in the monster's hand was straighter than the one in my eyes and straighter than Miriam's cannon and it pointed it at her head while its other arm reached out straight and pulled at her shoulder. When I reached my own arm out to pull her back, the monster moved its gun to the place where my daughter's heart beat at the side of her forehead. I dropped my arm and raised my hands, straight above my head in a prayer to all of the gods, all of the ones that maybe even this monster prayed to. But they did not listen. And now I kept the focus in my eyes, locked to Miriam's bright blue eyes as the monster pulled her away, towards the smaller line of smaller people, the ones that were too young or too old, the kind that the

monsters liked to eat. She reached her arms out straight towards me
and prayed. I don't know if she prayed to me or to our own god, but
there were no gods, none at all, listening that day and none for so
many, many days and nights after.

Bubby has covered her face with her hands and when she
shakes them free with her head, her eyes are greener than I
have ever seen them. Green and glittering with tears and
something even brighter. I don't know if it is pain or love.

'So, you want to know about Miriam?' She shuts them for a
moment. 'I should have told you all before, long ago, but I
never knew how.' She puts a hand over her eyes and pauses.
Maybe she still hasn't found a way. But then... 'She was
always there, but too far inside me to find a way out. *Mein
Gott*, so far inside me, where I told Henry and Dovid that she
must stay, so that we were the only ones ever to know her after
the war, and keep her memory just the way she had always
been.' Bubby's sigh sounds as if it has come from just as deep.
'Then when the little one was in the hospital, Miriam kept
coming back closer. Sometimes I didn't want it; the pain was as
sharp as the day she left me, and it pushed me away from that
poor child in her bed with all those wires. Please God she will
forgive me. But now my Miriam was telling me to bring her to
meet all of you.' She shuts her eyes again. 'Miriam was a *sheyne
meydel*. She was my *tochter*. And your clever *tochter* looks so
much like her.'

I reach out and take Arifa's hand.

'Bubby, you have ... you had a daughter?'

'I had a daughter, yes, *mamme sheyne*, I did. Here, I will
show you. Arifa, will you please pass me my bag.'

She does and Bubby pulls out an envelope. In it is the
photograph that made Grandpa David speak to his mother.

'This is the last piece of her I have. She was five years old when it was taken. You see how she looks like your *tochter*?' I nod, but my throat has closed too tight for words. 'The same age, same hair, same eyes. You can see here how they were light, but not how blue they were. Blue like the sky on the days she wanted to play outside the house, and blue like Amelia's. In our *meshpuche*, they say these eyes come back only for the blessed of the generation.'

Bubby runs her fingers along the curves of Miriam's cheek and smooths the wisps of hair that have come loose from the plaits curled onto her head. The way I do when Amelia is sleeping.

'But they were fools with their tales and their blessings. I was the blessed one to know her. I think you know when the war began, we were kept in the ghetto in Lodz. It was hardest on the children. No school, nowhere to play, nearly no food, the men with guns everywhere.' She shuts her eyes. 'Miriam was eight when they took us from the ghetto and put us onto those trains. She was so thin. These apple cheeks were gone; the smile was gone, but still the blue eyes. All four of us were like bones in a sack, in that train with no air, and the stink that stank in my nose for so many years after and thank *Gott* I am too old to remember now. And then we arrived in the place where they wanted to take us. And Dovid was old enough to do hard work and Henry was strong enough and I had the good sharp eyes they wanted that meant I was able to put together the tiny pieces and build their bombs for them. But not Miriam. Not our *sheyne meydel*. We were so frightened of their dogs when we arrived. Henry and Dovid were already gone with the men and they made Miriam climb down from my arms and walk, but still she wasn't big enough, strong enough. I told her, "Stand straight *Zieskeit*, you used to be the tallest of your class." So she tried—she stood so straight—but no, she could not stand straight enough for them. I was blessed to find my husband and my son again after a long time and a hard time. But the last thing I said to Miriam was to stand up straight. Stand up straight, as if I was angry with her slouching at the table. How could I say that to my girl, my *Zieskeit*, as if I was angry?' She puts a hand to her throat to stop the shake in her voice. Her next words are steady but almost soundless. 'I never spoke to her again after that.'

Miriam looks up at us from the paper. She never did grow old enough to work, but at least here, smiling out of the photograph, she is happy, as if she never knew the fear of being made to leave her mother. Her smile is as beautiful as Amelia's and as silent as this moment. But Bubby has not finished.

'And even so they have not stopped. They keep on with their wars to kill our families and make us into women with only half a heart to live with. Arifa knows this. She is like me; she doesn't like to talk about her war, but I know the story of tearing yourself into two pieces when you have to leave your home and one part of you can never follow. I know you carry your husband always with you, Arifa, just the way I do it with Miriam. We must thank *Gott* that Nasir is able to be here. That your child was spared and is growing into the fine man that he will soon be.'

I look at Arifa, but her face is unreadable and she says nothing. There is silence again for a moment, until her voice rises, clear but soft in a song that must be from her country. It sounds like a song for children, but there is something that pulls at me to remember it. I close my eyes and the song takes a fiercer turn. When I open them again, I know.

'That was the song you sang for Amelia, wasn't it? At the hospital.'

She nods.

'Yes. I told her that my mother used to sing it for me when I was a girl.'

'I remember.'

'And I used to sing it to Nasir and to his sister. To Amelia, that was the first time that I sang it since the day their bombs fell and killed Ranim.' She moves her chair to be closer to my great-grandmother and takes her hand. 'We are more alike than you knew, Nora,' she says. 'Not just women, but mothers with only half a heart to live with. Ranim was eight, the age of Miriam and she had the same smile, almost. Just with a dimple, a little dip, in the left cheek that her father loved to kiss.'

Bubby reaches out and cups Arifa's face in her hand as if the folds, wrinkles and knotted veins that hide over a century of strength could soak up some of her pain too. I wish I had an ounce of their courage, as Arifa leans in and their foreheads touch. Images of Amelia licking the honey cake bowl and lying still surrounded by machines mix in my head and I have no way of knowing how these two mothers ever found their way out of their pain and back to the other people who loved them.

'May I touch her?' Now Arifa takes the photo of Miriam from the table and smiles at her five-year-old beauty. She traces a finger around her apple cheek, and smooths her hair, just the way Bubby did. Just the way she must have done when Ranim was still alive. And just the way I do when Amelia is sleeping.

FORTY

Oy such a day!

Such a fuss everybody is making, but today is just another day. I am here in Arifa's bed in Arifa's flat with my teeth in, waiting for her to knock on the door to ask me what I want for breakfast, make me my breakfast which will be delicious, but I will not tell her this, and get me dressed. The same as every day these last days. But on the calendar, today is 24th April 2018. *9th of Iyyar 5778* the way Henry would say it. He would tell Dovid, 'How many days must there be in 122 years and 165 days? Go on! Count it out in your head. The children who know mental arithmetic are the ones with the good brains, the ones with the proud mother and father.' And he was right, we were proud of our boy; he had a good brain. But now it is gone. Ach, it is hard for a mother to see her son lost inside his own head that way. No way of talking, no way of understanding, just lying there so when the nurses come to clean him, they can pull his bones this way, that way, and he will not tell them stop. This is horrible; I cannot stand to think of it. But I can see that Dovid is still somewhere in there. When I saw him this week, he knew me and he knew his sister. A moment like this I thought I would never live again. A moment to sweeten the heart. So why should I not go now? I would close my eyes and think about Henry and Dovid and Miriam and just say goodbye. The whole of this long life *komt tsu a sof*, finished. *I* know it is the 24th April 2018 and that today I am the oldest woman and the oldest person ever to have lived in this world. I am the one who lived through their ghetto and their monster camps and brought the ones left of my family to London to make more family. I am the one to laugh at those angry, evil people and tell them, you see, I made it through. *We* made it through. We go to the *shul* and eat *cholent* and make children who grow up to be doctors and lawyers and *balaboostas*. This is enough. It is *my* world's record. They will put it in their books and their newspapers if they want other people to know it. Why such a need for a fuss? For a rabbi and a party and so many people there to say the chopped liver is too *gedacht*, the salted beef is too salted. So much of a fuss!

But then if I think about it differently; there will be vodka with herring and onions. This is something for a party. This is something to tempt me for one last taste even if I have to share it with that *meshuggeh* Sylvia woman and the lawyer son from America. Oy, the pity to have a boy become a lawyer and still such a fool. I knew that even *meshuggenehs* can understand that sometimes they must say they are sorry. But these ones? This is a miracle I wish Henry could have seen. And I wish he could join me for one last taste of the good vodka we bought and the real *schmaltz* herring, fat and juicy. He would tell me that going to their party to enjoy our favourites would be a blessing and all I will need to do after that is to tell them I am not feeling so good and they will have *conniptions* and that fine doctor-in-law of mine will come take a look at me and the party will be over.

'Nora?'

She is already here?

'Arifa? I didn't hear you knock.'

'I'm sorry. Should I come back later?'

'No, no, you can come in.'

'Good morning.'

'Good morning.'

'And congratulations, Nora. *Mabrouk* to you for becoming the oldest person in the world.'

She smiles the smile that I know well now, the way I know the smiles of my Henry and the children.

'The oldest in the world—ever. *Shoukran*, Arifa. Aren't you going to ask me what I want for my breakfast?'

'I have made you your breakfast. Eggs scrambled the way you like them and instead of the Aleppo pepper, a little of the fish you said you like so much. With the raw onions.'

'The herring? Bless you, Arifa.'

She smiles some more. It is the smile that told me she was the one to trust with my plan to get out of the Cedars and hide from my family. It worked out for a little while anyway.

'So, let's get you into your chair quickly, before the eggs go cold. I made you some of the hibiscus tea you like too, to settle your stomach before the party.'

'The *zouhourat*?' I like this word on my tongue. I like learning some of Arifa's words and sharing some of mine with her.

'Perfect Nora, you are making progress. *Mabrouk.*'

'Ach, stop with the fussing; it's just a cup of tea. Now help me out of this bed.'

Today is a day for the green silk blouse that Henry gave me. And a day for wearing my wig and the last pair of smart black shoes that I will ever own. The silk, I like. It is smooth against my skin, the way it felt in my heart when Henry told me the colour was almost as beautiful as my beautiful green eyes. Not like that rayon they were trying to sell for silk in the shop where our famous theatre used to be. The wig, I don't like so much. It scratches my head and the shoes squeeze my foot bones. But I will have to smile anyway and listen to them all telling me *mazel tov*, what a wonderful party, what a strong woman you are. When I think I will have to use this enormous strength for smiling and celebrating a world's record. *Oy vay is mir!*

'So, we're here, Nora.'

'What's that you say?'

'I said we're here. At the café. The driver will bring the ramp down and I'll help you out.'

Arifa. Very kind, but always fussing. I remember the day I came here with her and Nasir and some of my family. Deborah was there with the little one. This Deborah is a good girl too underneath all her joking and fighting and rolling her eyes. She reminds me a little of me. It was the first time I saw the shop since it was a café. All those colours and paintings where the shelves used to be and that big, big woman slurping her coffee on the wall. I could hardly recognise it. But Henry was still there and of course he will be here today.

'Ready, Nora?'

'You think I can be ready for a party I never wanted?'

'Maybe not, but I think it's time we should go.'

Arifa's smile tells me she knows I am ready.

'So what are you waiting for?' I say and smile back, and off we go down the *alte kacker*'s ramp and into the party.

———————

Oy, the place looks beautiful! Even without my glasses I can see the beautiful flowers all over the tables and on the counter. The food they have set out nice on the counter too. It looks good, very good, but of course I will need to taste it. The chopped liver and the honey cake I don't have to worry about, but the salted beef and the coleslaw I will try to see if they followed my recipe the right way. The herring and vodka only idiots could ruin. I look over to where our shelves were and I see there is a curtain over the part where they have their pictures, and a banner on top of it with words in red letters so big that even I can read them. Henry's Fruit, it says. Oy, the idiots! They want to kill me with some kind of heart burst?

'Bubby, you're here!'

'Of course I'm here, Deborah. This is my party, you foolish girl.'

'I know, you horrible old lady, and I'm so happy to see you.'

She leans down and gives me a kiss on the cheek. She is almost the only person left that still does that and I put my hand to her cheek. Good and round and smiling, like the *balaboosta* she is.

'So, what do you think? Do you like it?'

She swings out her arm and waves it around. She's going to start singing and dancing like in the musicals now?

'It's nice. They worked hard.' I tell her. 'I liked it better when it was a shop with the shelves and everything that people could think they wanted to find, but today it's looking nice.'

'Bubby, you really are a horrible old lady.' She shakes a fist in my face. 'Mummy and I spent hours arranging the flowers this morning. We nearly killed each other.' Now she laughs. 'And James almost fell off the ladder trying to put that banner up with Daddy directing traffic.' She leans closer to my ear. 'I know you love it really.'

I take her hand and use my enormous strength to pull her down to where I can put my arms around her.

'Yes, I love it and I love you too, Deborah Wojnawski.' She laughs again. 'OK, OK, I know your name is Levene these days. You and our family and Arifa have made a beautiful party. But what are you trying to do to me with Henry on that banner up there? Oy, somebody needs to pour me a vodka!'

'Vodka, we have,' she says, 'and I can get you a *bisl schmaltz* herring too if you like.'

'Ach, Deborah, you make me laugh,' I say, and we both throw our heads back and what do I care if all these people see my false teeth? 'You know, you have been spending too much time with this old lady, you are beginning to sound like the *balaboostas* I used to take tea and a small glass of vodka with back in the old days. You want to be careful you don't start to look like me!'

'Bubby, I know you were quite the looker in your day. I've seen your wedding photo, don't forget, and I don't think James would mind if I end up looking like you when I'm 122.'

We laugh some more and she kisses my cheek again before scooping up a couple of vodkas from a waitress with a tray. Very smart. Finally, they did not such a bad job with organising this *meshuggeh* celebration. Deborah and I raise our glasses. '*L'chaim!*' The herring really is the real *schmaltz* herring and, with the good sharp onions in the mouth, it is time for another small sip. I look around to see who the people are here. Machel and Sylvia of course, and today I think they are even smiling at each other, so they must have tried the herring too, or the vodka. And sometimes saying a sorry can help the smiles come back to the bedroom. Oy! I am not so old that I don't remember things that way with my Henry. But thinking like that could bring on the *conniptions* after all, so I look around some more and I see their sorry lawyer boy from America and some others who must be Dovid's relations from Canada. The ones from his girls, Judith and Sarah, who left for Montreal so long ago I cannot recognise them. And now they are back with all of their family. Unless they are the people who run the café or the ones from the Guinness World of Records or the newspapers. And there is Nasir. So smart he always looks in his uniform. But I will not let my heart burst twice in one evening. Maybe a *bisl* more vodka. Ach, and there is the rabbi. I see he has been looking out for me, because he is coming in my direction. I put down my glass and turn the button on my wheelchair towards my smart young man.

'I am a very happy woman to see you here this evening, Nasir.' I tell him. 'I thought with what my family said and what I did, you might decide not to come at all.'

'Well, I didn't get a chance to sign Amelia's plaster cast the other day, so I thought I'd pop in,' he says. 'And then I thought maybe you and I could squeeze in a game of poker.'

'Ha!' This boy is finally understanding the Jewish humour! 'You are right to tease me, but I know that really you are here for the chopped liver and the herring.' I drop my voice so that he has to bend down closer. 'And if you are careful, I will pour you a glass of vodka that your mother doesn't see.'

He laughs so loud that I am sure his mother will come over

and ask what the joke is, but no, I see she is talking to Deborah and her fine doctor husband, James, and they are laughing too. The little one is with them and she pulls at her mother's skirt and points. And now here she is, hobbling over to us on her crutches with a serious face, the little white teeth biting her lip.

'Hello, Bubby and Nasir,' she says, smiling now so her face is full of her apple cheeks. 'I like your party. Thank you for letting me invite Amelia B and Amber and Mae.'

'This is my pleasure, *mamme sheyne*,' I say. 'I don't want you to be bored with all these boring grown-up people.'

My little Miriam-Amelia is the prettiest thing at the party, in a green dress with purple patterns, and a shine that I think is my own butterfly brooch pinned onto a purple ribbon in her hair.

'You are looking like a lovely spring flower, Amelia. But what has happened to the Queen Elsa? No crown today?'

'Bubby, you are silly. Today is an important day, not a dressing-up party. I know how old you are today. The oldest person in the world. Ever!'

I think she would jump up and down as she says it if she didn't have her crutches.

'And you're my Bubby and I wanted to be me—Amelia Eve Levene—for you today. That's why I'm wearing my special jewellery you gave me. And my dress nearly matches your shirt.'

'Yes, it does, Miss Amelia *Zieskeit*. We are both very pretty today, the oldest and the youngest. Now you listen to me.' She comes close and her height is just right for me to whisper into her ear. 'I want you to make me a promise that you will grow very old like me and have many, many children. Maybe they will have blue eyes and maybe they will have brown, but I think they will all have that smile and those apple cheeks, just like you.'

'I promise,' she says, but then she has enough of me and wants to talk to Nasir. He crouches down to her and smiles, and with the two of them chatting and laughing, I have to stop myself calling to Henry to come out from the back of the shop to see how good we made our *kinder*. The two of them make my chest so full of *naches* and Henry's too, I know this. The big boy with the good brain and the small girl with the blue eyes like an angel and both with enough love for the whole family. So I will call Henry to stop fussing in the back and come out here to see them, maybe bring them a small treat from the storeroom. But now here is the rabbi, taking advantage of me going off into my dreams to creep up behind me. Oy, is there no chance for me to have some peace at this party?

'Mrs Wojnawski, what a wonderful occasion! What a wonderful party!' He raises a small glass of vodka in one hand and passes one for me in the other. '*Mazel tov*!' he says and the vodka is gone. I always did like this rabbi. He knows how things should be, with the men and the women apart in the *shul*, but together when we are sharing a celebration.

'Now, I know there are many people here who want to greet you, congratulate you. You are the star of our show today. But if you would come over this way, your great-granddaughter has something to show you.'

Such a fuss, but what can I do? He brings me over to the back of the shop, under the beautiful banner of Henry's Fruit, and Deborah is here and Amelia is back again with her. I didn't want to be the star of anybody's show, but maybe it was worth it because now I see Machel is bringing my Dovid in his wheelchair to be here with us, here in the shop where he worked every day after school, every weekend, to help us build a life together, such a good boy. Now, here we are both, wheel next to wheel under his father's banner. Ach, how can it be so long since we were both behind the counter and Henry up his ladder in the shelves or checking how many jars of pickles were left in the storeroom or talking his sweet talk to the ladies that came here to find just the special ingredient they needed? I know that Dovid cannot see the changes they have made to our store with its big, colourful woman on the wall and its coffee with berries in it, and I take the hand that is just bones in mine and hold it to my cheek. 'You see, Dovid,' I whisper, 'here we are, back at Henry's Fruit. If you listen, your *Tatte* may be calling you to help check the numbers in our Bible.' But I don't know if he will hear him because now there is too much noise and somebody calling out for quiet. Oy, such a noise. I keep a hold of Dovid's hand and see if I can tell what the fuss is about.

'My dear Bubby,' Deborah says and somebody starts a record with my favourite *klezmer* music, the clarinets and violins that I used to dance to with Henry back when there were still places for Jews to dance in Lodz, and later with the one or two new friends we made here in London, at the Luncheon Club and that beautiful Grand Palais theatre. Now somebody is tapping a knife on a glass and Deborah is talking for everyone to hear. 'My beloved Bubby, as everyone with us here knows, today you are a world record breaker. Ladies and gentlemen, today Mrs Dinora Wojnawski is exactly 122 years and 165 days old, a bona fide miracle, as my father once put it, and the world's oldest person ever!'

Now they are all cheering and clapping and shouting *mazel tov* at me and for sure I shouldn't have had that last drink of vodka, because my face is feeling hot and my wig is itching more than ever. There is some more tapping on a glass. Because she thinks she still has something else to say?

'Before I hand over to Rabbi Goldstein and Mr Sinclair of the Guinness World Records—and I'll leave it up to them to tell you about her life and why we are all so lucky to have her with us here, so lucky to be here at all for many of us.' *Genug!* These *shlemazels* think I am staying to listen to that? 'Before that, I would like to share a small tribute that Arifa and I have prepared for Nora, here at Henry's Fruit. Go on, Amelia,' she says and the little one pulls on a cord that opens the curtains hanging under the big red sign. And now I see that they have changed the pictures. I think they used to have some paintings of blue and yellow stars, but they are gone and instead it looks like some photographs. Deborah takes me closer and Arifa gives me my glasses. So now she wants to make me look even older. Ach, with all this fuss they've made I think I must wear them to keep them happy.

I look closer. *Mein Gott,* here is the old picture of Lodz that was hanging on my door in that *meshuggeh* place where Dovid still has to live and where they tried to kill me with their terrible food. Then I see my Henry and me on our wedding day, with all of the flowers, standing so still for the camera that we could not smile. Deborah is right, I was a beautiful woman that day. And I see the small photo taken outside our shop. Henry, Dinora and David Wojnawski of Henry's Fruit, the one from our Bible. Now I see a picture of Arifa, arm in arm and happy with a man that must be her Tarek and a too young Nasir and his sister. She is Ranim, so pretty with the dimples in her smile the way Arifa said, but she will always be too young, like my Miriam. Next, a picture of a city in her country that I do not know, old like Jerusalem. And then a drawing of an angel on a wall, dropping orange hearts from its hand. I don't know who this angel is supposed to be, but it is pretty, I like it. Now I see a picture of all of my *meshpuche* at some wedding somewhere—so many weddings, so much *meshpuche*! The ones who still live near me here where I made my new life, the ones who came here to my party, even from Canada, the ones who have gone from my life in Lodz and from this world. Ach, it is so hot in this shop that I must take off my glasses to wipe them. So. That is better. And now I come to the middle of all the pictures and a golden frame that I have never seen before. But I know the photograph the same way I know my own face. This one is my Miriam. My *tochter*, the girl that nobody here except me and Dovid has ever seen. She is the child whose hidden eyes have kept my old eyes from going blind for so many years, and now here she is, smiling. Here together are Miriam and Ranim, smiling at all of us with their apple cheeks and their dimples. And here comes the little Amelia, smiling at me too and leaning in to whisper in my ear.

'Bubby,' she says, 'Mummy says she knows you don't want a fuss, but maybe, if you like the pictures, you can say something.'

I try to look into her blessed blue eyes but now my glasses are so cloudy I have to put them in my lap and dab at my cheeks with my green blouse that has all the memories inside the soft real silk. I will say something to them all, these people, but I don't know if they will hear me with my voice that feels like now it is just an old memory too.

'*Meyne tayere mespuche and frenden,*' I say, because this is the way to begin a speech and the tapping on the glass starts up again so I wait and clear my throat to see if I can remember my voice again. 'I think I must thank you for coming to my old shop to tell me how I am a wonder for growing so old and tell me *mazel tov*. But my great-granddaughter Deborah here and my great friend Arifa, who wouldn't listen when I told them "no, I will not have any party", they know that I am a horrible old lady who doesn't like to make a fuss. So, yes, I will tell you thank you, but no, I will not give you a fine speech about the world's record or my beloved husband Henry and son Dovid and how we came to this shop where we learned to live again. Instead, I will ask you all to come look at these pictures that they have hung on the wall here. And then, please look at this lovely girl, this *mamme sheyne*, my great-great-granddaughter, Amelia. In the pictures, you will see a photograph of my dear Arifa's *tochter*, Ranim, and then you will see a photograph of my own beloved *tochter*, Miriam. I think many of you didn't know that once I had a *tochter*, but it is true, here she is. Dovid's sister, who left us long ago. My Miriam. So, please, come and see these two *tochters*. You will see that they are smiling, just like our little Amelia. They are smiling their beautiful smiles, the way that anyone in the world, anyone with even a *bisl* of a good brain and a *bisl* of a good heart, must know and could tell you that all of the children, anywhere in the world, should always be. Smiling, with apple cheeks, the way children are when they are happy.'

What's in a name

What's in a name?

In Romeo and Juliet, Juliet answers this question, saying: 'That which we call a rose by any other name would smell as sweet'.

Far be it from me to contradict Shakespeare, but I have decided to give my main characters a name that says something about who they are. Here is a short guide.

Dinora Wojnawski

- The character of Nora was inspired by my late mother-in-law, Norma Celemenski, née Kryger
- Dinora is a Hebrew name, meaning avenged, vindicated.
- Wojnawski is a free interpretation of Norma's maiden name. Kryger means 'warrior' in Yiddish. Wojna means 'war' in Polish, hence Wojnawski.

What's in a name

Deborah Levene

- Deborah is a Hebrew name, meaning bee: busy and sweet, with a sting in its tail.
- Levene is an Anglicised version of Levi. People whose surname is Levi are said to be descended from the Levites, one of the twelve tribes of Israel. The word itself means to join or connect.

Arifa Hashmi

- Arifa comes from the Arabic for 'learned, expert'.
- Hashmi comes from the Arabic for 'honourable'.

Nasir Khalil

- Nasir means 'supporter, helper'.
- Khalil means 'friend' in Arabic.

David Wojnawski

- David is a Hebrew name, meaning 'beloved'.

Miriam Wojnawski

- Miriam is a Hebrew name, meaning 'wished for child', or 'bitterness'.

Amelia Levene

- Amelia is derived from the Hebrew word meaning 'industrious, striving', or 'work of the Lord'. It was the UK's most popular girl's name in 2013, the year of Amelia Levene's birth.

Ranim Khalil

- Ranim is an Arabic name, meaning 'song' or 'singing'.

The names of the staff in the hospital where Amelia is taken are all borrowed from real NHS doctors and nurses. They were all immigrants who worked for the NHS and who, tragically, died of coronavirus. Arifa's quest to become a doctor in the UK and the use of their names are a small tribute to them, their work and their dedication.

They are:

- Philomina Cherian, a nurse at the John Radcliffe hospital in Oxford, who came to Britain from India.
- Carlos Sia, a health care assistant from the Philippines who worked at the Royal Worcester Hospital.
- Elsie Sazuze, a care home nurse working in Wolverhampton, originally from Malawi.
- Dr Karamat Ullah Mirza, a GP based in Essex, who moved to the UK from Pakistan.

- Dr Rajesh Kalraiya, a consultant paediatrician at the North East London NHS Trust, who was born in India.

Acknowledgments

Firstly, I'd like to thank the people who believed in me right from the start of my writing journey and who never stopped: Michel, Juliet, Francesca, Aurora, Rosemary and Louise. You've all read everything I've written and given me such loving, generous support and thoughtful feedback. A special thank you to Michel for always finding ways of giving me the time and space I needed. That takes me to Kerry and John, founders of La Muse, an incredible retreat in the beautiful, empty wilds of France's Montagne Noire, where Nora's story began and where I met fellow writers Bridget, Pete, Nell and Nicola. Thanks for the fun, the sounding boards, the fires and the sunset walks and a soupçon of extra gratitude to Nicola for helping me to see that my story needed Arifa's voice. A big thank you too to all the team at Jericho Writers. I was lucky enough to go to three of their Writers' Festivals in York quite a few years back and they were the place where I really began to feel confident about my writing and that one day I might be able to stop aspiring and be published!

Thanks of course to my late mother-in-law, whose indomitable spirit, physical and mental resilience in surviving the camps – but also stubborn bad temper – inspired Nora. Thanks to Mahbubeh and Imane, two women far from home, whose kindness and courage inspired Arifa.

Thanks to Dr. Daniel FitzPatrick-Watson, my nephew, for his advice on brain injuries, to Mohamed for checking my

Syrian Arabic, to Hicham for the poker tips and to Michel (again) for the Yiddish and Yiddishkeit.

I owe much gratitude to Margaret James, Cathie Hartigan and especially Sophie Duffy of the Exeter Novel prize for their encouragement and for putting my novel on the shortlist that led to the wonderful Broo Doherty awarding it first prize and becoming my agent. Thanks to Broo for falling in love with Nora and her story – what a luxury for an aspiring author to have her insightful and enthusiastic feedback and advice as I drafted the novel. I am also lucky to have a passionate, insightful and supportive editor in Charlotte Ledger. Thanks to her and all of the team at One More Chapter for bringing the story together as a book and for helping it fly the nest. I am also very happy to have found the 2023 Debuts group on Twitter in the run-up to publication – it's been great to share our journey and have you as cheerleaders.

There are too many other friends and family members to whom I am grateful to mention them all by name. A final thank you, though, to my three daughters, Rose, Claire and Ruby. We may sometimes drive each other mad, but you always fill my heart with love.

ONE MORE CHAPTER

The author and One More Chapter would like to thank everyone
who contributed to the publication of this story...

Analytics
Emma Harvey
Maria Osa

Audio
Fionnuala Barrett
Ciara Briggs

Contracts
Georgina Hoffman
Florence Shepherd

Design
Lucy Bennett
Fiona Greenway
Holly Macdonald
Liane Payne
Dean Russell

Digital Sales
Laura Daley
Michael Davies
Georgina Ugen

Editorial
Arsalan Isa
Charlotte Ledger
Jennie Rothwell
Caroline Scott-
Bowden
Federica Leonardis
Hamza Jahanzeb
Kimberley Young

International Sales
Bethan Moore

Marketing & Publicity
Chloe Cummings
Emma Petfield

Operations
Melissa Okusanya
Hannah Stamp

Production
Emily Chan
Denis Manson
Francesca Tuzzeo

Rights
Lana Beckwith
Rachel McCarron
Agnes Rigou
Hany Sheikh
Mohamed
Zoe Shine
Aisling Smyth

**The HarperCollins
Distribution Team**

**The HarperCollins
Finance & Royalties
Team**

**The HarperCollins
Legal Team**

**The HarperCollins
Technology Team**

Trade Marketing
Ben Hurd

UK Sales
Yazmeen Akhtar
Laura Carpenter
Isabel Coburn
Jay Cochrane
Alice Gomer
Gemma Rayner
Erin White
Harriet Williams
Leah Woods

**And every other
essential link in the
chain from delivery
drivers to booksellers
to librarians and
beyond!**

ONE MORE CHAPTER

YOUR NUMBER ONE STOP

FOR PAGETURNING BOOKS

One More Chapter is an
award-winning global
division of HarperCollins.

Sign up to our newsletter to get our
latest eBook deals and stay up to date
with our weekly Book Club!
<u>Subscribe here.</u>

Meet the team at
<u>www.onemorechapter.com</u>

Follow us!
 <u>@OneMoreChapter_</u>
 <u>@OneMoreChapter</u>
 <u>@onemorechapterhc</u>

Do you write unputdownable fiction?
We love to hear from new voices.
Find out how to submit your novel at
<u>www.onemorechapter.com/submissions</u>